Praise for A.E. Rought's
Slade and Kally

"...I found the Slade and Kally to be an enjoyable story that leaves thought-provoking images in its wake."
~ *Scandalous Minx for Literary Nymphs Reviews*

Blue Ribbon Rating: 4 "SLADE AND KALLY made me cry – and not just silent tears. ... A. E. Rought has a gripping novel... It shows the hero's loyalty of character, and the heroine's steadfast need to trust. I couldn't put it down."
~ *Natasha Smith for Romance Junkies*

"Riveting story of an abusive relationship and the healing power of true love found when all seems lost. ...This story will make you cry, worry, then laugh, and root for the hero and heroine as they work through Kally's trust issues."
~ *Susiq2 for Ecataromance*

"If you have never read a book by A.E. Rought, you have no idea what you are missing. Slade and Kally is that book that stays with you long after you have read it. ... there are moments of humor that are just so real, you'll feel as if you were there. ...Slade and Kally is a not to be missed read."
~ *Sandra for CK2S Kwips and Kritiques*

Look for these titles by
A.E. Rought

Now Available:

Nuermar's Last Witch

Slade and Kally

A.E. Rought

A SAMHAIN PUBLISHING, LTD. publication.

Samhain Publishing, Ltd.
577 Mulberry Street, Suite 1520
Macon, GA 31201
www.samhainpublishing.com

Slade and Kally
Copyright © 2009 by A.E. Rought
Print ISBN: 978-1-60504-418-7
Digital ISBN: 978-1-60504-246-6

Editing by Bethany Morgan
Cover by Anne Cain

First Samhain Publishing, Ltd. electronic publication: December 2008
First Samhain Publishing, Ltd. print publication: October 2009

Dedication

For Lisa.
With many thanks to Nels and Barbara for sharing their dream.

Chapter One

November 7th

"How could you let him take you down this far?"

No one replied. I might talk to myself, but I wasn't about to start answering my own questions. I did have a response, however, I felt it with every fiber of my being. In the bathroom mirror I examined the bruises around my eye and the split in my lip. There was no doubt in my mind, this was the last time he'd ever beat me. *Matt's not going to take any more of me. I've lost too much already.*

I pushed my hair back and spat blood on the bathroom floor. "It's the last bit of me you'll ever have, Matt."

Jaw aching, I wandered to the kitchen and pulled a bag of peas from the freezer. Pain ran up my spine when I sat on a stiff chair. Frozen vegetables held to my cheek, I stared at the stark, medicinal white wall—spotless, free of flaws, too damned perfect—like Matt wanted everything in the house. Perfect.

Great fantasy. Fucked up reality.

I couldn't stomach anymore of his Spartan views or iron fists. My gaze drifted to the shelves, to the orderly picture frames and the shades of gray lies they told of a happy couple. Blood spattered my sweater when I snorted. Those pictures were all black and white, but the little Kallys should have been black and blue. I flicked through the album pages of my memory, exploring the ugly snapshots of truth. Those images told a different story, one not so idyllic or attractive.

When did the violence start? And why the hell did I stay?

The first time he insulted me, I explained it away, but my actions only enabled him to keep hurting me. I should have packed and run then, but hope remained. Within a month of our engagement and me moving into his house, the verbal abuse turned physical. His vicious talk turned to violent outbursts and throwing or hitting things. I became the thing he hit. The hope I held for him to come to his senses and treat me like he used to was equally battered, and I clung to it. I lived in fear, scared of him, scared of the pain, until this afternoon when he choked the hope right out of me.

I didn't love him and hadn't for months. I refused to be his victim any longer.

My brain churned over what to do, where to go. I had no plans and only a short time to execute them. Then, the front door creaked, and my guts seized in fear. *Oh God, not him already!* I walked into the dining room, expecting to have a last showdown with Matt. Instead, I was face to face with my sister Susan. Her eyes were wide and fixed on my split lip.

"What the hell are you doing here, Sue?"

"I saw Matt's truck tear down our street and I knew he'd beaten you again." She reached a hand out, but I pushed it away. "How many times do you need to be kicked in the teeth before you learn?"

"Exactly this many."

The copper scent of my blood mingled with the ripe musk of embarrassment. I grabbed the last tissue from the box and blew snot and blood from my nose. Susan's gaze took in every movement, every nuance of color in my face.

My sister was concerned about me. She said that every time Matt wasn't around, but the last thing I wanted after another beating was to be tended to by Susan. I backed away from her, and she chased after me with a wadded kerchief in her hand. The doorjamb between the kitchen and breakfast nook blocked my escape, the distressed wood snagged my sweater. Susan took advantage of the moment and blotted at the blood still spilling from the tear in my lip. She sucked air through her teeth when I smacked her hand away and wiped the red onto the back of my sleeve.

"I'm a big girl, and I can clean my own messes."

"I've heard those words before." Susan's eyes narrowed. "So what are you going to do? Are you going to ice the bruises, put a steak on your eye and in a week take the bastard back?" Her voice rose to a cutting timbre. With the shrill tone, crossed arms and tapping foot, she resembled our mother. The only thing missing was the apron.

"This is the last time."

"Yeah, sure. Like the night of Oktoberfest? He beat the crap out of you and you said the same damn thing. Look at you now, hardly a month later and he's hit you again."

My frayed nerves couldn't handle another nag fest. Hands curled into fists, jaw muscles clenched, I turned away from her. Tears might have fallen, my eyes burned like they were filled with salt water, but I was past crying.

She didn't know what I'd gone through an hour before she walked in. Susan had no idea how far he'd dragged me into his hell. Matt convinced me I was the one at fault, his constant brow beating made me believe I was bad/stupid/slutty/fill-in-the-blank. He made me hate myself, and I had sworn I would never go there. The abuse had only gotten worse, his open hands had turned to fists, his fists took up objects. I knew weapons were not far behind. I would not allow him to take my life the way he'd taken my self-esteem and everything else. I turned on my heel and stalked to the laundry room with Susan right behind me and bitching all the way.

"Damn it, Kally, don't walk away from me. You cannot let him come back here. If things keep going the way they are, he is going to kill you."

My jaw locked on a torrent of cuss words, knowing they wouldn't do either of us any good. Instead of feeding her rant, I purged my frustration and pain, kicking a box of Christmas ornaments Matt had brought up earlier from the basement. Fragile globes cracked, the top popped open and shards of glass peppered the floor. Susan ducked behind the louvered door. "Jesus, Kally!"

"Jesus has nothing to do with this."

For good measure, I buried my foot into the other box of decorations Matt had hauled up from the basement before our fight. The first box was filled with my ornaments, some of them heirlooms. The second box was full of Matt's collection of penguins and his NFL themed decorations. The cardboard crushed beneath my heel and the plastic and resin inside crackled in complaint. I unloaded another kick at Matt's precious Christmas memories and sent the box skidding into the hallway.

Fuck you, Matt.

"Kally, you need to get a grip on yourself."

It was the last straw. I spun on her and with one step our faces were inches apart.

"Do not talk to me like Mom talked to Dad." I slammed my fist into the washing machine lid, denting it. "You have no clue what I've been through. I kept hoping he'd stop, that I could be what he wanted, that I could make things work. Matt broke my nose, sprained my wrist, split my lip more times than I can count..." I shoved my bangs back and wiped at the moisture in my eyes. My chest hurt, heart ached and I pushed against the pain. "Flesh heals, Sue. I'm not so sure about the rest of me."

Susan's mouth snapped shut. The frustrated expression left her face, washed away in a tide of sadness. Her loafers skidded on the layer of broken glass when she took the last step between us. I stood quivering, rage and a year of pain and stress surging through me until I was sure my skin would rupture and leak misery. Her silent embrace saved me. Susan's arms encircled my bruised ribcage, and her hand guided my head onto her shoulder. The dam holding back ten months of pain broke, and the hell within me flooded out in sobs, poured from my eyes in salty tears.

Limp and empty, I leaned against my older sister, a hollow shell of the woman I had been when I moved in with Matt. Susan rocked side to side, cradling me like an infant against her chest until the last of my tears dried on the shoulder of her blouse. She pulled my hair from my eyes and sopped my tears with the kerchief she'd never put away. I wanted to pull back from her tenderness when she held my face in her hands searching for a sign of fighting spirit remaining in me.

Susan nodded, a half-smile flittered across her lips and she wiped at the wet slicks underneath her eyelashes. She tucked the damp, bloody piece of cotton into her pocket, crossed her arms and leaned against the wall.

The legs of the utility stool ground the glass debris to powder when I pulled it to the washing machine. I climbed it and teetered on the top step until I braced a foot on the dryer. Straining, I reached the top of the cabinets above the appliances. The handle of my suitcase cracked from age when I grabbed it, and dust fell into my eyes when I yanked the luggage from the cabinet top. I wobbled on unsteady footing. The tapestry case might have fallen and taken me with it to the floor, but Susan was there, bracing me, helping me with the first step on my way out of this house.

"Thanks."

"You're welcome, hun."

Nothing more was said. I handed the suitcase to Susan, and she held it while I groped for the matching toiletries bag. We trudged up the stairs to the bedroom I shared with Matt. It was supposed to be a place of comfort, a place to express our love. It was nothing more than the room where most of my beatings had taken place.

I dropped the dusty luggage on top of the unmade bed. A gray haze rose from the fabric and settled on the bedspread. Matt would hate dust on his side of the bed. A dark grin cracked my lips, but the stinging of the fresh cut on my bottom lip wiped the smile away—even laughter hurt. Susan opened the cases for me while I rummaged in the closet. I returned with arms full of jeans, sweatshirts and sweaters, which I tumbled into the big case. Bras spilled from my underwear drawer when I pulled it from the dresser. I picked up the satin-clad wire contraptions and stuffed them into the case. The drawer I dropped to the floor. I gave my sock drawer the same treatment.

Susan appeared from the bathroom, a towel held by the corners and filled with brushes, shampoo and conditioner, deodorant and perfumes. She put the towel down on the bed and packed the items into the toiletry bag. She even dug the box of pads out from underneath the sink.

"Wait." I took the box of pads from her.

"Why? Kally, I thought..."

She quieted when I produced a wallet from the bottom of the box. I opened it and showed her the paltry sum of money and bankcard I had been able to stuff away without Matt knowing.

"It was the only place I could think of where Matt wouldn't look."

Susan patted my shoulder. "Smart girl."

We crammed the bag to bursting. I had to sit on it to snap the clasps shut. Then Susan wrapped my hand in hers and led me down the stairs to the coat closet. When she reached for the box on the top shelf, I stopped her, pushing it farther back. "Don't touch Matt's box. I don't even want your fingerprints on it."

"What the hell is it?" Her eyes widened. "Is he hiding a gun or something up there?"

I didn't need to speak. The expression in my eyes said everything.

"Jesus, it's no wonder you are always on edge."

"I told you Jesus has nothing to do with this. He doesn't come around here, Susan."

"You're still alive, Kally...I'd say you have evidence enough God has been watching over you."

I let the discussion drop and rummaged in the bottom of the closet instead. The fur of my boots was soft and warm when I shoved my feet into them. My jacket, however, was old and threadbare. I refused to wear the fussy fitted one Matt had bought for me last month. My purse hung from the nearby hall tree. I grabbed it, pulled open the main compartment and took out my cell phone and stuffed the wallet in its place. The plastic casing of my phone clicked against the band of my engagement ring when I walked to the polished expanse of the dining room table.

The ring was faded, the gold plating worn off, and when I tried to cut glass with the diamond, the damn CZ stone had chipped. Our relationship was a sham. So was this ring. I pulled it off, dropped it beside the cell phone on the table and then looked back into the house. There was no sense of loss, no sadness. I wouldn't miss a damn thing in the neat and tidy, wood and white house. I tugged on Susan's arm, and she looked at me, her maternal nature showing in her eyes.

"Ready to go?"

"Hell yes."

The door swooshed shut behind us, the weather stripping dragging on the tile floor of the foyer. Out of habit, I checked the mailbox mounted to the aluminum siding beside the front door. The envelopes were all addressed to Matt Stransberg. They always were. He controlled everything.

Not anymore.

Susan's Buick sat parked behind my old Toyota Celica. She tugged on my hand, pulling me toward her car. The door locks released when she pressed the button of the fob on her key ring. I stopped, my boots squeaking on the early November snow.

"No, Susan."

"What do you mean, 'no'?"

"I mean I am not going with you. I can't go to your house and risk Matt finding me there."

Entrenched, Susan refused to release me, still tugging on my hand in disbelief.

"Susan, no. Matt's crazy. Do you want to risk Joshua and Samuel's safety? I know you want to take care of me, to nurture me like Mom would, but Mom's gone and I need to leave this town."

Her lips twitched, then she nodded and brushed a tear from her eye. "Where are you going to go, Kally?"

"I think I'm going to go visit Ilene."

"Out in Wyoming?" Her voice rose again. "Kally, are you insane? It's almost winter, almost Christmas time."

Looking left and right along the street, I saw a neighborhood cluttered with dumpy houses. A rattletrap Datsun churned through the slush covered road, flinging slop from its tires. My arms crossed over my chest when I turned back to her. "I've heard Wyoming is beautiful this time of year, peaceful and quiet." I looked into Susan's brown eyes, silently begging her to understand this had to be about me, not about her or whatever holiday was closest. "I need some peace, Susan."

"Okay, okay." Her nod of understanding was almost imperceptible. She cracked open her pocket book and pulled out her wallet. "At least let me give you some cash for the road."

"I can't accept your money." I put my hand over hers and closed her wallet. "Use it and buy the kids something for Christmas—say it's from me."

"No. Now, Kally, damn it, you can take money from me. Who knows when I'm going to see you again?"

It was true. Even I didn't know when, or if, I'd be coming back.

"You win." I shrugged my shoulders. "I won't forget how you've helped me." I held out a hand turning blue from the cold, but she pulled me into a fierce hug. Before either of us cried, Susan pushed me away, taking every bill from her wallet and putting the wad into my hand.

A folded packet of hundreds and fifties lay on my palm. More than I'd ever held. Her generosity astounded me.

"Susan, are you sure?"

"I only wish I could give you more."

I tucked the money into my pocket and buttoned it shut. When I looked at my sister again, she held out the blood and tear soaked hanky.

"What's this for?"

"So you don't forget what he can do to you." She took my hands, folding my fingers over the constant reminder of my months of abuse. "Whenever you think about going back to him, take this out and look at it, remember what he put you through."

"I will." The sopping cotton went into the breast pocket of my jacket.

Susan looked at her watch and then tossed a glance down the street in the direction of Matt's favorite bar. "Okay, hun, this is it. I'm going to go home and hug my kids. You get your butt in your Celica and get out of here."

"Yes, ma'am. I'll stop and get a new cell phone and call you from the road."

Waving at her, I pried open the driver's side door of the Celica and pulled the trunk release. I packed the bags in and slammed the trunk down.

"You damned well better." Susan climbed into her sedan and then poked her head out of the window and into the fresh snow starting to fall. "I love you, Kally Jensen. Go and heal. Call me when you can."

Her car purred and then rolled smoothly down the drive. My Celica started with less grace, coughing and sputtering before it turned over and growled to life. Susan honked her horn when she turned north out of our drive. I waved again and then turned south, aiming the nose of the Toyota away from Matt's house and my hometown.

There was no telling how far my car would take me, but the more distance between the bastard and me, the better. I fastened my seatbelt, turned up the heater and stepped on the gas.

Chapter Two

Saint Joe shrank through the rear window of the Celica. An orange teddy bear sat beside the speaker behind the back seat, blocking part of my view, a gentle reminder not to look back. He was insentient and still smarter than me. He looked forward, out the windshield, while I looked over my shoulder and past him. Deep twilight shadows lay on Niles Road, the route which took me out to I-94, south toward Chicago. The sun dipped into the west while I sat at the intersection, shaking and nauseous.

Everything I'd ever known was in St. Joseph, Michigan. Everything. I was born at Lakeland Hospital, attended church there until I was old enough to know different. My sister and her family, my old school, the two friends I didn't lose because of Matt, my tormentor himself—hell, even my parents' graves were back there. My entire life was encapsulated in one small town. How could I leave it all?

Doubt swirled through me. A hand hovered near the gearshift, while the knuckles of my other hand tightened on the steering wheel.

I could go back, face Matt and pray I didn't end up dead at his hands. Maybe hide at Susan's house? No. It was silly to even entertain the thought. After walking in her door, I could hang a "VICTIM HERE" sign over my sister's front porch. Sue and Jerry's would be the first place Matt would target. I was already worried sick about them. My debate ended there, on the faces of those boys. Their safety was an irrefutable argument. My nephews would not become casualties of my dysfunctional relationship if I could help it.

A Chevy 4 X 4 pulled up in my rear view mirror, a black beast of a truck with enough chrome on the front to resemble teeth and its lights blazed into my low sitting car. It was similar enough to Matt's to give me the willies. Chills ran down my spine and flushed away any second thoughts I entertained. The gas pedal creaked when I stepped down on it again. It was time to leave Michigan. My heart and soul depended on it.

Traffic on I-94 was light. The early snowfall scared a lot of Michigan drivers. My little Celica slid on the curves, but it wasn't bad enough to stop me. I strained to reach the maps in my glove compartment and keep my eye on the road. Dome light on, I unfolded the Michigan map and traced the length of the major southbound highway, looking for a place to gas up. There was no way in hell under a quarter of a tank would get me to Michigan City, where I wanted to stop for the night.

The map didn't fold nicely, and I ended up jamming the damn thing under my purse on the front seat. The corners reached up and covered part of the view out of the passenger side window. I stuffed them down and gave myself an unobstructed view.

The rolling hills and sandy expanses of southern Michigan have a serene beauty and made for a peaceful ride. Its splendor, however, lacked in comparison to the Lake Michigan shoreline. St. Joe was beautiful. The snow clung to the pines like frosting on a Christmas cookie, white and softer than the moon's reflection on the Saint Joseph River. I left my picturesque hometown behind because of the monster it harbored. Give me wild, open ranges, where the challenges were visible, not swinging hammer fists.

I took the Stevensville exit, looped around and pulled into the Admiral station on the Red Arrow Highway. It was such a silly name. I never could figure out why they called it an arrow. The road was crooked as hell. It snaked along between the main highway and the lakeshore.

Standing with my hand on the door handle, I waited and watched the road. The roof over the fuel tanks was a welcome respite from the wet snow and, somehow, I felt safer with the lights of the gas station shining down. Even though I was exposed like a lab rat in an experimental maze and more vulnerable out in the open, a blindside attack from the shadows was less likely. Matt never fought with me in public. He waited until we were home, and then he usually came at me from the side, or behind, to catch me unawares. I plugged the nozzle into the fuel tank and watched the road while the price clicked higher and higher.

Over forty dollars in gas and a bag of road food later, I made my way back onto the main highway and pointed the Celica south. Unless I ended up in an accident, there wouldn't be another stop between Stevensville and Michigan City, Indiana.

After copious dial spinning and static, I finally managed to tune a radio station in. Two DJs chattered back and forth about the economy and politics and set my teeth on edge. "What hell is this? Talk radio?"

I cranked the dial again only to find, in the year the car had sat in the driveway, someone had switched the radio to the AM channels. "Oh my goodness, Matt even messed with the car radio?"

He was the only one to get into the car, and I could easily picture him changing the station to one spouting sports while he started up the car every few months. It was always him-him-him. His radio. His house. His diet. His fists.

For a second time I thought, *Fuck you, Matt.*

I switched to the FM dial and finally landed on a top forty station. Some nasal, high-pitched girl sang about her love for her man. It made me sick. With another spin of the dial I found a station playing angry rock music. I turned it up, howled along and dragged the bag of snacks from the back seat. Starving because I had spent the dinner hour at the intersection of I-94, I stuffed a cheese puff in my mouth. The thing was mostly air, with a little batter and a lot of fat. Just the thing Matt would not like me eating, and damn it if they didn't taste better when washed down with scorn. I was hating him and loving the hell out of the junk food.

The Michigan border passed beneath my wheels in silence. I did not whoop or shout, only sighed and released a fraction of the tension along my spine. Sooner than I expected, the Michigan City exits loomed ahead. I pulled off the highway and onto a smaller, much busier road. The summer before I met Matt, my girlfriend Ilene and I had spent a night in Michigan City and stayed at a Super 8. It was a familiar place and hopefully a safe one. I'd never spoke about the trip, or Ilene, around him. I drove in, walked up to the front desk and got a room with cash and an alias.

Room 210 was not the nicest appointed room I'd ever been in, but the door had two sets of locks, the shower was hot and the pillows were soft. I pulled back the bedspread, and sat on sheets smelling of bleach. With the hotel visitor guide in hand, I punched the appropriate numbers and dialed Susan's house. The phone rang three times, and then the answering machine picked up. I disconnected the call before the message finished.

What the hell? It's late, the kids should be in bed by now...

I waited a few minutes and dialed again. The message started once more. "Hi, you've reached the Nelsons. Sorry we're not in right now. If you leave a message, we'll be sure to return your call."

It wasn't safe to tell her what hotel I stopped in, but I couldn't leave her worrying like our mother had taught her to. "H-hi, Susan. It's me. Kally. I wanted to let you know I've stopped for the night, and I'm safe. I'll try to call you again before I set out."

Where was she? Were they all right?

I was tortured by sudden worry, thinking Matt had something to do with their late night silence. At the thought, I broke into a cold sweat and guilt swarmed through my guts like angry bees. I sat a moment, clutching the handset of the phone, debating on whether or not to call again, but acid burned in the back of my throat, and the cans of Diet Coke and snack bag of cheese puffs attempted to reappear. Hand over my mouth, I ran to the bathroom and fell to my knees beside the toilet. With every thought of Susan and the boys, my guts clenched. Visions of Matt terrorizing them flashed in my mind.

The junk food churned up through my throat and out into the toilet. I slumped back onto my heels, shaking and sweaty. I prayed for my family's protection and then rose on weak legs to splash water on my face. All my doubts about escaping Matt's tyranny evaporated when I looked in the mirror. My hair looked more like tangled hay than the blonde it was. A dark bruise ringed one of my eyes, and the split on my lip had scabbed over.

"It's no wonder the clerk at the gas station looked at me funny."

The hot water steamed, rippling along the sides until the sink was full. The rough-napped hotel washcloth was not the best thing on tender skin. I submerged the terry cloth, and then rung out the excess water. Even wet, the washcloth was cat-tongue rough. I wiped the sweat from my forehead, cheeks and chin, taking care not to hit the torn skin on my mouth.

I pulled the chain attached to the light above the mirror and watched the sudden shadows wipe away the signs of abuse from my face. The hotel was blissfully quiet and velvet dark filled the room after I shut off the lights above the bed. I curled up on my side and faced the door, half expecting it to get kicked in. It didn't.

The digital clock blinked with each minute ticking past. Faint red light splashed my pillow like digitized Chinese water torture. The empty side of the bed echoed the rumbles in the hollow pit my gut had become. I missed Susan. I missed my nephews. Hell, I even missed the fuzzy, snoring lump who had occupied the other side of the bed for a year. Matt was a monster, but he was a demon I had grown used to. In the vacuum of his presence, loneliness settled on me, comforter thick and spare pillow cold. I stretched out and slid to the middle of the bed, silencing the ghost lying there.

Sleep remained elusive. Paranoid, I rolled to the far side of the bed, pulled open the curtains and checked the parking lot. Matt's truck was not there. I knew it wouldn't be, but I checked anyway. The orange teddy bear in my back window matched my lonely expression. I grabbed the door key and stuffed on my boots. Damp, chilly wind buffeted me when I stepped outside and retrieved my bear from the Celica. At least we could be lonely together. I had to smile a little when I walked back through the lobby, I felt like an elementary school kid wandering down the hotel corridor in my flannel pajamas and clutching a teddy bear.

Back in bed, with the bear in my arms, I finally succumbed to a fitful slumber.

The room spun when I opened my eyes and, for a moment, all sense of place and time was lost. I rubbed my hands over my cheeks and pushed back my tangled hair. Then, my rational side awoke. I remembered where I was and why. The ceiling of a room in the Super 8 was above me, the right side of the bed was empty.

My vision was bleary and I knew I'd slept with my mouth open. My tongue felt like a cat had slept on it. I cupped my hand in front of my lips and huffed a few breaths. *Oh my... I need a toothbrush.*

My bags were far enough away to make it a nearly callisthenic stretch to reach them. After a good amount of rummaging and cussing, I fished out toothpaste, a tooth brush and my slippers. My orange teddy had rolled over and gone back to sleep. I shuffled to the bathroom and left him on the pillow. My fleece clogs were fuzzy and warm, and after I brushed my teeth my breath was icy fresh. The toiletries went back into the small bag, but I kept my slippers on for a quick foray to the lobby and the continental breakfast the sign at the front desk promised.

Two elderly couples sat at the tables by the windows, and a rather rumpled looking man danced from foot to foot, waiting for the toaster. After last night's gastrointestinal pyrotechnics, I knew cereal or sweet pastries would not sit well, and puking again was not an option. I walked past the thermoses of coffee, picked out an Earl Grey tea, plunked it into a carry cup and drowned it with hot water. Then, I joined the queue at the toaster, plain bagel and steaming cup of tea in hand.

The foam plate was hardly bigger than the bagel, and I had to stack the buttered pieces together to carry my meager breakfast back to the room. Then, there I stood, with bagel in one hand, cup in the other and room key in my pocket. "Duh!" I would've smacked my forehead if my hands weren't occupied.

A rustle alerted me to the presence of someone else behind me. *Oh God, no!* Every muscle clenched and my jaw locked on instinct. I ducked my head and curled my shoulders in an effort to protect myself. I waited for a voice to raise or a hand to fall. Neither happened.

"Can I help you?" A wrinkled hand came into my view, reaching for my plate.

The hallway closed in on me. I couldn't breathe, couldn't think, when I should have relaxed and accepted the help. Someone stood behind me and I hated it. Too many memories were attached to the fight-or-flight feeling I suffered from when someone was behind me. I suffocated there against the door, stubborn and unmoving.

"Are you all right, miss?"

The voice was feeble, the fingers resembled spindles covered with skin. A modicum of relief trickled through me, and the sick trepidation sluiced from my gut. But I shook my head and balanced the bagel plate atop the teacup. I looked over my shoulder and into the face of one of the balding old men who had been in the lobby moments ago. His glasses were thick, his eyes projecting clear concern. I managed a weak smile for him.

"No, thank you. I can manage."

Releasing a shaky sigh, I pulled the card key through the lock and the green light flared. My bagel tipped when I pushed the handle down, tea sloshed in the cup, but I made it back into the room without spilling. The door swung closed, and I deposited my breakfast on the table in the corner.

Silence overwhelmed the room. I reached for the TV remote and chewed my bland bagel. The available channels clicked past in rapid succession while I finished my breakfast. Local news forecasted better weather for the Chicago area. To the west, it was more of the weather I left behind. A storm advanced from the West coast, over the Rockies and into the plains. The upper east corner of Wyoming looked to get nailed with an early snowstorm. After the less-than-auspicious forecast, I pulled jeans, a turtleneck shirt and sweatshirt from my bag—better to dress warm and be safe.

The dry cleaning bag served for my dirty clothes hamper, which I smashed tight and shoved back into my bag. My packed bags sat on the bed, with the teddy bear looped through one of the handles. I dropped beside them on the rumpled blankets, and picked up the phone to try Susan one last time before setting out for Chicago and beyond.

One ring, and then two. But on the third, someone answered.

"H-hello?"

"Oh good. You're home! I was so worried about you."

Susan groaned, and I could tell by the thickness in her voice I'd awakened her. "Kally? What're you doing calling this early?"

It was only six forty-five a.m. when I looked at the clock. I'd forgotten about the early morning hour. I was always a morning person. Susan wasn't very civil until she'd had half a pot of coffee. "I'm sorry to wake you, Sue. I tried your number twice last night. No one answered. I was worried... I thought he—"

"You thought Matt came here looking for you?"

"Yeah." I choked back the fear rising in me. The tone in her voice told me he had been there. I didn't have to wait long for her to validate the assumption.

"He did. Jerry met him at the door, and Matt bellowed like a damned bull. Then, he just took off. I looked out the window an hour later and I could see the hood of his truck around the corner. He was there for hours so we took the kids and went for dinner and a late movie. Thank the Lord it's the weekend."

My guts seized. My throat tightened around a guilty cough. My sister was facing the brunt of his anger because I was a chicken ass and ran when I should've fought back. "I'm sorry, Sue. I got you into this."

"Don't be sorry. I've been telling you to leave the bastard for a year. We'll manage. Jerry's cousin works at the courthouse, so if it's necessary, we'll get a PPO on Matt. You just take care of yourself."

"I will. I'm headed out now." Stuffing my guilt away, I rose and checked the room one last time. "When I get to Chicago, I'll find a cell phone and call you with the number. I love you, Sue."

"Love you, too, honey. Call me when you can."

Disconnecting the call was like leaving Susan all over again. I hung on the line, listening to the dial tone and feeling like a fool. My hands shook, and tears welled up. Chicago was the point of no return for me. It was the farthest I'd been from home, and I knew if I went past it, there would be no return trip. Tears blurred my vision and fell. I dropped the phone receiver onto my lap.

"Goodbye, Susan."

I put the handset back on the phone, gathered my bags and took stock of my snacks. There wasn't much left, and I had a long way to go before the day was done. Gillette, Wyoming was at least a fifteen hour drive. A plan formulated in my mind. I could stop and get some food when I picked up a cell phone in Chicago. And with a small part of my path decided for the day, I slung my bags over my shoulder and left the room behind.

The perky girl behind the counter never questioned my alias when I checked out of the Super 8—cash works wonders, even in this credit card based society. I paid for the night's stay and my long distance calls. The money Susan insisted on me taking was such a blessing. I wouldn't have been able to afford to stay in a hotel, and I might not have had enough money to make it out to see Ilene. I gave the clerk a smile and then stopped at the little breakfast nook for another cup of tea.

Granted, I would have to stop for a potty break, but there are certain sacrifices to make when the weather is damp and cold.

An icy patch in the parking lot caught my foot and sent me sliding, the trunk of the Celica catching me before I fell. I leaned against the car, propped the bags up on the bumper and then stuffed them in the trunk. With one hand braced on the car for balance, I slid around to the driver's side, and then climbed into my seat. I sat clutching the warm teacup with the car running for a few moments until the engine warmed up.

The travel time from Michigan City to Chicago was negligible in comparison to the rest of my trip. I'd hardly finished my second cup of tea when the Chicago exits signs blotted out the sky. I stayed on 90/94, which turned into the Dan Ryan, the major artery pumping traffic through Chi-town and northward. There were times the highway was so clogged with cars the town could've had a coronary. My Celica was expelled into the stream of traffic aimed for the Des Plaines Oasis, which was a perfect place for me to stop for a potty break, fuel up and buy a cheap phone.

I stood cross-legged at the fuel pump, doing the pee-pee dance and groaning while the tank filled and my meager stash of money dwindled. At this rate, the fuel industry would relieve me of the majority of my sister's generosity. Even though I was terrified of horses, they were becoming an attractive alternative to oil based fuels, if I could ever get the guts to climb up on one.

My shoes squished into the wet mat by the door, and I damned near skated through the building to the bathrooms. The lock on the stall was missing, and I had to lean forward and hold the door closed when I used the commode. I could smell Starbucks' coffee over the soap at the bathroom sink and my guts rumbled in reply. The tea and bagel had long since vacated my stomach. When I walked out of the bathroom the smell of roasted coffee beans was enough to make me salivate. I ordered a Café Breve and biscotti, which I sipped and nibbled while I browsed the cell phones. Flip this. Take a picture of that. Bluetooth technology. It was enough to make my head spin. Why can't they just make a simple, no frills, no techno babble phone?

I found the cheapest phone possible with the least amount of techno babble on the package and bought extra minutes. Then I leaned against a counter and punched numbers until I had it activated and functional. The phone snapped shut, and I stuffed it into my pocket.

I patted the phone through my jacket. "You're nothing but a damned necessary evil."

Armed with a cell phone, water bottles, a couple sticks of jerky and a bag of dried fruit, I climbed back into my little car. I had a long ride ahead of me in unfamiliar territory and I did not plan to stop for anything other than bathroom breaks and fuel.

I rescued my teddy bear from the trunk and put him in the passenger seat. He would be my copilot and the soundboard for my inevitable bitching. *Poor little guy.*

I flipped the cell phone open and fumbled with the keys to dial Susan's house. Each ring set my heart to pounding faster. I knew Matt had watched their house last night. I wouldn't put it past him to watch the house every minute he wasn't working. Hell, I wouldn't be surprised if he slept in his truck around the corner from Susan's remolded Victorian.

"Hullo?" It was my youngest nephew's voice.

"Hey there, Sammy Whammy!" I tried to sound chipper. "Is your mom around?"

"Aunt Kally? Mom said you left Uncle Matt..."

"Yes I did, Samuel, and he is not and never was your uncle, little man. Matt and I weren't married." I heard cell phone minutes ticking away in my head. "Can I please talk to your mom? I don't have a lot of minutes on this phone."

"Sure. MOM, IT'S AUNT KALLY!" He yelled loud enough I was certain people heard him on the east side of Lake Michigan. "Okay, Aunt Kally, here comes Mom."

"Thanks, Sammy."

The hand off between mother and son was muffled, and then Susan's voice filled my ear. "Hi, Kally. How's the trip going so far?"

"I'm doing all right. The tank is full, I have some healthy snacks and water and I am on my way to Ilene's. Will you do me a favor and write down this cell phone number and then hide it in your purse or something?"

"Sure, hun." Her voice sounded confused.

"Sue, I'm worried about you guys. I'm afraid Matt's going to break in when you're not home and find the number or...or worse."

"Okay, sweetie. I know you're worried about us, but I told you we'll be fine. Now get on the road and call me from your next stop."

"It'll be late. I'm going to see how far I can drive today."

"Fine, then. Call me from Ilene's if you make it there."

"Will do. I love you—you and the boys. Take care." I snapped the phone shut, and entrusted it to the arms of my orange companion. He could hold it and I wouldn't have to fumble in my pocket it for it if Susan called.

The engine kicked over and groaned to life when I stepped on the gas pedal, then I eased the car back out of the mouth of the hypodermic entry lane and back into the artery of traffic flow. I pulled out a water bottle, propped it on the console between the seats and then switched on the radio. Bass thumped through the speakers, providing background music for my departure from all I'd known. Foot on the gas and heart beating with hope, I headed for the open range of Wyoming and my friend Ilene Rogers.

Chapter Three

Somewhere around Madison, Wisconsin, my ass went numb. I pulled off at the next available stop and walked around until the feeling returned to my butt cheeks. The weather had warmed since my departure yesterday, and sitting in the little car with an overactive heater was making me sweat. My limp jacket fell to the floorboards of the backseat when I peeled it off. I rolled my shoulders, twisted from left to right, wiggled my hips and then touched my toes a few times to get the blood flowing.

Ilene would laugh at me for doing stretches in public. With the thought of my old friend, I fished my little silver phone from the teddy bear's lap and dialed her number.

She wasn't shocked by my call, or by me finally leaving Matt. "It's about time you got smart, Kally."

"I'm not sure if I should thank you. I know I'm not—"

"I know you're not stupid either," Ilene cut in. "So don't go there. It's just none of us could figure out why you stayed with him after the first fight. I would have packed my crap and been on the next bus home."

"I don't know what to say, other than I loved him." I couldn't vocalize a better argument. After the first fight, I had been in shock, in pain and still weak-in-the-knees in love with Matt. I always hoped he'd change, or I would be good enough. That never happened.

"I know you did, sweetie, I know." Ilene was the only one who seemed to understand this side of me, and how I couldn't give up on the love I'd fought so hard to keep alive. "We all love you too. After everything we went through in school, how you stayed with me when I was sick. God, Kally, you're a sister to me."

Tears started. "I know, and I'm so sorry I didn't call, or write like I should have. I wanted to keep some part of my life separate, and you are the one person I most wanted to keep hidden from him."

"It's okay. I missed you like mad, Kally, but Susan called and kept me abreast of what was going on. It killed me the first time she told me Matt had hurt you. If I didn't have Steve and my job out here, I would have come back to Michigan and taken you away from him. Any guy who raises a hand to you isn't worth having. You need someone to love you the right way, to treat you like the goddess you are. And I'm just damned proud you finally realized it."

My leaving didn't have anything to do with a goddess complex. My self-worth fled beneath Matt's fists and my love for him had died in its absence. Yet I had stayed, hoping he would learn to love me, and I could love him again. "Well, I'm not sure about the goddess thing. At least I realized I should be able to live without fear of being beaten to death by a man claiming to love me."

"Whatever the reason, you took the first step back toward becoming yourself again. Now, hurry up and get to Gillette. I'll put in a good word for you at the store and hopefully get you a job."

'Back toward becoming myself.' What a wonderful concept. "All right, Ilene. I'll call you the next time my ass goes numb."

She laughed, and the noise tugged at my heartstrings. I'd missed her laughter, missed having Ilene in my life. "Just call me. I don't need to know what your butt is doing."

I smiled, put the phone back into the bear's lap and drove to the next exit promising gas. The gas gauge had been sticking since I left Des Plaines, and I wanted to make sure I had enough fuel and didn't run out somewhere miles from help. In short order, I was back on 90/94 and feeling better with every mile north and west I traveled. Some small part of the shadow overhanging my life lifted. If a compass direction affected the soul, the needle pointing toward Wyoming made my soul sing.

Clouds slowly scudded across my view through the windshield, reminding me of November weather in Michigan. Thanksgiving was in a couple weeks, and happy memories of dinners at Susan's came to mind. I could almost smell the turkey roasting and feel the weight of my nephew Samuel dozing in my lap. He had latched onto me from the day Susan had brought him home, and I loved the little booger madly. My heart thumped in a sweet melancholy way, bringing tears and a smile to light up the Wisconsin landscape.

Static or country music crackled from the speakers with each spin of the radio dial. I gave up on the radio, rummaged in the glove compartment and found an old Def Leppard cassette. I was surprised the cassette had survived since high school, let alone years of heat and cold exposure, but it played without a problem. Soon, Joe Elliot's voice rasped out *Love Bites*.

How true, how true.

Joe and the band kept me company through the Badger State and on into Minnesota, though after multiple replays, the music became monotonous. I stopped often for bathroom breaks, fuel and to stretch my legs through Minnesota, and more than once bemoaned my forgotten cassette collection. The farther past the Minnesota/South Dakota state line I drove, the antsier I became. I stopped off in Mitchell, South Dakota for gas, something hot to eat and a break from the rolling scenery. With the Celica fueled up, I drove into a Culvers restaurant for a burger.

The tray with my meal sat waiting on the counter while I checked my purse and pockets for my wallet. Each search was fruitless. A sick sense of embarrassment and loss quivered in my stomach, while my jaw fell and my gut plummeted into my shoes. I checked all the nooks and crannies where a wallet might hide, all to no avail. The cashier watched me with disinterest, a frown furrowing her brow when I shrugged my shoulders. "Can you give me a minute to check my car? I must've dropped my wallet in there."

My cheeks flamed red. I could see the high color in my reflection on the driver's side window. The rubbery feeling within filtered out to my fingers and I dropped my keys to the asphalt. There, stooped over in South Dakota, I saw in my mind exactly where I dropped my wallet—two stops back, at the really busy gas station on the eastern side of this state. I thought I had heard something fall when I climbed in the car, but had dismissed it.

So damn stupid.

Hundreds of cars had to have passed through there. Someone had to have found my wallet. Tears splattered beside the key ring when I bent to pick them up. My heart fluttered, and the air was suddenly too thick to breathe. What was I going to do without my wallet? How could I get along without an ID, or the meager stash I'd tucked inside the billfold? What would Matt do if someone called him about my wallet, or sent it to him?

Impotent tears burned up. I scrubbed them away with the cuff of my sweatshirt. Crying was useless, and I'd done enough of it already. I dropped into the front seat, hoping I was wrong about where I had dropped the wallet. I tore through the glove box, upturned my steadfast orange companion, looked down beside and between the seats and doors and clawed through every bag in the car. The trunk, which had remained closed since Michigan City caught a cold South Dakota breeze when I opened it hopelessly digging for my wallet. I had to face the facts. The wallet was gone. My ID, my money, all of it was gone.

At least I have Sue's money. It was still in my jacket pocket, beneath the bloody reminder of a handkerchief. I lifted my rumpled jacket from the back seat and took a twenty-dollar bill from my sister's money.

The cashier rolled her eyes when I returned sweaty, blushed and disheveled from my mini meltdown in the parking lot. I'm pretty sure the girl snorted when she accepted the money. She plopped my change on the tray. "Have a nice day," had never sounded so snide.

The table I chose faced the west windows and the waiting dark gray clouds. Culvers had become purgatory in between the hell at home and the frightening unknown. I wouldn't return to Saint Joe. Without my own money and important papers, I was suddenly hesitant to go any farther. I lifted the lukewarm burger to my mouth, and found I no longer had any appetite. The loss of my wallet and the ramifications had soured my stomach.

I took the iced tea with me and bagged the remainder of the uneaten meal. The door swung open in the swift breeze, and my bangs blew in front of my face like a blonde curtain. My hair settled when the gust died. For a moment, I thought Samuel was walking toward me across the parking lot carrying my orange bear, then I pulled stray bangs from my eyes. The little boy resembled my nephew, but his hair was not wavy or brown. He stopped, held out my teddy bear by one arm, his other hand tucked in the small of his back. "I-I found him on the ground by the car over there. Is he yours?"

"Yes, he is." I bent down to the boy's level and took my teddy bear from his hand. I ruffled his hair a little, and he smiled. It was an honest expression, and it tugged a little grin from me too. "Thank you for saving my teddy bear. He was a birthday gift from a boy very much like you, and I would have missed him terribly."

The boy didn't reply, just waved and then ran to a car parked beside mine. The crammed navy sedan backed out and then drove to the main road. The pale haired boy turned and waved through the back window, a sunny face in the dark car. The license plate had a silhouette of a cowboy on a bucking bronco.

"A Wyoming license plate...I know a good sign when I see one."

Even with the loss of my wallet, and hundreds of miles from home, my spirits lifted. My teddy bear in the hands of the little boy was a great blessing and I took the license plate to be a sign of good things to come. I'd left the darkest time in my life behind me, and my path led to a place of blessings and joy. My teddy bear molded to my chest when I hugged him, and then he reclaimed his post as copilot. The leftover dinner sat on the floorboard in front of the passenger seat, close by if I decided to eat. Then, cell phone in hand, I piled in behind the steering wheel.

Susan was disheartened by my missing wallet, but I knew she needed to be on the lookout for Matt if someone sent it back to the address on the driver's license. She advised me to find a place to stay for the night and to contact the proper authorities in the morning. Her advice fell on deaf ears. "I'm serious, Kally. The next time I talk to you, you'd better be in a hotel."

"All right, Sue. I'll talk to you when I stop for the night."

I'm sure she bitched at me. I refused to hear it. I disconnected the call and dialed Ilene. She needed to be informed of my situation. She was less surprised at my misfortune, and also less concerned. "I think you're right, hun, the little boy was a sign. You have great things to look forward to here. Just drive nice and easy, and keep out of trouble until you get here. We'll take care of your ID and money troubles tomorrow morning from my kitchen table. I love you girl."

"Love you too, Ilene."

I hung up the call and then silenced the ring tone. I didn't need Susan using up my remaining minutes nagging me. The echo of the cell phone hitting the floor bounced around the car when I dropped it behind my seat and on top of my discarded jacket. Then, I put the key in the ignition and started up the car. "Wyoming, here I come."

The money in my chest pocket dwindled the closer I drove to the Wyoming border, but it did not dampen my mood. A kind of schoolgirl excitement buzzed in my veins despite the worsening weather and darkening sky. I could hardly see a car length in front of the hood. Snowflakes swirled above the hood and melted against my windshield. The dark sky and white flakes were a beautiful contrast. I've always loved an overcast, snow filled winter day.

Past the Wyoming border, I pulled onto the road shoulder to knock the snow and ice from my windshield wipers. I lifted the wiper blades and let them whack back against the glass. The right remained in working order, the left blade broke into brittle shards. "Oh, fuck me running! What's next?"

Heavy wet snow pelted the windshield after I crawled back in the car and crept down I-90. I couldn't see a damned thing, even by driving with my headlights off so the light wouldn't be reflected by the snowflakes. It was no good. With the car creeping along, I pulled the maps back out, looking for a city big enough to have some place to stay. Estimating gas used, I guessed I was somewhere around Sundance, but I never figured it out. At an intersection, the Celica skidded, and instead of engaging my brain and thinking enough to turn the wheel in the direction I wanted to go, I jerked it and slammed on the brakes.

Like some tutu wearing ice queen, the car spun on the spot. I screamed and swore until the air was blue and the car righted itself. Out of instinct I looked for the compass Matt had mounted to his truck's dashboard. Of course, this was the Celica and I didn't have any of those sensible manly things. I climbed out of the car and wiped snow from the windshield and debated my crossroads' dilemma.

Each direction looked the same—whitewashed of any identifying markers. *What the hell? I'm bound to find someone,*

one way or another.

The wheels spun before getting a grip and moving forward on the road. It was a flat ribbon of white in a snow squall, and I squinted at every road sign I passed. They were coated with snow and not about to reveal their secrets. Shrugging and damned near snow-blind, I crawled along, resolved to travel to the first gas station I came across.

Then, with sick clarity, I felt another shift in the car's direction. The wheels skidded in the snow and my Celica spun an almost lazy circle and slid off the pavement. A jarring thump rocked the car when it pitched rear first into the culvert alongside the road. My head rocked back and the seatbelt strained against my shoulder. The vehicle teetered on its bumper, snowflakes settled on the glass above me and my belongings tumbled into the back of the car.

My only thought was to scramble in one piece from the car. I pressed the seat belt button, but the latch did not release. The fabric cut into my palm when I pulled. I yanked and tugged until my hands bled and tears fell more swiftly than the foul language pouring from my lips. Straining, I kicked the glove compartment and popped open the door. Papers fell past my face. The dull edge of my multi-tool hit me square in the jaw. Though pain burned along the bone, the tool rested on my upturned chin.

The blade reflected the dome light when I opened it. I cut through the belt and then dropped into the backseat along with the scattered papers and French fries. My shoulder crunched and my knees came down into my face. The sudden displacement of weight tipped the car onto the roof. I screamed, though no one could hear. The burden of the under carriage was too much, the metal frame crumpled and the windows shattered.

Pain spread in thick waves through my shoulder, up my neck and down my spine when I pulled myself through the back window. I lay in the cold snow, sweating with fright and exertion while snow melted on my face. I was grateful to be alive, though gratitude was the last thing I expected.

Cold sarcasm rose suddenly, given birth by the chills wracking my body. "Yeah, sure. Drive down a road to nowhere in the middle of a snowstorm."

A groan escaped me when I rolled onto my stomach. Pain

characterized every move when I clawed away from the vehicle and stood and I wasn't certain where it originated. Spots of light danced in front of my eyes and a detached numbness sluiced through me. I only wished it had taken the pain with it. Everything hurt, but somehow, I was disconnected from it. I wiped sweat and blood from my forehead and surveyed the wreckage.

"What the hell am I going to do now?"

My phone was buried beneath the mass of twisted metal, my clothes, or what was left of them, were in the trunk, which resembled an accordion. My snowbound surroundings offered nothing more than a picturesque winter night, a broad stretch of land and a long barbed wire fence.

"Fences lead to houses." *At least they do in Michigan.*

From where I stood, any house would be a long walk. Not one building was visible. I wiped the sweat and trickling blood from my face and set out along the fence. Chills crept up my spine and then trembled through my whole body. My teeth chattered, and I clenched my jaw to stop it from rattling my head. Every jiggle made my head throb. The uneven ground proved treacherous beneath my feet, but solid underneath my ass when I fell. I kept moving. Eventually, I would find someone who could help me.

Goose bumps coated my skin, my breath rose in thin plumes and my feet were numb in winter's grip. I kept looking for a house, a car, anything to show signs of life. I must have marched along the loneliest road in Wyoming, because my search proved to be more hollow than the new moon above me. Then, running on the inside of the fence and off into the property, I found a path. I took off my sweatshirt, threw it over the barbed wire and scrambled over the fence and face first into the snow.

The barbs released my shirt from their nettled grip, and I pulled the holey sweatshirt back on. The path was narrow, meandering over the uneven terrain and in-between stands of aspens and pines. Hillsides poured into little valleys dotted with scraggy bushes and full Christmas tree pines before climbing again. After the third or fourth incline and fast slide down the other side, I noticed my chills were gone. A detached feeling replaced them. I raised my hand to the cut on my head. It was dry. Either the cut had frozen, or the blood just wasn't getting there.

Even I knew in my frozen, muddled consciousness, decreased blood flow and no more chills were dangerous.

Drowsy weight settled in my limbs. My eyes drooped, then flew open wide at the sight of a light and a low roofline. It was a small building, maybe just a barn. At least it could provide shelter. I left the path I had followed and plowed through a flat field of pristine snow. Yards from a roofed cattle pen, my left foot slipped and sank. I didn't realize until icy water gushed over my calves and into my boots, that I'd floundered into a pond. Instinct ticked in my muscles, and I fell backward instead of face first into the frigid depths.

Mud seeped through my clothes, caked my scalp. Water dripped from my body when I crawled from the muck. I managed to collapse on the bank, where the damp mud held me in a wet embrace and fresh snow blanketed me. I panted, watching the plumes of my breath rise in the faint blue glow of the halogen lamp while the cold soaked into my bones, into my guts, which lay inert beneath my skin.

Irony struck me like an icy club. I'd left Matt because I was afraid he'd kill me. Now here I lay, dying. A sick, strangled laugh escaped me. Though a ray of light flashed across the pond, black fields encroached on my vision and a chilly invitation to a long cold sleep tempted.

"What in the world?"

A voice rang in the little snow filled dell. I lifted my head from my icy bed and saw a man in a low profile Stetson hat riding toward me on a white horse. The image of him sitting astride the horse framed in snowfall was etched like ice in my mind. He trained the beam of his flashlight on me and our gazes locked. "Gid-up!" He spurred the horse and it charged around the edge of the pond I'd stumbled into.

The man dropped from the saddle and pushed his hat from his head. He nestled his Maglite into the snow so that it shined on me. Steam rose from his dark hair, and his expression flared hope in me. His eyes were polar ice blue and angel robe soft. No matter how I wanted to look at his face forever, my eyelids sagged. His hands were clear in my hazy vision. Hands weren't always good. Matt had hit me with his hands. A little knot of fear tightened in my gut, but this man was gentle. "Come on, girl. Stay with me."

"Car crash." I muttered. I couldn't say more. Nothing came out but a shaky breath. He nodded, and a frown knit his brows together.

He pulled the gloves from his hand and patted my thighs and arms. "You're soaked to the bone and freezing."

I wanted to nod my head in agreement, but my fine motor skills were frozen too. His fleece-lined jacket smelled of Stetson cologne when he pulled it off, the scent of sweat sweetened with fabric softener rose from his long underwear shirt. "Let me help you."

I couldn't have fought him if I wanted to. I had no strength left. My field of vision narrowed when my eyelids drooped again. He wadded the shirt into a soft mass and patted my face dry. Despite the sting of his shirt against my cheek, I was grateful for his touch. My head lolled to the side while he wiped down my arms. I was less appreciative when he used the shirt to sop water from my shoulders and chest. Pain blazed from my shoulder socket and radiated through my arm and chest. A weak cry escaped my lips, but the onset of hypothermia had iced over my tear ducts.

"Hush now." He stopped, placing a warm hand on my cheek and shushing me. "We have to get you dry you before you freeze to death."

It might be too late.

He stood, more silhouette than man to my increasingly fuzzy vision. Putting his hat back on, he bent to wrap me in the clothing he'd removed. I couldn't feel him touching me. I was beyond feeling, slipping into the numb, quiet dark. The pain eased. The cold eased. My vision failed. There was only me and him. His chest was the last thing I saw when he wrapped his arm around my back. The last thing I felt was the warmth of his bare skin.

Me and him.

Me.

...black...

Chapter Four

He had always hated accident calls like this when he was on the force. The only ones he had hated worse were accidents involving little kids.

This girl was barely conscious and going hypothermic. Slade knew if she didn't get warmed soon her chances of survival were slim. Even her breath was cold on his skin. Whistling for his quarter horse Jack, he scooped his arm beneath her legs and lifted the limp woman. Despite the blood and mud, her hair still smelled like jasmine. At times like this, the small details made each call different, made each victim unique.

She was wet dead weight in his arms and slipped in his grip like his mother's oiled holiday turkey. Bracing her butt on his thigh, he trussed her up with his long underwear shirt, using the sleeves like handles. His boot slipped on the edge of the pond, and instinct made him squeeze her tighter. She struggled and whimpered. "No...please don't hurt me again."

Slade had been an officer with the Hulett P.D. only three months ago. There were times he had cared about the victims, and there were times he hadn't, but this girl's unconscious cries for mercy cut right into his heart. She was unlike any victim he'd ever helped before.

The blizzard solidified beside him in the form of his horse Jack. The stallion knelt and Slade eased the girl up into the saddle. She slumped over the pommel and against the horse's neck. Jack rolled a brown eye in her direction and nickered softly. Slade patted his neck. "It'll be all right. Up, Jack."

Jack stood and Slade pulled up into the saddle behind her. He knew he needed to contact the main house. He'd need help when he arrived there. This wasn't a normal call, and there wouldn't be EMTs showing anytime soon. Sundance was at least thirty minutes away in good weather. The girl in his arms didn't have an hour. He leaned to pull his radio out of the saddle bag and the girl pitched sideways. Slade dropped the reins, trusting Jack to take them home. He held the nameless young woman tight to his chest with one arm, smelling jasmine and blood while he paged the ranch house with the other hand. "Slade to home. Anyone there?"

His father's voice crackled through the speaker. "Pine here. What's the emergency, son?"

"I found the source of the cattle's fussing." He looked at the girl, her face had an eerie blue tint, and her features were almost elf-like. She looked breakable, a bisque porcelain doll in his arms. "There was a woman floundering in the cow pond on the back eighty."

Disbelief rang in Pine's voice. "Come again?"

"I'm bringing in a young woman. She's hypothermic, Dad. Please start my truck and get some warm blankets."

"Roger, Slade. We'll be ready."

His family's willingness to pitch in, to help out someone in need, was something to admire. He was always impressed with his parents' capacity to care. *I wish they just didn't care so much about the ranch.*

If it wasn't for the ranch and his brother Beau's dreams of expansion, he wouldn't have quit the force and come back to help his parents. He'd be out somewhere, maybe even in Gillette, in a cruiser, responding to an emergency call. He lifted his eyes to the sky. God, he loved the rush of stepping on the gas, heart racing with the thrill of the unknown. The excitement had been hard to quit.

The girl moaned, and his mind snapped back to the very real emergency call he clutched to his chest. Frail, blonde with blue eyes and bruises he knew damned well didn't come from the car wreck. She mumbled again and he shushed her, patting her shoulder. "It's okay, girl. I'm here."

And maybe I'm here because of this—to help Mom and Dad, and to find her. Slade knew his parents didn't check the perimeters like he did, and they wouldn't have noticed the stir the cattle were making on the back eighty.

The lights were on in the last house on Rancher's Row. The

small ranch house resembled the main house, just lacking the wing of guest rooms and office space. Jack whinnied when Slade's godmother stepped onto the porch. The woman in his arms flailed wildly at the horse's greeting and mumbled something unintelligible. Slade placed a hand on her cheek, holding her snug against him so she could not hurt herself or his horse when he spurred him forward toward the main ranch house.

She quieted, hardly responsive, and Slade knew lessened consciousness was never a good thing in a medical situation. Training told him it might take some of the suffering from the victim, but he knew from experience it sure as hell made reviving them more difficult.

Light bathed the snow in front of his parent's ranch house. It had a quiet beauty all lit up on a snowy night, it was a shame he hadn't paid the house much attention in a long while. He reined in Jack on the long side of the circle drive. His parents were waiting on the porch and his godparents drove in right behind him. His father hurried to help, stronger than his gray hair suggested he might be when he lifted the woman from Slade's arms. His mother met him beside the truck, her arms loaded with blankets and clean clothes for him.

His godmother scurried up, her dark eyes wide with interest. "So, you're bringing home strays now? This is the first girl you've brought home in two years, Slade."

"Yes, ma'am. Wasn't like I could leave her out there." *Please don't ask if I plan on keeping her...*

Humming voices rode the surface of my murky haze. His voice anchored me to some sense of reality, but jostling roused me from my stupor. I woke to find bright lights glaring down from a rooftop, snowflakes falling on my face and commotion all around. A panicky sense of suffocation rose in me, and then there he was, silent and soothing, holding me and wrapping me in a warm blanket. "I've died or I'm dreaming, because chivalry is alive and well in Wyoming."

His face warmed, a smile crept over his lips, and then he broke into a full laugh while he tucked the blanket corners around my face. "For being frozen silly, you have quite a sense of humor."

My brain was too sluggish to produce a smart retort. Even

my fears were quiet. I couldn't formulate a reply, or ask what was going on. I focused only on the connection to my cowboy hero and hung limp in his arms. He settled me into the front seat of a battered blue and white Dodge pickup and pulled the safety belt around me. A woman with graying hair and soft blue eyes appeared beside him with a thermal Henley shirt, which she hastily pulled over his head, and handed him a new jacket. Then, she turned to me, leaning into the cab of the truck to tuck a quilt scented with lavender and sage over the blanket swaddling me. She stroked muddy strands of hair from my face. "There you go, sweetie. Now, don't you worry, Slade will take good care of you."

Slade? What a name for a cowboy.

She turned to my dark-haired savior then, shoving him toward the truck. "Hurry up, boy. Get her to the hospital in Sundance."

Hospital? No! What limited consciousness I had screamed in revolt. I didn't have any money, any insurance, any way to pay for treatment. I shook my head. My eyes couldn't remain open and the fog of sleep took me back into its depths.

I slept through the drive to Sundance but awoke on a gurney beneath blazing hospital lights when my damp clothes were cut away. Hands attached to any number of ER attendants poked, prodded, jabbed in IVs and pasted sticky pads on my skin, connecting me to monitors. People shouted vital signs. A nurse with a kind face and strong hands dressed me in a scratchy hospital gown before they wrapped me in a heated air blanket someone called a "Bear Hugger".

The only source of true comfort in the storm of emergency room activity was Slade's face peeking around the curtain's edge. I kept him in my sight, the last familiar and soothing thing. He turned from watching me and the clock to looking through the crowd of ER attendants. A nurse in a pink scrub suit hurried past his point of observation and Slade caught her by the sleeve. "How is she, Leanne?"

"What are you doing in here, Slade? Get your butt out to the waiting room and I'll come out with an update when we have one."

"Bullshit. We've known each other since the second grade. The least you can do is tell me if she's gonna be okay."

Leanne cast me a swift, appraising glance. Her face

softened and then she scanned the clipboard in her hands. "Yeah. She'll be fine." She held the clipboard out toward him. "What's her name?"

"I have no idea. I found her dripping wet and freezing by one of the cow ponds on the back eighty. The girl could hardly talk, but my mom called her Fate."

Leanne snorted, cracking Slade on the shoulder with her clipboard. "And I'm an angel. Now get your rear out of the way!"

No! Slade, don't go...

He did. With one last look at me and a tip of his Stetson, he was gone. The room closed in, suffocating me, swarming with faces, wires and tubes. I tried to retreat into the sleepy haze swirling in the back of my mind, but the doctors and nurses demanded my attention. Answer this, blow into that, "don't worry, this won't hurt a bit..."

Yeah, right.

By the time I had been wheeled into a private room, my arms were flesh-toned pin cushions. I could have been a character in a Tim Burton movie. I lay in the dark room, trying to center myself. My life had become a whirlwind with all solid footing gone. Images of Matt and his fists swirled with views out of my car window and the picturesque ranch I had stumbled onto. The one constant in the storm of visions was the quiet strength, and gentle face of Slade. I latched onto his image and drifted off to a more peaceful, restorative sleep.

Fresh snow covered the trenches her car had dug, but they were enough to catch Slade's eye. He switched on his flashers and pulled off on the shoulder of Route 24, pumping the brakes to keep the Dodge from sliding too far. The spare flashlight in the glove box was ancient. He pulled it out and checked the battery. The beam of light cut through the snowfall. *Yup, works fine.*

Slade followed the tracks off the pavement, walking a straight line through her car's crazy loops, and then slid with one hand against the embankment wall for balance. The car was ass end down in the culvert, flames still sputtering in the crannies of the underbody. The front license plate was plain blue with white digits and in the middle of the line at the bottom it read "Michigan".

Skirting the flames, he scooped up everything he could

find—a jacket, cell phone and some girly stuff. He aimed the beam of the flashlight in a search pattern up, down and across the culvert. Nothing caught his eye.

Guess the fire got the rest.

Slade was wrong. Scrambling back up the slope he kicked the snow off from an orange teddy bear laying not more than a foot from the muddy trench in the side of the culvert. He brought the bear to his nose. *Jasmine.*

She had smelled like jasmine and bloody mud when he'd found her.

A girl from Michigan hypothermic in his pond...

Bruises not consistent with a car accident.

Traveling with a stuffed animal...

He piled her belongings onto the passenger seat along with the clothes and blankets Mother had insisted he bring home. Climbing behind the wheel, he tipped back his hat and scratched his head. The police officer side of him wondered what the hell a girl from Michigan was doing on the road to Hulett in the middle of a snowstorm. It just didn't make sense. The stuffed animal part he understood. It must have sentimental attachment. But Hulett? Hulett had great hunting. From what he found at the accident site, she wasn't here for hunting. They had a hell of a rodeo in the summer, too. It was far from summer.

Driving mostly on autopilot, Slade ignored the scenery. He knew the path home all too well. The Dodge dipped south on the hill she'd most likely slid down. He steered around the pine stretching over the drive while he fished out her cell phone. It must be fairly new, shiny, hardly a scratch on it, no consistent wear marks. When he rounded the bend in Rancher's Row, he lifted it close to read the display screen and the same floral perfume drifted up.

The scent conjured images of the girl in his mind. Vulnerable and blonde, she was like sunshine in the blizzard. The lost look in her eyes in the ER had touched him. She was scared. He read it on her face. Other victims had been equally scared, sometimes hurt worse, but Slade had lingered with this one, staying longer than he would for any normal call.

Why the hell did I stay?

To comfort her. Even though she'd only said a few words, something about the girl spoke to him and he knew she needed him to be there.

He clicked through phone's menu and found her contact list. There were only two numbers. Ilene Rogers, with an area code he easily recognized—Gillette, Wyoming. And, Susan Nelson, with an area code he didn't recognize. Going by the warped license plate on her car, he had a good guess where the number would ring. *Must be a Michigan number...*

The screen flickered with each click when he exited the contacts list and found the I.C.E. information she had been smart enough to program in. There was no home address, no phone number. Only a name.

Kally Jensen.

"What are you doing so far from home Kally?"

Of course the girl couldn't answer. She was sound asleep in the hospital.

The ranchers' drive was dark and quiet, just like it should be. Only a swirling snow devil moved through the cattle pen. The herd wouldn't be brought onto the house range until closer to Christmas. Everything was in order, considering the late hour. Then, his headlights shone through the gap in the barn door. Slade might ignore a pretty hill, but he never missed details like a door ajar, or an open window. *Dad must've forgotten to latch the door.*

He put the Dodge in neutral and dashed for the door. Jack whinnied in the shadows, and his mother's horse shook her mane. Nothing else moved. There were no new scents. Satisfied nothing was amiss, Slade stepped out in time for the rotten-tempered orange barn cat to shoot through his boots and around a bale of hay. "Damned cat."

The tabby peered from the shadows, his yellow eyes luminous in the starlight. Slade had the distinct impression the cat was thinking, *Fuck you, human.*

Feuding with a cat might be stupid, but the tabby had hated him from birth. Slade closed the door, got back into the truck and puttered up to the house. He rolled the last few feet without power or lights in case his parents were sleeping, and stepped lightly across the porch to keep his boot heels from thumping.

His mother met him in the foyer, however, her foot tapping and her arms crossed. "So, how is she?"

Slade dropped his boots onto the plastic tray by the wall

and then piled the laundry and other items into his mother's arms. She followed him into the main room and Slade knew by her quick breathing she was itching for more information. "She didn't talk at all, just laid there with this scared expression. I would have stayed longer. Leanne told me she'd be fine and chased me out. I sat in the waiting room until I got word they'd put her into a private room." He hung his Stetson on the antler peg next to his father's white Resistol hat and headed for the stairs.

"Well, I'm going to go down there. The poor girl shouldn't have to stay in a hospital in a strange city alone."

You're a stubborn one. You could convince a rattler it needed mothering. Slade knew enough not to argue with her much though. "It's past visiting hours."

"I know." His mother nodded. "I also know her doctor, so I'm going to go and sit with her. Do me a favor and fetch the quilt in the bedroom next to the bathroom please. It might do her good to have a little homey comfort."

"Yes, ma'am." He hustled up the stairs, ducking into the room two doors down from the stairs. The quilt was one of his mother's better projects, based on scraps of his flannel works shirts over the past few years and accented with other shades of white and blue.

She stood in the foyer, boots and jacket on, waiting. "Thank you, Slade. Please help your father pack tomorrow morning before you come back to the hospital."

Slade tilted his head. "How'd you know I was going to go back?"

She just smiled. "Because I know you, son. The look on your face, the way you held her..."

He stood, gaze locked with his mother's, but the girl and her meager belongings flashed through his mind. Kally had nothing, and they were in a position to help. "Mother, I didn't find a wallet on her and no purse or ID cards at the scene. I think the Fourth Moon should cover her medical bills. I mean," he kicked at fuzz on the rug, "we did find her on our property, after all."

She patted his shoulder before slipping out the front door. "Of course, son. I think it's right and proper. I'll see you in the morning."

"Good night, Mother."

His room sat on the second floor, spanning its width, at the far end of the hall he'd pulled the quilt from. The ceiling vaulted to the rafters. The top half of the outside wall was glass, a framed wildlife image of a soft Wyoming night, the tree line was deep in shadow and the hilltop he knew was behind it was obscured by the snowfall.

Slade turned his back on the view, chucked his shirt into the woven wicker hamper and then pulled his range bag from the closet floor. He removed the paddle-style holster from the waistband of his jeans and pulled his service gun from the molded leather. Following safety protocols, he pressed the release button, popping the mag out of the gun, pulled back on the slide to verify there wasn't a round in the chamber and then put them both into pockets in the bag at his feet. He knew there was a loaded rifle kept in both the house and workshop, but after years on the force, he preferred keeping his sidearm handy.

Better safe than sorry.

Pacing in front of his bedroom windows, Slade debated on whether or not to call her contacts. They needed to know what happened to her. The authorities should have been notified too. For some reason, he hesitated dialing the station. Sucking up his doubts, he pressed the number to call her Wyoming contact, Ilene Rogers.

The phone rang twice, and then a groggy female voice filled his ear. "Kally? Where're you? Why're you calling so late?"

I wish this was just a police call, then it would be easy. This, however, wasn't going to be easy. "Ms. Rogers, this is Slade Carlson. I hate to have to tell you this—"

"Who the hell are you and why are you using Kally's phone? There'd better be a good reason you're calling me in the middle of the damned night." *Good Lord. She went from groggy to grumpy in nothing flat.*

"Ma'am, I apologize for calling you this late, but Kally has been in an accident—"

"Accident?" The irritable tone was gone, replaced with panic. "Oh my God! What happened? Is she okay?"

"Her car rolled over. I found her on my parent's ranch. She was hypothermic and banged up." He paused, Kally's pale face in his mind. "I was scared we'd lose her, so I brought her to the hospital in Sundance. The nurse assured me she'll come out of it fine."

"Oh my." Ilene broke into tears. "The poor girl...after everything's she's been through..."

The faded purple bruises on her neck. Maybe this was a chance to get an answer about those marks, his curiosity, his need to solve the case overtook his sense of caution. "If I may ask, what did happen to her? I was very concerned when I noticed bruising around her neck. Those marks aren't consistent with a car accident."

She was quiet for a long time, and Slade wondered if she'd hung up. Her voice was soft and measured when she spoke. "It's not my place to say. If the accident hasn't been reported, please don't. Some elements of her past don't need to resurface in her future."

His mind was locked on the girl's mumbled pleas for mercy. "I'll do what I can. I'm sure Miss Jensen would appreciate a visit from you. You're only one of the two contacts in her phone."

"I'll be there in the morning. Thank you for letting me know, and for taking care of my friend."

"No thanks necessary, ma'am."

"Oh no, trust me, there is. Kally needs kindness. So, thank you, Mr. Carlson, and good night."

"G'night, Ms. Rogers."

He disconnected the call, clicked back to the contacts menu and dialed the second number. He held his breath, knowing it was even later in Michigan. Another woman answered the phone, but sounded like she'd been stalking it, waiting on the ring. "Hello? Kally? Where the hell are you? I thought I told you—"

"I'm sorry, Ms. Nelson, this is not Kally. My name is Slade Carlson, I'm calling to let you know Kally has been in an accident. She's in the hospital in Sundance, Wyoming."

Silence was his only answer. Then he heard a strangled sob. "I knew something happened to my sister. I just knew it." She lost it then, like so many other victims' family members had.

"Please don't be upset, Ms. Nelson." He wanted to comfort her, hated to hear a woman cry. "Kally has some bruising and was hypothermic, but I got her to the hospital in time."

She snuffled and then squeaked out a "thank you".

"I do it gladly, ma'am. I was a police officer, and when I canvassed the accident site I noticed she had no wallet." What was he doing? His brain mouth filter was broken. "So, our ranch will be covering her medical bills."

"I appreciate the gesture, Mr. Carlson." Her tone was tense. "Please just send me the bills and we'll take care of them."

"I don't mean to argue with you, Ms. Nelson." *Yes, I do.* She displayed the same argumentative traits his sister Joeley had honed to a fine art. "I insist. I'm the one who found her and I want to help her back to well."

"It's awfully kind of you, but I'm not comfortable with a stranger paying her bills." It was a battle of wills now. *What is it going to take to get her to listen?* "And I'm sure Kally won't be either."

"I'd probably feel the same way, ma'am. I assure you we only want the best for her. My mother's gone to sit with her tonight, and I'll go back up tomorrow. How about we let Kally decide about the bill?"

He could nearly hear the arguments churning in her, then she surprised him. "Okay, Mr. Carlson. Kally's trying to make a new life. I think she has the right to start making her own decisions."

"So, it's agreed. I will call you when I have any updates on your sister."

"Thank you, Mr. Carlson."

"You're welcome."

She hung up the phone, and he was almost relieved. *She must wear the pants in her family.* Kally's two contacts were both very concerned about her. Past that, the women seemed to be polar opposites. One concerned, caring about keeping her safe, and one who wanted to take control and mother the girl. And something in her sister's voice told him Kally had had a hard time of things in Michigan and was out West to escape.

The pieces were falling together in a puzzle not turning out pretty. Slade shook his head. His concerns hadn't quieted down. They had escalated after speaking to Ms. Jensen's contacts. Her friend had said, *"Some elements of her past don't need to resurface in her future."*

What would chase a girl six states away?

There must be monsters in her shadows.

A horror in her past made sense. Why she fascinated him

did not.

Slade's jeans fell to the floor with a jerk of his belt and a few snaps of his fly. He hooked his toes under the rumpled denim and kicked them into the hamper, then rolled his socks into a ball and threw them on top before climbing into bed. He tossed and turned, but couldn't sleep.

Her face, tinted an eerie pale blue and framed with blonde hair, haunted his mind.

Morning sunlight poured in the window. The heat bathed the side of my face. The comforting caress was welcome. I'd hardly slept at all after a night full of numerous visits by phlebotomists and nurses. And chills still crept along my skin even though the warm air blankets had done their job, bringing my core temperature back to near normal. An odd, fatigued dizziness swam behind my eyes and I wanted desperately to sit instead of lie. My fingers fumbled over the buttons of the bed controls and then it lurched to a less-than-upright position.

My shoulder throbbed with the new elevation. Groaning, I rolled to my side and the pain in my shoulder wrenched a cry from my lips. I flopped back onto the mattress, defeated and sniveling. Clothes rustled and a faux leather chair squeaked, alerting me to the presence of someone else in the room. I sucked up my tears and wiped at my nose with my good hand.

The woman with the kind face and pale blue eyes from the night before skirted the curtain beside my bed. She wore denim and corduroy from head to toe, and the clothes were creased with a night's worth of rumples. Her cheeks were tanned, and though wrinkles framed her eyes, she had a youthful appearance. She came to the side of my bed, looking down at me like I often looked at Samuel when he was sick in his crib. "Are you in pain, dear?"

I didn't know what to say. Yes, I was in pain, and her sitting in my room left me dumbfounded. Only family and friends sit with people in the hospital.

"If your shoulder hurts, you can ring for the nurse to bring you something." She stepped closer to the bed, her hand alighting atop the blankets over my forearm. My gaze fell to where her thin fingers rested over a patch of delft blue on the quilt. Its weight rivaled the comfort of the sun coming through the window. "And if you're wondering...my name is Bonnie."

"I-I'm fine, Bonnie." I lied. My shoulder hurt like hell. "I don't want meds. I can't afford this hospital stay." Sudden tears burned my eyes. I buried my face in my hands. Bonnie stood beside the bed, silent and comforting when she stroked my neck and back.

"Hush now, dear. Don't worry about the hospital bill. Fourth Moon is taking care of it."

"What's the fourth moon? Wh-why—"

Bonnie's soft finger on my lips silenced the deluge of questions. She reached around the curtain and pulled the chair close before she sat. She slipped her hand under the side of the blanket and placed her fingers over mine. "The Fourth Moon is our ranch. It's where my boy Slade found you dripping wet and freezing to death. And, to answer your question of 'why' the ranch is covering your bills, well, Slade insisted. He feels responsible since he found you."

Sick guilt gnawed at my guts. I wouldn't question her words or his feelings. A reason deeper than an accident had brought me to their ranch and Slade to my rescue. I believed coincidences were nothing more than the universe moving in unexpected ways. I nodded my head in mute understanding.

Bonnie shifted her weight in the chair, leaning closer to me. "Do you have any more questions, dear?"

My guilt grew a voice. "What can I do to pay you back?"

"It isn't necessary. We can just call it a gift."

"Forgive me for arguing, but it's an awful expensive gift. I don't want to start out my new life indebted to anyone."

She tipped her head, an unreadable expression on her face. "There is a vast difference between a gift and a debt. If you insist on repayment it will be between you and Slade to settle. We are leaving for an extended business trip overseas."

"Leaving?" *How could I pay him back if they were leaving?* "Is Slade going too? When will I be able to talk with him?"

Just then, Slade peeked around the doorjamb. Bonnie's face lit up with a smile and she squeezed my fingers. "Right on cue, my son."

"Good morning, Mother." He tipped his hat. "Morning, Miss Jensen."

My heart fluttered at the sight of him. His sheepskin-lined denim jacket covered a body I knew was lean muscled with wide shoulders. His Wranglers were tight on his butt and loose in the thighs just like I like them. I forced my mind to focus on speech, on dealing with the issues at hand and not drooling over a cowboy in my hospital room. "How do you know my name?"

He produced my cell phone from his jacket pocket. "I found this by the wreckage of your car. I checked the I.C.E. you'd programmed in. Smart girl to fill it out in case of emergencies." He placed it on the table over my bed, then reached into a gift bag he carried and pulled out my orange teddy bear. "I found him too. He was a tad muddy, being in the bottom of the culvert, so I washed him off. Thought he might be important if he came all the way from Michigan with you."

Oh, how considerate. This guy was melting my heart. I bit my lip to cap a fresh fount of tears, then nodded and reached a hand out for my orange companion. I wrapped the stuffed animal to my chest, tears falling into fur wonderfully smelling of the same herbal scent as the quilt over my hospital blankets. Finally, I mumbled a "thank you" through the arch of his ear.

"You're most welcome." Slade placed the gift bag beside me on the bed, and then walked to the far side and stood next to his mother. I sat there and looked at the bag, feeling like an emotional baby for clinging to a stuffed animal. "Go ahead, girl. It's for you."

"You don't have to give me anything. You've done so much already." I looked up into his brilliant blue eyes, so honest and unguarded. There was a familiarity between us normally only shared by longtime friends, and his presence and jovial attitude buoyed my spirits.

"Don't argue with the gift bringer, darlin'." He screwed up his handsome face into a façade of ornery toughness and then waggled a finger at me. "I might not bring you another."

I had to smile. Instinctively, I reached for the bag with my right arm, stopping short and wincing when pain surged through the socket and out to my fingers. The orange teddy bear was relocated to the crook of my right elbow, and I used my left hand instead. The bag rumpled the quilt when I pulled it close, but I smoothed the blanket. Then, I pulled tissue paper from the gift bag and exposed two wrapped parcels at the bottom.

The first package was soft and crinkled with an odd plastic noise. The wrappings came away to expose a plastic bag full of hand-tied tea bags. When I opened the bag a dusty sage scent wafted up, mellowed with the smell of berries and lavender. "It's my mother's special tea blend. I drank it after a horse bucked me off a few years ago. She can probably explain it better than I." He cast his mother a glance, eyebrows slightly pinched.

"Of course, son." Bonnie patted the back of my hand lightly. "I'm not quite sure how to say this, so I'm just going to give you the truth. I'm a bit of a kitchen witch, and the tea is my own blend of local herbs and berries with healing attributes."

"Witches are all right in my book, Bonnie. And thank you, Slade."

Slade tipped his hat, but his gaze did not leave mine. "You're most welcome, Miss Jensen." His gaze shifted to his mother's and gave her a knowing wink. Her smile broadened in reply.

"Call me Kally."

He tipped his hat down and peeked beneath the rim. "I'll take it under advisement."

One package remained in the bottom of the bag. It was limp and squishy when I lifted it out. I cast a swift look at Slade. His face was impassive, refusing to give me any clue of what the gift was. The paper came away to reveal a pastel tie-dyed stuffed bull, a perfect companion in size and color to the orange teddy bear resting against my arm. His horns were a peachy pink, and his silly/happy bovine face looked up at me.

"Y'see," Slade explained, "if it wasn't for the cattle bellowing I wouldn't have investigated the cow pond last night."

"Thank God for cows." I wrapped the two animals to my chest and snuggled into my pillow. A yawn escaped me and a warm, sandy weight filled my body.

"Aw, the poor girl is exhausted. Come on, son." Bonnie shooed Slade from my bedside and toward the door. "Let's skedaddle so Kally can get some sleep."

"No, wait please." I tried to sit up, to chase the sleepiness from me. Slade and his mother stopped at the door. Another yawn escaped me, and I shook my head, rubbed my face with my free hand. "Did you contact anyone on my cell phone list? I need to tell my sister where I'm at. Need to call my friend Ilene..." The sentence ended in another yawn.

Slade came back to my bedside. No matter how happy I

was to see him, how handsome I thought he was, when his hand rose toward me, I flinched, cringing inside. His hand and expression were gentle when he placed his palm against my chest, pinning me to the bed while he pulled the quilt up to my chin with the other. "You've been through a lot, Miss Jensen, and you need your rest. Yes, I used your phone. Yes, I called your sister and your friend Ms. Rogers. They are both very worried about you, but I promised we would take good care of you. Your sister didn't settle down until I promised her an update today. Are you going to pitch a fuss and keep me from calling them?"

I felt better the moment his hand lifted from my chest. Sleep settled over me, draping my limbs like a quilt. "Call me Kally. And no, sir, no fuss."

He stroked my hair. "That's my girl."

His touch was the last sensation I felt before I drifted into a sound nap.

A familiar laugh filtered into my dreams and eased me toward consciousness. The face I saw when I opened my eyes was sweeter than any memory. Her dark blonde hair and sunny smile were unmistakable. My heart soared at the sight of my friend Ilene Rogers. "Hey, look who's here."

"Hey! Look who's up."

"Hi, Weenie."

"Oh sure." Ilene winked at me and then draped herself over Slade's shoulder like a cheap suit jacket. "Just because I'm talking to this hot cowboy in your hospital room doesn't mean you get to pull out my old nickname."

Slade shot a look at me, shuffled his feet and then looked out the door. "Well, this is awkward."

"Don't worry about me, Slade." Laughter bubbled up in Ilene, then she steered him closer to my bed. "I'm spoken for. Kally, here, on the other hand is recently single."

"Ohmygod, Ilene!" I sat up quickly and pain throbbed through my shoulder. I couldn't suppress the wince.

Slade almost looked relieved. "You're in pain. Let me find a nurse." He shot out of the room, and the clatter of his boots danced off the walls.

Ilene dropped onto the end of my bed, wiping her brow. "Wow. Did you get a good look at him? His eyes...his Wrangler butt?" She held her hands out and cupped them, like she was testing the curve of his buns. "He is gorgeous."

A hot and sudden blush burned my cheeks. My heart pattered. I twined my fingers around the knot between a deep blue and ivory patch on the quilt. "I...I hadn't noticed."

A sarcastic snort escaped Ilene.

"Well, what do you expect? I've been unconscious for the majority of the time I've known him." Images of his chest against my cheek and the wonderful, warm smell of Stetson cologne and fabric softener magically formed in my sinuses. "I guess he is kind of handsome."

Ilene sobered. She took my hand in hers and her green eyes suddenly took on the same shadow Slade's had in the ER. "He's a good guy, Kally, and was horribly worried about you. What kind of spell did you weave over him?"

"I didn't do anything." I looked out through the doorway recently vacated by Slade. "When I left Matt, I only wanted freedom, to be happy and breathe without looking over my shoulder."

"Well, maybe you didn't ask for a new love. I really feel something between you two though. Promise me, if opportunity knocks, you won't shut an opening door."

I looked down to the flannel quilt Bonnie had draped over me, but her son's image was all I could see. "All right. I won't. Just don't expect me to run through it either."

The phone's ring cut into the silence between us. Ilene caught my gaze and mouthed the words, "Want me to get it?" to which I nodded.

She picked up the phone. "Kally Jensen's room." Then, her face softened, and she nodded her head. "Yup, Susan, she's right here. I'll hand you over."

Oh, Susan! My sister was always the one to nurse me back to well when I was sick or hurt. When I needed mothering, I wanted my sister. A sudden ache gripped my heart and tears fell when I took the phone from Ilene. "Hi, Sue."

Her voice sounded so far away. "I heard you got yourself into an accident. Honey, are you all right?"

I grabbed a tissue and wiped snot from my nose. "Yeah. I got tumbled pretty hard, but the doctors say nothing is broken..."

"If I'd known you'd end up in a ditch in some godforsaken

state, I would never have encouraged you to leave Matt."

"You couldn't have known, Sue." And she didn't know the good I'd found here. She didn't know how wonderful Slade and the Carlsons were to me. "This isn't a godforsaken state, either. I had the great blessing of being rescued by the nicest family I've ever met."

"If the rest of the family is like him, you certainly are blessed." She paused, and I heard her sip on something I was sure was strong brewed black coffee. "Slade was terribly concerned about you when he called and has called since then to reassure me you're all right. It's good to know you are being taken care of... I just wish I could be there." She took another sip. "At least Ilene is with you."

"Yeah, seeing her was good for my heart."

"Well, you just do what's good for your body now. Make yourself well, okay?"

"I'm working on it. I love you, Sue. I'll call you tomorrow, okay?"

"Sounds good, sweetie. Bye-bye." I handed the receiver back to Ilene and she hung up the phone while I abandoned my nest of hospital blankets for a trip to the bathroom.

I'd just finished washing up before Slade's boots announced the arrival of a nurse who came bearing gifts of painkillers and water. Her tray appeared first, then her ample bosom crammed into a tight uniform and finally a kind, round face.

Slade peeked around the door at Ilene and me. "Is it safe?"

I nodded, and Ilene stepped to the end of my bed and motioned him in.

The nurse came up beside my bed. She took up my wrist, two fingers on my pulse point. She nodded her head and pulled out a stethoscope with a singular, well-practiced motion. "Are you having much pain, dear?"

"My shoulder does hurt..."

"What's your pain, on a scale of one to ten?"

How the hell do I know? I had never equated hurt with numbers. "I don't know... Seven, maybe." It was a statement, but my voice rose in pitch at the end of it, demonstrating my confusion.

The stethoscope from the frozen depths of Dante's hell

against my bare back was by now routine. The "breathe deeply" had gone past the point of annoyance to blind indifference. Inhale, exhale. A new point of skin is flash frozen. Inhale, exhale. Restrain from cursing the nurse.

"Well..." The nurse replaced her stethoscope over her neck and then gave Ilene and Slade a warning glance. "These will make her drowsy."

I don't want to sleep. I haven't seen Ilene in so long. My lips turned down. My eyebrows furrowed when I met Ilene's gaze.

"It's okay, hun." Ilene patted my leg. "I'll come back tomorrow."

The nurse held out the tray. I took up the little paper cup and then tossed back the meds. I wrapped my lips around the straw and drank down water cold enough to be frozen solid. I felt the polar temperature water pour down my throat and sit inert in my stomach. Someone had straightened my bed while I was in the bathroom, and placed both stuffed animals beside my pillow. I scooped them up into the crook of my left elbow and eased the bed back.

Ilene retrieved her purse and jacket from the chair beside the window, then she kissed my forehead and promised she would return. Slade turned off the lights and followed Ilene to the door, but I wasn't ready for him to leave. "Slade?"

Hand on the doorjamb, he looked back. "Yes, Miss Jensen?"

"Can you please stay with me for a while?"

"Of course." He walked to the chair recently emptied of Ilene's things and pulled it closer to the bed before sitting. Leaning forward, he propped his elbows on the rungs of the bed. Internally, I shied away. Externally, my body warmed and relaxed as the drugs kicked in. "What can I do for you?"

"I don't know." A frown furrowed my brow. "After everything I've been through in the past few days, I'm confused, overwhelmed, scared."

His smile was tender, the corner of his eyes softened. "I can fix that. Just tell me where to start."

"I wish I knew." I nestled into the pillows and turned my head to him. "I think even your treatment overwhelms me right now. I'm a stranger, but you and your mother are taking such good care of me."

His smile faltered, and his gaze fell to a paisley patch on

the quilt before finding my eyes again. "I don't rightly know what to say, Miss Jensen. I'm the one who found you and brought you here to the hospital. I guess I feel responsible for you getting well again."

"So it's just a savior thing, then? When I'm better, you'll give me the bill and send me on my way?"

"No!" His answer was fervent and fast, and his eyes narrowed. "I want you to get better and...and... We'll go from there." His gaze plumbed the depths of my soul and touched a part withered beneath Matt's abuse. Trust? Faith? I didn't dare to give credence to the silly narcotic-induced thoughts of love.

"I'm sorry. I meant no offense. I just feel like a bat, flying blind and, after the cave I took flight from, I'm struggling to find my bearings."

"Well, your car was headed directly toward the Fourth Moon Ranch, under a new moon. You left pain behind to search for happiness, and I found you when you strayed from the path."

"New moon?" My sluggish brain grasped at the connection he laid before me. "New beginnings. A new life. And you..." My mind let go of thinking, but my hand reacted to the truth in me, reaching out and wrapping his fingers in mine.

"I'll be right here."

The medicine won, taking first place in the race from conscious thought to peaceful dreams. And once more, I fell asleep with Slade touching me.

Chapter Five

A waxing crescent rose above the Fourth Moon Ranch. Slade looked through the windshield at the sliver, a hook in the sky he'd once hung his hopes on.

Those hopes had died. His opportunistic girlfriend had cheated on him and he ended their relationship over a year ago. He had left the Hulett P.D. to help his folks a few months ago. Slade's life was in flux, stuck in one long-ass waning cycle.

But this new moon had truly brought new life with it. He had found Kally when his hopes were lowest and the hollow moon was highest.

He put the truck in park, leaned his head against the steering wheel and closed his eyes. She was there, in the shadows of his mind, waiting for him. The delicate porcelain doll he'd cradled on his horse had become a complex girl, hiding the cracks and damage behind a new layer of sass-colored paint. She was unlike any girl he'd ever known, and she fascinated him.

A cold gust of November wind blew into the cab when Slade opened the door. The icy air poured over his neckline and down his skin like her cold breath had the first night. Chills spread across his skin and he pulled the jacket tight, tucking his chin into the collar so his Stetson blocked the wind chapping his cheeks.

What is in her past? Why does she make my heart pound?

He barley noticed the doorknob in his hand. The luggage in the foyer, however, was hard to miss. His mother's matching floral cases sat neatly stacked in the corner beneath the stained glass window of running horses. Pine's and his brother Beau's were less orderly. A hodgepodge of olive drab lumps tumbled up against the opposite wall and beneath a colorful window depicting the Devil's Tower at sunrise. Both Beau's and Pine's bags were military issue. Pine's were old and duty worn. Beau's were military surplus. Slade had to snort. *Beau is Dad's clone.*

His mother's presence filled the living room. Slade didn't have to see her to know she was there waiting for him. "Good evening, Mother."

"Hello, son." She placed her carry-on bag atop of her stack of tapestry bags. The latest addition reminded Slade of the trellis in the garden behind the house. He eyed the stack appreciatively. "I see you've been busy."

"Of course I have." She patted his shoulder. "We are all packed, and with your father's help I even managed a shopping trip to pick up a few things for Kally."

Slade recognized the glimmer of anticipation he saw in her eyes. *Don't get your hopes up—either of us.* He forced the thought away. "What a kind thing to do, and coming from you, Mother, I'm not at all surprised."

She lingered over straightening the pile of luggage, her eyes averted. "From what I've seen and you've heard, the girl could benefit greatly from some kindness."

Like a mama bear adopting a cub. "Her friend and sister said she's had a tough time." Slade removed his Stetson, dusting melted snow from the brim and running a hand through his hair. He fussed with his jacket, needing to talk and hating it at the same time. "Mother, I've been thinking about Miss Jensen a lot."

His mother wrapped her hand around his and led him to the squishy armchair beside the fireplace. Her concerned expression was heightened by the soft lines around her eyes when she smiled. "Do you want to talk about it?"

What is it with women wanting to talk? It's a jumbled mess in my head and I don't want to talk about it. Still, he couldn't stop the truth from coming up. "She sticks in my head like no other emergency call."

Her smile softened, her eyes held the wisdom of the Wyoming countryside. "Maybe it's because she isn't *any other call.* You weren't working for the police, dear. You didn't have the 'it's just a job' expression on your face."

He rolled his eyes, the corner of his mouth hitched up like it did when he thought someone was full of crap.

"Don't you roll your eyes at me. Maybe you didn't recognize the change when you were working on the force. You did change, put shields up. I saw it in your eyes, on the lines of your face."

Was it just my guard?

No. There was more to it. He gazed into the flames while his mind drifted elsewhere. Slade was vulnerable, not in the same wounded sense Kally was, but in a more essential, natural manner. His life was poised for change, ready to settle down and something about her captivated him. Finding her, making sure she received proper medical treatment was everything he had trained for. She was nothing he had ever expected to find.

"Slade?" His mother's eyebrows were pinched together as she tugged on his shoulder. "You still in there?"

He wrenched his gaze from the fire in the grate. "Sorry, Mother, just thinking. Kally came out here and ended up on your ranch..."

"Our ranch, Slade." Her eyebrows lowered a fraction. "There are four 'C's in the Fourth Moon brand."

For the first time in a year, the term "our ranch" sounded good. "All right, 'our ranch'. Kally was looking for a new life and her path stopped on our ranch. I want to offer her a job here. It will help her out and me too."

Her damned "mother knows best" expression crossed her face. "Who will it help most?" She tipped her head, and an impish grin bloomed on her lips. "I doubt she'll want to move the cattle."

Slade snorted and shrugged his shoulders. He wasn't sure how to answer the question. The truth was there, but he couldn't quite track it down. A smile, nervous and fleeting crossed his lips. He furled and unfurled his fingers before pulling out his knife. He opened and closed the blade with a flick of his wrist. *Open. Close. Avoid eye contact. Open. Close.*

Nodding, Bonnie stood and ruffled his hair. "Don't fret, son. I understand..." Her sentence trailed off when she looked at his father, who'd walked into the room unnoticed. Pine was a large man, thick arms and a tree trunk of a body. Slade always felt the thinning gray hair looked out of place atop his head.

"Did I hear right?" Pine's smile was part smirk. "You want to bring the girl home?"

The knife opened and closed, and then Slade pocketed it

before he stood. "Yes, sir."

Pine wrapped Bonnie in his arms. She nodded when he looked at her, and Slade knew instinctively they'd already discussed the subject. The expression in their eyes spoke volumes. "It would be nice to a have a younger girl around here. Even with all the guests, this house has been too quiet since your sister left." He kissed the top of Bonnie's head. "Don't you agree, darlin'?"

"Of course I do." Then she leveled her gaze on Slade. "Job or not, the Fourth Moon will be a good place for her to heal." She pulled Pine's arms tighter around her. "This place has a way of growing on a person. She may really like it here."

His father took Bonnie's hand in his and stepped closer to Slade. "You just make sure to take good care of her."

"I learned from the best, sir."

Pine smacked Slade's shoulder. "Good answer, boy." Pine laughed and Bonnie rolled her eyes.

"I'll drop in on her before our plane leaves in the morning." With Pine in tow, she crossed the large rug anchoring the living room furniture. "Why don't you give her the room beside the upstairs bath? She'll be just down the hall from you. You can keep a good eye on her."

"I'll do my best, ma'am." His parents stopped at the bottom of the stairs. "Good night, sir. G'night, Mother."

Slade pitched a couple of logs onto the fire and dropped back into the cushy armchair. He spun the chair and propped his feet on the hearth. Quiet settled on the house. The shadows spread from the corners when the stairway light shut off. Slade's gaze ran over the stones making up the hearth and wall. He remembered building the fireplace with his father, remembered many holidays in front of it. This would be the first holiday season without his parents, a silly sense of loss kept company with the late dinner in his gut.

Slade looked forward to the possibility of sharing a ranch Christmas with Kally. He looked into the shadowed corner where they always put the Christmas tree. He was determined to make this a special holiday, one of healing and happiness for both him and the girl brought to them beneath the new moon.

A knock on my doorjamb roused me. I rolled to my side to see Bonnie standing in the doorway, beating the sunrise and my breakfast. Her silver-gray business suit complemented her gray hair, which seemed a premature color when it was wound back into a neat French twist. The plain paper sack she carried was bulging, and completely incongruous to her sleek, stylish new appearance. "Good morning, Kally. Are you up for company?"

"Of course." I motioned for her to come in. She left her perch at the door, drifted across the floor in her pumps and then settled on the end of my bed. She placed the bag between us and then nudged it closer to me.

Her sophisticated attire made her appear like a corporate bigwig. When she spoke, however, she was the same Bonnie I'd grown attached to. "The bag is full of odds and ends, dear. The ranch hands towed your car to the barn." She took my hand in hers, a gentle pat with her fingers. "I'm afraid there wasn't much left. An electrical fire destroyed whatever was still in the vehicle. They managed to find a few things in the snow around the culvert..."

Her voice fell away, but I gained hope and encouragement from her eyes. I pulled the bag closer, covering my favorite patch of fabric on the quilt. At the top sat my small jewelry bag, other than the water marked satin, my mother's pendant and the few other trinkets were intact and unharmed inside. Beneath the jewelry bag sat a couple of cassettes, a hairbrush, a bottle of shampoo and some perfume.

There, beneath the sundry items was my jacket. Hands shaking, I checked the breast pocket. Tears welled up and ran. Susan's money was still there, what little was left. And, when I pulled the meager stash free, I found Susan's hanky. The bloody spots had stiffened. It crinkled in my fingers. It was a tangible message from home, a reminder to never allow Matt to hurt me again. For a moment I forgot about the woman sitting beside me. I could only imagine the storms crossing my face.

"Are you all right, dear?"

Tucking the money back in the pocket above the kerchief, I tried to pull myself together. "I'll be okay, Bonnie. I'm just very relieved. The money in the pocket was from my sister."

"Well, then you better hold on to it tightly." Her smile reminded me so much of her son's.

A layer of tissue paper disguised the remaining contents, the paper crinkled beneath my fingers, but I did not pull it out.

Bonnie's gaze flickered to the clock and then back to me. "I guessed at the sizes of the new things. The receipts are at the ranch house in an envelope. The sweater is a gift from one of the timeshares."

She bought me new clothes? The kindness this woman and her family poured on me made my heart swell and thump in a sweet painful way. But to receive a sweater from someone else, someone I didn't know? "Timeshares?"

Bonnie's rather monochromatic color scheme brightened with her smile. "Yes, Kally, timeshares. Y'see, we own a four thousand-acre functioning cattle ranch. A couple hundred groomed near the big house are divided into twenty-acre mini-ranches we divided into timeshares—like condos in Florida or ski resorts in Vale."

"Wow, I've never heard of a timeshare ranch before." Being raised in Michigan suburbia, I struggled to grasp the concept of why someone would want to buy a timeshare on a cattle ranch. The closest thing I could think of was the "finding yourself" film with Billy Crystal. "Is it like the movie *City Slickers*, where people help with the cattle drives?"

Bonnie's smile changed to a hearty laugh. "No, Kally. The people come for various reasons, but none of them are hired hands. The timeshares are like our guests. They are more than welcome to work when we drive cattle. They are also welcome to stop by for a bite to eat or whittle on our wraparound porch all day and spit chew."

"Well, there's an image I've never had before." It was silly and somehow very quaint.

She sobered a little when she rose. "Maybe not in this life, but I believe country is in your soul." She cast another look at the clock. "Well, dear, we have a plane to catch and I need to hurry out of here. It was a pleasure to meet you, Kally and I hope to see you again."

"Me too, Bonnie." And I meant it. I'd grown fond of her in the past three days. "Have a safe and successful trip."

"Thank you, dear."

Bonnie's shadow had hardly left my door before my breakfast arrived. The eggs were lukewarm, the hash was not crisp, but the coffee was hot and I was thankful for small blessings. I wolfed the food down and then sat back to sip the coffee and look over the clothes Bonnie had brought. The jeans were the right size, so were the tops, only none of them were my style. The jeans were boot cut and the shirts were button up, and flannel. I hadn't worn flannel since I was in elementary school, and then it was only with nightgowns.

I pulled out an ivory/sage/forest green plaid shirt. *Oh, it's so soft.* Just as I rubbed the shirt on my cheek, Ilene rounded the corner. She stopped dead in the doorway. "Oh, honey, if you need something to snuggle, grab hold of your sexy cowboy when he comes in."

"Bite me, Weenie."

She huffed and tipped her weight back onto her right hip. "What the hell? You haven't used my nickname since we were kids."

"I know. And it's still cute, even with both my front teeth and no lisp."

Ilene stepped to the little wooden closet, and fretted over my meager personal belongings, stuffing them into a bag. I could've sworn I heard a sniffle. "Well, it used to be cute. But then in middle school, we were awkward kids thrust into a new school and out of our element. Those nicknames kind of lost their cuteness in high school."

"Your cute never wore off to me, Ilene." I got out of bed, wrapped my left arm tight around her and hugged her fiercely. Then, Ilene giggled. She looked at me, her eyelids slanted, teeth puckering her bottom lip and the corners of her mouth twitching. I sniggered and we ended up laughing like howling monkeys.

"So, what am I going to do now? They're discharging me today, and I have damn near no money, no car, no ID..."

Ilene's arm remained around my shoulders. "We'll figure things out. I'm sure I can find you a job in Gillette—"

"Or, you could come to work for me at the Fourth Moon," Slade cut in. He stepped into the room and tipped his hat. "G'morning, ladies."

My heart pounded and my jaw dropped. Ilene's, however, rose slightly when she smiled. She patted me on the back. "Well, there ya go, Kally. You can sleep on my couch and find some job at a department store or work for Slade on his family's ranch."

I had left Michigan intent on staying with Ilene. I had looked forward to renewing our friendship. Her presence in my life was a blessing and brought such joy. But here was this handsome man, without whom I would have died, offering me a job on his ranch. My thoughts whirred with new opportunities and old friends. Plans stood in juxtaposition to an element of fate. Torn and dizzy, I turned from Ilene and dropped my rear on the bed. Slade hurried to my side, while Ilene took up the bag of clothes from Bonnie and began transferring things.

I wiggled a few inches away from Slade. The heat from his thigh beside mine didn't help me make a decision. What he said next did. "My mother said you insisted on repaying the Fourth Moon for your hospital stay." I nodded my head, and he continued. "With my parents and my brother gone, it's basically down to me to do everything. I thought it would help us both out if you came to work for me.

"If you find a job elsewhere, you're welcome to go. It doesn't have to be permanent," he added.

"What about lodging? Transportation?"

"You can stay at the ranch house. We have more rooms than we need and plenty of vehicles."

I mulled over the options and the very reasonable plan Slade offered. I could work off my debt, which would lift a burden of guilt off my heart. The Carlsons did not hold me responsible for the bill, but I was not comfortable with accepting such an expensive gift.

"Honey, you'd be foolish not to accept his offer." Ilene's green eyes searched mine. "Gillette isn't too far from Hulett. We'll still see each other plenty. And, like he said, it's not permanent. You can always look for work elsewhere too."

Slade looked from Ilene to me and then loosed a strangled laugh. "How is it you two girls always manage to make things awkward for me?"

"Sorry." Ilene winked at me. "We're quite a pair."

"So it would seem."

I inched closer to him, our thighs brushing. "Slade?"

"Yes?"

"I'll come to the Fourth Moon, at least for a while."

He slapped his thigh and then headed for the door. "Great! Then I'll rustle up a doctor and get your walking papers."

Ilene hurried to the door and peeked into the hall. "You just made him a very happy man."

"How can you tell?"

"He was damned near dancing down the hallway."

"Oh for goodness sake, Ilene. You're just trying to hook us up."

"I don't think I'd have to try very hard." She winked at me and then returned to help me pack. I handed her clothing, and she packed it into a sturdier bag. Then, I found the sweater at the bottom of the bag. It was an oatmeal-colored cardigan, with cable stitching and earthy tones knitted in a band along the bottom and the wrists, before the ribbing. The patterned band mimicked a Fair Isle sweater but was more Native American in style, with a star-in-moon design knitted in the center of the back like a pentacle.

"Wow! Kally, where'd the sweater come from?"

"Bonnie said it was a gift from one of the timeshares on the Fourth Moon."

"What in the world is a 'timeshare'?"

"It's a long story. Suffice it to say, Slade's family ranch is kind of a resort ranch, with timeshare ranches similar to timeshare condos."

"Oh cool. Working for the Carlsons is sounding better and better. Maybe I should get a job with them too." Ilene grinned when she stuffed the last of my belongings into the bag, leaving out a pair of jeans, new white socks and the flannel shirt. Then, clothing draped over my arm, I ducked into the little bathroom to get dressed. The jeans fit well enough to be snug where I wanted and loose where they needed to be and the shirt was slightly fitted. Pleasant surprise piqued my interest in western wear. It was a damned comfortable outfit. *Maybe life on a ranch would be a good thing.*

Pondering the thought, I shoved my feet into new, fur-lined mukluk boots courtesy of Bonnie, and then pulled on the heavy sweater from a generous person I hoped to thank very soon. Ilene whistled appreciatively when I emerged and dropped to the bed. Picking up the phone, I dialed Sue. I didn't have time to prep a story, an explanation, anything. She picked up halfway through the first ring. "Kally?"

"Yeah, Sue. Um, I'm not sure how to say this, so I'm just going to say it. I am going to the Carlsons' ranch for a while, to work on paying them back for my hospital stay. I'm not comfortable with—"

"I understand, honey," she cut in. "Their generosity is overwhelming. I even offered to pay for the bill, and he shut me down, absolutely refused. Mom didn't raise us to take things easily. Everything had a string attached. So, if you're looking for me to say it's okay, then, Kally, it's okay to go to the ranch to pay them back and make the start of your new life on your terms, even if they are stubborn."

Relaxation flooded me, spreading further from my heart with every beat. Sue's permission, or at least her understanding, meant the world to me. I was ready, at least I'd convinced myself for the moment.

The balding Doctor Johnston who had admitted me and administered the majority of my breathing tests came into the room with a clipboard, a pen and Slade in tow. "Good morning, Miss Jensen. It's good to see you up and around. We were very worried about you when you came in." He held the clipboard out. "Read the after care instructions, and then sign the discharge papers and you're a free woman again."

The after care instructions were an itemized list of common sense things. I breezed through them and signed the papers. Handing them back, I tucked my two stuffed friends into the bag and then hoisted my sack. My shoulder ached, but I soldiered through to the door. Slade stopped me there, taking the bag from me and signaling to the wheelchair just outside the door. "Not so fast, Miss Jensen."

"You're kidding me. I have to ride in a wheelchair?"

"Yes'm." He wouldn't take "no" for an answer, tipping me back into the chair and onto my butt. Ilene took my bag, and the doctor occupied my hands with a prescription for an anti-inflammatory and a painkiller. "Fill them both at the pharmacy downstairs. Take the anti-inflammatory twice a day, but take the painkillers when needed for your shoulder."

"Thank you, Doctor Johnston." I nodded my head, and we were on our way out. The hall led to elevators and my stomach flipped. *I hate elevators.* It was a silly irrational fear, and I owned it. The dangling, weightless feeling reminded me of my life with Matt—no solid footing. The doors swished open, and Slade rolled me in backward. The elevator lurched beneath me, and I grabbed the arms of the wheelchair. When the lift reached the lobby it lurched again. This time the wheelchair rolled forward before Slade could catch the handles. *Okay, now I hate wheelchairs too.*

The nurses at the desk waved over the counter to me when Slade drove the chair past their station. Slade took the prescriptions from me and dropped them off at the pharmacy before he left me in the care of Ilene. We watched him hurry out to the truck, the crepe soles of his boots skidding on the icy cement. The second he was out of sight I stood, and Ilene drove the heinous wheeled contraption over to a cluster of them by the front door. I mouthed a silent "thank you".

The blue and white pick-up drove under the enclosure, and Slade hopped out with an ice scraper in hand. He went to work cleaning the remainder of the windows, expanding the teensy weensy window hole he'd cleaned on the windshield for himself. I could never understand why men make such tiny clean spots on the window. I scraped and wiped off everything.

While we waited for Slade to straighten up the front seat, my day nurse ran up to me, her arms full of the quilt from my bed. She piled the warm blanket into my arms. "Mrs. Carlson left strict instructions for this quilt to go home with you."

"Thank you! I can't believe I forgot it."

The nurse patted my arm. "It's okay, honey. Slade Carlson is a walking distraction."

I just smiled and folded the blanket in two then wrapped it around my shoulders. "So it would seem." He was rubbing off on me, at least verbally.

"Speak of the devil..."

The automatic doors slid open, and Slade breezed in on a gust of cold air. He stomped his boots on the rubber mat inside the doors, then whacked his gloved hands together. "Ready to go?" He took the bag from me and reached out his free hand. I leaned back from his hand but looked at his eyes. "If we hurry we can get back in time for a reasonable dinner."

"Sure." I wasn't ready to leave. A question burned in me Slade could not answer. "Can you give me just a minute?"

"Yup, I can."

I rushed over to the front desk to the nurse who'd brought down the quilt. I tapped her shoulder. She turned her attention to me, and I pulled her within conspiratorial distance. My voice was hardly above a whisper. "Why does Slade have all the girls gaga?"

Her smile was indulgent. "Oh, honey, he's one of the area's

most eligible bachelors. Sure, he's handsome in a gasp-and-swoon kind of way, and his parents' ranch is worth millions. I think what makes the girls crazy is he is a good man. He's not some boy on a pony. There's a man in the saddle. His parents did right by him in raising him the way they did."

"Wow. I guess I'm a lucky girl then."

"Until the local gals find out he's smitten."

I rolled my eyes. "Something else I hear too."

"Anyone who knows Slade would tell you the same thing. I may be in Sundance, but I grew up in Hulett and believe me when I say you will meet a green-eyed monster or two there."

"Oh goody." My sarcastic outburst was brief. "Thanks again for bringing me the quilt."

"No problem. Take care of yourself."

Ilene met me at the door. Chills crept over my skin and a sudden sense of loss swirled in me. I'd only had Ilene back in my life for a few days, and now we were parting again. Some part of me wanted to hold on to her forever. I reached out with my left hand and took hers in mine.

"I'm going to take off now, Kally. I'd like to get home in time for dinner. Steve offered to take me out tonight."

I hugged her fiercely. "Well then you best scoot. I love you, Ilene. I'll call when I get settled."

"I'll be waiting on the call." She patted my back and then pulled away to look me. "I love you too, sweetie."

Slade scurried past with a quick wave to Ilene before ducking into the pharmacy. He emerged with two little white bags, one for each prescription. Then he offered his arm for support. Giving me the power to make the decision made a huge difference in my reaction. I wrapped my left arm in his and he led me to the truck while Ilene went toward her Jeep. My teeth chattered when I waved to Ilene, and then Slade helped me up into the cab. It was an awkward climb with one arm and a man trying to help me in. Eventually, I settled in beneath the seatbelt and tucked the quilt around me. My riding partner and newest friend climbed in and shut the door. He looked me in the eyes when he pulled his seatbelt over and clicked it home. "Are you ready for this?"

I thumped my feet and pulled the quilt tighter. "Y-yup."

"Cold?"

"I'm freezing." My jaw shook with chills, and I gave him an embarrassed, apologetic look.

Slade started the truck, steered out of the parking lot and turned up the heat. "This old beast might heat up slow, but when it does, it can roast your butt right out of the truck."

"Sounds g-good right now." I thumped my feet up and down and nestled farther into the quilt. Sundance passed by the window in a blur of buildings and snow. I only half paid attention to the town as I peeked over the edge of my quilt cocoon. Soon, another Wyoming highway—a tangible example of my changing path in life—stretched before us, leading northward. The pavement was dark and wet, snaking into a landscape obscured by snowfall and shadowed by the setting sun.

I rode in silence beside Slade, struggling with chills and knowing I was stepping away from everything I had ever known with a man I knew very, very little about. The choice to leave Matt and the fear and pain he dealt out came with sweet clarity. Going to live with Ilene seemed like such a good choice. Ilene and I had remained close despite the distance between us. And, for nothing more than geographical distance between me and my obsessive abuser, Wyoming was far removed from Michigan.

Instead of an easy trip to my girlfriend's in Gillette, fate had delivered me into the arms of a cowboy. I cast him a sidelong glance. Black Stetson, dark hair and icy blue eyes, rugged jaw line, tempting lips. *He looks like an angel in Wranglers and fleece. Do I really know anything about him?*

Some part of my soul sang when Slade was near. But I'd been through so much, been beaten so far down by Matt, that trusting any man completely would be damned difficult. Slade returned the glance, a gentle smile on his lips.

The dry petite snowflakes of earlier changed to fat fluffy ones hitting the windshield while the rustic landscape rolled past the windows. Even Kenny Chesney coming through the radio could not chase away the awkward silence sitting between us like a third passenger. Slade cleared his throat. "Um...so..."

"This is awkward, huh?"

"Tell me about it."

We both laughed. The release was sorely needed between the two of us. A little tension left my spine, and the cowering posture I had around Matt finally relaxed a fraction.

"Well, now the ice is broken. No pun intended. Can you tell me about the ranch? I'm a small town girl, so I'll need all the help and guidance you can give me."

"Well, there's dirt and trees, hills and valleys. We have cows, lots of cows, a few goats, chickens, barn cats and a couple hounds for hunting."

"Don't forget the ponds."

Slade laughed again. "How could I? You're the best thing to come out of one of them."

Laughter bubbled up again. I relaxed back into the seat. For all the questions, the great unknown we traveled toward, being with him was easy. Slade sitting beside me was like suede on my skin, soft and comfortable. I asked questions, not only to know what I was getting in to, but to hear him talk. He was my lifeline.

The Fourth Moon, he told me, was his father Peter Carlson's dream. They'd only owned the property a short time before his father had earned the nickname Pine for his love of the evergreen trees on the ranch. Bonnie stood by Pine's side, adding a woman's touch to the rustic lodge house, and Bonnie named the ranch after the phase of the moon the contract was signed in.

"A few years later, the first four timeshare houses were built. In less than two years they were sold or rented and another four were built. We have a dozen timeshares now. I swear I grew up with a hammer in my hand instead of a football."

"It sounds wonderful. I can't wait to see it."

"You won't have to wait long. We're nearly there." He pointed at the roadside, to the trenches my car had dug into the dirt of the culvert. "Our back driveway is a mile down the road. I found you wandering in there, on our back eighty."

I was silent while the truck rolled through a dell, up a small incline and then into the drive. Fuzzy images of the first night shadowed my mood. "Some of this looks familiar."

He patted my thigh, a gentle human motion of comfort. I wished it hadn't sent a jolt up my nerves. "I thought it might. I took this way driving you to the hospital."

"Ah." Not much else came to my mouth even though myriad images and displaced fear occupied my mind.

Pull yourself out of it, Kally. This is an excellent opportunity to grow and learn. And Ilene is not far away.

The drive wound in between stands of evergreens and over a rise or two. An occasional aspen waved a pale gold leaf it refused to release. Snow-capped pines covered much of the landscape, though white-clad clearings stretched across the flat lands—a winter wonderland for cross-country skiers or snowmobilers. The woods gave way to a broad open range rumpled by a few small hills and dotted by houses with lights burning in the windows. It was a *Saturday Night Post* cover made real. The earthy aroma of wood fires suffused the cab of the truck.

"Wow, something sure smells good."

Slade cocked an eyebrow. "What does?"

"The wood smoke, silly. Don't you smell it?"

He shrugged his shoulders. "I guess I'm used to it."

"Really? How could you get used to it? It's wonderful. I love the smell of a fire. It reminds me of Christmases at my aunt's in Kalamazoo."

"Forgive me in advance, but where the hell is Kalamazoo?"

A snort escaped me. The word sounded funny coming out of him. I held up my right hand, thumb out and fingers straight up. "Y'see, the bottom half of Michigan is like a mitten." I pointed to the edge of my palm, below where the life line starts. "Here is Saint Joseph, where I lived my entire life." I moved my finger in toward the lower third of my palm, about one third up from the wrist. "Right about here is Kalamazoo." I gave him a teasing sidelong glance. "You'd like it there. It's a big agricultural area...lots of cows."

Slade returned the snort. "Ha ha. I thought you thanked God for cows."

"I am thankful."

"Good because you'll be living near a herd of them." He turned the corner and a large empty field and a long, low barn came into view. "This here is one of our winter pastures. And there," he pointed through the windshield at a rambling log cabin style house, "is our house."

The cattle pen was nearly a city block away from the main ranch house. A small barn, a tool shed and another outbuilding stood between the cattle pen and the house. Wooden siding covered the buildings. Forest green trimmed the windows and doors. Black tiles supported the snow disguising the rooflines.

Slade parked in the front drive. The house was a rustic, hewn-log home with a huge wrap-around porch. Strings of white lights circled the entire porch, and lights flickered on the floor level to the left of the main door.

I took the handles of the clothes' bag, which Slade then took from me. "Let me, okay?"

"Sure." I answered him, but I couldn't take my eyes from the house. It was beautiful, inviting in a cozy, rustic charm sense. Before I knew it, Slade was at my door, with it open and his free hand extended to me.

"Come on, Miss Jensen. How about you stop looking at it and come in?"

He offered his hand once more and helped me from the truck, where I stood a moment and absorbed my surroundings—the smell of wood fires, a horse whinnying in the small barn, a Black and Tan Coonhound lying beneath the cover of the porch roofline. When the truck door slammed shut, a ginger tomcat appeared from the shadows of the barn to investigate. He paraded past Slade like he was nothing more than boots on a used scratching post, and then wound his orange body around my ankles before disappearing beneath the porch.

"Contemptible animal." Slade took my hand and led me across the icy patch before the steps. He scuffed his boots across the heavy natural fiber rug spanning from the steps to the double door. The tracks he wiped his boots in were worn, an obvious path. I stomped my feet, too, knocking the snow loose from the treads.

The double doors were stained glass windows on top with four C's linked in a circle in the center and a finished oak panel on the bottom. Slade opened the left door, and warmth poured out, along with the smell of a wood fire, hearty stew and fresh baked bread. The smell was enough to make my stomach growl.

The foyer was cozy, warm with wood tones and brightened with high-set stained glass windows. Slade kicked his boots off at the door, setting them on one of the empty boot mats lining the wall. He stepped onto the foyer rug, which was emblazoned with the same linked "C" design. I followed his example, leaving my new boots beside his. Beyond, in the great room, slate floors ran throughout and the ceiling vaulted, mimicking the hillside framed by the windows in the back wall. The walls and trim were all stained a medium pine finish. Plush scatter rugs ran between the furniture and caressed my stocking feet when I drifted in, touching this, stroking that.

The wooden furniture was Missionary Oak, and the upholstery was earthen tones of rust, browns and greens. Lights twinkled from decorative ficus trees and across the hearth, winding through swags of natural pine branches and dried berries. Slade pulled two pairs of slippers from a basket beside the sofa. The over-padded armchairs begged to be sat on, and the end table beside the sofa suggested a romance novel and a cup of coffee. The fireplace took up much of the back wall with the sides, chimney and hearth of natural field stone. A warm crackling fire danced in the hearth and seemed to whisper to itself.

"Oh my. This is beautiful."

"Glad you think so. Welcome home, Kally."

Chapter Six

What did I just say?

Slade swallowed hard, but the words had already escaped. He could've kicked himself. It wouldn't have been an exactly sane exhibition for her first moments in the house. He always used her proper name. Calling her "Miss" kept distance between them. Distance was comfortable. Distance was easy. The heat he felt rising when they were close was not. Her proper moniker had become his shield. Her first name had just slipped past it and his gut somersaulted. But then it settled.

He flexed his fingers, fidgeted his toes, while his gaze coursed her face and body, registering her reactions. The elfin look returned when she inhaled—small, delicate and vulnerable. Air from the ceiling fan pushed stray strands of blonde hair past her eyes. Her gaze flitted around the room, first alighting on a piece of furniture then watching the dance of the flames before looking back at him. In her irises he saw strength and fear, freedom and lingering doubts. He lived a lifetime in that moment, trying to reassure Kally without saying a word.

She exhaled and her total demeanor changed. Kally softened. Tension left her face, her shoulders dropped, her lips parted, full and kissable soft, before the corners turned up in a slight smile, and he was glad.

Slade hoped she would be comfortable at the Fourth Moon. He hoped she'd stay. The hard lines of the Mission furniture benefited from her feminine curves. The firelight looked good flickering over her face. She was a very beautiful addition to his home and life.

A.E. Rought

Home. I hadn't felt "at home" in a year. In simplest terms, Matt's house was his, not mine. Susan's house was the closest thing I had to a home, and it wasn't mine, wasn't even decorated in a style I felt comfortable sitting on. This house, so new to me, offered a real sense of comfort. A sense of settled love exuded from every corner, every piece of furniture.

"You all right, Miss Jensen?"

"Yeah. I'm sorry. I can get kind of quiet when I'm taking things in, and this house is a lot to take in. It's so much more than I'd imagined. I can see myself curled up by your fireplace, sinking into one of the armchairs."

"How about seeing yourself at a table with a bowl of stew in your hands, first? The fire will be there all winter."

"Only you using my first name sounds better."

Slade, for the first time, seemed shy. He tipped his hat, hiding a half-smile and blushed cheeks. He looked at his feet, and then back up to me. "I'm working on it. We were raised to address a lady properly."

"Well, then relax, cowboy. I'm far from a lady."

"I don't believe that."

He'd called my bluff with playful banter and our gazes locked. My mouth ran dry of quick retorts and I stood open and vulnerable, no verbal weapons and no place to retreat in this new environment. Slade's hand rested on my jaw line, the warmth of his skin sent pleasant tingles through me when he rubbed my cheek with his thumb. His lips parted, but he was cut off by a loud clatter, which echoed in the great room, followed by a muffled curse. "Damn it!"

Slade hurried to the left, past a painting of a Wyoming sunset and into the kitchen, with me directly behind him. He skidded to a stop, inches from a pile of pots and pans on the floor. "Rosie, are you okay? Didn't I ask you to leave the cleaning up to me?"

A petite, dark haired woman of Native American descent stood beside a butcher-block countertop, apron askew and long dark bangs tumbled forward and covering her eyes. "My apologies, Slade." She pushed stray hair away from her face. "I just wanted the kitchen to be clean, and everything just right when Ms. Jensen arrived."

"A house isn't lived in if it isn't a little dirty, Rosie." He stooped to gather the dishes. "Mother always believes a perfect

76

house won't win over a person. It's the hospitality that will keep them around."

She pushed a lid on to an empty storage bowl. "But, still..."

I was eager to reassure her. "The house is beautiful, Rosie." I smiled when she met my gaze. "And the stew smells amazing."

"Oh, Miss Jensen." Rosie pushed her hair back and wiped her hand on the apron before stepping forward to shake my hand.

"Rosie." Slade placed a hand on my shoulder. "Please allow me to properly introduce you to Kally Jensen. Kally, this is Rosie Thompson. She's like a second mother to me."

Rosie's hand was warm and strong when she shook my hand. "It is good to see you walking and talking instead of shivering in Slade's arms."

"I certainly can't shiver in such a wonderful sweater now can I?"

"How did you know I made it?"

"I'm not exactly sure." I shifted my feet, ran my fingers down a cable of knitting. "When my gut speaks so strongly, I know it's right, and I just know you knitted this sweater. Thank you so much!"

Her eyes sparkled, giving her a bird-like appearance. "You are most welcome, my dear. Like you, I just knew I needed to make it. I started knitting that sweater this summer."

Rosie acted on the whispers in her soul—I liked her. "Is the stew ready? I'd love to eat something other than hospital food."

Slade took three pottery bowls from the dishwasher and balanced them against his arm while he wrapped spoons and butter knives in his other hand. "Can you grab some glasses, Kally?" Slade nodded his head in the direction of a cabinet. "They're in the cupboard to the left of the sink."

Being included in daily tasks instead of doing them all was a treat. "Gladly. What's to drink?"

"There's water, milk, sweet tea. Rosie, is there any coffee?"

Rosie nodded her head and pulled the pot out of the coffee maker. I shook my head. "Oh, no coffee for me, thanks. I don't want to ruin my sleep tonight."

"Well, can you fill one up for me, Rosie?" Slade carried the bowls to the table, while Rosie and I stayed in the kitchen to fill two mugs with coffee and a glass with water. She nudged me, and I turned to her while I waited for the water to run cold. "I am very glad you came back, Miss Jensen. It will be so nice to share the holidays with someone new."

"Thank you, Rosie. I'm happy Slade invited me here. I bet this place is beautiful when it's decorated for Christmas."

"Oh it is." She leaned close, her voice in a whisper. "Last year, Slade drank a few too many at the decorating party. He staggered out the back door, and—"

"Hey, you two." Slade's voice was muffled through the wall. "I hear whispering. Rosie, you aren't telling her the decorating party story already, are you?"

She put a finger to her lips and I nodded. "Of course not, Slade."

We gathered the drinks and carried them to the table along with a loaf of bread and dish of butter. I sat for a moment, a thick slab of buttered bread in my hand enjoying the quiet, peaceful feeling from being in a real home, with real food and people who intrigued me. The bread was warm and honey sweet. I ate the entire piece and buttered another. Slade, however, shook a layer of Tabasco on his stew thick enough to choke a lesser person. "Holy cow, Slade. How do you even taste the food?"

He stopped, spoon in mid air, looked at his bowl and then at me. "Y'know, I'm not sure if I do anymore."

I cocked an eyebrow at him but said nothing. Rosie, however, had a good laugh. "He's always used lots of Tabasco. His brother uses lots of pepper."

"I haven't heard much about a brother."

"Beau is a feisty, headstrong type. You'll like him. And I have a sister too." He shoved another spoonful of stew in his mouth and chased it with a swig of coffee. "Never get to see Joeley anymore. And Beau is off with my parents on business, so it's just us and the guests."

"Sounds like great company." I stuffed a spoon full of stew in my mouth. One delicious bite led to another, and then another. "What's in this stew? It's the best stew I've ever had."

"Our own ranch-raised beef and venison, then just the regular vegetables."

"Venison?" The food lumped in my throat. "Deer meat?" I struggled to swallow. When I'd forced it into my stomach, I drank half of my water.

Slade stifled a laugh. "Yes, Miss Jensen, deer meat."

Suddenly I was fuller than on any holiday. The stew sat like a rock in my stomach—a heavy, gravy covered deer-meat stone. Images of Bambi's mother ran through a repeating loop in my brain.

"I'm sorry. I guess I should have made it with just beef." Rosie offered me more bread. I was certain nothing short of a surgical sponge would help soak up the nasty feeling in my stomach.

"No, it's okay. I've just never eaten," I shuddered, "deer before. No one in my family is a hunter."

"Well, the good news is, until you knew what was in it, you were liking it just fine." Slade set his spoon down. "So, it's just a mental thing."

Oh, yeah, thanks for that. A lot of good it does me now. "I think I'm done. I haven't eaten much in the past few days and, um...the stew and bread was an awful lot."

Slade leveled a finger at me. "Shouldn't you take your medicines, Miss Jensen? The pamphlets say to take them with food."

Medicine on top of deer meat? Oh dear God. "I think I'm going to skip them tonight. It's nearly bedtime and I am tired of taking medicines. They were always shoving a pill at me in the hospital. I think I can make it through the night."

My body, however, displayed solid evidence of my lie. My shoulder ached, the strained muscles tired from all the activity. Right arm tucked tight to my side, I folded my napkin and put it back on the table. Slade rose before I could even push my chair back.

"Let me help you." He reached out to support me by my left arm. "We'll take your stuff up to your room, and then I'll show you the bath."

It wasn't possible to wash away the creepy-crawlies in my stomach. But a hot bath at least provided an escape from a deer meat dinner I couldn't stomach more of. I clung to the hope it would soothe my achy body too.

"Yes please. A bath sounds wonderful." I turned to Rosie. "Please excuse me, Rosie."

"Of course, dear. I'll see you in the morning."

"That would be nice." I shook her hand again. "We'll have coffee and talk."

Slade scooped up my bag and led me back through the great room and up the stairs that rose behind the fireplace to the second floor. The wooden stairs creaked with each footfall, and the warmth from the smoldering fire radiated through the wall and filled the staircase. I didn't realize how tired I was, how drained, until the penetrating heat washed over and through me. Exhaustion went in front of me, and I had to push it up the stairs.

At the top of the steps, a long hall stretched across the length of the house. Slade turned to the right and stopped at a door two doors down from the stairs. "This will be your room."

A bed occupied a corner, and an entry to the adjacent bath stood past the foot of the bed. Moonlight poured through the window and spilled over the rug in the center of the floor. Near the window sat a Mission Oak rocking chair and a highboy chest of drawers.

I looked at the quilt hanging from Slade's arm. A pang of separation anxiety wavered through me. The quilt was one of the tangible constants I'd had since the accident. "Slade, can I keep the blue and white quilt in here with me?

"Actually, the blanket comes from this room, Miss Jensen." He stepped into the white moonlight and laid the quilt on the bed along with my bag of clothes. "I believe Mother hoped you'd be coming back here."

Woman's intuition? I thought. *Witch's intuition?* It might have spooked some people. I took comfort in a hint of metaphysical connections.

"Works for me." I opened the bathroom door and peeked in. "Is this my bath?"

"Well, in warmer weather, when the ranch house is full of guests, it is a community bath, but you and I will be the only ones here for the winter. It is fully stocked with towels and such in the cabinet and soaps, shampoos and lotions on the shelves by the tub."

"Oh...okay." *Mental note—lock the hallway door.* I turned to Slade then, wanting to express my appreciation for all he and his family had done for me. "Slade, I just want to thank you for giving me a job and a place to stay. You are a good man."

"You're welcome, Miss Jensen." His smile was warm, and his eyes blazed.

I batted my eyelashes. "Please, call me Kally."

"My, aren't you insistent?"

"Yup, I am." I inched closer, his dark bangs brushing the blonde wisps before my eyes. "And I can be a downright ornery kind of stubborn if I'm ignored." Tipping my head, I gave him a warning smile.

He winked. "Well, I do appreciate a challenge."

"Yeah?" I took a step back. The heat rising between us made me dizzy. "Well, right now my challenge is getting washed up and into some pajamas." I inclined my head toward the bathroom door, an obvious hint for him to make himself scarce.

"If you don't need me for anything else, I'll take my leave and see you in the morning."

"I'm a big girl. I've been bathing alone since I was six years old."

"What a crying shame." His smile was playful when he tipped his hat. "Good night, Miss Jensen."

"Good night, cowboy."

His absence left the room empty and cold. I watched him walk out and then go to the door at the end of the hall. The door closed behind me with a soft click, and then I rummaged through the bag and found a package of panties. I did not find pajamas. A search of the bureau only turned up spare blankets. The long underwear shirt Slade had wrapped me in the first night lay folded at the bottom of the bag.

Close enough, for tonight, anyway.

The tub was old, a claw-footed porcclain one with a deep basin. I loved tubs like this. The hard rubber stopper plugged the drain, and hot water was soon filling the tub. Nosing through the cabinet, I found a washcloth and towel. The shelves yielded a grand assortment of bar soaps, body washes, shampoos and conditioners. I rounded up a selection of lavender products and returned to my bath. I hung my clothes on a waiting rack of antlers, and stepped into the bath. My toes tingled with the heat, but I settled into the hot water and drew the warmth in.

All the tensions, the traumas I'd experienced in the past week came crashing in when I should have been relaxing, enjoying a hot bath in a resort ranch. The last beating by Matt...his hands around my throat, his breath heavy and wet in my hair... The relief at finally finding the strength to leave the bastard. Losing my wallet. Crashing my car. Hanging helpless in a cowboy angel's arms...

Tears bubbled up. The washcloth soaked up my tears. Nothing, however, could contain my sobs. I was indebted to a stranger, sitting in the bathtub of his home, tired, aching and bawling like a baby. My right shoulder throbbed when I tried to raise my hand above my head. I dropped my hands back into the bubbled bathwater, clutching the shampoo bottle and sobbing.

Knuckles rapped against the hallway door. I had forgotten to lock it. "Miss Jensen, are you all right?"

No!

I couldn't lie and tell Slade I was fine. My self-pitying sobs took all my breath. Slade knocked again. I sucked in a breath and tried to steady myself. I wiped my tears with the washcloth, but only succeeded in wiping more water across my face.

The doorknob turned slowly, the latch clicked and the panel eased inward. A draft breezed through the open crack, and I saw the crown of Slade's wavy dark hair. I was naked, so exposed, and more of his head appeared with each escaping sniffle. Frantic for cover, I reached for another washcloth, spreading them across my breasts before Slade peeked around the door. His eyes were shadowed. "I heard you crying. Is everything all right?"

I should have said yes. He would've left me alone then. Instead, I held up the shampoo bottle, sobbing. "My sh-shoulder hurts and I c-can't wash my own hair."

"I can fix that."

The shadow left his brow, and a soft smile warmed his cheeks. His eyes sparkled a snow-bright blue. The expression was hard to resist. He opened the linen cabinet and took out a few towels. He unfolded and held a hand towel out for me. I held it a moment, my eyes locked on his. His lashes dipped only a little, but the minute expression spoke volumes. I nodded, laying the towel on top of the thin washcloths to cover my breasts. The second towel cushioned his knees when he knelt behind the tub.

Oh God, he's behind me. Matt was behind me, his hands around my neck. Fear rose up in me. My muscles tightened, and my shoulder hurt more.

Slade saved my life. He has only ever offered kindness.

"Tip your head back."

A knot of fear sat in my gut, keeping company with the venison rock. Numb and disbelieving that a man would help me with something so trivial, I obeyed. Slade emptied a porcelain pitcher of its collection of hand towels, and then he sank the pitcher's mouth below the water's surface. I closed my eyes when the pitcher's lip passed my face, and he poured the hot water over my hair. The heat soothed my skin and muscles—his quiet presence soothed my frayed nerves. He lifted the shampoo from my hand, and the herbal aroma swathed my sinuses when he poured it on my hair. Then, he worked gentle circles along my scalp and neck.

If I had been a cat, I would have purred. I could only manage a murmured "thank you".

"I'm happy to help." His hands drifted to my shoulders, his strong fingers working out knots from months of hunching my shoulders in self-protection. My stomach flipped and my nipples tightened in an odd mix of excitement and misplaced fear when his fingertips brushed my collarbones, but there Slade stopped. He retrieved the pitcher, dipped it and then doused the bubbles from my hair. He rinsed my hair a second time, dried the pitcher with the towel he had knelt on, and then replaced the pitcher and contents at its decorative post.

"Next time you need help, don't hesitate to ask. I hate to hear a lady cry."

Could you be any more perfect?

"Thank you, Slade. I promise I am usually very self-sufficient." My gaze fell despite the smile on my lips. "I normally wash my hair just fine."

He wiped stray bubbles from the back of his hand and turned to leave. He paused with his back to me and his hand on the door. His bangs slipped forward slightly when he turned. "Well, I don't mind helping." Then, he stepped into the hall and shut the door.

I quivered in his absence. The fear I fought came back and sickened me with my inability to control it. Shell shock? Gun shy?

Abused.

The fact was, I was battered and bruised, both outside and in. Matt had beaten me so far down I couldn't relax beneath the caring hands of a cowboy who intended nothing more than my aid. I had flinched when it wasn't necessary and I felt so foolish.

I needed to learn an elemental truth in this life. Not all men are bad, not all men are attached to fists. Some men care and protect. The lesson I needed to learn? Slade wasn't Matt.

And I couldn't do a damn thing about it until I learned who I was. A year under Matt's tyrant rule had changed me, stolen my confidence and sense of self.

The drain unplugged with a firm tug and a gurgle. The lavender had not cleansed away all of my tensions, though in my heart, I felt better, more settled—a broken bone in a cast. I'd found solid footing beneath me for once. I allowed the drain to take away the water and hopefully the negative energies cluttering my aura. The nap of the towel could not scrub away the conflicting emotions in me. I pulled on a clean pair of panties and Slade's shirt and then walked back into the bedroom.

The quilt Bonnie used to swaddle me was spread out over the bed, and the blankets were turned down. Even my two stuffed friends were propped before the pillow. *Oh God. He is such a good guy.*

I dropped yesterday's clothes on the rocking chair in the corner. Sitting atop of the highboy was half of a peanut butter sandwich, a glass of milk and one of my pain killers. A tear, for once of happy origins, welled in my eye. I never wove a spell, but he was weaving one of simple human magick on my heart. The sandwich and milk soothed the icky dance my stomach did around the venison, and the medicine was fast acting.

The pillow cradled my head and my two stuffed animals lay beneath my right arm, propping it up. Sleep crept through me, warm and fuzzy like bunny slippers on a cold morning. My eyelids fell and I slipped into a deep, healthful rest.

Washing her hair...
Touching her skin...

Breath hitched in his throat. Slade leaned his head against his bedroom door. The handle was in his hand. He wasn't going to use it, but he needed to hold onto something.

Kally was naked. She was beautiful. And she was so vulnerable he didn't dare touch her any more than he had, no matter how much she'd flirted beforehand.

His heart slammed, his blood pulsing behind his eardrums and the fly of his jeans. Yes, he was definitely male. He was horribly aroused and didn't want to be.

Pacing the confines of his room, Slade struggled to derail the desire surging along his veins. He was taking care of Kally, nursing her back to health, back to wholeness. This was not the time for sexual wants to get in the way. There were too many clues, too much evidence saying Kally had been abused. Slade knew she needed to find herself before he should even consider intimacy, let alone lust after it.

It's going to be a tough night.

He kicked a stray sock at the hamper. It dangled on the edge and then flopped down in front of the door. One look at light under the door conjured images of her soft skin beneath his fingers. The scent of lavender and jasmine drifted down the hall, torturing him. The fist he curled rivaled the tightness in the front of his jeans.

Yup. A very hard night.

Desperate for a distraction, Slade dragged his range bag from the closet, laid a towel out on his bed and field stripped his gun. He pulled patches of cotton and cleaning products from a pocket and forced his mind to the task of cleaning. He might be able to chase out thoughts of Kally. He wasn't sure about his dreams.

Morning came early and quiet. I would have easily gone back to sleep, but those new room jitters shook me awake when my eyes opened. I wasn't scared, I wasn't sad. It was a tad unsettling to be in a fourth room in a week's span. A yawn rumbled through me, followed by an upper body stretch stopping at my right shoulder. Then, I climbed from the bed and straightened it before walking to the window.

Weak light filtered through the panes when I pulled the muslin curtains back. A ceiling of gray rose above the vast landscape. Snowflakes danced an erratic ballet. Even with the overcast sky, the Wyoming countryside stretched forever, a visual expression of endless possibilities.

"It's a fairyland." I reached out and drew a heart in the ice on the windowpane.

"Don't know about a fairyland, but Jack Frost certainly visited last night."

Slade stood behind me, his presence warm and comforting on a cold morning, yet I flinched when he touched my shoulder.

He pulled his hand away, leaned forward and drew an arrow through my heart on the window. Slade turned from me, offering up a perfect view of his Wrangler butt. No jeans had ever fit a man better. His T-shirt clung, second-skin tight, white and displaying his lean muscled upper body. My heart flittered, jumping into a stilted rhythm.

"I thought you might like some fresh coffee."

He held out a mug of steaming coffee with one hand, and the other returned to his hip, the thumb tucked into the corner of his jeans pocket. The vapors drifted up, obscuring his face, and then he blew the aroma of roasted Arabica beans toward me. My stomach growled and a weak smile bloomed on my lips. "The coffee smells really good."

"So how about you drink it and then come and help me with breakfast?"

Ah, normal life.

I was acutely aware of my bare legs. Slade's long underwear shirt only hung far enough down to cover my butt. "Can I get dressed first?" I nodded to my clothes still sitting in the rocking chair. "My legs are a little cold."

"How about you pull on a pair of my pajama pants and take it easy this morning? After breakfast, we can discuss what you can do here at the Fourth Moon and call your sister and Ilene. Then, I thought we'd take a ride into town for supplies and maybe some more clothes."

Mentally, I added clothing onto the list of things for which I intended to pay the Carlsons back. "Deal."

Slade held out a pair of flannel pajama pants, gray with dark blue pinstripes. He turned his back when I bent over to pull them on. The waistband sagged. I tugged on the cords running through the casing at the waist and tied them tight. I wiggled my butt in them, settling the soft, warm cloud of flannel around my legs. "Okay." Slade turned back to me. "I'll take the coffee now."

"Watch it, I brew it rather strong."

"Watch it yourself. I'm Dutch, I like it strong."

"Then you came to the right place."

I smiled at him, a full happy expression. "So it would seem." The Fourth Moon already felt a little like home.

His ice blue eyes were even brighter without his Stetson perched above them. And his hair begged to be touched. *Later, I* promised myself, *maybe later. Right now, I want food.*

"So, about breakfast…"

"Oh, yeah." Slade held open the door for me. "We won't be alone."

Oh my.

Chapter Seven

The kitchen and dining room bustled with activity. Rosie was setting places for at least eight people, while a mid-height heavy-set man with blond hair followed her around the table with napkins. Two more women were in the kitchen, one a brunette, the other gray haired and both of them looking at me through their glasses. Everyone stopped what they were doing to stare.

I feel like a zoo exhibit.

I tugged Slade close, my voice hardly above a whisper. "Shouldn't you be charging admission for this?"

"Let 'em get a good look at ya." He took on a bumpkin accent. "Y'know it's not often us country folk get to see a purdy city girl come back from the dead."

I gave him a "you're lucky you're cute" look, to which he seemed impervious. For the time of a breath, no one spoke, and the energy between me and Slade sizzled. I fell into the burning plains of his ice blue eyes, my heart beat harder and softer at the same time. He smiled placidly, a playful devil in cowboy cologne.

"Good morning, everyone." Slade nudged me forward. "I would like to introduce you to the Fourth Moon's newest resident, Miss Kally Jensen."

A chorus of "welcome's" and "happy Saturday's" filled the air while they surged forward. The blond gentleman, I learned in the ensuing onslaught of handshaking, was Rosie's husband George and the two women in the kitchen were Emma Edwards and Grace Porter. Rosie and George were retired educators in the Wyoming schools. Emma, a retired librarian from Iowa, was brunette and bereft of a husband who had left early in the morning to hunt. Gray-haired Grace said she was "never anything more than a housewife", and was a "hunting widow" like Emma. All of them were long time guests of the Carlsons' and terribly excited to see Slade sidle up to a "filly" like me.

Slade cleared his throat. My gaze fell to a piece of fuzz on the floor, which I poked at with my toe. His feet shuffled on the rug beneath us. "There's currently no sidling, Emma."

"Yet," Grace bantered back. She flashed us a grin and then busied herself with dicing potatoes and onions.

My eyebrows arched, Slade shrugged his shoulders and then he guided me toward the kitchen. Emma returned to her post at the stove, stirring ground sausage in a massive skillet. She waved with her free hand toward a large container of eggs and brick of cheese which sat on the counter beside a mixing bowl. *Sausage, eggs, potatoes, onions and cheese, and only one pan?* "So, what's on the menu today?"

"We call it breakfast mess."

"It's Pine's favorite," George chimed in.

"It's basically an unconstructed omelet." Slade picked up where he'd left off. "You brown the sausage, add in the potatoes and onions and cook them until they're soft, and then scramble in the eggs. Most of us like it topped with shredded cheese."

"Sounds delicious." I couldn't resist getting a barb in on him. The guests had him unsettled already. "And then you add Tabasco and fry your taste buds, anyway?"

"Yes, ma'am." He leaned closer, his voice hardly above a whisper. "And if we weren't going into town this afternoon, I'd have an extra helping." He fanned a towel past his behind. "I don't want to be cruel."

"You are too kind." I snorted and then pulled the plastic layer from the 18-egg package. "So, how many eggs should I crack?"

Grace shooed Slade off toward the toaster and a loaf of bread, then came over to answer my question. "Nine eggs today."

Holy cow. "Nine?"

"The recipe is pretty loose, but we use 'one egg per person, plus one' for a guide. It helps to bind all the goodies in the pan together."

"Gotcha. Thank you, Grace." I busied myself cracking eggs into the mixing bowl while Grace murmured a welcome and stirred the sausage again. Emma and I crossed paths when she carried her bowl of diced vegetables toward the skillet. She smiled, and her brown eyes twinkled in their frame of wrinkles when we danced in a half-circle to avoid collision.

"In case you're wondering, Kally, it's always busy like this on the weekends. Saturday breakfasts together are a Fourth Moon tradition. It makes for a wonderful family atmosphere."

"Uh-huh," Grace agreed.

Rosie appeared by my side at the refrigerator. She snaked an arm around my waist and gave me a quick side-to-side hug before pulling a large pitcher of orange juice out of the fridge and heading back toward the dining room. I took a gallon of milk back with me, and poured a measuring cup worth into the eggs. George swooped through the kitchen, taking the milk jug and cap from me on his path to the table.

The chaos settled into a comfortable uproar when the breakfast mess skillet was carried to the table and the group settled into seats to eat. Neither Grace's nor Emma's husband arrived, but before Slade poured a cup of coffee two men walked through the back door. They were total Paul Bunyan look-alikes. Both of them tall, brawny, blue jeans and red-and-black plaid flannel shirts with the sleeves rolled up. Slade pushed his chair back from the table and greeted the men at the dining room entrance. "Ah, the infamous Billings brothers."

The three men shook hands, and then the newcomers took up seats across the table from Slade and me. Slade introduced me to Mike, the brother to the left, who at current moment wore a black shirt under his plaid flannel. Mike nodded. "Morning, Miss Jensen."

Mark, the brother to the right, wore a red T-shirt under his flannel, and was even less vocal. "Morning."

Rosie, a full foot or two shorter than the Billings twin, promptly smacked Mark on the shoulder. "Next thing we know, you'll be grunting instead of speaking."

"He already does." His brother ducked a mocked swing at his head.

Slade shook his head at the antics, then tapped my hand where it rested by the mug of coffee. "Don't let the gruff exterior fool you. These guys are big softies and would throw themselves in front of a bear to save someone else." Mark snorted at Slade's glowing praise. "If they don't shoot the bear first."

Mark and Mike, I was to find, were avid hunters but never missed a Saturday breakfast. They were also the only actual timeshare guests at the table. They owned the fall/winter hunting seasons, while a family from Florida came up for the summer season. Rosie and George had bought their ranch the first year. Emma and her husband Stewart spent two years in repeat visits before buying a ranch of their own. Grace and Alan had bought theirs the following June. Most of the remaining twelve houses were sold, and many of the Fourth Moon residents went home for the holidays.

The holidays. Thoughts of Thanksgiving without my sister and the boys made my heart flip uncomfortably. I might have wallowed in the melancholy moment, but brooding wasn't possible at the Fourth Moon. Rosie could sense my mood, and she spun the conversation onto suggestions of which outfits to buy to complete my cowgirl attire, and where to shop for the best riding boots.

"Oh, I don't ride, Rosie. I don't know the first thing about horseback riding."

It was the first quiet moment at the table. Not a fork moved. Not a mouth chewed. Everyone turned to me, and then to Slade, their eyes wide. Slade coughed in the middle of a swig of coffee and nearly choked himself. "You mean you've never ridden a horse?"

"I didn't realize lack of saddle time was a bad thing... I told you I was a small town girl. The only thing I rode was a bus."

One of the women muttered, "Oh, dear."

"Well, then we'll fix your horse riding inefficiencies. You'll be barrel racing before we're through."

"I still have my doubts."

He looked me straight in the eyes. "And, there's your problem, Miss Jensen."

Cuts right to the heart of things doesn't he? I poked at an elusive piece of sausage on my plate. "Maybe it is."

Slade seemed to pick up the fact I no longer wished to talk about my lack of riding time. He dropped the subject completely, and instead rose, stacked our dirty dishes in one hand, and grabbed the coffee mugs with the other. "Why don't you ladies have a chat by the fire while I'll refill your coffee for you? Leave the dishes for the fellows to take care of."

The ladies and I retreated to the great room, where last

night's fire had been reborn into a crackling blaze. I tucked my left foot underneath my butt and sank into the armchair closest to the fireplace. Rosie occupied the nearest corner of the sofa, and Emma took the other. Grace sat in the armchair across from me. Though we'd left the table and dropped the subject, Slade's ability to read me, to see self-doubt reining me in like any harness, was unsettling. I wanted to curl into myself and disappear into the furniture, or fling my insecurities at his feet and run to Ilene's.

I was determined to stand my ground.

"Kally, is everything okay?"

Rosie's face was shadowed with a frown, but I didn't get the chance to reply. Slade returned with fresh coffee, a small plate with a glass of milk, and my medicine bottles. "She's just quiet when you throw her into new situations, Rosie. Miss Jensen said so herself last night." He handed Rosie her cup, and then brought my mug and the plate to me. "Dessert, Miss Jensen?"

"Oh goodie." I rolled my eyes in feigned despair. "More medicine."

The plate remained stoic in front of me. Slade's voice dropped a timbre. "It's better than hearing a lady cry."

I could have cried again, knowing the emotionally intimate moment we'd shared when he washed my hair and took away my tears. I blinked away the wetness in the corner of my eye, took the medicines and chased the bitter pills with milk. My "thank you" was met with a wink, and then he handed me the mug of coffee. "Enjoy your coffee, ladies."

Grace was the first to speak and reminded me most of my grandmother. "So, Kally. What did you do back in Michigan?"

"Well..." I stalled. How could I tell them, anyone here, an abusive relationship had me on the run? "I used to manage the ladies' clothing section of a department store in Saint Joseph. I did the ordering, the scheduling and designed displays. Anything they threw at me."

Emma was the one to drive the knife of family into my heart. "Did you leave any family, or anyone special behind?"

"Just my sister and her family. My parents and grandparents all passed years ago. It's been pretty much Susan and me for years."

"Then leaving must have been a hard decision."

"More than you know." I still feared Matt finding me, or my

wallet showing up in his mailbox with a Wyoming, or North Dakota return address and then he'd know where I'd gone. Matt didn't know Ilene but he knew Susan. I wouldn't put it past him to press her, to hurt her for information.

Rosie watched my face through the entire conversation. I knew, in the pit of my gut, she knew I withheld information. When she caught my eye, her bright gaze cut through my façade and into the part of me I kept walled away. I felt her peeking into the memories of Matt beating me, felt her reaching in and cradling the scared girl who cowered in the corner of my mind. Rosie pulled me out of myself and reassured me life would be better now, without saying a word. She nodded when she saw the cloud lift from my face.

The chitchat after those questions was light and short lived. One by one, the women pardoned themselves and returned to their homes, leaving me to Rosie's company. Rosie walked to the chair where I sat, and I rose into her embrace. She hugged me, rocking side to side like a mother soothing a child. Tears welled up and fell silent into her dark hair. Then she held my face in her hands. "You are loved. You are safe here."

Blinking tears away, I nodded and whispered, "Thank you."

"Anytime, sweetheart."

With a final smile, Rosie left, exiting through the back door. I dashed off into the east wing bathroom. After washing my hands, I patted my cheeks dry and smoothed my hair. Slade sat on the hearth when I returned to the fireside easy chair. He had a pocketknife out, trimming his fingernails with the blade. Once I was settled, he closed the knife with a flick of his wrist and then pocketed it. "Are you ready to talk about working, Miss Jensen?"

"Ready as I'll ever be." I slid my butt into the far corner of the chair and then turned it to prop my feet on the hearth. My stomach, full of breakfast, insisted on dancing like I was a teenager at my first job interview. I crossed my arms over my chest. Why did I feel so skittish and giggly around him?

"You know my parents are on a business trip. They have meetings scheduled with possible investors and will be spending Christmas with one of the families who are also close friends of ours. If they land the financing, we will be buying another four thousand acres and adding on a lot to the Fourth

Moon. Plans are drawn up for true resort-like expansions, everything from a golf course to an old time western town."

"Wow. You'll never have to leave the ranch."

He suddenly sobered. His pocketknife came back out, and he opened and closed the blade. His voice was softer when he spoke. "I'm not all that happy with being trapped here. There's a big world out there and I only got a piece of it when I worked on the force."

He had been a police officer? Why is this coming out now, when he's trying to convince me to stay? "Force?"

Visible pain passed like a shadow over his eyes. "I was an officer with Hulett's police department for a few years. I was looking to transfer to Sundance and then maybe out of here altogether. But my parents needed me, so I left the force and came home."

How could he leave so perfect a place? I was learning much more about this cowboy than I ever expected, and a lot about myself. I liked it here. "Well, Slade, I'm glad you came back to the ranch. Otherwise, you wouldn't have found me."

"Maybe it was fate's ultimate plan...the real reason I came back."

Only the fire spoke. I saw before me a man conflicted, harboring a pain I wanted to heal. He forced a smile and patted my leg where it rested next to his. "Now, back to my parents, the ranch expansion and your job."

He was skirting the issue of his discontent, and I wasn't about to push him on the subject when he didn't know the truth on me leaving Saint Joe. If I wasn't willing to talk about Matt, I couldn't ask him about surrendering his dreams to come home. I nodded, encouraging him to go on.

"Until my parents return, Mother has the monthly bills set up on an auto-payment system. I am taking over the rest of the ranch's business, moving the cattle and such. What I'd like you to do is take care of incoming mail, separate it into the appropriate files. Answer the phones if I'm not around, and help out where you can."

"So, basically, you want an assistant?"

"I prefer to call it 'Jane of all trades' or my 'go-to-girl'. Besides, it's a lot better than admitting I want to keep you around because you purdy up the place. Such a statement could be construed as sexist."

"Ya think?" It was a sarcastic comment, but Slade seemed amused rather than offended. "I wouldn't feel right taking payment for it anyway."

"So we're settled then?"

I nodded. "You've got yourself an assistant, cowboy. I'll run up and get dressed and then, if you want, we can head into town."

"I'll get the truck warmed up." He lifted his Stetson from its perch on an antler rack attached to the fireplace. "And what's up with calling me 'cowboy' all the time?"

"Well, you call me Miss and I'll call you cowboy."

He smiled, and he tipped his Stetson to hide his eyes. "I like you, Miss Jensen. You've got spunk."

"I like you too, cowboy."

Maybe too much.

Slade liked her for more than her spunk, but he wasn't about to let his desires cloud the issues. She was sweet, sexy, funny and sad, and damned captivating. He wanted to know what made her tick, what her lips tasted like, what the hell she was running from back in Michigan.

His key ring weighed his pocket down when he pulled his jacket tight against the cold, and a stiff breeze threatened to steal his black hat when he opened the door. A beautiful Wyoming morning greeted him on the wrap around porch. Blue sky stretched above and sunlight danced in burning diamonds on the snow. It was a good day for a drive. Slade's boots skidded on the icy drive. He regained his balance without pinwheeling his arms and looking like a fool. The door stuck and he slammed it with his shoulder. Snow fell from the roof and down his back.

Dancing boot to boot he shook the snow from his shirt and jacket. "Damn it!"

The orange tabby hissed and jumped from beneath the truck near the engine. The cat scrambled for solid footing on the hard packed snow, thumping into Slade's boots before skittering away from him and into the barn.

"Well, excuse me." Slade kicked snow in the cat's direction. The cat had stalked the main farm and ranch house ever since Kally showed up. Hell, she had every one on the ranch stirred up, from him to his mother to his godmother.

But why?

He climbed behind the wheel, checking in the rear view for any obstructions. The Dodge started with a shudder. He sat behind the wheel until the engine settled into its dependable rhythm. He pulled the truck around to face the porch and found Kally there, bundled up and waiting for him. Her blonde hair danced on the breeze, her cheeks and nose pinkened by the cold.

His heart thumped and a silly smile crept across his face. *Yup. A good day for a drive.* Slade leaned across the bench seat and opened the door for Kally. He hoped to get a few answers to his questions on the way to Gillette. Even though they hadn't had much time to talk, Slade felt a connection to Kally. It flared up the moment he scooped her into his arms, and he wondered if she felt it too. Time alone would be a good way to see where her heart and head were.

The drive to Gillette was filled with Slade asking questions and me dodging the personal relationship ones. By the time we'd reached Ilene's store he knew everything there was about Susan and the boys, about my parents passing, even about my embarrassing chubby years in middle school. When it came to Matt and our dysfunctional relationship, my response was short. "We just weren't good for each other."

"Then why'd you stay?"

Everyone asked me the same question. The longer I was away from Matt and around a good man like Slade, the more I asked myself the same thing. "I'm not sure anymore. I used to love him."

"So what happened?"

"Lots. Too much. Not enough." I locked my jaw and turned to the window. I wanted to growl, release the churlish temper scorching my guts. "How much longer till we're there? Going anywhere takes forever out here."

"Yup. Welcome to Wyoming." He chanced a long look at me before turning down a side street to look for a place to park. "I'll leave the subject alone for now, Kally."

He used my name, not the formal moniker, but my real name. The tension brought up at the mention of Matt melted. Tears formed, and I wiped them with my sleeve. "Say it again?"

"What? To leave it alone? Gosh, girl, if I'd know it was such a touchy subject I wouldn't have—"

"No, silly, when you said my name."

"Oh." A blush reddened his cheeks. His voice slipped from husky to suede. "It just felt right, Kally."

He parked the Dodge on the ground floor of a parking garage. Dark shadows swathed the truck, but a shaft of light caressed his face, brightening his eyes, heightening my reaction. My pulse raced, my lungs locked up and blood rushed to my cheeks. I was falling into him, falling for him and I never moved. He unlatched his seat belt and leaned in, his cologne tingling my nose. His gaze trailed over my face, my throat, my body. His hand brushed my cheek. "I truly am sorry if I've upset you, Kally. I want to know you, know everything about you."

I wrapped his fingers in mine. Desire for him rose in me, but I begged him to stop with my eyes. "Please give me time. It's not very easy to talk about."

Slade nodded. "Time moves slowly on the ranch, so you have all you need."

"Thank you." His fingers remained on my thigh after I released his hand.

"No." He shook his head. "Thank you, for staying, for showing me new life on an old ranch."

"There's no need to thank me, Slade."

His smile returned; he was a rogue in Wranglers. "Likewise."

A high-pitched, annoyingly nasal female voice cut through the sporting goods section of Ilene's workplace. "Slade Carlson! Fancy meeting you here."

Her high set, platinum blonde hair resembled a shark fin on the other side of a rack of fishing supplies. Then she rounded the corner and only reinforced my killer shark visual. A wide, flat nose spread like the snout of a great white over a mouth full of teeth, which were bared in a predatory smile. "Good afternoon, Slade." Her eyes tore over me while she extended her hand. "And who is this?"

"Hello, Cissy." The name hissed through his teeth. "This is Kally Jensen. She's a guest at the Fourth Moon."

"Oh, really?" Her hand snapped over to me, which I shook once. She honed in on me, a seal swimming on the surface of her hunting grounds. "Cissy Rawlings, pleased to meet you. So, Kally, are you a new timeshare?"

Slade shook his head when I shot him a questioning glance. "No, Cissy. I'm actually staying in the main ranch house. Slade invited me."

The savage grin became a sick pantomime of the friendly tone in her voice. "Oh really?" Her pupils dilated, taking in her prey before the kill. "How fascinating."

Slade wrapped my hand in his and nudged past the woman. "It's been nice catching up, Cissy, but we have a lunch date."

Her hand waggled above her hairline like the flash of a tail fin. "I'm sure we'll be seeing each other again."

God, I hope not. There was a distinct "kill the interloper" sense about the woman. I tugged on Slade's hand. Continuing to plunge through the sporting goods section, he cast a quick look back. I pointed in Cissy's general direction. "Who the hell was she?"

"Cissy Rawlings. She's another Hulett area native. Her father has tried five times to buy property in Gillette. They have aspirations of world domination."

I shuddered and Slade laughed. "My thoughts exactly." He pointed to an escalator. "Ilene's office and the Ladies' clothing are just past the Housewares' department."

Ilene was on lunch break when we found her department. Knowing the long drive we had to return home, I started shopping without her. Slade was lucky I'd lost my purse, or he would have been holding it while he sat in the little chair by the fitting rooms. He sat patiently through a half a dozen jeans but started to fidget and sigh loudly when I debated on flannel or fleece tops. "If it makes any difference, I like the T-shirt and flannel combination you tried two outfits back."

"Aww." The lady in the next stall peeked out, looked Slade over and then gave me the thumbs up. "He's a keeper, honey."

"You think so?" I winked at Slade and then dashed off for a couple more shirts.

After I ducked back into the fitting room, Slade knocked on the door and then whispered through the slats. "If she liked that, then let's see what she does with this..." His boots moved back away from the door before he spoke louder. "While you're at it, girl, why don't you get some new boots and a purse to match?"

My neighbor's gasp was audible. My Cheshire grin was private, Slade shushed my giggle, however. Shoulder aching, I pulled on my old clothes, bunched up my new ones and then stepped out. Slade took part of my burden and then I aimed for the register closest to Ilene's office.

Slade stopped in the middle of the main aisle. "Hey. Where are you going?"

"To check out."

He shook his head. "No, you're not. You're going to go find boots and a bag."

Scrambling to catch a pile of shirts, I stopped and turned. "I thought you were just joking around."

"I was serious. You're going to need boots—or shoes—and a bag, right? You should get them now and get all the shopping done at once."

I couldn't get past the shock. A man was encouraging me to shop? "You're not kidding are you?"

"Serious as a heart attack, darlin'." He shifted the mess of clothes to one arm and pointed back down the aisle. "The shoe department is over there."

I followed his direction, passing the loafers and dawdling through the sneakers. They all looked the same, and none of them spoke up and said, "Buy me". I turned to make a second pass through the athletic shoes and I heard an obvious snort. I spun on my heel and looked at Slade. He whistled and looked off at hardware. His hint was only slightly less subtle than a 2 X 4 to the head. *Okay. I can take a hint. Maybe a pair of boots would be nice.*

When it came to boots, I was a lost cause. I didn't know crepe soles from composite, leather uppers from snakeskin. I knew which ones looked pretty. How sensible would pretty be on a cattle ranch?

"Slade? I don't know anything about boots. Can you help me?"

"Sure thing."

After trying on a few pairs and a lot of sensible advice, I settled on tan boots with synthetic soles and floral embroidery on the uppers. The trim along the top resembled cut lace. It was almost a shame to pull my jeans down over them. I walked down the aisle, sashayed past Slade and watched a smile of a different kind bloom on his face. *Now I know what they meant by "walking tall". I think I could learn to like wearing boots.*

We put the boots back into their box and toted everything toward the register. On a special display stand I found the perfect bag, with leather colored similar to my new boots, a big silver buckle and fringe. The old me wouldn't have been caught dead carrying it in Saint Joe, but the old me was gone. I stood in the aisle, running my finger on the buckle. For all I know, I could have been drooling.

"Quit fondling it and just grab it, Kally."

I wrapped my fingers around the strap. "You don't have to tell me twice."

Slade made me walk back to Ilene's office while he paid for the purchases. "I don't want you feeling guilty, now scoot!"

He was right. I'd feel guilty as hell when the final tally came up. *He knows me so well already.* It was an oddly comforting feeling and made my heart swell even though an element of fear accompanied it. Letting him know me was letting down my guard. Letting him in was something I wouldn't fight. I knocked on Ilene's door and waited.

Ilene squealed when she opened the door and found me on the other side. She saw Slade feet away at the counter and then wrapped my hand in hers and pulled me in. There was no preamble, no "Hi, how are you?". "So, tell me everything. Did he kiss you yet?"

"Slow down, Ilene. No, he didn't kiss me yet." Pausing, I shuffled my feet and peeked around the door and back at my cowboy. I melted a little inside when he smiled. "He did something better, Ilene, something so much more intimate."

"Ohmygod!" Her eyes were wild, almost rabid. "What?"

"While I sat bawling in his bathtub because my shoulder hurt, he came in and washed my hair for me."

Her voice rose. "He did? Did he see you naked?"

I shook my head. "He handed me towels to cover myself before he knelt behind the tub."

Ilene's jaw fell, then she pulled it up into a soft smile. "Oh, Kally, how kind and thoughtful could he be?"

"Ilene, he is wonderful. I like him and I don't want to. I don't want to fall too fast, like some rebound crush, and then find myself stuck with another Matt."

Ilene motioned to stop what we were saying. I cast a quick glance around the corner. Slade was weighed down like a pack animal and headed for the office. Ilene whispered. "He is not another Matt, Kally. I'm telling you, I think you were meant for each other."

My heart said one thing. My mind said another. "Maybe."

Slade turned sideways to ease the packages through the doorjamb. "Maybe what?"

Ilene scrambled for an answer. "Maybe we can get together next weekend. I heard Butch's Roadhouse has great food."

He turned to me, and I smiled weakly. Lying would be impossible with him. *Please don't ask me what we were talking about.*

"Next weekend? The Friday after Thanksgiving?"

"Sure. Will Friday work for you?" Ilene and I exchanged glances and she shrugged her shoulders.

He looked at her calendar on the wall. "Should work just fine. And if you want, you can spend the night at the ranch and then go with us in the morning to cut a Christmas tree."

"Sounds great. I'll have to clear it with the hubby at home."

"Heck, bring him too. We have plenty of room."

Ilene tilted her head toward the phone. "Let me make a couple of calls, and then I'll call you at home later, okay?"

"Oh, Ilene, I can't wait." I hugged her, and then we parted. Ilene went back to work, and Slade and I headed for home. By the time the parcels were loaded into the bed of the truck, my stomach was growling, and my shoulder ached. Slade ushered me into the cab of the truck and then shut the door for me. A huge growl rolled through my stomach and Slade laughed.

"Hungry?"

"Starving." Another rumble just enforced my answer.

He gave me a quick look before starting the Dodge. "Mind hitting a drive-thru so we can eat on the way home?"

I pressed back against my gurgling stomach. "Actually, a burger sounds damned good."

Slade laughed. "A girl after my own heart."

"Just don't let the secret out." I knew I didn't need to say it, but it was fun to play.

The Burger King drive-thru wasn't busy for mid afternoon. We both ordered the biggest meal they had. The juicy beef felt good going down. It warmed my guts and quieted the grumblings. Slade however finished his off and belched before I could eat my last five fries. "I win."

"Well, if I'd know it was a race..."

He gave me a sidelong glance. "I still would have won."

Nodding my head, I had to concede. "Probably."

I settled into the bench seat and leaned against Slade's shoulder. Even though my shoulder ached, the hum of the tires on the pavement and the warmth of the sun hitting the back window soon lulled me into a comfortable doze. I snuggled against him and then, in a brash moment, unbuttoned his jacket and smelled his cologne. I curled my arms into my jacket. "Hey, Slade."

"Yeah, darlin'?"

"Thanks for today."

"No thanks necessary. Now, you go to sleep for awhile and we'll be home before you know it."

Kally adjusted herself while he held the steering wheel with one arm and wrapped the other around her. She pulled the bag with her pajamas onto the seat and then packed it between them like a pillow. A comfort settled in him with his arm nestled on her shoulder and her silky hair beneath his fingers. "Right" was always an abstract concept for Slade, but just then, with her body next to his and the sun coming through the window, he understood what it meant.

He never felt it on the ranch after the wanderlust hit. It was the feeling he had missed with his past girlfriends. It took a girl from outside of the ranching life to show him what he was missing. Slade squeezed her softly in thanks and was rewarded with her resting a hand on his thigh.

At Moorcroft, Slade turned left onto Highway 14 toward Keyhole State Park. There was no longer a lingering doubt for Slade. Kally's head, and her heart, were here with him and her friend. The uncertainties he had about the abuse in her past were gone too. The evasive manner in which she answered questions about her past boyfriend, and her defensive manner when pressed, told him this girl's heart needed healing just as much as her body. It was up to Kally to admit it and Slade knew. She needed to feel comfortable enough in herself and with him before she would shine a light on those shadows in her past.

The hard part was waiting. Something he was never good at.

The area past Kanode Road, north of the reservoir was one of his favorite areas in the northeast corner of Wyoming. It reminded him of the less wooded areas of the back eighty acres of the Fourth Moon; only the ranch lacked the grandeur of Keyhole Reservoir. He debated on waking Kally, but her comfort and the soft expression on her face was nothing he wanted to disturb. She lost her broken doll appearance when she slept.

The intersection of Cabin Creek Road and Route 24 was deserted when he reached it. He aimed the Dodge north again, traveling the last few miles to home. Evening shrouded the ranch when Slade turned onto the back drive into the ranch. Right about Rancher's Row, where the smell of wood smoke permeated the cab, Kally awoke. She inhaled deeply, yawned and stretched, running her hand up his chest. "It's good to be home."

Yes it is. Good to be home with you.

The house was quiet and dark when he parked the truck close to the front porch. Slade handed Kally the keys to the front door in order to free his hands to grab her bags. He hoped she would learn he was a good man and good men treated their women like royalty.

Kally's eyes searched his boots instead of his face when she spoke. "I'm sorry for sleeping so long."

"Don't be sorry, silly girl. I told you to take a nap."

She shrugged her shoulders and turned into the broken doll. "But, still..."

"Still, nothing." In a frozen moment, his hand passed the point where she normally flinched. She didn't. He exhaled a breath he didn't realize he was holding and rested his hand on her shoulder. "You have nothing to apologize for, Kally."

"Well, if you insist." Her smile returned. The porcelain doll disappeared.

"I do insist." He bent and gathered her bags to his chest. "Now come on, let's get your new things squared away."

"Right behind you, cowboy." He turned in time to catch her ogling his butt. Her deep blush told him she was right behind him and enjoying the view.

Yup, I like you a lot, Miss Jensen.

Chapter Eight

I had hoped for a quiet evening. Susan's phone call shattered my fantasy. After dinner and dessert of an anti-inflammatory and painkillers, we retired to the great room to watch the fire and stare out the windows at the hills. The ranch's main phone line lit up, blinking its red light into the office shadows, and the phone's ring interrupted our fireside chat. Slade and I held a locked gaze for a sequence of rings.

"Hardly anybody uses the main ranch line." Trepidation soured the air when he scrambled into the office, set off from the great room, and grabbed the phone. His form was shadowed, a silhouette in the office doorway. "Fourth Moon Ranch, how may I help you? Yes, Susan." Slade cast a quick glance at me. "Kally's fine. Okay, I'll hand the phone over to her."

His eyes were shadowed, storms passing over the blue ice. There was no light on his face. His smile was gone. My stomach flipped and then sank. I suddenly dreaded taking the phone from him but found myself reaching for it anyway. My mouth was dry. I had to swallow twice before I could talk. "Hi, Sue. What's up?"

"Honey, I have some news." The tremor in Susan's voice ran through the phone line and into me. "Someone in South Dakota found your wallet. They mailed it and all your papers to Matt's house yesterday. He stopped here this morning and threw it through the living room window."

"Oh, good God, Sue! Is everyone okay? Were the kids hurt?"

"We're fine, Kally. Jerry boarded up the window. I think Matt's lost it. He stood there in the front yard screaming and throwing the rest of your things at the house and car. Jerry opened the door and told him he was calling the police and Matt charged up the front steps, shoved Jerry into the house and shouted at me."

A lump formed in my throat. Fear, sick and familiar, flooded me, and the rubbery feeling I'd had when I lost my wallet returned. I dropped into the chair beside the desk. I could picture Matt's face, his brown eyes black with rage. *How did I live like this?* "What did he say, Sue?"

"He was wild, screaming at me, 'Tell your damned sister I will find her and drag her home by her effing hair'. He knows you're out West now, Kally, and I don't think he'll stop until he finds you."

I was silent. Every bit of panic and pain I suffered boiled up and then over within me. Slade reached out, his hand hovered over mine. His need to comfort me was visible in the lines of his face. Tears falling, I reached for my cowboy, wrapping my fingers through his. "Hang on a minute, Sue."

Covering the mouthpiece, I explained Matt's actions to Slade. I told him about the present, not about my past with Matt. It was enough to light a fire in Slade's eyes and set his jaw on edge. His brow furrowed, his chest heaved and his free hand clenched into a fist. "Give me the phone, darlin'." His voice was steady and darker than the shadows in the corner. "I'll take care of this."

I shook my head. "I need to handle this myself, with some help from you."

He nodded, his gaze locked on mine. "You know I'll make sure you have anything you need."

It was the truth. Looking at Slade, seeing the conviction in his expression, I knew I could trust Slade with my life. He was my cowboy, and he was an officer trained to handle situations of stress and violence. The thought of Slade's past on the force brought an idea to mind. "What's the address of the Hulett P.D.?"

Slade scratched the address down on a writing tablet. I gave it to Susan over the phone. "Please ship my things here. Matt won't get the ranch's address."

"But why the police department? What are they going to do?"

"Slade used to be an officer in Hulett's P.D. He has friends there. And this way, even if Matt's friend Scott sees the package at the Saint Joe Post Office, the address will only lead Matt to the police."

"Good idea, Kally."

"I'm learning. Sue, I am so sorry about what Matt did to your house."

"It's just a house, no one was hurt. We were expecting something like this out of him. Don't you worry about it. I'll hold the fort here, you forge a new life for yourself in Wyoming."

My gaze fell to Slade's hand, which I'd taken back into mine. "I think I've made a good start."

"Me too. I love you, honey. Call soon."

"I will. Love you too."

The miserable bastard was still affecting my life, even out here. My stomach returned, dinner roiling in it like a coming storm front. I clamped my jaws shut and tears soaked my eyes. I released Slade's hand and wiped at the water on my cheeks. Slade stood beside me, one hand on my forearm while I pulled myself back under control. He lifted my chin until our eyes met. "Do you want to talk about it?"

"Talking won't fix what's happened, or what he did." I looked away. "I knew Matt would be upset, but I didn't think he'd break my sister's window and scream at her."

He rubbed my arm. "Losing a good woman can make any man go mad."

"You don't get it, Slade." I shrugged off his hand and stepped away. "He was already crazy—always crazy."

After spilling a little of the venom poisoning me, I crossed my arms, walked out of the office and took the remainder of my fears and misery with me. Slade called my name, but I shook my head and hurried to the stairs. At the bottom step I stopped. Slade stood at the office door, his hands raised in a gesture of confusion. I wanted to run back, bury myself against his chest and tell him everything. I withdrew and ran away instead. Shaking my head I whispered, "I'm sorry."

The staircase was disguised in a blur of tears. My jacket crinkled in my hands when I opened the pocket and pulled out Susan's hanky. The room dissolved in my tears. I could see nothing except the damned blood-crusted kerchief I twisted in my fingers. My heart ached, my throat was tight and I wanted badly to step out of myself, to lessen the wretchedness I felt.

I pressed my ear to the door while Slade stomped down the

hall. Images of his face, those beautiful blue eyes rose in my mind. I wanted to nestle my face next to his neck and smell his cologne. I couldn't. Ghosts held me back and I didn't know how to get past them.

My hot bath did not help my shoulder or soothe my misery, but how could it? I harbored the hurt, horded it like a miser, keeping it from the one man who genuinely wanted to take it away. My new pajamas only reinforced Slade's gentle, comforting presence in my life. Curling into bed, I clung to the pillow, wishing it was my cowboy.

Face wet with tears, I realized how broken I had become under Matt's iron fist. He'd hurt me to the point even healing carried its own fresh pain. The love I had for Matt was never the same after the first beating. Fear kept me in his house. Fear muffled my cries. And fear confused life with existing. The truth of it all settled on me while I lay beneath my quilts. At one time, I had loved and hated Matt with equal measure. Somehow, the scales tipped and I was unaware. The passionate love I felt for him had long since died, and I had clung to hope it would revive, and called the hope "love" instead. I had not been truly in love with Matt for nearly a year. I survived on hope, misguided and false, for things to change.

At least a relationship with Slade wouldn't be a rebound. You can't bounce off from nothing. I embraced the revelation. It blanketed my mind and finally coaxed me into sleep.

Stubborn girl. Why are women so complicated? Onc moment they're right there, soft and sweet, and the next minute they're miles away and grouchy.

Slade dragged his range bag from the closet. He rolled the tattered, stained towel across his comforter, opened the main compartment and sighed. *If I keep cleaning guns when I'm frustrated, I'm going to run out of firearms.*

He understood why Kally would be upset about what happened at her sister's house. Hell, he'd have been pissed off, but anger wasn't what had put the fear in her eyes or sent her storming out. She had held his hand one moment, and the next moment she had withdrawn into her cracked porcelain shell. Her behavior was a textbook response of an abuse victim. And her ex-fiancé Matt's actions were classic signs of someone with a liking for abuse and an obsessive complex.

Slade lifted his father's revolver from his bag and some cotton patches and oil. He also grabbed his cell phone from the dresser. He looked at the gun and held the phone, debating on how far to stick his nose into where it hadn't been invited. Waiting and wondering were never high on his list of things to do. Slade sat with his back to the door, not wanting to even see the hall light peeking beneath the oak panel. The light would remind him of her room beneath the light fixture, and his night would go down hill from there.

Blue light glowed around the keys when he flipped open the phone, and then flashed in the half lit room when he clicked through the menu to *Baxter, Red.* He pushed the green phone button and held the speaker to his ear while it dialed and rang.

Red's voice was restrained. "Hullo?"

"Hey, Red. It's Slade. I need ya to do a favor for me when you roll into the department tomorrow."

"What's up?"

"I want you to run the name of a Matt Stransberg in Saint Joseph, Michigan through the computer and see what comes up. If you get so much as a hiccup out of the system, call me."

"You betcha." He paused, and Slade knew by the way he sucked air through his teeth Red had more to say. "Can I ask what this is about, Slade?"

"Call it a hunch." Slade pulled absorbent cotton swatches from the small plastic pouch. "I'm sure you've heard about our guest at the ranch."

"You mean the cute little blonde the town is buzzing about? Yeah, I've heard some, mostly gossip from Carly up at the Trading Post."

Slade groaned. *It sure didn't take long for tongues to get to wagging around these parts.* "Yeah, she's the one. Miss Jensen is staying with us, and I believe she may have had trouble with Stransberg before she came here. The girl is scared, and I want to know why."

"She won't tell ya?"

"Let's just say I don't want to push too hard." He dripped oil onto a few pads. "I think the girl's been hurt. She won't even give her sister the ranch's address. We're having her things shipped to the P.D."

"Roger. I'll check into him, and I'll keep it quiet for her sake."

"Thank you, Red."

"Glad to help, Slade. You know we miss you up here."

Oh, drive the knife in, why don't ya? Et tu, *Brute?* He'd hoped to get through a conversation with his old partner without Red reminding him how the Hulett P.D. was doing without him. "I get to missing the place too. Give me a holler when you hear anything, or if Miss Jensen's packages arrive all right?"

"Will do. Good night, Slade."

"G'night, Red."

He snapped the phone shut and replaced it in the wicker do-dad basket on his dresser. Slade turned back to the bed, the damned hall light caught his eyes and churned up all the feelings he had tried to squelch. Part of him wanted to stomp down the hall, wake Kally up and drag the truth out of her. The other part wanted to hold her in his arms, run his fingers through her hair and drown in her jasmine and lavender.

Waiting was inaction, but when it came to Kally, he had to. Despite his suspicions and his call to Red, the abuse in her past was her truth to tell. It was up to her to find the right time to tell it, and if she couldn't, there wouldn't be any peace for her, no matter how hard he tried to provide it.

Slade dropped back to the bed and turned to the task of wiping a thin protective layer of oil over his father's gun. A good weapon should be well taken care of, cherished, respected for its power and protected for its value and permanence.

Kind of like women.

He nestled Pine's gun back into the protective sponge-lined case and then stowed the rest of his gun cleaning gear. A yawn rumbled through him, and he was damned tempted to rub his eyes. The oil on his hands made it a bad idea. Stifling another yawn, he wrapped his hand in the towel, turned the doorknob and braved the hall light and the emotions it illuminated in him. He stopped below the light and outside of her door. He stood with his fingers hovering next to the wood grain, suppressing the urge to knock.

Her room was dark and quiet. A soft snore filtered through the wood, and Slade nodded. Kally was sleeping, and she should be. He should be, too, but there he stood listening to her snores and imagining her beneath the quilt of blues with the stuffed animals supporting her sore shoulder. It was a better image than of her face, contorted with emotions, before she had retreated up the stairs.

He shrugged. Trying to figure women out was like asking Mother Nature "Why?" There was never a reasonable answer.

A well-placed nudge with his shoulder opened the bathroom door, and then Slade stood at the sink, steam obscuring his reflection while he lathered up and rinsed his hands. The passage back down the hallway was quick, and then he was under the covers and waiting for sleep, his fickle fair-weather friend.

Hours from dawn, he gave up the quest for elusive good dreams and set out to busy his hands with something other than guns. He crept down the hall after dressing and aimed for the stairs. The stairwell was cold, and the steps creaked, sending Slade dancing gingerly down the outside edge where he knew the boards were screwed into the framework. He stopped at the base of the staircase and listened, but the second floor remained quiet.

Bypassing the kitchen, Slade held the handle of the back door to keep it from slamming shut and then walked to the workshop where he and his father had spent so much of their time building the furniture for the Fourth Moon's main house.

The door swung inward, and sawdust kicked up in the breeze. The lights came on with a click and a hum. The shop was just like he had left it, chairs in different stages of assembly or repair, including the rocker he'd started years ago, and when he turned, the rifle still sat in its place above the door. He chucked a few logs into the wood burner stove and fiddled with a tool while the warmth spread. In some ways, he hated this place. Carpentry had carved out a huge chunk of his teens and twenties. In other ways, it was a place to lose himself in the shaping and building to find himself again. And reshaping his moods was always good.

The house was empty, and the early morning shadows lay long and wispy on the floor. I rose and stood in the chilly, pre-dawn air. The door creaked and the oak panel swung in over the rug. I grabbed my quilt, Bonnie's handiwork I'd learned, and wrapped it over my shoulders and crept out into the hall. Slade's bedroom door stood open, and his room was vacant. The bed displayed the evidence of his troubled night. The blankets were twisted and the fitted sheet was rumpled in the middle.

Looking out his window, I saw lights on in the little outbuilding between the house and horse barn. The staircase was cold. Slade must've let the fire die. Mounted mule deer heads in the great room regarded me with somber silence when I walked past. I pulled the quilt tighter around my shoulders and ran in stocking feet through fresh fallen snow to the small outbuilding. Frigid air bit my exposed flesh when I rapped my knuckles on the door.

Slade's voice was garbled when he answered from the other side. I didn't have a chance to ask him to repeat it, or knock a second time. Light and heat poured out when he opened the door. He was sweaty and shirtless, sawdust covered his jeans and he hastily wiped his hands on a work towel. Light poured over the contours of his chest and arms, displaying his lean muscles in high relief. If I wasn't so wrapped up in feeling sorry for myself, I might have swooned right there.

"You're up early. Are you feeling any better?"

"I'm fine," I lied. The misery brought up from the night before had not left me completely, and the chills I'd thought finally gone had returned. Shivers climbed my spine and shook out through the hand clutching the quilt.

"No you're not." He stepped to the side, a hand extended to guide me in. "Come in here where it's warm."

Movement eluded me. I stood with my toes in sawdust and warmth, and my heels in snow. Slade's eyebrows pinched together, and his extended hand reached forward to pull me into his workshop. His hand made it no farther than the blanket around my shoulders before I flinched in a knee jerk reaction. My gaze plummeted and I felt a sudden blush burn my cheeks. This man had been nothing but nice to me, and I still shied away.

"Don't be so skittish, girl. You flinch like someone who's been hit too many times."

You have no idea.

It was the truth I had kept hidden from him.

The misery, a wound reopened by Susan's news, bled out, seeping through the bandage I tried so hard to hide it beneath. A tear beaded on my eyelashes and I wiped it away on the corner of the quilt.

After my actions last night and the expression on my face,

the truth was evident. His words were slow and heavy with shock. "You have been beaten."

I dragged my focus from the sawdust on my socks back to his face. The emptiness of my reply spoke volumes. I clutched the quilt like a security blanket and fought tears. Slade stepped back a pace, his gaze locked with mine. Compassion burned bright. The warmth radiated from him. I yearned to reach out and take it. I evaded it instead. His hand, once reaching for me, clenched on air and then pushed his wayward bangs back from his face. An awkward moment hung between us. His shoulders sank, and Slade turned back to the workbench.

A draft blew up the confines of my quilt cocoon and ushered me into the warmth of the cramped workshop. I reached for some safe topic of conversation, and then my gaze fell on a half-constructed piece of furniture. "I noticed all the Mission Oak furniture in the ranch house." I waited for him to respond. He cast a quick look over his shoulder. "It's beautiful."

"Yeah? Thanks." Slade turned toward me but shrugged his shoulders. "My dad made a lot of the big pieces. I made the end tables and the headboard in your room."

"Where'd you learn to make furniture? Carpentry is a dying art."

"Not around here." He picked up a hand sander and passed it back and forth over an edge that no longer needing sanding. "Carpentry's nothing special."

Why didn't he think it was something significant? I would treasure such a skill. "It *is*, Slade. Why don't you see it?"

A shadow passed over his eyes, and he dropped the sander to the seat of the chair. He looked over his shoulder, jutting his chin in the direction of a project resembling a combination of rocking chair and giant 3-D puzzle. "My dad taught me. Like I said, it's nothing special."

"It is a skill, and your father teaching it to you is a gift. It's a blessing."

I stepped up to the workbench and let go of the quilt with one hand. I ran my fingers over the runners of the rocking chair, tracing the clear grain of the wood. He stepped closer. "I guess you're right, if I look at it from your point of view."

Smiling, I shook my head. "Not always, Slade. I see the beauty you forgot in this ranch, but you see the truth in me I try so damned hard to hide. And, somehow, it's wrong."

"You're not hiding it, Kally. The pain is written on your face. The misery comes out in waves. I guess I was just waiting for you to find the right time."

My heart ached for relief. Still, I hesitated. "Is there ever a right time?"

"Your heart will tell you, Kally." He turned toward the workbench, and the new dawn light poured through the window across the muscles of his back. The light clung to his skin, his sweat. He glanced at me over his shoulder. "You just let me know when the time comes, and I'll be there to pick up the pieces if you fall apart."

A sob broke loose. "I'm already falling apart."

His tool clattered on the bench top. Slade turned, fresh sunlight and sweat. He reached for me and I did not flinch. I crumbled against his chest, broken and vulnerable in my cowboy's arms. Slade held me together when the truth of Matt's abuse ripped free in wrenching wails. He held me while I recounted the months of suppression and bruises, belittlement and broken noses. Cradling my face in his hands, Slade breathed new life into my wounded soul. "No woman deserves to be treated the way he treated you, Kally. You should be loved and protected. You should be cherished."

He was close enough for me to taste his breath. I felt the familiar tumbling sensation. The only things holding me upright were Slade's hands, and they pulled me to him. He brushed a delicate kiss against my forehead, and I buried my face against his neck. Slade crushed me in his arms. "If I could take away your pain, I would."

"You are." With the poison purged, his embrace was a bandage on a wound finally able to heal.

He held me until the sunlight of a fresh winter morning bathed the inside of his workshop. "Come on, girl, let's get some breakfast. Then, I'm going to take you on a ride."

"Please tell me it's a ride in your truck. I don't ride horses." Fear of horses might be foolish, but it was very real to me. I pulled back from his embrace, a frown forming on my lips.

Slade's head tilted to one side. "So you say now, Kally. If you can trust me with your pain, climbing up in a saddle and sitting with me should be a breeze."

"You mean I can ride with you, not along side on another horse?"

"Yup." His smile was infectious.

"If you're with me, I'll try it."

He wiped sawdust from his pants with a clean paintbrush and grabbed his jacket from a peg by the door. The fleece lining slid over his skin like I wished my hands could. On some level I craved to touch Slade, to caress him and savor the simple intimacy of human touch. Impulsive, I ran a finger down the cleft between his abs. Slade twitched, his eyes widened and he grabbed my hand at his beltline. "You're tickling me."

"Oh? I'm sorry."

"Don't be." His eyes smoldered. His pull was so sudden and strong, I thumped against his body. One arm cinched around my waist, and with the other Slade reached up and tangled his fingers in my hair. He pulled my head back. The warmth of his words bathed my neck. "I like it. You can tickle me anytime."

"Yes, sir." It was a promise, not a threat.

The workshop darkened with a flip of the power switch. He held me another moment, lips only a breath away from mine, our bodies burning in the cool shadows, then a rooster crowed in the nearby barn. Slade sighed, snorted something about ranch life and then released me and opened the door. Slade stepped into the snow and motioned for me to follow. But I stood in the doorway, my socks sopping wet and pasty with damp sawdust. He extended a hand, waving me forward. "Come on. Breakfast isn't going to make itself, darlin'."

My gaze fell from his face to my feet. His gaze followed.

"You should always wear boots on a ranch. You never know what you're going to step in."

Without further discussion Slade scooped me into his arms, which is where I yearned to be. He carried me toward the ranch house, and in the circle driveway a red Jeep 4 X 4 drove past. Mark Billings tooted the horn, and Mike pumped his fist in the air. I snorted, unable to suppress my smile. Slade looked down at me and laughed. "Hell, if the Billings boys had you, you'd be strapped over the hood."

"Then I'm glad you have me." I nestled my head on his shoulder.

He squeezed me tighter. "Me too."

Chapter Nine

Slade set me down on the porch, and I swear I felt his eyes on my butt when I bent over to strip off my dirty socks in the foyer. I stood and looked at him. His face was covered with the impassive mask he knew drove me crazy. He whistled a few notes and then asked, "What?"

If he wasn't going to admit looking, I wasn't going to push him about it. Shrugging my shoulders I stepped into the living room. The house was quiet, full of sunbeams and shadows, the fireplace empty of the homey blaze. The kitchen was still dark and utterly devoid of life. "Where is everybody?"

"Many of the Fourth Moon's residents attend church services on Sunday mornings." Slade flicked on the kitchen lights. "It makes Sunday breakfasts a simpler affair, good time for the family to reconnect."

"You don't go to church?"

He shook his head. "Nah. My mom meant it when she said she was a kitchen witch. She," he paused, "well, we believe in a Great Spirit, a holy energy in all things."

Interconnected—part of one great whole. I'd always held a similar theology, and knowing we had similar beliefs gave me a richer sense of comfort. "A quiet meal would be pleasant." I tugged on Slade's hand. "If I start coffee brewing, will you start a fire?"

He agreed, and we parted company. Not long after, a new fire snapped and sizzled when sap leaked from the logs. The smell of fresh coffee spread through the house and Slade joined me in the kitchen, making a mess of the countertops when he mixed ingredients for a batch of hoecakes. I took over the skillet, flipping the golden cakes while he fried a pound of bacon. Coffee mugs steaming, we settled with our meal in the little breakfast nook off from the kitchen.

The nook occupied a large bay of narrow windows. The padded benches were covered in saddle leather, and the tabletop was distressed wood with a shiny finish. The high gloss sealer on the table looked like spring run off, and our rustic pottery ware seemed to float above the wood grain.

I leaned back beneath a painting of running horses and between two narrow windows. The window across from me opened on the nearby barn. Goats rooted through the snow in the pen, and in the shadows of the barn a golden tail swished outside a stall door. Saddles, bridles and things I didn't know the names of cluttered the upper left corner. I had to smile, reclining and sipping the dark brew. This was never a life I would have intended, but I felt more comfortable in the moment than I had since I snuggled on my father's lap while Mom read fairytales.

Slade tore through his breakfast like he hadn't eaten in days. His plate was cleaned and heaped with seconds, yet I'd hardly touched my hoecakes. "What's the matter? Aren't you hungry?"

I nipped off a bit of bacon and then took in a fork of the rich, buttered cake. "Nothing's wrong, Slade. In fact, things feel pretty near perfect."

"Oh, well you could've fooled me, going all quiet like and not eating."

"Just taking it all in—the peace and quiet, the horses whinnying in the barn. Feeling like I can breathe deep and freely."

After my revelations in the workshop and the way he held me, I knew things would never be the same, and Slade did too. His face warmed with a tender smile. "Then take your time, darlin'."

I finally finished my breakfast by the time Slade's plate had been emptied twice. We cleared the dishes together, filling the dishwasher and turning it on before I choked down my morning meds and headed upstairs for clothes. The stairwell was the warm channel I had missed in my morning descent, but I could not linger with Slade following me. He was a man on a mission, and he rushed me mercilessly.

Slade tapped my shoulder at the top of the stairs, and then

spoke while he hurried down the hall to his room. "I'll meet you back in the great room in five minutes."

"Okay, Mr. Hasty Pants."

He snorted. "Hurry up, Ms. Dawdle Butt."

I stuck my tongue out at him and then ducked into my room. Panting, I leaned against the door, my heart pounding in a mix of excitement and fear. I hadn't been on the dating scene in over a year, and it had been at least a year or more since I felt such a consuming attraction for a man. Riding a horse was the least of my worries.

Somehow, his arms felt empty without her in them. Slade's forehead rested against the door panel, his hand drifting down the wood surface. The thumping of his heart echoed in his ears. Her face, tear-streaked in the early dawn light, was all he could see.

He'd waited, given her the opportunity to open up to him. Slade never expected the full depth of her suffering. He'd suppressed the urge to pummel the abusers on every domestic abuse call he ran on the force. Not one incident report compared to her experiences. Those reports were cut and dry, filled out behind the safety of his badge, behind his buffering wall. Kally had passed his defenses, and her tale cut them both, raw and bleeding. It brought him to the edge of tears and anger at the same time. Anger not at her, but at the asshole who had dared to hurt her.

His hand curled into a fist when he inhaled. Anger. Frustration. He felt them, acknowledged them and then released those emotions when he exhaled. There wouldn't be room on the horse for them.

His Hulett P.D. uniform hung in his closet. It commanded his attention every time he reached for a shirt. This time, his glance slid past it with hardly a tick of emotion. It was nice not to want or need the excitement. His smile was lopsided as he grabbed a heavy flannel shirt and pulled it on.

He closed the closet door on the memories of the force.

Kally stood in the hall, right outside his door; her hand was poised to knock, and a silly smile brightened her face. "Knock, knock."

He laughed. "Ready to go?"

Her gaze fell, recouped quickly. Her bottom lip, however,

sank just a little. "Ready as I'll ever be."

He resisted the urge to pat her on the back, tell her everything was going to be just fine. Her automatic flinch slowly faded, but was not gone yet, and it hurt him to see.

They walked together through the hall, Slade a couple inches behind and watching her body, liking the way her butt wiggled when she didn't know someone watched her. He stopped at the top of the stairs, following the unwritten cowboy code demanding, ladies first. Kally passed him with a breathy "thank you", drifting down the stairs until the bottom window near the landing. She always stopped at the window and looked out. Today was no different. "Whatcha doing, darlin'?"

She looked up at him, light from the window caressing her face. "I don't know. I just like the view from this window. It's so rustic, so different from the views out of..." Kally's voice trailed off and her gaze fell. She shrugged her shoulders and covered the last couple of steps. "Well, it's not like the views I'm used to seeing."

"Hopefully nothing here is like what you're used to." He regretted it the moment he said it. Truth was it was exactly how he felt. From what she'd said, he wanted everything about her life at the Fourth Moon to be different from her life with Stransberg in Michigan. Kally's expression was one of surprise and something close to happy. Slade just smiled.

His cell phone came to life in his pocket, singing the chorus of "She Thinks My Tractor's Sexy". *Oh God, how embarrassing.*

Kally's eyebrows went up, and a smirk colored her cheeks. "I didn't know you had a tractor."

Really embarrassing. "Um, yeah, it's in the big barn." He fished the phone out of his pocket on the third refrain. The display screen read, *Baxter, Red.*

He flipped open the phone. "Hey, can you hold for a second?" Slade covered the little microphone hole. "Kally, I need to take this call, can you give me a minute?"

"Sure." She moved from the stairway and took a seat by the fire. Slade excused himself again and scooted past into the office, easing the door closed behind him.

He held the phone up to his ear. "What's up, Red?"

Red spoke in his business tone, which was his method of delivering less than good news. "Ran the name you requested."

Slade damn near tasted the adrenaline dump when it

flushed his body. He could feel the squad car seat beneath his ass and the steering wheel in his hands while Red continued with a litany of crimes and convictions.

"Stransberg definitely has priors, and there's a pattern emerging." He heard Red shuffle papers. "It started out with a B&E in his teens, and a date rape charge by a girl, but the charge was later dropped. At twenty-two, Stransberg was held over on a domestic abuse charge—that one stuck— misdemeanor with less than a year in lock up."

A fire blazed in his gut similar to the one after Kally's sister's last call. *No wonder Kally was so damned skittish.* His jaw was on edge while he listened to the rest of Red's report. "And then there was a felony aggravated assault charge with a weapons violation. The weapons charge was dropped in a plea bargain. He did less than the two-year maximum sentence, released early on good behavior."

Slade forcibly unclenched his jaw. "Thanks for the info, Red."

"Glad to help, partner. Keep your eyes open, Slade. I have a bad feeling about this guy."

He inhaled, forcing himself to relax. "Me, too, Red. Me too."

They disconnected the call with a promise to keep in touch, and then Slade eased open the office door. He stood, watching Kally poke the fire's coals with a cast iron rod. *She was certainly playing with fire before she came here.* The look on her face, the manners she displayed told him she didn't know what kind of guy Stransberg really was.

He didn't plan on telling her, unless it was necessary. No use in adding insult to injury.

His gaze slid over Kally, riding the dip of her waist, climbing the round curve of her butt when she bent to tuck the fireplace tool back in the rack. *How could anyone hit a girl like Kally?* He knew the spirit inside her was bigger than the Wyoming sky. Physically, she appeared to be the embodiment of her delicate floral perfumes. Slade was determined to help coax her inner spirit out. He took his Stetson from its peg and settled it over his head. "Ready to go, Kally?"

"Sure." She dusted soot from her hands onto her jeans. Her brow narrowed. "Was it an important phone call?"

Evasion is never a good thing. An honest life meant you didn't need a good memory, but in this case, Slade felt it was warranted. "Just my old partner from the P.D. We were discussing a case."

She handed Slade's coat to him. "Is everything okay?"

"He's concerned about a guy with prior convictions causing more trouble." *I am too.*

"Oh my." Her bottom lip turned down and a shadow settled over her eyes when she pulled on the jacket he held out for her. "I'd hate to think someone might get hurt."

He shook his head and opened the door. He was both relieved she was clueless, and worried as hell. "Me, too, especially in this case."

Kally had her hand on the doorknob when Slade cleared his throat. "Remember what you said about chivalry?"

She turned her head, while she maintained her grip on the doorknob. "Are you saying you want to open the door for me?"

"Yes, ma'am."

Instead of arguing, Kally stepped aside. Slade turned the knob and opened the door, standing to the side with the knob in his hand. Kally gave him a puckish grin, smacked him on the butt and then breezed through the door while she pulled on a pair of mittens. Slade smiled at her back. *That's my girl.*

The winter chill nipped my skin beneath my jeans, but my new lined barn coat and sweater kept me quite warm otherwise. I watched Slade put the bit and reins on the same white horse he'd ridden the night he found me. Standing outside the barn, I sneezed twice and wondered if it was the hay in the barn, or the unfamiliar, persistent aroma of poop. Slade laughed while I danced foot to foot around a steaming pile when he beckoned me forward. He handed me a round, flat brush while he wrapped the stallion's reins around a post.

Reaching out and grabbing the hem of my jacket, Slade pulled me toward him and the horse. "His name is Jack and he is very gentle, just don't walk behind him."

"Why not?" It was a stupid question, but honest.

"Horses can be brats. I don't want you to get kicked because Jack gets spooked."

"Okay, thanks for the advice." Unfortunately, it only fueled the fear racing through me.

Slade tugged me to him. Holding my fear was difficult

beside Slade. He instilled confidence without even trying. "Put your hand through the leather strap over the back of the brush." I followed his instructions and he nodded. He eased me closer to the horse and then wrapped his fingers over mine, guiding my hand along Jack's shoulders downward. "Brush him in the direction his hair grows. Just like this. Jack likes it and it makes sure there's nothing in his coat when we put the blanket and saddle on him."

The brush smoothed the hairs, running easily over his coat. Slade stood near, coaching me through a few more strokes before removing his hand from mine. The simple motion and the warmth of Jack's body were soothing. Relaxing, I enjoyed the honest, natural connection between the horse and me. I soon found my left hand on Jack's sides, stroking his coat while I brushed his haunches with my right.

I walked in front of Jack to his other side, brushing him from his neck down and back, while Slade rounded up a blanket and saddle. Stroking the horse's neck, Slade settled a thick, plush blanket on Jack's back. The saddle was large, covered with deep brown leather, and creaked when Slade set it carefully on Jack.

While he tightened the straps, he explained proper saddling procedures. "First you need to make sure the horse is not a puffer." He settled the saddle and pulled down the stirrup. "Because some horses will puff up when you tighten the straps, so then when you put your foot in the stirrup, the saddle slides and you fall on your ass. And make sure the stirrup is over the saddle, and doesn't smack them when you put the saddle over." He fed the straps through to me. "Here, hold this."

Slade came around to my side. He patted Jack before tightening the straps. "Jack, here, is my pal and he isn't a puffer. But I still tighten the straps twice." The coarse hair of Jack's neck slid beneath my palm when I stroked him. Slade gently tugged all the cinches again.

Boot in the stirrup, Slade grabbed the pommel and pulled himself up onto the saddle. He turned to me, eyes bright, sky blue when he smiled. The barn, the snow falling outside, the orange tabby cat winding through my feet—everything—fell away. The world became my cowboy, his horse and me. Jack's heartbeat danced across the skin of my palm, his warmth bathed my face, my gaze, my heart, were focused on Slade. The nurse's words echoed in my mind. "He's not some boy on a pony. There's a man in the saddle."

My man in the saddle.

With Slade's help and only a little shoulder pain, I scrambled up onto the saddle, between his pelvis and the pommel. A tremor of discomfort blossomed in my chest, then withered beneath the heat of my healing heart. Reins in hand, Slade wrapped an arm around my waist. He chirped to Jack, a short whistle sound. "Gid-up, Jack."

The rolling gait was something to get used to, especially pinned between Slade's body and the leather covered pommel. I focused on the horse and getting used to the rhythm of his motion before I could enjoy the scenery. By the time Jack carried us to the mouth of the timeshare drive, I had settled into the pace.

The ranch was even prettier in the daylight. The dark wood houses nestled in the blanketing snow and rolling hills. A ragged tree line circled the broad open range, the deep color of the evergreens muffled with white. Wispy gray plumes drifted up from fieldstone chimneys. A chestnut horse stood outside a barn, swishing its tail, and a black-and-white cattle dog chased a chicken into a coop farther down. "The ranch is so beautiful." I leaned back against Slade's strength. "I love it here."

Slade squeezed me tighter, a physical response to my spoken word. Comfort enveloped me, warmer than any jacket. Jack trotted down the center of the lane, while I looked at the ranch houses. They were similar in structure, but each was unique. I knew Emma and Stewart's house immediately by the large bookcase in the front window. I nudged Slade. "What's up, Kally?"

"Remind me to visit Emma sometime and mooch some books from her."

He laughed, chirped to Jack again and the horse picked up speed. "I most certainly will. Emma would love a visit from you."

The chilly air rushed against my cheeks and chest. Slade kept my back warm while we rode past Grace and Alan's house, and up a hill to Rosie and George's ranch at the end of the long lane. The wonderful scent of fresh winter air mixed with the smell of smoked meat. Rosie stood on her porch, shaking out rugs. I would have known it was her house regardless. Native American carvings decorated the porch walls, and a large dream catcher hung in the center of the plate glass window. I held the pommel with one hand and waved with the other. She returned the wave before shaking another rug.

"Do they have a smoker?"

"Yup." Slade inhaled deeply. "Smells good doesn't it? Rosie always smokes a venison roast for Thanksgiving." He pulled the reins to the right, guiding Jack up a hill and into the tree line. Before I could voice a concern, he quieted my fears. "Don't worry, Kally, we'll have a turkey, and Grace always has a ham too. There's always a huge meal on Thanksgiving."

"Thank goodness."

We continued on a narrow path leading along a ridge toward the hunting cabin. When I started to speak, Slade shushed me and spoke with a suppressed voice. "This is the path to our hunting lodge. I try to be quiet and not spook the deer."

Oh no. We wouldn't want to scare them, would we? Silently, I hoped the animals had moved out of shooting range.

We crested a rise, where the land fell away to a little dell lined with aspens. The hunting cabin was in sight, but Slade pulled back on Jack's reins. "Shhhh." He pointed across the dell to where an incline leveled off before rising further to the hill's peek. His voice was nothing more than a whisper. "Look. Those are mule deer."

The hill was a blur of snow and tree trunks until I squinted. Then, the antlers I had mistaken for branches moved when the male deer lifted his head. I could make out the movement of three deer when a doe and a fawn moved in closer to the buck. Their ears were much larger than a Michigan Whitetail, and their coats were darker. *They're such beautiful animals.* "I see them!"

"Yeah. If I had a gun with me they'd be breakfast, lunch and dinner."

"Slade!" I twisted around and smacked him on the shoulder. The sound of my elevated voice scared the deer, and they thundered off into the brush around the far side of the hill.

He snorted, tipped his Stetson down over his eyes and aimed Jack for home. "Remind me not to take you hunting."

I pushed back hard against him, matching his snort with one of my own. "Not a problem."

Instead of getting mad, like Matt would have, Slade

laughed, long and hard until I laughed too. We'd ridden nearly back to the timeshare lane before the last snickers subsided. He let go of my stomach and pushed me square between the shoulders. "You're a feisty one."

"I warned you before I could be an ornery kind of stubborn."

"Yup, and I said I like a challenge." He leaned back, and before I knew it, he'd tipped me off from Jack and into the snow bank beside the barn. Thankfully, the snow was soft and deep. My shoulder didn't even hurt. "There, now you don't have to worry about falling off a horse anymore." I came up sputtering, but he dismounted to the other side and led Jack back into the stall.

"Oh, ha ha." I packed a snowball. "Thanks for that. You're lucky the snow was soft and your little stunt didn't hurt my shoulder more."

"Soft, you say?" When he peeked out of Jack's stall, I nailed him full in the face. He blinked twice and then wiped the snow away with his sleeve. "If I didn't have to take all this off Jack and get him fed, I'd whitewash your hind end."

I thumped my chest like a male gorilla. "Bring it on, cowboy." *I pitched softball for six years. I'm a damned good shot.*

Slade shut the stall door, and I hit him in the chest with another snowball before he wrapped me to his chest and landed us both in the snow bank. I huffed and blew snow and hair from my face with Slade still pinning me to the snow. His gaze devoured me. His hand slid up my side and along my arm to wrap in mine. Neither of us moved. Then he brought his face close to mine, the brim of his hat brushing my forehead.

"Be careful what you wish for."

The energy between us built. A heated desire for his lips rose within, no matter how cold the snow was beneath me. Slade would not push the moment farther, and I wasn't sure if I was ready for him to. Slade seemed to sense it. He rocked back onto his knees, and then extended a hand after he stood.

Slade stayed behind in the barn to curry Jack while I walked to the main house. In the office I checked the phone messages, there was only a call from Ilene. She and Steve would be happy to come to the Fourth Moon the night after Thanksgiving. A ranch hand had dropped off the postal mail on the desk in the office, and I sifted through the envelopes sorting them into the appropriate bins. On the chair sat a small box, no bigger than a box of tea, addressed to Slade personally, so I brought it out to the kitchen with me while I brewed a pot of coffee.

Stomping his feet by the back door, Slade knocked the barn muck from his boots before coming in. He hung his coat on the row of antler pegs by the back door. "The coffee smells good!"

"I thought you might appreciate a cup." I met him in the doorway, package held out. "This package came for you."

He turned the small parcel in his hands and read the return address. "Oh good. It's here." He tucked the little box under his shirt hem and hurried past.

"Well, what is it?"

He turned crafty eyes on me. His grin was the most mischievous I'd seen. "Never you mind, Kally Jensen."

Well, now my interest was piqued. Turning to busy my hands with the mug and coffee pot, I pretended the box didn't matter. "I sorted the rest of the mail in the office. And Ilene called."

"Are they coming after Thanksgiving?"

"Yep."

"Butch's should be a blast then." Slade hurried through the great room, and his boots clattered up the stairs. He reappeared a few minutes later, taking his coffee into the breakfast nook. We sat with a notebook and planned out the Thanksgiving meal and Ilene and Steve's visit. His voice was soothing, and I found myself lost in the lines of his face, swimming in the blue of his eyes. He noticed me staring and smiled. My heart flittered. Matt had never bewitched me like this before.

Chapter Ten

Thanksgiving Day's Eve

Thanksgiving caught them sooner than Slade believed possible. Life's pace was hectic. There was always something to do when they had actually settled down to a more normal ranch life. Kally busied herself learning the ins and outs of the ranch business. While he was out tending cattle, feeding the livestock or dealing with timeshare issues, Kally made all the preparations for the holiday meal. She even rousted out Bonnie's special table linens, washing them and pressing them. The night before Thanksgiving, Kally set the good china out and polished the silverware.

Bundled up in jackets, boots and quilts, they took their dinners of chicken stew out onto the porch, which was one of Kally's favorite things to do. Slade took up one half of the porch swing, and she snuggled in next to him. At first he thought eating in the cold was silly, but when she scooted closer he decided he liked it just fine. He enjoyed the wistful expression she had when she looked out at the ranch under the moonlight.

She nudged him under the blankets. "Slade?"

He gulped his last spoonful down. "Yeah, darlin'?"

Her elfin look returned, only lit with an inner strength instead of seeming so fragile. "Thanks for sitting out here with me."

"My pleasure, Kally."

Her smile was huge when she whipped the blankets off him and the cold air rushed in. "Mine too." Laughing, she grabbed up the blanket and hurried through the door before he could gather up his quilt. "I get the bathroom first."

Racing him in for a hot bath after sitting on the porch was

one of her other favorite things to do. "Oh, ha ha, Kally." He stuck his tongue out at her.

Slade rinsed the dishes and stowed them in the dishwasher. Switching off lights, he walked through the house and stoked the fire before he followed Kally's path up the stairs. The scent of lavender suffused the hall and he knew she was in the bathtub. He inhaled deeply when he passed the bathroom door, images of washing her hair rose in his mind, and he entertained them, instead of chasing them away. He hardly saw the doorknob or the carpet of his bedroom. The small box in the basket of his dresser had his attention.

The hinges creaked when he opened the box. The stone wasn't perfect, never was, but the imperfections were a great part of its charm. The white metal shimmered in the moonlight coming through his window. He lifted the ring from the box, and polished the band with his cleaning cloth.

Thanksgiving was hours away. Slade, however, looked forward to Christmas.

Thursday morning came early, with Slade knocking on my door well before sun up. I groaned, rubbed my eyes and rolled to the wall. The knocking did not stop. "Come on, girl. We've got to get the bird in the oven."

"All right. Keep your drawers on." I pulled loose from the tangled sheets, shuffled over to the bureau and shoved my feet into slippers. Bleary eyed and smoothing my hair with my hands, I opened the door and followed Slade down the stairs and into the kitchen.

"Birdzilla", as Slade affectionately called the turkey, sat in the fridge, taking up a damned good portion of the cubic meters of space. Pine's favorite recipe for sausage stuffing had been prepared the night before, and I crammed the cavity full while Slade crosshatched strips of bacon over the bird. We wrestled the monster into a custom-sized roaster pan and then into the oven.

I yawned and stretched. "Can we go back to bed now?"

"Not really enough time, but how about a snooze on the sofa?"

I needed no more prompting and steered clear of the ingredients for Susan's garlic mashed potatoes on my way to the fireplace and the sofa. Dropping down on one end, I fluffed a pillow and nestled in. Slade, however, disrupted my comfort zone with his long legs when he stretched out in the other corner. With some blanket tugging and leg twining, we ended up tied in a knot from the waist down and covered with the same fleece blanket. I watched one movement of the fireplace ballet before nodding off.

The timer on the stove *ding-ding-dinged* into my dream of Susan's pumpkin pies. Startled, I sat up, afraid we'd snoozed away the day and it was time for dinner. "Ohmygod! I don't have the table set." I tried to extricate myself from Slade's legs and only ended up on the floor.

"Calm down, darlin'. I set the timer so we wouldn't sleep too long." His blue eyes were all mirth and laughter while he helped to untie our tangled limbs and blanket.

"You set the timer to wake us up? You're a pretty smart guy, Slade."

"Thank you kindly. Though I prefer 'genius'."

Of course you do. "Okay, smart guy, we need to get a move on."

Soon, we were showered, dressed and eating a light breakfast. Slade produced a coffee mug with the epitaph "GENIUS" slathered across the front. I raised my eyebrows, pretending not to notice when he purposefully held it up in front of me. I drifted into the dining room and busied myself with setting the most beautiful table in my life. The wine glasses sparkled. The silverware cast a beautiful gleam.

Our guests appeared two-by-two, laden with trays of food. Rosie brought a smoked venison roast and cheesy potatoes, Grace brought a ham and green beans and Emma brought three kinds of desserts.

The dining room table appeared ready to collapse beneath the weight of the food when we sat to dinner. Slade to the seat on my right side and Rosie to my left. Thankfully, he'd left his braggart coffee mug in the kitchen. Emma and Grace's husbands actually showed up for the meal, although the word was they planned to go back to the hunting cabin after dessert.

Slade held out a teensy weensy bite of Rosie's smoked venison. The dark meat hung before my face when I gave him the "you've got to be kidding me" look. I shook my head, but with Slade begging me and the entire table watching, I eventually crumbled beneath the pressure. It was rich, smoky and warm, so much better than I had expected. When he offered me a second bite later, I accepted it. Of course, when eyes were averted, I chased it with a big fork of mashed potatoes and gravy, and washed it all down with sips from my glass of wine. *Okay, so venison is not so bad. It's still not better than ham.*

I really missed Sue and the boys when the desserts came out. Pumpkin pie was Sammy's favorite and mine too. The plate sat before me, smelling of pumpkin and spice and slathered with whipped cream. A tear welled up. I wiped it away before Slade or Rosie caught sight of it.

The group migrated to the great room with cups of coffee or tea, and a few of the men, Slade and the Billings mostly, had seconds on dessert. Grace, in her grandmotherly way, asked how I liked Wyoming, and I had to admit I loved it, other than the culverts. Emma invited me over for tea and to troll her sizeable library. But I think the best invitation, by far, was Rosie inviting me to her house to learn how to weave baskets. I used to love crafting before Mom died, and the offer to try a new craft intrigued me.

Evening shadows settled outside of the ranch house, and the guests slipped, one by one, through the back door. I watched through the steam rising from rinsing the dishes while they loaded their vehicles with leftovers and then drove through the squeaking snow and out of the circle drive. Rosie turned and waved before they left for home. I waved back and then wedged the last dirty dish in the dishwasher and sighed. "This Thanksgiving has been my best holiday in at least two years."

"I'm glad." Slade hung his dishtowel over his shoulder before placing a hand on mine. I reached across my body and covered his hand with my own. We stood there a few moments in the quiet kitchen, enjoying the silence and each other's company.

The orange tabby cat walked out into the circle of light cast down by the lamp atop the barn. A breeze buffeted his fur, and a part of me yearned to bring him into the house where it was warm. Acting on impulse, I grabbed a dish from the cupboard and filled it with turkey scraps. Slade tipped his Stetson back and scratched his head. "What're you doing?"

"Just watch!" I hurried out the back door, and stood on the edge of the porch with the bowl between my toes. "Here kitty,

kitty, kitty."

The tomcat stood and loped toward the house. His orange fur was nearly the color of pumpkin pie filling in the shadows. Stopping before the porch steps, he sniffed at the dish with his ears back. "Come on, kitty."

He climbed the steps, ears back and eyes wide. "It's okay. Come on, kitty."

I stood still while he crept up and took a tentative bite. He looked up at me and then wolfed the food. Bending over, I petted his back before he retreated to the barn.

Slade met me in the kitchen. "Well, look at you, wild cat tamer."

"Yep, I am." I walked past and he cracked my left butt cheek with a towel corner. The home phone rang then. I picked up the line expecting it to be Susan or Ilene. "Hello. Fourth Moon, this is Kally."

"Well, hello, Kally." The voice was deep, rich and happy. "This is Pine, Slade's father. We just wanted to call and wish you both a happy Thanksgiving!"

"Well, thank you, sir. Happy Thanksgiving to you too. Slade's right here, would you like to speak with him?"

"Bonnie wants to talk to him actually, dear. It was nice talking to you finally."

I had to smile. "Nice to talk to you too. I'm handing Slade the phone." I held the phone out to Slade. "It's your parents."

His eyes widened slightly, and a faint smile grew when he took the phone. "Can you excuse me, Kally?" Slade didn't wait for me to answer. He covered the mouthpiece and walked into the office with it. Surprise bubbled up when he cast me a quick glance through the door and shooed me away.

Slade held the phone up. "Hello?"

His mother's voice was close to his heart and so far away. "Hello, son. How are things working out with Kally at the Fourth Moon? Is she healing well? Did the package arrive safely?"

"It's so good to hear your voice, Mother." He dropped into the chair behind his mother's desk, fiddling with the letter opener. "Yup, Kally is healing up really well." *In more ways than one.* "And she fits in here just fine. She's kept up with the mail and has been a great help." Slade watched the shifting shadows beneath the office door, the movement was suspicious. He turned the chair away from the door and spoke softly. "And, yes, the box came. Are you sure about this?"

Her voice was soft but assured. "Yes, I am. If she's the girl, then the ring is yours to give."

The chair squeaked when he turned it back to the desk. The shadows had not moved from the hinge side of the door. He poked at a cow figurine with the business end of the letter opener. "She's the girl." The cow tipped and nearly fell. "I can't explain it, don't want to get all...soft on the phone..."

His mother laughed. "You are just like your father. So, when are you going to do it?"

He stowed the letter opener and rolled the chair back. "I'm thinking I'll do it at Christmas. Give her time. Give me time too." Kally had captured more than Slade's imagination. He wanted things to be right and know they wouldn't change.

The shadow outside the door moved, drifting closer to the door handle. Slade was certain if he pushed the door quickly, he would ram Kally onto her butt on the other side. He'd be damned tempted to laugh then. But he didn't want to get under the porcelain shell he knew she still held. He didn't want to hurt her feelings in any way. Slade stomped his boots to give Kally a clue to back away from the door.

The clatter of boots cued me to step back from the door. I moved back to a more inconspicuous distance, and Slade came out of the office looking like the cat that swallowed the canary. "What're you smiling about?"

Shaking his head, he crossed his arms. "Nothing you need to worry about."

"No." I feigned a pout. "I have to wait until Christmas."

He patted my shoulder, false consolation in the light of his impish grin, and then his hand slid down my spine and rested on my hip, a perfect natural fit. "Christmas is going to be great. I'm really looking forward to having you here with me."

I gave him a sidelong glance and the mischievous smile I'd learned from him. "Yeah? Well, I'm looking forward to the infamous upcoming decorating party!"

"Oh..." A slight blush reddened his cheeks. "The party's actually this Saturday."

"Saturday?" The timbre of my voice rose. "So soon?"

"It's not some fussy affair, Kally. We just pull out all the leftovers, throw some crackers and cheese on the table and haul out the beer. We play loud music, put up decorations and share a few drinks."

"Sounds like fun." Decorating at Matt's had been horrible. It was a job, to be done to his specifications, not as a group effort, and certainly never fun.

"Yup, usually is." Slade tipped his Stetson back. "And, we've got Butch's tomorrow night."

Time with Ilene and her husband Steve. We were going on a double date, like a real couple.

"I can't wait."

Chapter Eleven

Butch's Roadhouse was the busiest, loudest questionable establishment I'd ever been in. Music poured out of the windows, the scent of beef and beer permeated the air—and that was just in the parking lot. Ilene and Steve met us at the front door. Peanut shells littered the floor. Mounts of small game lined the walls beneath garish neon signs touting the different types of liquors sold there. Waitresses strutted by, wearing tight jeans and tighter T-shirts. The dance floor was filled with whooping, yee-hawing line dancers.

I cast a nervous look at Ilene, but she flowered beside me, her jacket coming off and a smile blooming on her face. Steve took Ilene's jacket from her, tossing it over his shoulder in a fluid motion I was certain he'd made a thousand times before. Slade slapped him on the shoulder and then tipped his hat when a man shouted his name from the nearest corner of the dance floor. "Howdy, Tom."

Fidgeting beside Slade, I stepped back to hide behind him. He turned to me then, eyes shadowed by his Stetson. "We don't have to stay..."

I shook my head. "No. It's okay, really. Just a little louder than I expected. Besides, Ilene and Steve look like they're already having fun."

"And Kally could use a beer," Ilene hooted. She grabbed my hand and dragged me toward a table to the left of the teeny dance floor. Steve had taken up a corner and cleared space for Ilene to sit beside him. She slid beneath his extended arm like a flower petal beneath a breeze.

"I didn't know you drank, Kally." Slade cocked an eyebrow at me and then smiled. Passing beneath the brim of his hat and dangerously close to his large belt buckle, I sat in the corner opposite of Steve and right next to a bucket of peanuts. Slade dropped onto the leather padded bench beside me and put his arm across the back of the seat, close to my shoulders, still not touching.

"I tied one on a few times in my college days. But," I tossed a peanut at Ilene, "unlike some of us, I grew up."

Ilene stuck her tongue out at me. I returned the favor, and both men laughed.

A pert little blonde waitress with a high-set ponytail came up to the table. "Hi, I'm Suzy. Can I get y'all anything to start?"

Slade and I shared a menu while Steve and Ilene ordered burgers, steak fries with gravy and a couple of beers. I handed the menu to Slade. "A burger sounds good. Put me down for one too. Just give me ketchup for the fries please."

Slade folded the menu and then snorted. "No one out here uses ketchup, darlin'. It's ranch dressing, fry sauce, or gravy—"

"Slade Carlson?" Suzy interrupted. She devoured his face with her gaze. "Long time no see!"

His blue eyes rolled when he grimaced, then he turned to Suzy with a fake smile plastered across his face. "Suzy Mitchell. How the hell are ya?"

She blushed, batted her eyelashes and shimmied closer. Her thigh brushed Slade's where it stuck out into the aisle. He pulled his leg back in beneath the table. "I'm fine, Slade, thank ya for asking. Just got the job here to help with the bills." She looked me over in the same predatory "kill the interloper" sense Cissy had done in Gillette. "And who's this? You got a cousin in town?"

Ilene kicked me under the table, jerking her eyes toward Suzy. Slade dropped his arm from the back of the bench to drape on my shoulders. He pulled me closer. "She's not a cousin. Kally is my..."

"Special guest at the Fourth Moon," I filled in.

"Oh really?" She backed away a step, ignoring me and thrusting her order pad between her and Slade. "So what can I get for you, Slade?"

He ordered the same burger combo we all did, but added jalapeño poppers and a bloomin' onion. Suzy tucked her tablet into her tight, low slung apron and then nearly tossed her butt into Slade's face when she left to fetch our drinks and the appetizers. Slade backed away in mock fear and then took a sip of his water. The topic of tomorrow night's decorating party came up, with Ilene and me begging for a second night. Steve shook his head. "Sorry. Ilene and I have to get home tomorrow morning. Mom is only going to watch the dogs for so long."

"Bummer." I pouted and Ilene surrendered with a shrug of her shoulders.

Suzy returned with a tray full of beers, the battered, deep fried onion and Slade's poppers. She stepped back without trying to chat up my cowboy. I watched her make a beeline away from our table to another at the other end of the dance floor. Cissy Rawlings sat there with what looked to be Cowgirl Barbie and her dark haired, less attractive but equally plastic friend. The three women leaned in and then followed Suzy's finger right to me.

The nurse said I'd meet green-eyed monsters in Hulett. I didn't think they ran in packs. I nudged Ilene underneath the table and then pointed to the table of feral females looking this way. She rolled her eyes and turned her back on them. "Just enjoy yourself, hun."

"Agreed," Steve chimed in, and raised his beer bottle like a champagne flute for toasting. "Here's to new friends and having fun."

Slade raised the neck of his bottle, clinking it against Steve's. "To new friends."

Ilene and I toasted, "New friends. Having fun."

As a group we drew swigs off our beers, the men turning it into a race, draining their bottles. The bottles banged on the tabletop and Slade belched loud enough for the residents of Saint Joe to hear him. Ilene and I exchanged bug-eyed glances and then laughed out loud. I dropped a hand onto his thigh. "Great hang time."

"Thank you kindly." Slade asked Steve about his job while he unscrewed the cap of the Tabasco sauce bottle and dosed his side order of poppers. The tangy fumes were enough to knock a smaller girl on her ass. I looked at him, searching for sanity in a crazed man. "Are you kidding me?"

"Ain't much can't benefit from a little Tabasco."

"But, Slade, those are jalapeños."

"I know. I love 'em but they're kind of fumy." He waved his hand over the plate and then winked. "Good thing you sleep alone, eh?"

A deep blush singed my cheeks. If sliding under the table could be considered appropriate, I would've been gone. Ilene smiled, her eyes taking in every nuance of body language we displayed. She elbowed Steve, and he nodded.

Steve excused himself to go to the restroom, saying he'd order another round of beers before returning to the table. Slade nodded. "I'll keep the ladies safe until you get back."

In Steve's absence, Slade leaned in over the center of the table toward us girls. A mischievous twinkle danced in his eyes. "Ever been stopped by those guys who smell like mint at the kiosks in the mall?"

Ilene cocked an eyebrow. "Occasionally. Why?"

"Well last time I was in the mall over in Spearfish, those guys stopped me twice." He leaned back and waggled his hands over the table like a girl drying her nails after a manicure. "They just shouldn't be asking a man if they want a 'hand treatment'."

Ilene snickered. I giggled, then laughed out loud. Tears beaded in the corners of my eyes, and I laughed so hard I snorted.

Slade faked a shocked expression tainted with a slight grin. "What?"

"I'm sorry." I hiccupped for breath. "That really struck me funny."

His eyes settled on mine. "I know." He smiled, broad, with his blue eyes sparkling in the down turned light. Slade dipped a French fry in his puddle of fry sauce and then popped it in his mouth. Steve returned, and we settled into our meals. Our plates were emptied by the time Suzy returned with four beers. I took one drink off the new bottle and the "drink one, pee one" rule took effect.

"I've got to go to the little girls' room. Need to go, too, Ilene?"

"Yep. I could use a little bladder relief."

We worked our way out of the booth and wove through people to the bathroom. A sign above one door read "Colts" and another read "Fillies". Ilene plowed through the Fillies door with me in tow and then banged into an empty stall. I danced foot-to-foot, waiting for the other stall to empty. A portly girl with a too tight shirt tied in a knot under her breasts walked out, and I ducked in. Ilene and I met at the sinks, where I tapped her shoulder.

"Do I look okay?" I turned on the heels of my boots, so Ilene could gauge my outfit.

"Oh, honey, you look great." She waved a hand, dismissing my clothing concerns. "It doesn't matter what you're wearing, every girl in this bar is glaring at you with envy because of who you're sitting with. And speaking of Slade..." She cornered me. "Are you in love yet?"

I squirmed, tapping my toe and fussing with my blouse. "Oh, Ilene, please."

She balled her hands into fists on her hips. "Come on, Kally. 'Fess up. Do you have feelings for your hot cowboy or not?"

"Would you feel better if I said 'yes'?"

She leaned against the wall with her arms crossed. "At least then I'd know you were telling the truth."

I tucked my thumbs in my pockets. "Okay, fine. I like him. I like him a lot."

She smiled and grabbed my hand. "Kally, I think you should go for it. Next time he gets close enough, wrap your arms around him and kiss him."

I quoted Slade. "I'll take it under advisement."

We walked out of the bathroom in time to see Cissy Rawlings and the Barbies heading our way. Refusing to dignify their nasty glares, I tossed my hair over my shoulder and walked back to the table. Slade and Steve stood when we returned, Ilene smooched her husband, and for a moment I considered kissing Slade. But I didn't want to kiss him just to prove a point to those other women, or even Ilene.

I stroked his cheek with my fingers, drawing close to him before sliding against his body and sitting in my seat. A new plate mounded with fries took up the center of the table, along with bowls of gravy, fry sauce and ranch dressing. Slade encouraged me to try a fry with gravy, holding it for me to bite. "Okay, fine." I took the offered fry. It was damned good. "I think I've found a new favorite."

Slade smiled, running his fingers along my arm. "Me too." A slow dance song played, and Slade took my hand. "Are ya dancing?"

"Are you asking?"

He pulled me from the booth and onto the dance floor. I melted against him, his embrace more intoxicating than the beers coursing through me. Sighing, I stroked the back of his neck, playing with his dark hair. He emitted something close to a groan and held me tighter, one hand slipping down to cup my butt. Losing track of the lyrics, I clung to the rhythm, following the motion of his body and the rocking of his hips.

I could have danced with Slade all night, but eventually the song ended. He drew both hands up the side of my body, cupped the sides of my face and drew me close. My heart beat harder, my breath seized in my throat. *Yes! Kiss me, press your lips to mine.*

He didn't. Slade stopped, his eyes leaving mine, his gaze aimed over my shoulder. "Oh God...here she comes."

"Who?"

"Adelle Crawford—the ex-girlfriend from hell."

The bleached-blonde Cowgirl Barbie swaggered to us, rolling her hips and thrusting her breasts at Slade in an obvious vie for attention. He held up his hands in a gesture of annoyance while she circled us, her muddy green eyes scouring me. I maintained my ground, fingers curled in his, while a new sensation of stubborn will rose within me. Slade shifted his weight onto his left hip, his body brushing mine. Her painted lips parted. "I heard you brought home a stray, Slade. I never expected you to keep something so scrawny..."

I stepped up to face her and shocked myself. "And what's your problem with it?"

I didn't have time to ponder the newfound strength. Adelle turned on me. "My problem? This is my territory and he's part of it. Always has been, always will be."

She sounds like Matt. Her attitude only fanned the flames inside. *No one owns someone else.* "Then why don't you cock your leg and piss on him?"

She snorted and rolled her eyes. "Only male dogs cock their legs, idiot."

"Oh? Then you're just a bitch."

Inwardly, I was shocked with myself, but I maintained a solid stance. Her eyes widened. Her mouth fell open, then snapped shut again. The blush on her face flushed her body, even staining her cleavage and breasts an angry red. She cast a glare back to the table she'd recently left and then turned back to me. "I am not a bitch, and I sure as hell ain't no female dog!"

Just then, the two women who'd traveled in her pack to the bathroom and back to their table came to the dance floor and stood beside her. Things weren't going her way, so she had to call reinforcements? Sarcasm simmered to a boil in my mouth. "Oh look, the rest of your dog sled team has arrived. Did you leave your harness outside?"

Ilene appeared by my side to join the verbal fray. "So, which one of you is the lead dog, and who are the ones left looking at ass all day?"

A round robin chorus of "you bitch" and "how dare you" ensued. Adelle seemed ready to charge in and rip out my throat with her manicured nails, but then the lone man at their abandoned table shouted, his voice cracking like a whip over the churlish pack. "Hey, Adelle. Get me a beer, would ya?"

Silence fell and a grin cut into my cheeks. "Better hurry, Adelle, your musher is calling..."

The color drained from her face, leaving red splotches of blush on her cheekbones. She growled half curses and glared at Slade. His smile remained placid and unaffected by her anger. Her bravado faded, but she leveled a finger at me. "No one insults me like this. You'd better watch yourself. I'll come at you sideways. I'll make you miserable for even looking at him!"

"Impossible."

I motioned for her to run along, and then I tugged Slade's hand and led him from the dance floor, leaving her chewing on the bone of her embarrassment. Slade stopped at the edge of the polished oak expanse and pulled me to his chest. He came close enough to kiss me a thousand ways and didn't. The energy between us crackled. I was torn. I couldn't turn away, but I didn't want our first kiss to be because of Adelle. Then his lips moved, a breath away from mine while his hand encircled my back, cinching me to his body. I would have given in then. I couldn't resist his embrace. His heart beat for us both.

"I love it when you're feisty." His voice was husky, a secret for just us.

The heat of his lips scorched mine. "I love your liking me feisty."

We returned to our table, and Steve patted Ilene on the back. "I thought for a minute I was going to have to break up a fight. Good job, honey."

A rather crestfallen Suzy showed up at our table and I ordered rounds of shots for the table. I swilled my beer down before she returned. The little glasses were passed around and tossed back before she was out of earshot. "Hey, Suzy!"

She turned, and Slade ordered another round. Steve shouted for more beers too. Between the bourbon and beer, I was buzzed. I leaned against Slade, stuffing a fry into the fry sauce from him, and then dipping one in the gravy for me.

Around one o'clock, people filtered through the roadhouse and out the door. Adelle shot me a scathing glare, which I met with a stoic expression of indifference. Ilene came up beside me in a show of solidarity. The pack of bitches passed through the door, followed by their musher Tom. He cast Slade an apologetic expression and shrugged his shoulders. "Adelle's a spirited one."

"Yup. She is." Slade tipped his hat, then spoke only loud enough for us to hear. "And I'm glad she's his burden."

I left a good tip on the table for Suzy. She was a fine waitress, and I wasn't going to hold her poor choice in friends against her. We filed out a few couples behind them. Waving, Ilene and Steve headed to his car. "Meet you back at the ranch."

Turning on my heel, I aimed for Slade's truck. There was no warning, not even Slade caught wind of the attack. Adelle hit me from behind, slamming me into the tailgate of his truck. Stars exploded in my vision, and air *whooshed* out of my lungs. The stubborn will that had flared on the dance floor flooded me. I pushed off the tailgate, clipping her jaw with my elbow when I spun to face her. She covered her jaw with a hand, and her fingers came away bloody. "You witch!"

"And?" I clamped my jaws shut and widened the stance of my feet, bracing myself for another round. Adelle swung out, fingernails bared. I blocked it with a hard outward swing. She was framed by the moon before I struck back, shoving her in the middle of her chest, pushing her back on her ass in the muddy parking lot.

She scrambled to her feet and balled her fists. I taunted her, stepping back and baiting her in. She swung and I sidestepped, letting her smash her pretty nails against the tailgate of Slade's truck. The metallic bang echoed off the vehicles and caught her escort's attention. Tom's head popped up like a prairie dog in a field of cars before he stood in the doorframe of his Suburban. "Adelle! What the hell're you doing?"

She spat at my feet and then backed away. "I told you I'd come at you sideways."

"No, you hit me from behind, like a pathetic little bitch."

Adelle's face contorted, and her eyes widened, pupils dilating like a dog tracking a target. Tom appeared out of the shadows, wrapping his arms around Adelle's stomach and holding her back. Slade placed a hand on my shoulder, fingers digging into my jacket. "Doesn't matter what you want, Adelle. In the end, you're with Tom and I have Slade."

Her shoulders slumped. Tom released her then, wrapping his hand around her wrist and leading her back to his vehicle. Slade tapped my shoulder. "Come on, Kally Cat. Let's go home."

I climbed into the front seat and buckled in. "Kally Cat?"

"Well, yeah." His smile was broad when he turned to me. "You get into a cat fight outside of a bar and not expect me to say anything?"

I snorted. "Well, she started it."

He laughed and smacked my thigh. "And you finished it."

"Damn straight."

I slumped on the seat, bracing my knees on the dashboard and wrapping my fingers in Slade's. The normal Wyoming travel time warp was quickened in an inebriated blur. The roads slipped by in a snowy haze of hills and trees, flat lands and the occasional house with lights on.

We turned into the Fourth Moon's main drive, closest to Devil's Tower. The Missouri Butte was framed in snowfall and moonlight. I turned in the seat, climbing up onto my knees to watch the landmark shrink in the back window before the trees swallowed the picturesque view. Slade parked near the house. I opened the door and got out, but my legs had turned to mush. I staggered toward the porch, slipping on an icy patch and nearly pitching face first onto the drive.

"Good lord, girl." Slade hurried to my side and looped an arm around my waist. Turning sideways, he ushered us through the front door and foyer.

Ilene and Steve were waiting for us in the great room beside the fire. "Hey you two. What happened back there?"

My tongue felt thick in my mouth, and I still couldn't stop

it from wagging. "Adelle attacked me."

Steve didn't seem the least bit surprised. Ilene jumped from her chair. "Oh, hun! Did she hurt you?"

"Kally's a pretty good scrapper. She shut Adelle up in a hurry." Slade released me and I drooped forward, catching myself on the back of an armchair. The floor rocked and the walls wavered. The chair I clung to tipped unbelievably sideways, and Slade caught me before I fell. "Right now I think this little scrapper needs to go to bed though."

Ilene laughed and agreed. "We'll show ourselves to the room and then meet you in the morning."

I waved my hand like a goon. "Night, Ilene. Night, Steve."

"Come on, you." Slade guided me toward the stairs. The shots caught up with me climbing the steps in the warm stairwell. By the time I'd reached the hallway at the top my head was doing loops, and my feet had somehow become detached from my body. They moved beneath me of their own accord, aiming toward my bedroom. One hand trailed the wall for support while I stumbled along to my bedroom with Slade holding up my other arm.

"You can certainly hold your bourbon." He grunted when I pitched forward through my open door. "But it comes around and bites you in the ass, doesn't it?"

"Yep!" A sober thought burned bright in my sluggish mind. *Ohmygod, I'm sloppy drunk in front of Slade!*

I tried to stand without swaying. My "fuck Adelle" shots of bourbon had destabilized my equilibrium. My ass hit the mattress, and I flopped over to pull my boots off. One boot came off with a lurch and I hit myself in the forehead with the embroidered flowers of the upper. Slade stopped me from making myself twice the fool by removing the other boot for me. I reached out and grabbed hold of his hand. He kept my world from spinning. "Slade?"

"Yeah, Kally?"

"I'm drunk." I tugged on the wrist of my top, but couldn't navigate its removal.

"Yes, you are." The lines of his face softened when he wrapped the hem of my sweater in his fingers. I hiccupped when the cotton stitching of my sweater passed over my face and off from me. My hair poured over my eyes and his gentle touch wiped it away.

I blinked hard, trying to clear my vision. "The room is spinning."

"Maybe it will stop when you go to sleep."

I turned when he directed me to, and slid beneath the blankets. The world failed to adjust with my new position and I felt certain I'd fall through the bed and floor. "I don't want to sleep alone tonight. You're the only thing holding me steady."

"Then tell me what you want, Kally."

"Will you sleep with me?"

He cocked an eyebrow, and I wished to God I didn't have so much bourbon in my veins. I wanted to say something smart, wanted the walls to stop wobbling, wanted to feel his arm around me. But nothing more. I waggled my head from side to side and my gift of clear speech deserted me. "Not like *that*, though..."

He put a finger to my lips. "Sure thing, darlin'."

My eyelids drooped and I clutched the bedpost, watching him pull off his boots and remove his big, shiny belt buckle. His snowy white socks stood out in high relief to the sour mash shadows in my eyes. My brain/mouth filter was broken. "Nice socks."

"Hush up, your bourbon's talkin'."

I put a hand over my mouth and Slade climbed into the bed behind me. The bed shook while he settled in, then everything righted itself, like a ship after a swell, when he wrapped his arm around me and pulled me to his chest. My dizziness quieted to a wiggling at the edges of my vision and a gentle rocking when I closed my eyes.

I wriggled back tight against Slade, nestling my head on his other arm. He kissed the top of my head, and bliss spread in waves from the place where his lips touched me. Releasing me, he pulled the blankets tighter to my chin. I dragged the orange teddy bear into my arms and looked at the two pairs of boots by my wall. His breathing was regular, deep and soothing. I sighed, and then, warm and fuzzy, I relaxed into sleep.

Chapter Twelve

Slade awoke to the curtains filtering weak dawn light and Kally snoring softly. A morning stretch tempted him. The need to move burned along his spine, but he lay still beside her afraid to move, afraid to lose the quiet moment to the busy day he knew was coming.

Propping himself up on one elbow, Slade's gaze poured over her face, her throat. The broken doll was gone. Kally was a whole woman again, though her delicate features still reminded him of an elf.

Stray strands of blonde lay over her eyes. He brushed them away. Kally twitched, her eyelids fluttered, then she settled back into sleep. He kissed her head and nestled in the pillow where he could smell her bouquet of floral scents mingled with the unmistakable smell of Butch's Roadhouse. He had to smile at the thought of last night's date. Kally had loosened up, let her hair down, and he loved every minute of it.

She laughed, she flirted, and when pressed by Adelle, she fought back. Each new aspect of her evolving personality intrigued him. Kally had so many sides. She was a gem revealing herself one facet at a time.

He thought back over his time on the force and being wrapped around Adelle's finger. Slade choked back a sarcastic snort. Was he really so happy then? Looking at Kally asleep beside him, his heart swelling with each breath she took, he had to say no. Delusion was not happiness. The fight for advancements, the fights with Adelle were nothing but stress and adrenaline. They were beguiling and deceitful, just like the green-eyed Crawford she-devil. The emotions he felt with Kally were so much stronger, more honest and real than any crush he'd ever entertained.

The stretch he'd suppressed came back, and he could not fight it anymore. Slade leaned away from Kally while the movement traveled from his neck, through his shoulders and arms, down his spine and out his toes. Slade shuddered and a yawn escaped him. The girl he had tried not to disturb began to stir.

Morning came roaring into the room and my skull. My brain pulsed and ached with each beat of my heart. The sunlight through the window hurt my eyes, and I wasn't sure if the bright spots were sunlit dust motes or my ocular nerves screaming in agony.

"Oh God." My hands went to my head, pressing back against my temples.

Slade moved beside me, taking his warmth with him when he sat. The bed-wiggles went right into my brain. "Regret is a bitch, isn't it?"

"Oh yeah, a heinous bitch."

I groaned, and his fingers brushed my eyelids closed. He stroked my forehead, along my cheekbones and down my nose. My hands dropped to the mattress and I lay beside him, blind and drinking in his ministrations. Stroking his fingers on my skin, Slade took some of the pain away. Misery shrank beneath his hands, and then he cupped my chin with his palm and kissed my forehead. His butterfly kisses alighted on my cheeks, my closed eyelids, my nose, and then settled on my lips, briefly.

Was it real? Lights went off behind my eyelids. My heart slammed in my ribs. I could have been floating and not even on the bed. He brushed stray bangs from my face. "Want me to run a hot bath for you? Then you can soak while I make some coffee."

"Sounds good." *Even though I'd rather have you kiss me again.*

The bed rocked when Slade climbed over me and out of bed to stand on the rug. Wild, wavy dark hair stood at odd angles on his head, and his clothes were rumpled. The most beautiful man I'd ever been blessed to look at. My heart fluttered when he held out his hands, I used them to pull myself upright and then off the bed and into his arms. Nothing was stable. My legs felt like putty, my head ached and heart refused to pick up a regular rhythm. "Whoa! The world is spinning again."

Nestling against his chest, I inhaled his scent of day-old Stetson cologne and warm skin. The world steadied, the beauty returned to the grain of the wood paneling and the sun through the window was a blessing once more instead of a curse. Within, my soul danced and sang to the tune of my pounding heart. Was the world spinning because of my hangover or Slade's kiss?

"All right now, Kally." His grip loosened, and he pointed toward the Mission Oak bureau. "Fetch yourself some clothes. We have a party to throw and a house to decorate. Now scoot."

I walked toward the dresser, but not before catching a playful spank on my right butt cheek from Slade. I gasped and he ducked into the bathroom when I spun to give him a shocked expression. The dresser drawers gave up jeans, a long underwear top and pastel flannel shirt when I rifled through them. I folded the clothes while I watched him lock the hallway door and plug the tub. By the time I joined him in the bathroom, he'd dropped two of his mom's tea bags into the water. "Take two and call me in the morning."

Tea in the bathwater? "I never thought about putting the tea into a bath."

"It's kind of an aromatherapy thing." He swished the teabags around and then winked. "The lavender and sage are very soothing. Might help your hangover."

"Ah, well I can use all the help I can get." The icky feeling in my head had trickled down into my body while I stood. "Thanks for starting my bath, and for thinking enough to put the tea in there."

He ran a hand through his mussed hair, his pale blue eyes focused on mine, piercing into my heart. "I'm always thinking about you."

With one sentence, he turned me to goo. Warmth flooded me, bringing up nagging questions I tried so hard to ignore. I looked out the window, at the snow-clad trees and beyond to the hills. The ranch was so beautiful, the life here was utopian. "But why, cowboy? I'm just a horse-fearing small town girl with a painful past."

He closed the distance between us, one hand resting in the small of my back, and the thumb of his other hand tracing the line of my bottom lip. Those icy blue eyes had softened again, shifting from polar to baby blue. "Why?" He paused, his heart spoke in loud percussion, echoing in my own chest. "Well, for about one hour it was the whole 'wounded bird' thing. Carrying you home on Jack's back, you limp and leaning against me, mumbling, begging me not to hurt you. God, girl, you cut right into my heart and left me aching.

"Then, you woke up in the hospital, and everything changed. Your vulnerable side got buried beneath your feisty personality. When you interact with Ilene," a grin warmed his face, "you girls drive me crazy. By the way, you're all happy and act like you can take on the world. You're so respectful of my mother and our guests. But when you're with me, your soft side comes out. You bewitch me with all of your facets. Like turning a gemstone and seeing all the different sides.

"And when I think of the gift you gave me when you reminded me of the beauty of this place, the good honest blessings of this life, well it makes me fall even harder." The distance between his lips and mine was excruciating. I was malleable in his arms.

I blinked away happy tears. "You're falling for me?"

He placed a feather-light kiss on my lips. "Falling so hard."

The world no longer spun. Everything fell away, except me and Slade and the pressure of his lips on mine. His hand slid up my back, fingers tangling in my hair while the other hand traced the neckline of yesterday's shirt. My heart beat stronger and softer and the sound of it echoed in my ears. The emotion, the need for him was sweet nectar in my mouth. Emotions I could not control rose and swirled within. His eyes slipped closed when he came in to kiss me again.

Reality flooded back, cascading with the bathwater to the floor and dampening the heat of our embrace. Laughing, I scrambled for the faucet while Slade tossed towels on the floor. We both dropped to our knees mopping up the water, and then he winked at me, gathered the towels and tossed them down the laundry chute.

"All right, Kally." He opened the door to the bedroom. "I'm going to leave you to your bath and get some dry clothes. I'll meet you downstairs, because I believe the ranchers are down there whipping up breakfast already."

Fingers on the fly of my jeans I nodded. "Okay, I'll try to be quick." Slade hovered at the door, his eyes coursing my body.

"Go on, now. I'm not taking off my clothes while you're in the room."

His kissable lips twisted downward in a mock pout and he gave me a great imitation of puppy dog eyes. I shook my head and pointed down the hall. With a final whimper, he winked and then shut the door. The tiles were cold beneath my feet when I hurried over and locked it. I returned to the tub, letting out enough water to make room for me without overflowing it again. Then, dropping my clothes, I stepped into the bath, inhaling the herbal vapors and soaking my achy shoulder in the heated water.

Saturday morning chaos churned inside the kitchen walls. The lady ranchers were all busy with a pan or skillet, and George was setting places for ten. Kally slipped in like she was the pinch hitter for some kitchen sports team. She relieved Emma from her post at the fried potatoes and Slade stepped into flapjack flipper position. He cast sidelong glances at her butt while she shimmied to some internal tune.

Rosie walked past, her shiny black hair tied back on top and a turquoise beaded choker circled her neck. She nudged Kally, her dark eyes sparkling when she mouthed, "Watch this."

Slade's guts clenched and he rolled his eyes before wincing. Sure enough, Rosie puckered up and whistled the chorus of "Deck the Halls" and winked at him. His cheeks turned crimson, making his dark hair look even darker, and then he focused intently on the pancakes.

Yup, Rosie. I figured as much.

Kally giggled. When Slade gave her an exasperated expression she tipped her head to the side and smiled.

You're lucky you're cute, Kally.

The ranchers adjusted the seating arrangement, leaving the seats directly opposite of Slade and Kally open to accommodate their company. Chatter about where to cut this year's Christmas tree floated around the table. Breakfast was served, the coffee was poured and there were two empty chairs. Kally gave Slade a sidelong glance and then shrugged her shoulders. He searched the hall and through the arch into the great room. Their guests weren't to be seen. "Would you like me to get them?"

"Nah, I'll go." She shoved a strip of bacon in her mouth and pushed away from the table.

Kally had hardly disappeared beyond the mouth of the stairwell before his godmother turned on him. Pinned by Rosie's gaze like a bug to sponge board, Slade squirmed, took too big of a bite of bacon and nearly choked. He sputtered and chased the meat with a glug of coffee. Her dark eyes never left him, and his silence was not accepted. She cleared her throat. "Well? What happened last night, Slade?"

He couldn't shrink far enough into his collar. There was nowhere safe to rest his gaze. Slade's swig of coffee only forestalled her second throat clearing and his confession. "Well...Kally got a little drunk and asked me to stay in her room." Rosie's eyebrows rose appreciatively. Slade cut off any possible thoughts of impropriety. "We didn't do anything inappropriate."

No matter what craving his body had had, Kally's bourbon had shut him down. He wouldn't dream of taking advantage of an inebriated woman. He'd seen too many abuse and date rape victims.

Rosie's grin grew, covering her face like the Grinch in Dr. Suess's *How the Grinch Stole Christmas*. "So," she leaned across the table, inches from him, "you at least kissed her, didn't you?"

The answer was written in the moony expression on his face.

If it was possible, her smile grew. "I knew it!"

"Well, it doesn't mean anything's going to come of it." He pressed the butter knife straight through a slice of toast.

She leaned back in her chair, arms crossed in a pose of comfort. "It definitely means something." She placed her napkin on her lap, and her gaze drifted over his shoulder to the living room. "You don't do anything half-assed. And I don't believe you're kissing her was half-hearted either."

He couldn't deny it. His gaze fell and then returned to Rosie's face.

She gave him a knowing wink. Then, the other men at the table stood when Kally returned to the dining room. Slade stood, too, and pulled out her chair. She wound her lithe body between people and chairs, and his heart picked up its tempo. His affections for Kally weren't half-hearted.

I had the distinct impression I had been the main topic of

conversation until the moment someone spotted me in the living room door. I would've grilled Slade about it if Ilene and Steve hadn't appeared beside the table.

"Good morning, all!" Ilene took Steve by the hand, leading him to the seats across from Slade and me.

Rosie smiled and lifted her coffee mug in salute. "Good morning!"

"Happy Saturday."

The noise level rose with the addition of our new guests, platters circulated at a happy speed and the Tabasco bottle flashed back and forth. My friends fit in with the long time guests, nearly mistakable for timeshares at the Fourth Moon. Vampires from a Southern romance author were all the rage at the girls' end of the table, while firearms and wild game were discussed at the other end where Steve and the majority of the Fourth Moon's male contingency sat. After clearing our dirty dishes, we returned to the table with fresh coffee to discuss finding the tree.

The Billings twins, however, swilled their coffee and retreated to the backdoor, saying their good byes and promising to return for the decorating party after their evening hunt. After the group arrived at the consensus of taking a tree from the back eighty, Emma and Grace both decided to stay where the house was warm, and offered to clean up the kitchen. Rosie and George planned to go. Rosie said they'd "never missed a tree cutting and weren't about to."

Bundling up in the foyer, I reached for my fur-lined mukluks. Slade stopped my hand and shook his head. "You'll need your riding boots, Kally."

"We're riding?" I didn't intend panic to come through, but the timbre of my voice rose quickly.

"Yup. And you'll ride Sunny, my mother's mare. She's Jack's older sister. We'll need both of the quarter horses to pull the tree."

Oh God. Doesn't he remember that I'm scared of horses?

Ilene was well aware of my fear of horses, and she stood with a shocked expression on her face. She looked from me to Slade, who stood firm, his normally expressive face stoic.

My voice was hardly audible. "I'll get my boots."

My fears were trapped in my chest. My throat would not cooperate, and I couldn't scream at him. I pulled off the mukluks and dropped them to the floor. Hurrying through the great room I heard Slade excuse himself. He chased after me, a few steps behind when I blundered up the stairs. I made it to the bedroom first, where I leaned against the windowsill, shaking. Slade banged through the door a second later. "Kally, don't you trust me?"

My head fell. "Yes." He knew me better in the weeks I'd known him than anyone in my life, with the exception of Ilene.

"Then, if I tell you everything will be all right, will you believe me?"

"Yes." A mouse could've spoken louder.

"Sunny is Mom's horse. She's gentler than Jack and will follow without you having to do a thing other than stay in the saddle."

Still I quivered, the sick fear turning my breakfast to acid. "But..." I turned to him, my arms crossed and bottom lip tucked between my teeth.

Wyoming sunlight washed his form when it peeked through the window, and it highlighted the slumping of his shoulders. He turned from me to pull on his boots still sitting by my wall. "If you're scared, Kally, you can ride with me." He wove his belt through the loops of his jeans. "I'll call George. I'm sure he'll ride Sunny."

Why not just call me chicken? Calling in reinforcements would be a serious affront. Willful pride rose in me, straightening my shoulders and my spine. "No, I'll do it." *I'll probably puke on my boots, but I'll do it.* "It's time to face my fears head on instead of running from them."

Slade's expression was softer than his hand on my arm. "Only if you're sure."

I nodded. "I'll be okay."

Chapter Thirteen

Blue peeked through the snow clouds, sending sun through the crystal flakes falling down. The hills and hidden hollows of the Fourth Moon beckoned. With the fresh snowfall, the softened landscape suggested hours of winter fun. The snow squeaked beneath our boots, a sure sign of frigid temperatures. Most of the animals were in their stalls in the barn or their coops, except for the orange tabby cat trailing behind the four of us. Slade looked back over his shoulder at the tomcat. "Holy cow."

Ilene spun around, her fashionably long scarf swinging. "What?"

"The orange cat never comes out unless Kally's around. I swear she's gonna tame the obstinate beast."

"Never mind him calling you names." I stopped and petted the cat. "Obstinate is a whole lot like stubborn, so we have something in common. You can just be my tomcat." The ginger kitty circled my ankles and then disappeared into the shadows of the barn.

The particular aroma of hay and poop suffused the air in the barn. My sneezing started after the first stall was opened and drove me back out in front of the cattle pen. I stood with Ilene, who tried to comfort me while the men saddled up the horses. Saying, "If you're scared, you don't need to" fifteen times, fifteen different ways did a good job of banging me over the head with my insecurities, but didn't do a tinker's damn to calm my fears. Ilene's arm ended up around my shoulder, even though I did my best to convince her I wouldn't ball up and cry like a baby. Somewhere in my soul the decision had been made to stay at the Fourth Moon, and I would do whatever it took to make a strong and happy life here, even if it included choking down my fear of horses.

My heart jumped into a familiar patter when Slade led Jack and Sunny out of the barn. The West never looked so good. The mountains and barn, his Stetson and blue eyes. He was my cowboy, and I would brave any obstacle to be with him.

Bonnie's horse Sunny was a beautiful chestnut mare with blonde mane and tail, white socks and a white blaze on her forehead. The horse's quiet nature was obvious when Slade brought her reins to me. Then, he cupped my chin in his gloved hand. "I'm proud of you." His words meant so much. The tender kiss he gave me next, in front of my friends, meant everything. "Sunny, this is Kally. Kally, this is Sunny."

Sunny's eyes were large, the color of coffee with too much cream, and her nose was velvet soft when I removed my mitten to pet her. I stroked her coat, my hands gliding along her neck and shoulders, mimicking the moves of the curry brush while I tried to connect to the horse. The steam from her breath bathed my face when she inclined her head and nudged me in the chest. The motion was simple but broke a little laughter free. Then, with Slade's assistance, I clambered onto the saddle.

"Good girl." I patted her neck, disguising the feeling my stomach had fallen into my boots.

Sunny fell in step with Jack when Slade urged the horses forward along the drive to the timeshare ranches. I managed to keep my nervous tendencies under control if I didn't look down at the road beneath the horse's hooves. Scanning the tree line, I caught sight of a hawk. The bird spread its wings, flying over and I followed its arc across the sky. A large patch of blue opened overhead, and the sunlight bathed the range of mini ranches. The light bouncing from the snow made the back of my eyeballs ache. I squinted and wiped away water in the far corners until Ilene mercifully handed me a pair of sunglasses she had stashed in her jacket. "Thanks, Ilene."

"Well, if you weren't locked up like a hermit inside the house for the last year then the sun wouldn't bother—" She stopped mid-sentence and slapped a hand to her mouth. She pointed at Slade and raised her eyebrows.

"It's okay, Slade knows. I told him everything, Ilene." And I realized then how relieved I was, knowing I could trust Slade enough with the hurt and fear I had suffered under Matt's abuse.

At the end of the drive, in the front yard of the house with the large dream catcher we met up with Rosie and her husband. His horse was sturdy and brown, while Rosie's horse resembled her sleek, black hair. She cantered up to Sunny and me, her face all smiles above her sheepskin jacket. "Well look at you, Kally! Up on a horse and riding by yourself."

"*Shhh.*" I clutched the pommel of my saddle with one hand and shook a finger at her with my other. "I do much better when I don't think about it."

A soft grin highlighted her dark eyes. "I understand, dear."

Slade and I rode at the front of the group while Steve and George took the end of the line. Rosie and Ilene, however, chatted in conspiratorial tones behind me. I cast a look back when we crested a rise, and Ilene made a big show of shushing Rosie and pretending they weren't plotting about me. I just shook my head. *Yeah, right.*

Leaning forward in the saddle and copying Slade's chirping sound, I ushered Sunny forward. Jack whinnied and Sunny snorted in reply. Drawing even with Slade, I leaned back a bit in the saddle, and Sunny slowed to keep pace with the larger, lighter-colored horse. We rode in silence, him looking ahead and me openly admiring my riding companion. Tall, dark Stetson and denim, black leather boots—all I wanted was to be wrapped in his arms. An increasing desire for his embrace chased away the chilly, late-November air.

His questioning glance brought a silly smile from me. His grin was infectious. "Hey there, girl. Looks like you're getting comfortable in the saddle."

I patted Sunny's neck. "Actually, I am. I like Sunny." I had not intended to talk about horses however. "So." I paused, scanning his face, hoping he'd be open to discussing the subject I wanted to broach. "What's up with Adelle anyway?"

He reined in Jack and guided him a little closer. "Remember a horse bucked me off a few years ago?"

"Yes. What does Adelle have to do with it?"

"Everything and nothing." He rocked back in the saddle. "Her horse bucked me off, some high-spirited stubborn beast she wanted me to break for her when we were dating. He threw me. I ended up in the hospital with a broken arm. I wheeled into recovery and there's Adelle, making out with the male nurse.

"And, somehow, it was my fault. Like if I hadn't been tossed and broken my arm, she wouldn't have been thrown into the arms of the first asshole with a paycheck."

I blinked my eyes and sucked in a shocked breath. It was the strongest word he'd used around me. It unsettled me and I didn't know what to say. "I'm sorry."

"Don't be. I sure the hell am not. I'm as loyal as a dog. If I hadn't caught her red-handed, I'd still be with her, miserable and sitting in a police car or bar somewhere." He held out his hand, and I leaned over a little to hold it. "You're the best thing to ever happen to me, Kally."

I took off the sunglasses and plunged into the cool depths of his icy blue eyes. "I know what you mean."

He released my hand, guiding Jack up an incline. The terrain looked very familiar when we rounded a bend and then beyond the next hill. Memories swirled up like snow around the horses' hooves. We were on the edge of what looked to be a little dell. A long, low roof stretched along one side, which I knew now was a remote cattle pen with a roof to help protect the animals from the elements. The flat expanse of pristine snow, I had learned from experience, was a pond. A small herd of Black Angus milled in the pen beneath the suspended roofline, their low *moos* echoing off the inclines ringing the dell on three sides.

"Whoa." Slade reined in Jack, and Sunny stopped beside them. Ilene, Rosie and the men rode up behind until we were close enough to talk. Slade rose in his stirrups to address the group. "This is where I found Kally. Rosie and I thought it would be fitting to find our tree here this year."

He's so sentimental. His thoughtfulness could bring smiles and tears. I was thankful for the sunglasses disguising my eyes.

We skirted the edge of the pond, fanning out to search the pines. Beside a trail on the southernmost edge, I found the perfect tree. It was at least twelve feet tall, a perfect shape, with good space between the branches. What sealed the deal for me was the strip of my sweatshirt waving from one of the lower branches by the chilly breeze. I nudged Sunny with my thigh and leaned toward Slade, and she followed my cues, pulling close to Jack.

"There's our tree."

Slade followed the line of my arm to the tree and then

nodded in agreement. With a lift and swing of his left leg, he dismounted, tying Jack's reins to a nearby aspen before rummaging through the saddlebags. Soon a tarp, rope and a small hand ax lay in the snow. The rest of our group dismounted, tethering their horses to nearby branches.

The tree came down onto the tarp with minimal spitting and cursing from the men. I needed Slade's help to get back onto Sunny's saddle, then Rosie and George led the way back out of the dell, with Ilene and Steve following. The tree took up the last position in line, dragging behind Sunny and Jack on the tarp.

Emma and Grace met us on the porch with mugs of hot cocoa. I thought for a minute Grace was going to pinch our pink cheeks, my grandmother would've. Instead, she smiled and patted my shoulder. The foyer contained the commotion of six adults stripping off their winter wear, and then we gathered in the great room before the fireplace. Wood heat had never felt so good. It has a way of soothing and penetrating that gas or electric does not.

I stood by the hearth, hands out, soaking up the warmth until Slade took my favorite armchair. Sitting between his feet, I propped my feet on the hearth. His hand settled on my shoulder, fingers twining in my hair. It was a surreal scene compared to the hell I had left in Michigan, and I wished the moment could last a lifetime—my best friend with me, a cowboy who cared for me and a new sense of peace in my heart. Ilene and Steve got up to leave all too soon.

Pouting threatened to sour my mood and I couldn't wipe the expression from my face when I stood. "Oh, Ilene, I hate to have you go."

"I know, hun." Ilene wrapped me in a fierce hug. "But I'm not far away, and we'll be back for Christmas."

"Really?" Hope soared in me. Slade smiled and gave me a nod. Steve's motions were nearly identical. "Woo hoo!"

Slade laughed and then tapped my thigh. "Is that Michiganite for 'yee-haw'?" I wrinkled my nose at him. He returned the expression, then stood and shook Steve's hand. "It was pleasure meeting you. I'm glad you accepted my invitation to return."

Steve ran a hand through his blond hair. "How could I not? Those two fillies would hang me from the top of the Christmas tree if I didn't."

"Damn straight." Ilene winked at me. Then she and Steve climbed the stairs to pack their bags. Slade rounded up the mugs and brought them into the kitchen while the two women, who were fast beginning to feel like aunts to me, disappeared with promises of returning with food and decorations. Rosie and George, however, remained at the ranch house. Rosie stepped into the kitchen and George assisted Slade in dragging the tree into the great room and getting it to stand upright.

Broom in hand, I swept snow and needles through the foyer and off of the porch. Ilene and Steve met me on the outside steps for one last hug, and then they piled their bags and butts into Steve's Jeep Laredo and headed out for Gillette. Ilene poked out of the window at the tree line and waved before the afternoon shadows beneath the Fourth Moon's trees swallowed the vehicle.

Slade and I parted in the hall by the kitchen. I cluttered the granite countertops with leftovers from the fridge, and stacked trays with meats and cheeses while he pulled boxes of ornaments and decorations from the storage room in the attic. Sunlight faded from the range and early evening shadows cloaked the vehicles when the ranchers parked in the circle drive. Even the Billings twins showed up, laden with jerky, meat logs and beer.

"Looks like a good time tonight," Mark blurted when he plunked the meats down on the dining room table. At the far end, a large washtub filled with ice and bottles of beer, wine coolers and sodas sat on a sideboard. Mike drew three bottles from the tub before adding their contribution. He twisted the caps off, handing one to his brother, one to Slade and keeping the third for himself.

I wriggled beneath the tree with a string of white lights. Despite the restful, clean pine smell, banging my head and limbs against the branches and pokey needles, I developed the understanding of why the men had spat and swore while cutting the tree down. Needles in my hair, I scrambled out of the tree and came face to face with Rosie. She smiled, a little crook in one corner of the grin. "Don't you just love decorating real pine trees?"

"Not so much anymore." I rolled my eyes and then smiled. Even if decorating it was a pain in the ass and other places where the needles poked in, or it stretched my shoulder too far, the energy a real tree gave a house was beautiful. Surveying my work, I gauged how many more strings of lights I needed and then foraged through the boxes. The lights went on in levels, first the inner and then outer branches, until seven hundred lights draped the tree. When I stepped back I could appreciate my hour's worth of work.

"Wow!" Slade smacked me on the butt. "The tree is awesome. Kally, you have a new job. It's you and the lights from now on."

"Oh goody." The sarcasm was not lost on anyone. A collective giggle rose in the great room. I picked a needle out of my hair and pitched it at him.

He deflected it with his bottle before draining it. "Want a beer?"

"God, yes. I need one before you boys drink them all."

"Ha. This was only my third. Come on then." He extended a hand. "Let's get you a drink and some snacks."

Following Slade weaving through people and boxes, I noticed he was less than solid on his footing. In the dining room he loaded a plate with veggies and dip, crackers and cheeses, but his hand hesitated, hovering over the meats. I nudged him. "I'm not a girly girl. Go ahead and give me the meat and a beer."

His smile was enormous. "A girl after my own heart."

"Yes, I am."

He stood blinking and clutching the plate. His eyes searched mine and then, as if the truth of my growing affections settled on him, Slade dropped the plate to the table and pressed me to the wall. Rosie in the hallway, the ranch—everything— dissolved in the heat building between us. I wrapped my arms around him. His hands roamed the sides of my body while his lips and tongue entangled mine in a passionate slow dance of touch and taste. Breathless, I clung to him, depending on his strength to keep me standing.

His voice was husky, suede on my ears. "You have no idea how badly I wanted to kiss you."

Tipping my hip and shifting my weight, I spun him around and pressed him to the wall with a kiss equally fervent. "No, I really think I do."

The gathering we'd neglected erupted into cheers. Even the Billings brothers raised their bottles in salute. "It's about time."

A blush burned my cheeks. I hid my face against the flannel covering Slade's chest. He tipped his head down, those lips kissing my head and then he laughed, not a light giggle but a deep belly laugh. His laughter was irresistible, and I succumbed. Hands on my shoulders he turned me to face the conglomerate family who had welcomed me when I was a newcomer and now embraced our "couple" status.

Mike Billings handed me a beer and Rosie took my hand before we made our way to great room. The once cozy, earthen-toned room was now alive with natural pine boughs, berry sprigs and Bonnie's rustic Santa collection. Burgundy velvet runners topped the tables and accented the sprays of pine and berries placed on them. The ornament boxes, however, were full, awaiting the gathered women. Emma hung the crocheted snowflakes, Grace placed the berry sprigs and Rosie and I hung candy canes and red blown glass balls. The overall effect was simple elegance.

I plopped onto the sofa with my second beer and first plate of snacks. Rosie sat beside me, casting glances over her shoulder before she leaned closer to talk to me. I expected her to tease me for losing myself and kissing Slade in front of everyone like I did. She didn't. Rosie had much more embarrassing things to discuss. "So, like I was saying the first night..."

Emma squealed but stifled the sound with her hand.

"The decorating party story!" Grace closed the lid of an ornament box and joined us.

"Last year, we had a heck of a party under way. Even Grace there, who only drinks coffee and eggnog, was feeling pretty punchy.

"The men were outside stringing the lights on the roof and porches, and Slade had refilled his plate and grabbed another beer. He popped the top and sucked it down right there." She pointed to the doorway between the dining room and great room. "Then, he announced loudly he needed the restroom. I watched him stagger down the hall, knock on the back door and then walk outside like he was walking into the bathroom."

Hands settled over my ears before I even knew someone was behind me. The scent of Stetson cologne and smoked venison gave me clear indication of who the culprit was. "Slade Carlson, you best get your mitts off my ears."

He released me, his hands falling to my shoulders. "Sorry, Kally. I was trying to spare you the story and me some dignity."

I patted his hand. "No one is perfect."

He sighed. "And this is one of my defining 'not perfect' moments." He clasped his hands together in a gesture of supplication. Rosie just smiled. Throwing his hands in the air, he hunkered behind the sofa. "Okay, fine then, go ahead."

Rosie inhaled a deep breath. "Like I was saying, Slade walked out onto the back porch, unzipped his pants and peed on his mother's car bumper just after she'd parked in the driveway." I cast a look at Slade, but he pulled his Stetson down over his eyes, his cheeks flaring red. "Bonnie blew the horn and scared poor Slade sober. He hiked his drawers and turned to run into the house, then slipped on the steps and knocked a ladder off from the house sideways, sending his dad and a string of lit Christmas lights into the snow bank."

I clapped a hand over my mouth and Slade took off his Stetson, hiding his face behind my back. Laughter rose like a tidal wave within me, and I struggled to dam it behind my teeth.

Slade's voice was muffled behind my back. "Go ahead and laugh. Everyone else does."

My chest ached with the pressure. I released a giggle or two to lessen the pain. "It wouldn't be so funny if you weren't so damn perfect all the time."

Slade emerged when the laughter ebbed. "Can't fight years of raising, darlin'."

I patted his cheek. "It's okay, Slade. I like you just the way you are, flawed perfection and all."

His wink softened my heart even more. "Thanks, Kally."

The rest of the evening was spent enjoying the beautiful, rustic Christmas decorations while we chatted, ate and drank. Around midnight, Rosie and Grace stood by the fireplace and led a round of Christmas carols. I slid closer to Slade, and he wrapped an arm around my shoulders while we sang my favorite Christmas song, "Silent Night". My soul lifted, my heart sang and though I wished for the moment to last until dawn, I knew it couldn't. After the last chorus, we plastic-wrapped the leftovers and the ranchers headed home.

Nestled in the crook of Slade's arm, we stood on the porch, braving the chill to wave goodbye to our guests. I leaned my head on his shoulder. "This has been the best night."

He squeezed me tight. "Just one of many to come."

Wrapped in his arms, surrounded by Christmas glory, the hope for a happy future blossomed in my heart. Only my body kept my soul anchored to the ground. It was the closest to heaven I had ever come. Slade shut the door and at the foyer entrance switched off the house lights. Candles flickered. The lights twinkled on the Christmas tree as he led me into the great room and in front of the hearth. He wrapped me in his arms. I melded to him, chest-to-chest, hip-to-hip while he hummed a song and held me in a sweet, loving slow dance. The flames danced in the background, a muted version of the fire burning in my heart.

Chapter Fourteen

They were on Highway 24, headed toward Hulett on Monday morning. The snow of yesterday had given way to sunshine, and Slade watched from the shade of his Stetson while Kally fished Ilene's sunglasses from her bag and put them on.

His heart pattered, and other regions swelled with the increased blood flow. With her blonde hair, delicate beauty and those wide frames, she could be on the runway at a movie premier. Slade couldn't resist teasing her. "So, should I call you Miss Hollywood? How about Miss Daisy?"

Kally snorted, and he was certain she rolled her blue eyes behind those shades. "I'd stop now while you're ahead, Slade, or you won't be driving me anywhere."

"Well, on the possibility of losing my," he coughed, "driving privileges, I will cease and desist further teasing."

Her eyebrow arched over the rim of the sunglasses as she responded to his vague sexual reference but refused to comment. "So..." She redirected the conversation. "What's on the agenda for the day?"

Dread over their final stop, anticipation of showing Kally around his town and joy at having her beside him wriggled together in his chest like a ball of snakes. "Well, we have to go to the Police Department and pick up your things, and I figured you might like to do a little shopping, maybe pick up something for your nephews for Christmas."

"Ah." Kally fell quiet then, and Slade knew she was lost in thought by the way she pulled her arms together over her chest. The slight downturn of her lips whispered of negative thoughts. He followed the line of her gaze to the Devils Tower, which dominated the landscape. His research had told him there was nothing like it in Michigan. She wrapped her fingers around his hand, her thumb rubbing his.

Slade pulled into the parking lot of the Devils Tower Trading Post, a long building with wood siding reminiscent of an old western movie. The sign was large and yellow, with tall black letters on it, and chainsaw-carved bears stood at either side of the steps. Kally looked through the truck window. "I half expected to see one of those animatronic smoking Indians seated on a bench by the door." An excited expression replaced Kally's reminiscent one of moments ago, and Slade was glad. She gathered up her purse. "The boys would love this place."

"I thought they might." He climbed out and then opened the door for her. "It's just chuck full of souvenirs too. There are books and T-shirts, and little alien bobble heads. This area is famous for the *Close Encounters* movie..."

"I remember the movie," she said, removing the sunglasses and tucking them back in her bag. "Hated it..." She stood in the parking lot and looked from the Trading Post to the Tower. "Joshua would get a kick out of this place. He loves alien stuff!"

Slade had to smile. He had never liked the movie, either.

They stood, hands on the handle, reading the signs with the scent of chili wafting beneath the door. The warning on the door advised patrons of their seasonal closing on November 30. "Wow." She peered through the doors. "We just made it."

"Yeah, I know." Something close to a pout crept across his lips and felt very unnatural. "I stop here all the time for lunch and beer runs. It's a pisser when they close." He opened the door for Kally, stomping snow from his boots and holding his Stetson against the gust of wind.

"Hey, Slade." A hand waved from the snack bar.

"Howdy, Carly." Slade tucked his arm around Kally's middle and guided her toward the racks of souvenirs. He preferred to avoid the youngest Crawford if at all possible. "Come on over here, Kally. They've got these really cute souvenirs. I love the stuffed horses."

The knickknacks did not hold Kally's interest for long. She tilted her nose up, sniffing the air. Her stomach growl was loud enough for Slade to hear. "These are great, Slade. No matter how cute the aliens are, I'm not going to be able to focus on shopping if I'm hungry. Can we get a bowl of chili and then shop?"

He shuffled his boot, fidgeted with his hat. He hated going to the snack counter and the little gossipmonger who worked there. Maybe he could bait her with the promise of fancy food... "Well, I had planned on taking you to the Golf Club at Devils Tower. I thought you might appreciate a nice meal after getting your things. Distract you from any negative energy it might bring up."

He knew the second those words left his mouth he'd said something wrong. She turned to him with a shocked expression. "*Golf Club?* Fussy set tables and ladies in tight dresses? I got enough of that waiting tables at the River Yacht Club back in Saint Joe." She cocked an eyebrow, tossed him a curious look over the rack of books. "Don't tell me you...golf?"

There was something close to dislike in her voice. It struck Slade as funny. "Nope. But my parents do. My parents are into a bit of everything out here—line dancing, golfing, watching the rodeo. Hell I saw 'em at a concert in Sundance once." Smiling, he held up a T-shirt with a picture of Devils Tower and an alien on it. "What do you think of this shirt?"

"Shirt's cute. Joshua might like it." Kally walked past, headed for the snack bar. "I look forward to getting to know your parents. I also look forward to some chili, so how about it, Slade? Chili at the Trading Post, in a casual setting where I could sidle up to you, or a fussy meal at the golf club where we sit at a table all proper like?"

His chin dropped, he pinned her with the sexiest gaze he could manage. *Sidling sounds damned good.* "Since you put it that way..."

He grabbed her hand and pulled her close, inhaling her jasmine and lavender. Kally's eyes nearly cast sparks, setting fires within him, fueling his desires. Her hands slid around his rib cage and she leaned on his chest. Then, she surprised the hell out of Slade by reaching up and taking off his hat, turning it sideways to hide their faces. Time stood still, trapping him in the heartbeat before their lips met. The rising desires turned to consuming lust when he pressed her lips apart. Her tongue wrapped his in an intimate embrace before she pulled away. "I like how you sidle, Kally."

She tipped her head, gave him a naughty come-hither expression. "I haven't even started."

"Ha. Don't threaten me, Miss Jensen."

Slade was suddenly thankful for the privacy of the little nook they were in when she slid her hand down his stomach, wrapped his belt buckle in her fingers. "I don't threaten. It's a promise, cowboy."

Handing him his Stetson, Kally wriggled past and aimed for the snack counter. Carly was a mousy high school girl who talked too much but held a striking resemblance to her older sister. "Carly Crawford, meet Miss Kally Jensen—"

"Slade's girlfriend." Kally cut in and extended her hand.

His eyes widened and his jaw dropped when she vocalized his hopes. He wanted to say it, call her his girlfriend for the longest time. He just didn't think it was his place. Hell, he hadn't formally asked her. He certainly wasn't going to complain about her taking the initiative. Being claimed was a nice change.

Carly's gaze clawed across Kally's face like Slade was sure her sister Adelle's nails would have, given the incident at Butch's. Slade knew the sisters well enough to know Carly had been schooled about Kally's evil ways the night Adelle returned home with her proverbial tail between her legs. Her expression hardly disguised her predatory posturing. She looked ready to leap the counter and attack. "Hi, Miss Jensen." She turned from Kally and focused on Slade. "What can I get you today?"

Slade wanted desperately to set the little snipe straight, but he bit his tongue, played nice and ordered two bowls of chili, "cheese and sour cream, please", and two Cokes. The dishes were served up without another word, and then the girl disappeared into the back. *Good place for you, Carly. The more distance between you and Kally the better.*

Slade handed Kally a bowl and then doused his in hot sauce before they walked back to the souvenirs and ate while they browsed for gifts. Kally cast a glance at the back room door. "I wonder where she vanished to so quickly."

"She's probably going to call the Gossip Chain and start spreading the news I have an outsider girlfriend."

Her eyebrow twitched in the way he knew meant her interest was piqued. "Dating an outsider is a bad thing?"

"Hell no. I would've called them myself if I knew where the central intelligence hub was." He winked and stuffed a spoonful in his mouth.

"Girls, gossip chains and intelligence don't necessarily go hand-in-hand."

"Good thing you're not one of them girly girls, eh?"

"Ain't it the truth?" She smacked his shoulder and drifted off into the alien-related trinkets while Slade perused the male-oriented hunting and fishing magazines. He kept his eye on her, his mind stuck on Adelle and the convoluted way she had regarded him. Some days, he wondered if he would ever be free of the Crawford girls.

When the door opened, Kally peeked over a shelving unit. Slade half expected to see Adelle walk through, responding to the emergency call on the Gossip Chain. The bone white hat, however, announced Red Baxter, his friend and old partner from his years on the Hulett police force. Her gaze followed his path through the store and up to Slade. They shook hands, and Kally's face sank beneath the top edge of the shelves. Red mouthed the words "is it safe?" and Slade rose up on his toes. Kally was busy thumbing through a book. "It's clear. What's the word?"

"Your Michigan guy came up on the radar again. He was picked up in a Saint Joe on a Drunk and Disorderly, then was released the next day. And a PPO has been put against him."

The hope Slade maintained for no trouble from Stransberg faded. Run-ins with the law were picking up in frequency since Kally had left, and any lawman worth his badge knew the situation could easily escalate to violent attacks, even murder. Red cleared his throat to speak, and Slade shook his head, held his hand up, needing time to digest the new information. His time was short however. Kally came around the corner with her arms full.

She looked directly at Red, an odd, strained expression on her face. Slade's insides turned into a wriggling ball of snakes again. *Damn it! Kally must've overheard us.* Inwardly, he cringed. *Here it comes...*

"So, Slade, who's your friend?"

Red's gaze fell. He was never good at lying. Slade took a little too long to speak. "This is Red Baxter. He's a friend of the family." And then, compounding matters, he heaped a lie on top of withholding the truth about digging into Stransberg's record. "Red's going to help with the cattle drive closer to Christmas."

She seemed to accept his story, but the cracked porcelain

lines around her eyes were evident to Slade when she spoke. "Howdy, Red. I'd shake your hand, but mine are kind of full."

"It's okay, Kally, I'm sure I'll be able to shake your hand another time. It is nice to meet you," he smacked Slade's arm in a chummy gesture, "finally."

Then, she turned to Slade, a shadow settling over her eyes. "Look what I found, T-shirts for both boys, an alien bobble head and a book on Devils Tower for Joshua, and a stuffed horse and toy cap gun for Samuel." She attempted a smile. "The boys will love me. Susan will probably walk to Wyoming to pistol whip me with the cap gun."

He laughed a little, more of a snort, at her half-hearted joke, then turned to Red, a pleading "keep your mouth shut" expression in his eyes. "Excuse me, Red." Then, Slade fished his wallet out of his back pocket. "Let me give you some money, Kally."

She shook her head. "No. I'm going to pay for these." Slade opened his mouth to argue. She shut him down. "Remember the money Susan gave me? I told her then to use it to buy the boys Christmas gifts, so I'm going to, and then send the rest back to her."

"Well, if you insist, who am I to argue?"

"All righty then." She gave Slade a curious expression, reminiscent of the broken doll he'd held in the carpentry shed, then excused herself. "I'm going to leave you boys to your cow wrangling plans and pay for this stuff."

He should have been relieved, but Slade feared the shadows over Kally's eyes would turn to storms later on. He turned back to Red. The wince on his face must have been obvious. Red's voice was suppressed. "What's the matter?"

Slade's gaze drifted to Kally and then back to his old partner. Red's face blanched. "Crap! You still haven't told her you were checking into Stransberg's history?"

Slade just shook his head.

"Oh, man. Slade, I'm sorry. I hope I haven't got your ass in a sling."

Slade's gaze slid down Kally's back, nearly a loving caress. His sigh was deep. "Me too."

Red scuffed his boot on the floor. "So...did you need help with the cattle drive? I can spare the time. I've got the week before and week after Christmas off."

Wrenching his gaze from Kally's profile when she turned to pay for her items, he looked back at Red. "Yeah...I would appreciate the help, actually. With Dad and Beau gone, we're down two men at the ranch."

"All right, then. I'll see you at the Fourth Moon. Just gimme a buzz and let me know when." Kally was the only thing on Slade's mind. He hardly nodded in response to Red. His old partner read him too well. "Hey." He nudged Slade's shoulder. "If you're so concerned about her, maybe you should go talk it out."

"Yup. I plan to." Slade and Red said their goodbyes, and Slade hurried to Kally's side at the register.

Kally mumbled a "thanks" when Slade took the bag from her. She trailed behind him while he walked to the door, and he felt his heart dragging behind her boots. The weight of his hat was too much, and his head tipped forward. He swallowed but couldn't push the lump from his throat, or loosen the tightness in his chest. He'd shoveled a lot of crap in his day, and he fully empathized with it now.

Kally stopped beside the truck, looking back over his shoulder at the Devils Tower behind the Trading Post. Her face was haunted, the earlier joy lost. "Kally, darlin'...are you okay?"

Her gaze dropped down to Slade's boots. "Sorry." Her lips trembled. "I heard you talking to Red when I looked at the stuffed horses..." Her voice faded, and Slade knew she had more to say. She drew in a shaky breath and then put her hand on the door handle. "Can we just get going and talk about it in the truck?"

"Of course." He shifted the bag to his other hand. "Let me get the door for you."

Kally pulled the door open and climbed in by herself. She might as well have slapped him in the face. *Oh, yeah, this is not going to be pretty.*

The Devils Tower loomed over them when he climbed in. Key in the ignition, he cranked it, but left the truck in park when he stepped on the gas pedal to get the motor running. There was no way he wanted to engage in a car fight with Kally. "All right, Kally, we're in the truck now, so you want to spill it?"

Her eyes were hard, blue glazed irises over white bisque. Her lips were down and trembling. "I don't know. Maybe you should spill it. Seems I'm not the one keeping things to themselves anymore."

His hand fell from the gearshift to his thigh, and then he removed his Stetson and shoved his fingers through his hair. The call to Red had been a simple act of assessment. Following leads and assessing further threats was ingrained into his cop nature. Now he had to explain it to Kally and make the fact he never told her seem okay. It was for her peace of mind. What did she expect? How was he supposed to tell her?

He cleared his throat. "Okay...maybe you can tell me what you heard."

Her jaw shut, and her lips tightened.

"Okay, maybe not." Slade hated the silence sitting between them. "I wanted to know what happened between you and your ex. And the night of your sister's call...with you so upset and not talking to me, well, I reverted to the 'chase down the leads' side of me.

"I called Red and asked him to check into Matt's criminal record."

Kally's eyes widened, and in the shade of the truck's roof she regained her elfin appearance. Her jaw trembled, or perhaps she chewed on words she wanted to say, but she remained silent.

"You didn't know he had a record, did you?"

She shook her head, and her gaze dropped to her tangled fingers. Kally retreated completely behind her porcelain doll exterior. Her voice was tiny, cracked. "I had no idea." She pushed further away from him, turning her back to the door. "Why did you have someone look into Matt's record? And for God's sake, why didn't you tell me?"

"Well, I-I..." He searched frantically for a viable reason. "I didn't want to upset you any further."

"How could I not be upset? You lied to me."

His jaw set on edge. If there was one button to push and make Slade angry, Kally had found it with deft grace. His voice was close to a growl. "Excuse me?" Tension built in his shoulders. "You want to explain that one to me? I never lied to you."

"You withheld information—important information. You lied to me without saying a word."

Why is this all falling apart? His eyes rolled to the ceiling in search of answers. Reason left him, chased away by the rising frustration that tightened his muscles. "Well, you've got messed up reasoning."

"Call it what you want." She crossed her arms and looked through the windshield. A hard, cold voice issued from her. "Can we go please? I don't want to sit here and argue."

Oh, sure. Just stick your head in the sand...

"Are you done then?" Slade replaced his Stetson. The shifter was cold when he moved the gearshift from park to neutral.

"Oh, I'm done." Her voice fell to a dark, thick tone.

A sick feeling she may be done with more than this tiff overtook Slade. The truck rolled from the parking lot and back onto Highway 24, but Slade felt like they drove from the happy place they'd found at the decorating party back toward the dark she had run away from. His eyes strayed from the road to Kally, who was withdrawn and curled in on herself. White teeth pinched her bottom lip, and a tear shimmered on her eyelashes. His frustration faded, replaced with an impotent ache to hold her and soothe away her hurts. "Kally, I'm sorry, I just—"

"Don't say you're sorry." Her words were void of emotion. "Matt said 'sorry' hundreds of times. It started to lose its meaning after a while."

"Don't compare me to him." His knuckles clenched over the steering wheel. "I haven't hit you, haven't even raised my voice..."

Sullen silence answered him. Her arms circled tighter around her chest. Slade yearned to pull her out of herself, to goad her back to the Kally who touched him and was touched by him. His fingers twitched a physical echo of his emotional desire to hold her hand. "Kally, come on..." *Please be reasonable.*

"I know you're not like Matt." Shadows veiled her eyes when she finally turned to him, and her bottom lip had softened. "And maybe that's what hurts so much. You have thrown me for a serious loop, and my head is spinning."

Maybe she'll come around... "It'll settle after we get home. A hot bath and good night's sleep and you'll be just fine."

"I doubt it." The weight of her gaze deserted him, leaving an empty ache. She readjusted in her seat, her lovely profile aimed up the street instead of at him. "Are we close to the P.D.?"

"Yeah, it's not far now." Slade had hardly noticed the turn

from Highway 24 onto Route 112 and Yukon County Road. It was about the time his knuckles tightened enough to crack. These roads had rolled beneath his wheels so many times he could drive them on autopilot. At the intersection of Cont-Moore County and Hulett-New Haven, autopilot shut down and Slade realized how close they were. Anxiety welled in him, spilling over the containment wall behind which he'd dammed it.

He'd walked away from the job and regretted it, craved the ever-changing pace of things until Kally had come along. Preoccupied by their argument, Slade could not stop the sudden rush of adrenaline spilling through his veins. His respiration sped up, pulse, too, his mouth ran dry.

He loved it. He hated it. And it was the last thing he wanted to deal with. Kally's words, "I doubt it" drifted through his mind, a ghost bent on haunting him. What did she mean? Why did it sound so...final?

Time for dwelling on those questions ran out like his patience on last season's cattle drive. The Dodge rolled to a stop in his normal parking space, stirring up more memories. He put the truck in park and pulled the keys. Kally sat in her seat, tucking her hair behind her ears like he knew she did when she was nervous. He empathized with the sensation. Adrenaline jitters danced in his muscles and his jaw ached from clenching it. But inside, he was hollow, gutted by the fires of stress and disagreement. Hopes of Kally's support were gone, smashed beneath the stampede of Red's words.

Shock could've knocked him on his ass when he got out of the Dodge and Kally didn't. He skated around the hood of the truck, pausing to cast an apologetic glance through the side window. A pensive tilt to her eyebrows concerned him when she looked back, but then she gave him a weak smile.

Okay, maybe things aren't so bad after all... Hope flickered in the darkness in his chest. A mumbled "thank you" slipped from her lips when he opened the door. She drifted behind him, scuffing her boots across the lot and up to the entrance.

He stood there at the door, calm on the outside, storms raging within. Brains buzzing and chest tight, he stood dreading the first step past the threshold. The minute the handle chilled his palm he knew his defenses were down. The realization nearly slapped him in the face. His mother was right. Finding Kally was not necessarily any different than any other call he'd run. *He* was different. He didn't have blinders on. The night he had found her he saw and felt more than he had allowed himself to experience on the job.

A heavy sigh behind him reminded Slade of why he was really there: not for a trip down Nostalgia Lane, but to pick up Kally's belongings. He withheld the pain from his expression when he looked over his shoulder. She seemed shrunken, hunched with her shoulders curled in, her stubborn will still seeped through the cracks in her porcelain façade. "Are you ready for this?"

It was a question he asked himself, and her.

"Let's get it over with." The dark surly tone in her voice suffocated whatever little hope he'd entertained for things to right themselves quickly.

He was a ship without a mast or cannons for defense. A distinct sense of lurching seasickness rode along with him through the doors when the building's familiarity washed over him in a seductive wave. Shouts of "Slade!" and "Welcome back!" rang from the lockers and chief's office. Those shouts were a siren's song without Kally's calming influence, and Slade drifted off to talk to Richter, his favorite rookie.

Kally melded into the background, a gull caught in his storm. He hardly noticed her slipping along the outside wall and up to the reception desk.

The joy of returning to the fold was tainted. Without Kally by his side, or at least in his line of sight, the hubbub was somehow hollow. The old stories lacked their former glory, the smells failed to seduce him, and eventually he extricated himself from the shoulder-whacking gaggle and made his way back to the desk near the entrance.

Unease wriggled through him, and one of the snakes in his gut made its way into his throat. Red Baxter arrived for his shift and stood at the desk, locked in conversation with Kally. Slade trusted Red with his life. He knew the man wouldn't intentionally cause harm, but after Kally's response to Red running a scan of Stransberg's records, he didn't know how Kally would react. Judging their body language, Slade knew Red was trying to convince the girl of something, and by the tilt of her hips and pinched tight curve of her ass, he knew she was being obstinate still. *Poor Red.* He'd learned in the last hour arguing with Kally was an exhausting experience.

Kally's arms were crossed. Red's hand was out in a gesture of supplication. "Give the guy a chance, Ms. Jensen. He asked out of concern for you."

"And he went behind my back to do it." The flat tone had not left her voice, and her eyebrows seemed weighted toward the floor. "Altruism and secrecy shouldn't go hand in hand."

Yup. Slade shook his head. *She's using big words. She's still pissed.*

Red's hand fell, flipping in mid air to smack down on the desk surface. Shaking his head, he stuffed his hand in his pockets. "I'm sorry you feel that way. Whether or not you've listened to a word I've said is your choice, but please don't be angry at Slade for doing what he thought was right to protect you."

Fists on her hips, Kally seemed even more entrenched. "I'll keep it in mind."

Two boxes sat on the desk, both of them clearly addressed to Kally. Slade attempted to be chipper when he walked up. "So, I see you two have had time to talk. Thanks for keeping Kally company, Red."

"Happy to be of assistance." Certainty filled his voice. Red's expression said otherwise.

The two men shook hands, and then Red excused himself and disappeared into a conference room when Slade wedged his way between Kally and the boxes. "Let me get these."

"Of course."

Hooking the toe of his boot in the door, he forced it open and then used his butt to hold the door open for Kally to pass through. An unreadable expression masked her face, and her hair was tucked behind her ears. He had the worst urge to run his fingers through the blonde strands and set it loose like it was when she had kissed him in the dining room. It felt like silk over the back of his hands, and silk would have been so much better than the cardboard boxes he carried. And sweet, soft, floral Kally would be so much better than hard, dour Kally.

The top box slid when he jumped out of the way of the swinging door. He tipped back to counter the skid. The awkward thing bumped against his chest, and he found carrying the boxes and opening the Dodge's door impossible. Kally strode to the end of the truck and dropped the tailgate for him, but by the time he'd bungee-strapped the boxes in, she'd walked around and let herself into the cab.

Slade shook his head and then lifted the tailgate with his knee before finishing the action by pushing it with his hands. He almost dreaded the drive home. Road salt left a dry film on his hands, which he dusted off before adjusting his Stetson and rounding the side of the truck. She was stoic when he climbed in, quiet when he started the truck. On some level, he had to agree with her about why.

He had been her main support in healing after her accident and from her abusive relationship. Kally had put all her faith in him and only kept from him what was too painful to deal with at the time. He, on the other hand, had intentionally kept information from her. Yes, he had the best of intentions. In retrospect, she should have known what he did, whether it scared her or not. Now, he was dealing with the aftermath.

Hindsight was truly twenty-twenty.

Chapter Fifteen

After everything I'd shared with Slade, every way he'd helped and healed me, he had lied to me? Not just lied, but compounded the falsehood—buried it, hid it, mounded pleasantries on top of it.

Why? In the name of protecting me from the truth?

I looked at him, so handsome and desirable in the late November sun. My body screamed to be near him, to inhale his cologne and wrap his fingers in mine. It didn't matter now. My angel in Wranglers was sporting some kind of horns under his Stetson. The savior had fallen from the pedestal I'd put him on, plummeted, rather, like Lucifer cast out.

Get a grip, Kally. I squeezed myself tighter. *He felt he had a good reason.*

I was being hard on him. Unfair in comparison to the generous, self-sacrificing treatment I'd received from him, from the Carlson family. Slade had saved me from a frigid death. He had cradled me when I cried. Hell, he'd even washed my hair. On a physical level, I craved the intimate closeness we'd found. My mind wailed for distance. How could I sift through all this when he was right next to me?

I'm sorry for being a grump ass. Those words hung on the end of my tongue, but when he turned the truck under the black metal, laser cut Fourth Moon sign, words of a different nature came out. "I want to go to Ilene's."

His head whipped in my direction, the brim of his hat cutting the shadows underneath the truck roof. Eyes wide, the sky blue plains of his irises were unnaturally large. Everything froze. The world stopped turning, my breathing seized, my focus narrowed to his face and the procession of shock across it.

Every nuance of his visage changed when his jaw dropped. Blinking his eyes took forever, and then he focused his surprise into speech. "What?"

The same question echoed in my mind. *What?* I had surprised myself. I'd never entertained the thought. The truth slipped out while my mind was otherwise occupied.

At Ilene's I could have the distance I needed to work through Slade's lie and my emotions. He wouldn't be around setting my heart to a pitter-patter and my mind into a tailspin. The ranch, its creature comforts and quiet beauty couldn't seduce me. My voice had lacked conviction before. This time, it was evident. "I want to go to Ilene's."

"I was afraid you said that." His gaze fell.

Slade was quiet longer than I expected, and the enamored part of me longed to stuff away my feelings and focus on his. I really wanted him to be happy. I just couldn't be happy with him right now, and it hurt. I had to say something, soothe the wounds somehow. "Slade, I—"

He waved my words away, turning his head and sighing before he got out of the truck. I should've expected it. I hardly understood why I was hurt, so how could he? If the tables were turned, I would have been upset too. Cool winter air blew into the cab when I opened my door and jumped down. My boots skidded on the packed snow and I nearly fell over the orange tabby who had appeared the moment the Dodge shifted into park. The cat yowled and ran for the boot-free safety of the barn.

"Sorry, kitty." Add a dash of embarrassment to the frustration I stewed in. I grabbed the second box from the bed of the truck. "Maybe we should talk about this."

"Looks to me like the talkin's done if you want to go to Ilene's." Slade peered into the shadows of the barn, where a pair of yellow eyes watched us and then he back-kicked the tailgate shut. "Let me get the box for you."

"I've got it." Impotent tears formed in my eyes, and I shuffled my boots across the drive to the front door without looking at the scenery or Slade.

He stepped in the foyer and turned his gaze on me. The rift between my rational self and the idiot reaction self tore wider still. Part of me was tempted to drop the box and run to him. The other part was ready to storm past and snarl. Clutching the box tighter to my chest, I fought the sob caught in my throat. A mix of emotions passed over his face. His hand raised toward me then balled tight on empty air. His fingers unfurled, and I did not fight when he took the box from me.

The sherpa lining of his jacket curled up and exposed his rear when Slade turned and stacked the boxes in the corner. My heart rate picked up, the increased pressure in my chest pushed against my ribs and my throat. Moisture shimmered in his eyes and his lip stiffened when he faced me. He inhaled and then closed the distance between us.

Collapsing against his chest, I inhaled his cologne and drew on the strength I'd come to count on. One arm encircled my back, and another hand cupped the back of my head, holding me in a fervent, aching embrace. Shudders ran through me, shaking tears loose. His cheek moved against my scalp when he spoke. "I am truly sorry for hurting you, Kally."

"Me too."

No lights burned in the house, shadows sat on the furniture and the fireplace had grown cold, even though a flame still blazed in me. I had fallen for Slade, which made leaving the Fourth Moon and my cowboy damned difficult, but necessary.

The tension left his arms, and face averted, I wriggled from his grasp. "I'll go call Ilene."

"And I'll stay out of your way." He stepped back and then headed for the stairs, bypassing the rack where he normally hung his hat.

Shaking, miserable, I dropped into the chair in the office and called Ilene. Steve answered on the second ring, and Ilene was quick to get on the line after he hollered about trouble at the ranch. "Kally? What's wrong? Did Matt find you?"

"Well, hello to you, too, Ilene." I sighed and she gave me a nervous sounding giggle. "Matt is not the problem. I don't think I could handle him right now. Could I come to your house, at least for a while?"

Ilene knew me too well. "Oh, honey, did something happen between you and Slade?"

I sniffed back moisture in my nose and batted away useless tears. "Yeah...I guess."

"Say no more. I will be in the Jeep and on the road in five minutes. Have your cell phone with you. I'll buzz you when I'm on Highway 24 and getting close."

A sob broke free from the containment system in my chest. "Thanks, Ilene."

"Don't mention it, sweetie. I'll be there in a couple hours."

"Okay. See you in a while."

Silence lay in the ranch house thicker than a year's worth of dust. I stood in the office doorway, surveying the place I'd grown to feel was home and planned on leaving. A soft voice whispered in my heart. *No move is permanent.*

Skirting the armchairs beside the fireplace I cast a look over the living room and the Christmas tree. Even with the lights off, it was the prettiest tree I'd ever seen. Decorating party memories flooded my mind—the fresh scent of pine, the ladies laughing, Slade kissing me. The passion, the emotion in our kiss washed up in me like a high tide. I leaned against the wall and let the torrent surge through me.

Empty in the wake of those emotions, I stepped on the cord switch and turned on the tree lights before climbing the stairs. I craved the light and happiness of the upcoming holiday. I could use a little Christmas. The lights twinkled in the shadows, a gentle beckon to take up my corner of the sofa and day dream about the coming holiday. I wasn't going to sit. I wasn't going to stay.

Cool air hunkered on the stairwell giving a sense of discomfort and the wood creaked beneath my feet when I climbed the long cold incline to the second floor. A suitcase sat in the hallway, in front of my door. Only one person could have put it there. My gaze trailed down the carpet runner in the hallway and stopped at the puddle of artificial light beneath the oak panel of Slade's bedroom door. The bright light was the one he used to clean his guns, a task he told me he used to place some distance between himself and something upsetting.

I cried when I was upset. At least I did when I was alone. And those tears fell in my room, splattering the quilt and my clothes while I packed things into the suitcase. My butt held the case closed while I snapped the latches. The stuffed animals nestled into the bag of gifts for my nephews, and then I closed the door on the room not the memories. They haunted me down the hall and to the door where a new moment was burned indelibly in my mind.

The sound of Slade crying was unmistakable through the wood panel and distance lying between us. My heart ached for him and for me. Holding back tears, I knocked on his door.

"Just a minute..." Soft rustles filtered through the wood, metallic clicks I was certain were guns and ammunition magazines being hastily packed away. His eyes were red when he came to the door, but he tried to make his voice light. "All packed?"

Awkward tension wavered between us. "Yes. Ilene should be here shortly."

"Do you want me to come down with you? I could help with your luggage..."

"No, I think Ilene and I can manage. Thanks, cowboy."

His voice was somehow hollow. "Don't mention it, Miss Jensen."

He could have slammed the door in my face. Hearing the formal moniker felt the same. My gut plummeted and a rubbery feeling flooded me. My voice was hardly a whisper. "See you around, Slade."

"I'll be here."

I couldn't walk fast enough to leave my breaking heart behind. It followed me down the hallway, into the foyer and returned to its place of torture in my chest. I paced the confines of the entry until Ilene arrived. Evening shadows cloaked the ranch, and I was grateful for Mother Nature saving me the misery of seeing the Fourth Moon's beauty and then leaving it behind.

Snow crunched beneath the Jeep's wheels when Ilene pulled to a stop by the front steps. Jumping from the driver's side, she rushed around to open the tailgate. I closed my eyes, thinking through my decision one last time. No matter how I reasoned, I still came back to leaving the ranch. The familiar creak of the fifth step echoed through the living room and I knew Slade was on the staircase. Waiting for him to appear, to beg me to stay was fruitless. If he was there, he stayed out of sight. I whispered beneath my breath, "Goodbye, cowboy."

The ginger tabby scurried to the driveway and wound around my feet in a constant procession of step-and-dodge while we loaded the Jeep. He had never been this persistent. He seemed intent on thwarting my departure. After the last bag was stowed, I bent down and stroked the kitty's back.

A familiar silhouette shadowed the living room window. Tears welled and I wiped them away before waving farewell. He returned the gesture and, without looking back, I climbed into the passenger seat. Ilene slipped in behind the steering wheel with a pinched look on her face. "Are you sure about this, Kally?"

There was no room for questions. I was leaving, and I was leaving the man who held my heart behind. "Just drive, please."

Ilene's sofa was far from comfortable and fairly close to hell. The material was sage colored, scratchy tweed and smelled vaguely of Lysol and wet dog. Support bars prodded my back and legs, and the narrow cushions hardly gave me room to lie on my back. Lying on my side was a pipedream. Either my knees hung off or my butt did. I spent more time on the sofa trying to get comfortable than I did sleeping, and the last time I slept enough to dream, Ilene's damn Pomeranian Tinker stuck her fluffy tail in my face.

Morning, a week later, found me achy and bleary eyed, propped in the armchair and covered with a blanket. Ilene shuffled through the living room, yawning and scratching her head. She stopped by the chair and ran a hand across my forehead. "G'morning, sleepy head."

Good thing she didn't say 'good'. "Morning."

"How'd you sleep?" The rumpled sofa held both of our attentions. "I see you ended up in the chair again."

"Well..." I stood and folded the fleece blanket. Tinker's hairs floated to the oatmeal-colored Berber and a small shudder ran up my spine. "Let's just say the sofa is great to sit on."

Ilene's yesterday make-up gave her comical raccoon eyes when she pouted. "Aw, I'm sorry, hun. We'll get an Aero bed until we can insulate the sun porch for you."

Insulated sun porch? My empty gut dropped into the cushy pile of my bowels. *Oh goody...* "Let's worry about it later, okay?" The last thing I wanted to think about was sleeping on the veranda, with the branches creaking on the glass and the funky wet smell that currently inhabited the room. "What's on the agenda for today?"

"Lots. Let's start with some breakfast."

Ilene's slippers never left the floor when she walked into the kitchen. The bunny heads lolled from side to side with each shuffle. If I weren't so damn tired I would have laughed at the bun-bun cha-cha. The coffee maker had started at 6 a.m.

automatically, and a fresh pot waited. Steam from the rich Italian roast curled above two mugs of dark brew—one thing about Ilene's, she had damn good coffee—which we took with us to the table. I buried my nose in the steam and willed myself awake. "Can I help you with breakfast?"

She cast a glance at the counter where dessert plates and wineglasses cluttered the white tiles. "How about we go out and grab something?"

"Works for me."

"Deal." She pulled a long draw off her mug. "I've got first dibs on the shower and then we can bug out."

A copy of the *Gillette News-Record* lay loosely folded on the table. Ilene pulled the paper to her and opened it to the job listings. Sliding the paper at me with one hand, she swigged more coffee and stood. "Here, hun, you can look these over while I shower. Not saying you need to run out and get a job, but if you're going to stay here you'll want to get one soon. You'll go crackers sitting in the house all day."

"Very true." *I can only take two Pomeranians for so long.*

Instead of leaving for the upstairs shower, Ilene did a perfect impression of Susan, standing behind me, scanning the paper. "Looks like there's lots of construction and electrician openings." We both knew those weren't an option. Her fingers trailed down the page. "Here's a promising one. 'Hard working, dependable stylist, Monday through Friday nine to six. Apply with resume, including three references'. Too bad you gave up cosmetology school when you started dating Matt."

Matt. My hackles rose. I had nearly forgotten about the bastard. "He fucked up a lot of things in my life in a short period of time."

Ilene rubbed my shoulders and then stroked my hair, a perfect mini-Sue. "At least you got smart and left him. And time on Slade's ranch brought you back around to the strong happy girl I always knew you were beneath the bruises."

Did she have to mention the ranch? The familiar melancholy heartache spread through my chest. God, I missed Slade. I was a pathetic puppy, mushy and whiney without him. It only made me more determined to survive without him. Dependency was...dependency. I wasn't going to be dependant anymore.

The phone ring jarred me from musing. Ilene picked it up,

looked at the caller ID and then handed it to me. "It's your sister."

I took the phone and Ilene excused herself to go run out the hot water like she used to do when we were teenagers. I gave her a smirk and then answered the phone. "Good morning, Sue."

Her voice had a not-enough-coffee tone. "Hi, Kally. How are you holding up?"

I looked over my shoulder, peered down the hallway in the direction Ilene had taken. Her blonde hair and swishy booty was gone. My sister was on the phone and I didn't need to keep up the tough girl front. "I'm a wreck, Sue. I miss Slade, miss the ranch. Hell I miss the orange tabby cat."

"It's been a week, honey. Have you talked to him?"

"No." The coffee washed out the melancholy taste in the back of my throat. "I dialed the ranch the other day. The line was busy."

"And you didn't try again?"

"No. Ilene and I ended up going to the store. What is this, Sue, the Great Sister Inquisition?"

She laughed. "I don't have a wrack or thumb screws. But I think you should call him. God, he even called here just to ask if you were all right."

I could have growled. "He called you, and he hasn't called me? What's wrong with this picture?"

"He wanted to make sure you were okay, and the one time he tried to call, the phone was busy." Her tone was maternal. "Now, Kally, I don't want to get your knickers in a knot, but I really believe you need to give the poor guy a chance. At least let him explain his side of things. Then maybe you'll have a good reason to stay away, or a better reason to miss him."

She was so sensible, and I hated it. "I'll think about it. Right now I need to find some clothes because Ilene and I are going for breakfast."

"Fine, hun, get on with your day. Promise me you'll think about what I said."

"Okay, Sue. I'll call him."

I disconnected the call and then cast a look down the hall. Still no Ilene. She was an hour shower kind of girl. Drawing in a deep breath, I dialed the Fourth Moon for the second time in a week. The only answer was from the answering machine. Hope's small blossom withered within. My hand shook and in a fit of foolishness, I hung up the phone. *How stupid can I be?*

The phone vibrated, ringing while I held it and debated on whether or not to call him back. The caller ID read *Fourth Moon*. The shivers in my hand grew to shudders and suddenly nervous, I closed my eyes and held the phone to my chest. *What do I say to him? Do I ask for forgiveness? Ask him to explain what he was thinking?* I raised the phone to my cheek, but my concerns died the moment Ilene appeared behind me and took the phone. She looked from the ID screen to me, with a savior expression on her face when she pushed the 'talk' button. "Hello?"

She looked at me and smiled while listening to Slade. I knew it was him by the suede tone coming through the earpiece. "Hi, Slade. No, Kally isn't available right now. She's in the shower."

Her damp hair swung like over-cooked noodles when she nodded her head. "I'm sure our number did show up. I programmed the Fourth Moon's number into our speed dial while Kally stayed with you, and I pushed the button accidentally when I tried to dial Steven at work."

His voice faded away. Ilene's features softened, and a sad shadow glowered over her eyes. "I am sorry, Slade. I'll tell her you called."

She turned to the wall and I missed her expression and his voice. "Of course I will. I think she'd appreciate it." She paused. "Okay. Goodbye."

Her shoulders slumped when she returned the phone to its cradle on the wall. "Slade wanted me to tell you he's very sorry to have upset you, and would like to make it up to you, if you'll give him the chance."

He was honestly sorry. I was sure of it. The fact remained he did it in the first place. He went behind my back, dug into Matt's past and never told me, never even told me the kind of criminal I'd lived with for over a year. How was I to get past it? Ilene distracted me from musing, grabbed my hand, guiding me to the stairs. "He also said the orange tabby cat misses you."

My heart ticked a sad beat with just the thought of the orange kitty. Slade had watched while I had slowly taught him to trust me and won him over from the half-wild barn cat. I had just told Susan I missed him moments ago. *Is he psychic? He knows how to cut me to the quick.*

Hands on my shoulders, Ilene ushered me up the stairs. I stopped halfway, the carpeting tickling the underside of my toes. "Get up there and get cleaned up, Kally. We've got lots to do today. Don't forget about Michelle's spa party tonight!"

"How could I forget?" I'd put massive effort into letting the girly party slip my mind. The last thing I wanted, after a week away from paradise on the ranch, was to endure a conclave of the pack of prissy females Ilene worked with. I would be happier in the corner of the sofa at the Fourth Moon.

Chapter Sixteen

The phone didn't ring again, no matter how Slade willed it to. The silvertone thing sat inert in his hand. He'd learned to trust his gut instincts while he was on the force, and he propped the handset on his shoulder knowing in the bottom of his gut it had been Kally who had called and then hung up. If he hadn't been out milking cows, he'd have been in to catch the phone when it first rang. He could have talked to Kally, and maybe her voice would've filled a little of the emptiness she left behind. He sighed and hung the phone back on the base.

Nothing felt right without Kally. The house was quiet, he'd been moody as hell and the past two days he'd walked past the Christmas tree without turning the lights on. Standing in the office doorway, Slade looked back at the phone, the partial connection to the woman who held his heart. The familiar longing rose, and he stuffed it down. "I love you, Kally." Then, cursing his ranch operating tasks, he shoved on his Stetson and stalked to the foyer.

Crinkling rose from the cat food bag when he fished out a bowl of kibble for Kally's tomcat. He didn't feed the critter table scraps often since she had left, but the next morning, he had purchased a bag of dry food and started putting a bowl of it inside the barn door. The cat was one of the few links he had left to Kally, and he planned to take good care of it, even if it still behaved like Slade was a nuisance to his feline existence.

The early morning air might well have had teeth for how cold and biting it was when he stepped out the front door. Bowl of kitty chow in one hand, he pulled the sherpa-lined jacket collar tight to his chin and shuffled across the drive toward the barn. Silence blanketed the ranch like new fallen snow, except for the tarp over the hay bales flapping in the early December air. It was an eloquent reminder of how soon he and the hired hands would be driving the cattle to the main shelter from the upper pens.

Mental note—call Red about helping with the drive.

Jack nickered softly from the pewter shadows of the barn when Slade pulled the doors open. "Hey, boy." The horse's rump was warm when he patted it. The horse flicked his tail.

Beneath a bale of hay the yellow lantern eyes of the tabby cat watched Slade. He put the bowl in its normal place, beside the rack of bridles and gear in the tack corner and then walked backward out of the barn. When he reached the corner of the cattle pen the ornery cat scurried from hiding to wolf down the food. Slade shook his head. *Cantankerous animal. Just need a comfortable distance, don't you?*

Just like Kally.

He buttoned the neck of his jacket against the cold wind whipping down Rancher's Row. The rustic Christmas wreath rocked on its peg. Slade was hardly in the spirit to fix it. He turned to stomp back to the house but stopped to admire the scenery Kally had reminded him to appreciate. Dawn lit the drive and the vehicle coming toward him. Slade didn't need to see the make or know the model. He knew whose vehicle it was by the sound of the engine. A heavy sigh expelled from his chest in a snow-white plume. *Yup. Here comes Rosie.*

Slade was certain his mother and honorary mom were in cahoots. He could picture his mother calling Rosie, plotting long distance on how Rosie could smother him with double the normal mothering in Kally's absence. They treated him like a broken hearted individual, someone to be coddled and cooed to, and it was the last thing he wanted. He shrugged his shoulders, then tipped his head in acknowledgement of her rather than retreating to the carpentry workshop or his bedroom to clean his guns.

Distancing himself from Rosie was separating himself from the support and nurturing she needed to give. Slade wouldn't deny her the chance.

Tires crunched on the gravel churned up by the snowplow. She put the vehicle in park and left the motor running when she climbed out. Her smile was genuine. His wave was half-hearted. "Morning, Rosie."

"How are you managing today, Slade?"

His gaze fell but recouped quickly with a sense of implied strength. "I'm managing just fine. My socks could be whiter, and the answering machine catches more calls than me. Otherwise..."

Her dark eyes were more piercing in the fresh light of sunrise. "Well, that's not saying a whole lot."

Another sigh escaped him. "What's to say? There's work to do and no time to waste on moping. Pouting doesn't get a damn thing done."

"Very true." She slapped his shoulder good-naturedly. "So what can I help you with today?"

Mischief crept into his voice. "Well, we could muck out the stalls..."

"Um...no. I think I'll pass." Her laughter was a familiar unguent to soothe his wounded spirit. "What else is on your to-do list?"

Slade tipped his Stetson back and scratched his brow. "Reckoning on the date on the calendar, we need to plan the annual sleigh ride, start thinking about a Christmas dinner menu, then there's cattle feeding, stall mucking..." He attempted a weak smile. She, however, raised an eyebrow and tapped a foot. "And then there's forgetting about Kally for a while."

She patted his forearm and then turned to the passenger side door. The hand-embroidered bear on the back of her jacket was emblazoned by the morning sunlight, and always reminded Slade of the story she used to tell, one of the legends of how Devils Tower was created. "Hey, Rosie?"

"Yeah?"

"Can you tell the Devils Tower creation story this year at the Christmas party? Maybe a bit of the old might wash away new hurts..."

Her sharp, almost bird like features softened. "Of course I can. Now how about we get the sleigh ready?" She opened the passenger side door. "Climb in. I'll drive."

He shrugged, not willing to argue with a preheated car in the December chill. Tilting his hips, he slid into the warmed seat. "Works for me."

"I thought you'd agree."

The heater circulated air scented with sage and George's pipe tobacco. It was a warm and earthy combination, reminiscent of when he had worked side-by-side with his parents and their friends the Thompsons to build the first timeshare ranch houses. Things were simple then, even though there was always work to be done. Since graduation, he'd gone to the academy, taken a position on the Hulett P.D. and sank into a questionable hell when he started dating Adelle.

"You've gone quiet." Rosie prodded his thigh. "Where's your mind? On Kally?"

"Actually, no. I was wondering what the hell I was thinking when I started dating Adelle."

"Probably wasn't thinking. With her figure and blonde hair, I doubt many men do think around her."

Slade snorted. He couldn't articulate a more appropriate response to Rosie's commentary on the base nature of men around the blonde she-devil. Slade wasn't impervious to Adelle's powerfully feminine mystique. He'd once worshipped at her feet. He might still be with her if he hadn't caught the girl in a lip lock with Tom Masters. Thank God Tom shined the true light on Adelle's nature. If Slade had stayed with Adelle, she would've driven him to the top of the P.D. ladder while she sucked his soul dry and siphoned off all his money.

If he was honest with himself, he fully expected Adelle to have pushed him off the top of the ladder if they'd stayed together long enough. Shortly after his parents had asked for his help, she had wandered off to Tom's greener pasture.

Better him than me.

Rosie took the back way to what his father Pine called the "big barn". The monster of a building had taken months to construct and housed the majority of the ranches equipment and vehicles. It also sheltered his dad's prized possession—a hand-built sleigh his father and grandfather had built together.

Grandpa Carlson and his dad had spent many summers tinkering, cutting and shaving, getting the sleigh ride worthy. The finishing year was marked by Slade's grandfather losing his battle with cancer. He had chosen to spend his last day before entering hospice care beneath blankets, riding on the sleigh while Pine drove. The entire Carlson family rode with Grandpa. They all shared Grandpa's smile and not one eye had been dry. Slade wiped away a tear and ran his fingers along the runner.

So many memories. He had hoped to add new ones to the list when he brought the sleigh out this year. One of the gifts he wanted to give Kally this year was a quiet, moonlight ride with her piled beneath the blankets and a cup of hot cocoa in her hands.

Rosie derailed him from his melancholy track when she switched on the old radio on the tool bench and cranked up Madonna's version of Santa Baby. She shimmied down the length of the tool bench, to the bag of shop rags Pine kept in the corner. With a dramatic roll of her hips, she pulled the bag open and fished out polishing cloths for them both, draping them over her shoulders like tattered feather boas when she sashayed back to him and sang the chorus, badly.

The frown he'd sheltered under for days dissolved. A smile rose, high and hard until he was squinting back tears and laughing himself sick. "Interesting spin on Christmas. Rosie. I think my mother would be shocked."

"Yeah, well it got you out of your funk. Come on, boy, grab the polishing creams and let's get this baby shiny."

Rummaging through the cabinets beneath the worktop for the tins of Pine's handmade polishing creams, Slade let go of his worries and left the past where it belonged. He tossed the leather treatment tin to Rosie, who climbed into the sleigh and worked the softener into the bench seats while he kept the wood wax and buffed the outer walls until the white oak boards shimmered. The rails would be the last things touched, a check of all the solder points and a fresh coat of black paint on the struts and supports.

Rosie dragged the piled blankets back around to the tailgate of her SUV and placed them in. She shut the tailgate, pushed closed the window and then dusted off her hands. "I'll get these washed and use your mother's herbal linen rinse." Hands on her hips, she admired their morning's effort. "The sleigh looks damn good. Your dad would be proud."

"And Santa Baby would be jealous." Slade laughed and tipped his Stetson to hide behind the brim.

"Ready to head back to the house?"

"Yup. I hear lunch calling my name."

"I'm surprised you didn't say Tabasco was calling."

"Tabasco depends on what I end up eating. Flapjacks and syrup don't pair so well with tangy heat."

They rode back in silence until Rosie pulled into the main circle drive. She placed a hand on his forearm. "Slade, honey, I will be the first person to tell you to forget about a girl like Adelle. I've encouraged you to focus on something other than Kally. But she is so deep in your heart there won't be any cutting her out without killing you."

The ache, the emptiness bloomed in his chest, forcing a sigh out of him. He didn't need to speak. Rosie saw right into his heart.

Her fingers tightened on his arm. "Call her, Slade. Apologize. Even if you don't think you've done anything wrong."

"I tried." He kicked at a lump of sawdust on the floor. "Kally shut me down, told me she'd heard 'sorry' too many times before." The statement still sat in his craw, irritating the hell out of him. He was being punished for what that bastard Matt had done.

"Then find a way to say it, or don't. At least call her. And don't give me crap about getting her voice mail, or Ilene's answering machine. If the machine picks up, leave a damn message."

"Okay." He opened the door, and she loosened her grip on his arm when he climbed out. Slade gazed back into the vehicle. "Thanks for helping today, Rosie. And for kicking my ass just now. I promise I will call her."

"Good deal." She nodded, and he closed the door.

Sun and shadows chased Rosie's vehicle down Rancher's Row. Slade stood on the front step, looking out over the ranch Kally had taught him how to love again. Snow covered the rolling landscape and coated the trees in an image Kally had called "frosting on a Christmas cookie". It was a phrase he would never forget. Rustic, beautiful and with the sun shining on the hollows, so very empty without her. Turning his back on the Fourth Moon's winter beauty, he scuffed his boots across the mat and opened the door.

An air of expectancy hung in the office, as if even the phone had been waiting for him. Slade took the handset, carried it into the living room where he stepped on the clicker cord and turned on the lights of the Christmas tree before dropping into the armchair by the fireplace. His gaze followed the strings of lights around the tree while he drew a deep breath and punched in Ilene's phone number.

His guts twisted into an uncomfortable ball, and there was suddenly not enough air in the living room. Each ring brought a renegade thump of his heart and pushed the knot in his throat higher. The let down of the answering machine message was almost a relief. "Hi, you've reached the Rogers. We're not in right now. Please leave a message, and someone will get back to you."

"Hi, Kally." *What do I say now? God I feel like such an idiot blubbering a message anyone could hear.* "Things haven't been the same at the Fourth Moon. Even your tomcat misses you. I've been feeding him lately. He likes the food but still hates me. I hope you're all right. I..." *Just say it, Slade.* "I miss you and would like to talk sometime. Call me, okay?"

He disconnected the call but hung onto the phone. "Love you, girl." She wouldn't hear those words, not yet.

Chapter Seventeen

Ilene and I hit the Starbucks at Camel Drive and S. Douglas Highway. After the weird flipping in my stomach and dark Italian roast coffee, I was ready to put some food down there. The Top Pot apple fritter melted in my mouth before Ilene had the car in park and fished her cheese danish out. We sat in the car, nibbling doughnuts and sucking down caramel macchiatos while she laid out the day's plans.

"First, we need to hit a grocery store and pick up some food for the party tonight." She penciled a checkmark on the list in her hand and nibbled her danish while I tore into my second doughnut. "Then hit a liquor drive-thru and get you some," she shuddered, "beer. And then figure out what to do with it all after we get home."

I balled up my wrappers and napkins like I'd done with Slade, slam dunking the wad into the bag on the seat. "Done." I swigged down another gulp of the syrupy sweet drink. "With food in my tummy, we can do whatever you want."

A smirky half-smile bloomed on Ilene's face. "Well, I see you've picked up a few interesting traits from your cowboy."

My chin fell nearly to my chest. "He's not mine anymore. Never really was..."

"Yes he was, and yes he is." She grabbed my hand and forced me to look at her. "I know what Slade did upset you, Kally, but he did it out of love and instinct." My chin dropped again. I didn't want to look into her eyes, so earnest and unguarded. She refused to allow me to shy away from reality, lifting my chin until she could pin me with her gaze. "He loves you and you love him. Sooner or later you're going to have to face it."

"I'm trying."

"You are going to have to talk to him and work through this."

If I heard his voice, talked to him, I'd turn to mush. The resolve I called on to move to Ilene's would melt away. "I'm not sure I'm ready."

"Maybe not, but you two will talk...eventually. You know you are welcome to stay with us indefinitely. I have a gut feeling you will be going back to the ranch."

Sarcasm reared its ugly head. "From your gut to God's ears."

She stuffed the last of her danish in her mouth, stowed the coffee in a cup holder and pulled back out on the street. "Grocery store, here we come!"

We ended up at Ilene's favorite store, a fussy, foodie kind of place where even the vegetables had aristocratic names. Ilene, in her glory, disappeared into the produce section, while I went straight on to the protein and cholesterol-laden meats and dairy. When we met near the checkout, she had an elegant arrangement of fruits on a clear tray. I held a black-bottomed platter of meats and cheeses. Ilene eyed my deli tray with amusement. "Going for the old 'heart attack on a plate' thing tonight?"

"Only if I eat the whole thing." I winked and she laughed while she wiggled her skinny butt into the express lane. Our last stop was a drive-thru liquor store, a terribly western source of fascination for an old Michigander like me. It was an exhilarating sense of getting away with something, like being a teenager at a dirt two-track party out in the woods. We giggled for blocks. Ilene's eyes sparkled. "That just never gets old."

"Tell me about it."

Back at home, we stuffed the trays into the fridge and left the beer in the garage where it would stay cold and not take up any more room. Ilene whistled for Tinker and Zip, the Pomeranian terror twins and then pointed at the phone. "How about you check the phone messages so I can put the puppers out?"

"Why don't I take them out? I need to bond with the little blighters if I'm going to be staying here."

Ilene laughed. The silent war between me and the Poms was news to no one. "Deal."

Tangerine balls of fluff danced and yipped at my feet. "Come on you two, let's go brave the elements." Bending down, I scooped the wriggling dogs to my chest and then eased the back door open with my butt. The backyard was sheltered from the wind, and was riddled with paths Steve had dug for the dogs. The Poms disappeared off into the labyrinth, barking at everything. In small doses, Tinker and Zip were cute and endearing, but after the lights went out and they stuck their tails in my face and barked at shadows...well, the cute wore off.

Ilene stood in the center of the kitchen, holding the phone out to me when I brought the dogs back into the kitchen. "What's up?"

"You need to listen to this message." I took the phone from her. "Just press the '1' button and the message will play again. It's so sweet, Kally."

I pushed the button and pressed the phone to my ear. Slade's voice came through, a little melancholy, but still hopeful. *"Hi, Kally...Things haven't been the same at the Fourth Moon. Even your tomcat misses you. I've been feeding him lately. He likes the food but still hates me. I hope you're all right. I...I miss you and would like to talk sometime. Call me, okay?"*

His recorded voice was enough to melt me. Blinking back tears, I held out the phone for her. "He is such a sweet guy."

"Yes he is." She had an "I told you so" expression when she ignored the phone and moved past to the sink. "I'm going to take care of these dishes. I think you should go and call him back."

"Ooo-kay." I took the phone into the living room and dropped into the armchair by the window. Sliding my toes along the windowsill, I pulled the curtains back and looked in the direction I imagined the ranch to be. My throat was tight, my mouth dry and my hand trembled. I braced the phone against the chair padding and dialed the Fourth Moon's main number.

After the third ring, the artificial, tinny voice asked me to "please leave your name and number after the beep."

"Hi, Slade. I'm okay, despite the craziness here at Ilene's. I'd gladly take my tomkitty over two mouthy yapbox Pomeranians any day. Thanks for taking care of him. It means a lot to me." I drew in a shaky breath. "Maybe we'll actually connect on the phone one of these days."

After dinner, Ilene, our trays, my beer and I piled back into her car. The directions were taped to the dashboard, and the corner buzzed with each gust of heat from the vents. I curled my arms in over my chest and sighed. "Oh, come on, Kally." A high blush pinked Ilene's cheeks. "This will be fun. The girls are all excited to meet you."

She parked on the side street, one house down from Michelle's festively decorated bungalow-style house. I picked my way along between the snow bank and string of parked cars. Serious doubt sat in my chest, keeping company with the sarcastic snort I stifled when I saw the deflated pink balloon dangling from the mailbox instead of floating. "Tell me what kind of party this is again?"

"It's a spa party. A bunch of girls, some snacks and cocktails, lots of make-up and lotions."

Oh goody. "Sounds like a blast." The thinly veiled sarcasm was evident, even to me.

Laughing, Ilene skated past a lit-up reindeer. "Somehow you don't sound too enthused."

She could always see through me. "I'll be fine."

"I'm sure you will. I want you to have fun too." She skittered down the front walk, her bag swinging from one hand and the party platter of meats and cheeses, my contribution to the party, teetering in the grip of the other hand.

Rock salt crunched beneath the heels and soles of my cowboy boots, but I was sure footed in comparison to Ilene. Her patent leather high heels were more like ice skates than shoes on the shoveled path. I reached for the platter, dangerously close to losing its payload of food. "Want me to carry the tray? We don't want to lose it."

"Oh yes, please."

I took the tray in my right hand and wrapped my left arm around her waist. Relying on my cowboy boots, the two of us made it to the white light icicle-drenched house. Ilene's friend Michelle opened the door, her obviously bleached platinum blonde hair swept into a side part. The hairstyle framed her smile when she broke into giggles. "Good lord, Ilene. Have you been drinking already?"

"Hey, Michelle. You know it's five o'clock somewhere." Ilene took the tray and wriggled through the door. "Michelle, this is my life-long friend, Kally Jensen."

Michelle's voice was high, saccharin sweet when she offered her hand for me to shake. "Hi, Kally. It's nice to finally meet you."

Her hand was limp in mine. I fought the urge to drop it. "It's nice to meet you too. Happy holidays."

Ilene hung her jacket on the coat rack by the door. I followed suit, stopping short of pulling off my boots. Heels of various sizes and colors cluttered the floor beside the door. I scuffed my boots on the mat and stepped onto the tile. "Do you want me to take my boots off?"

Michelle handed me a cold beer and then winked. "Only if you want to have a pedicure."

"I think I'll keep my boots on for a while..."

Michelle's false smile stretched her lipstick to its limits. "Isn't she the cutest?"

Suddenly I felt like a country bumpkin who'd moved in with her city slicker cousin. Ilene clapped me on the shoulder, nearly dislodging the beer bottle from my lips. "She's a doll." Then Ilene dragged me toward the Christmas tree, pretending to look at the ornaments. She spoke out the side of her mouth. "You are going to loosen up, aren't you?"

Growling wasn't appropriate, but I considered it. My gaze locked on a frilly swan ornament with real feather wings. Begrudgingly, I walked back to the door, removed my boots and stood them next to Ilene's shiny black heels. *Inhale. Exhale. Release negativity.* "I am loosened up, Ilene."

I lied. The tension in my jaw might damn well give me a headache before the night was through. I drank a few hearty swigs of beer to forestall brain pain for a few hours anyway. Girly stuff was never my thing, and to be picked on by the most feminine female in the room irked me. Michelle reminded me of Adelle Crawford. I wasn't sure if it was the fake hair color, the obvious false boobs or the Catty Bitch shade of green eye shadow they both wore. *God, please don't let them put that color on me.*

Michelle carried the trays over to the table covered with heavy winter treats and crystalline snowmen. Ilene led me into a living room churning with women and reeking of artificial perfume. The pungent odors reminded me of how I missed the handmade natural lavender soaps at the Fourth Moon. Looking at the artsy furniture and poofed and painted women in the room, I yearned for the natural tans and crows-feet wrinkled ladies at the ranch.

I tried my best to enjoy the games and circulating lotions and smellies. A shade of nail polish reminded me of the teeny pink roses on the quilt in my room back at the ranch, and after finishing my first beer, I offered my nails up for a manicure and paint job.

The nail polish wasn't even dry when Teresa, the over-done demonstrator, suggested a matching pedicure.

I refused.

She insisted.

It could have become a vicious cycle, but she pushed the chair back, stopping dead at Slade's snow-white tube socks on my feet. "Oh my word, honey. Those socks are...are they men's?"

My defensive side grew a voice. "Yes." The "s" was a bit of a hiss.

Michelle spoke up. "Don't you have some trouser socks, Kally?"

I curled my feet beneath the folding metal chair. They were my favorite socks. The ones Slade had worn the night he slept in my room. No Gillette priss queen was going to talk me out of them or insult them either. "I like these socks. They're warm, soft and make my boots fit better."

Her brown eyes tilted, affecting an expression akin to pity. "Oh, hun, there's your problem right there. Ilene." She waited for Ilene to clamber from her seat and negotiate the female body obstacle course. "Ilene, don't you have heels and hosiery on sale in your department?"

Ilene handed me another beer accompanied with a plate of snacks and an apologetic, "never mind her" expression. "Yeah, we have our annual sale going right now. In fact, Kally got her boots at our store too."

Michelle was quicker on the pick up than I expected. She climbed back into her seat. "Well, Kally, if you ever want a pedicure, you can come to my salon. We have all the same products there too."

"Good to know." I made a big fuss over my manicure to make up for my snit. The pink dried prettier than I expected, with a soft sheen. In the back of my mind I wondered what Slade would think. His voice haunted me, his suede timbre in my mind. *"Pretty, if ya like girly stuff. Is the paint chip-resistant?"*

Though I was two beers down, the female bonding session had lost its appeal, and Ilene could sense it in me. I yearned to be in the car, on the way home, past Ilene's home and all the way back to the Fourth Moon. Taking my plate and a new beer, I curled into the corner of a sparsely populated sofa, but my serenity was short-lived. Ilene motioned from me to move my feet, and then wedged her little behind close enough to be sitting on my lap. "I spoke to Michelle..."

"Oh? Does she think I'm an antifeminist nutbag?"

"No, not at all. I told them you've had a rough few months. She said there is going to be a chair opening at her salon when one of her girls goes on maternity leave." I wasn't catching on to whatever Ilene hinted at, and looked at the beer bottle like I accused it of clouding my thoughts. "She wants you to come to work at her salon. Of course you'd need to be licensed here in Wyoming."

"Very nice of her." I yawned. "Can we get going? I'm getting tired."

Ilene smiled, patted my shoulder. "You never could make it far past the second beer, could you?"

My nose wrinkled in a yawn, my eyes squinting shut. "Nope, not sitting on my butt with a bunch of girls anyway."

Ilene left me in my comfortable corner, talked with Michelle a few more minutes and then packaged up the tray of meats and my last few beers. She stood in the doorway between the kitchen and living room, waving at me. "Come on, Kally, let's get you home and put you to bed."

I stood and wove between the girls while they shouted their goodbyes and waved their hands like they were drying their nail polish. "Bye, all. And Michelle?"

Her head popped up from a pow-wow at the table. "Yeah?"

"Thanks for having me and for the job offer. I'll look into schooling."

Her smile was enormous. "Great! See ya around, Kally."

One battle with the boots and a slippery track to the Jeep later, Ilene clambered in behind the steering wheel. I dropped into the passenger seat and closed the door "So...what's on tap for tomorrow? Another busy day?"

"Well, it's a Saturday, so Steve thought you might like to go to his favorite sports bar for a nice, laid-back meal." She looked at me, yawning and rubbing my eyes. "Remind me not to let you drink any beers tomorrow."

The cloud of steam from our laughter obscured the windows, and we sat with the Jeep idling until the defroster cleared the windshield. The dark roads slipped beneath the tires while I struggled to stay awake. After a week of not sleeping well, I lost the battle. Ilene roused me when she parked the Jeep. "Kally, honey, we're home."

My first thought was a fleeting hope of seeing the porch of the Fourth Moon. The back wall of the garage met my eyes and obliterated my dream.

After stowing the meat tray and beer on the bench in the garage, in a spot easily visible to Steve, we kicked off the boots and shoes and staggered in. Steve stood in the middle of the hallway shaking his head, then laughed when he wrapped an arm around Ilene's shoulders. I mumbled goodnight when they climbed the stairs to their bedroom. I tucked a sheet over the scratchy sofa fabric, pulled a blanket over me and crashed into sleep despite the Tinker hair on my pillow.

We spent the following day huddled around Ilene's computer desk in the corner of the living room. Screen after screen flashed by while we searched the Internet for information on procuring a Wyoming driver's license and locating cosmetology schools and funding, all of which required a proof of legal Wyoming residence.

Though I wanted to move forward with my life, I was not certain where I wanted to live. My heart longed for the hills and trees and loving company of the Fourth Moon, but a small part of my mind still argued against it. Following my heart and loving Slade was what got me here in the first place. If I hadn't loved him, he couldn't have hurt me, even though his crime seemed less and less severe. The more I thought about it, the more I could see his side, how it could very well have been him following his cop instincts to check a violent man's background. What still bothered the hell out of me was he didn't tell me.

A phone call shattered the relatively easy afternoon. I expected it to be Slade and prepared myself to for an emotional conversation. Ilene looked at the caller ID, mouthed "my mother" and then took it into the other room to answer. Every fiber of my being shouted something was wrong. Ilene's estranged mother never called her, the woman hadn't even shown up for Ilene and Steve's wedding. *Why the hell was she calling Ilene now?*

By the time I'd logged out of my new email account and made it to the kitchen door, the conversation was over. Ilene sat at the table, ashen and shaking. I shouted for Steve and rushed to Ilene's side. Steve's feet thundered down the stairs and hall announcing his arrival in the kitchen. "Honey, what's wrong?"

Her gazed passed from Steve's face to mine. An unreadable shadow hung over her eyes. "She was calling to warn us. To warn you, Kally."

I dropped to my knees before her feet and took her hands. "What're you talking about? Why would she be calling here to warn anybody?"

"A private investigator forced his way into her home. He threw a copy of our yearbook and some newspaper articles about the girl's volleyball team on her table and grilled her about our friendship back in school." She twined and untwined her fingers. "She refused to say anything and he threatened her, said his client was not a patient or reasonable man..."

My gut clenched around my lunch. "Oh God...Matt. He's still trying to find me."

"And by the looks of things, Matt's figured out we were best friends through school."

"And marriage certificates are a matter of public record, Kally," Steve, always logical, chimed in. "If the P.I. could track things down to Ilene's mother, he can certainly follow the paper trail here."

A panicky unease bubbled through me. "When did this happen, Ilene?"

"Today. Just now. Right before she called me."

Steve put a hand on Ilene's arm and one on my shoulder. "Don't worry, girls. There has to be something we can do, some way to protect Kally." Ilene attempted a smile. I'm sure mine looked more like a grimace. "And what you two nervous Nellys need is a night out. My treat. There's not much we can do on a Saturday evening anyway. Monday morning, I'll call an attorney and see what legal route we have."

Ilene looked at the clock and shrugged her shoulders. "It is damn near dinner time. We could sit here, worry ourselves sick, or we could go out, hide in a dark corner and force a couple beers down Kally's throat..."

I nodded. "I did sleep better last night than I have since I came here."

Steve's eyebrows rose. "So we're agreed then?"

Sighing first, I quoted a very famous pirate movie. "We have an accord."

We were supposed to be going out for dinner, a fun, relaxed evening at Steve's favorite sports bar. Passing under the neon sign festooned with ridiculous Christmas garland, I knew my fantasy was not coming true. Steve stopped a guy who looked every bit like a village snitch, the one who knew all the information and just where to leak it to his advantage. He looked over Steve, Ilene and me with a sense of disinterest before Steve asked him if Scott had arrived yet.

"Oh yeah. He's at the bar waiting." His eyes turned bright and piercing. "So this is the girl? She's cute..."

"And you are moving on, Dave." Steve pushed the mousy man on past us and out the door, giving Ilene the perfect opportunity to give me an apologetic glance before socking her husband in the shoulder. "Scott Weston from accounting? Good Lord, Steve. What were you thinking?"

He shook his head, locking Ilene with a silencing gaze while I swirled down the drain of despair and Ilene simmered to a boil. One thing I loved about Ilene, you couldn't shut her up if she thought something was wrong. "Damn it, Steve. Don't you go all silent on me. Tell me you didn't just set Kally up with that bookworm."

"Don't call him a worm. There isn't anything wrong with being smart."

"Smart? Smart?" Her voice rose sharply, her eyes widened. "He's past smart, Steve. He's in the goddamn—"

"Okay, now stop it. There he is." Steve pointed past a sparse branched, pitifully decorated artificial pine tree to a sandy haired guy of average height. His light brown hair was brutally short and his bangs had been forced into some sort of a Princeton style. It did set off his owl-like glasses nicely though. His refined features gave him an austere, almost snobby appearance. I rolled my eyes and sighed. It was going to be a long night.

Scott was not the dark-haired, light-eyed rugged cowboy who made my heart sing. He wasn't unattractive—just wasn't attractive to me.

With his head forward, Steve led the way to the bar, not realizing he had lost us steps from the door. I hung back a step and tugged on Ilene's arm. "Scott's in a what, Ilene?"

She heaved a sigh and patted my hand. "He is in a think tank. All the guy talks about is books and world politics. You want to know the real price of tea in China? He's the guy to ask."

"Oh my..."

"Yup...oh my." She tugged me forward. "Let's get this over with so we can crucify Steve in a snow bank on the way home."

Picturing Steve white washed and spread eagle beside the road was a pleasant image. Only going back to the ranch could sound better at this moment. "Deal."

We wound our way to the table. Both the men fell silent and slid over to allow us to fit in. Scott's voice was mild, bordering on meek when he extended his hand. "Hi, Kally. It's nice to meet you. Steve's told me so much about you."

"Oh really?" I shook his hand. "Hopefully some of it was good."

"All of it." His gaze wandered my face and upper body. "He said you were intelligent and high-spirited. However, he left out how attractive you are." Smiling, he passed me a menu.

Nice try, smart guy. "Well, he's biased. He has Ilene to look at all the time."

We all laughed. Though there was no energy, no chemical attraction and no interest. Scott did wear some damn nice cologne. It was a fussy, complicated scent, nothing like Slade's musky Stetson. When the waitress came, three burgers platters and one Asian salad were ordered. Steve poked every bit of fun at his salad-eating friend he possibly could. "Oh, ha ha," Scott snickered, but took the ribbing good-naturedly.

The meal proved to be a perfect distraction from talking. It did not, however, keep my mind from straying back to Butch's Roadhouse and the dance with Slade. I was so wrapped in memories, I didn't notice the arm Scott slid across the back of the bench seat. I could not, however, miss the busty blonde with the Catty Bitch shade of green eye shadow who walked slowly to our table and stopped even with our bench. Adelle

Crawford's shiny lips parted in a leering grin. "Well, Kally Jensen, look at you! I heard you left Hulett. I never thought you'd end up here underneath the arm of another man days later."

I fought to stand, to throttle the mocking tone out of her voice, but Scott's arm shot from the bench and his hand clamped vice-like on my shoulder. I turned on him, pinning him with a scathing glare and growled. "Get your hand off of me."

He shook his head. "I don't like violence."

Smacking his arm away, I stood and faced the last person I expected to see here in Gillette. "What does my location matter to you, Adelle? And what the hell are you doing here?"

"Sweet little out-of-towner Kally." Her grin was feral and mocking. "Didn't Slade tell you my daddy owns this bar and a bunch more like it?"

Scott's hand materialized around my wrist when I stepped forward and tugged me back. "If I had any clue who owned this bar," I wrenched my hand from Scott's grasp, "or who I'd be dining with, I would never have come here."

"Kally, please sit down," Scott pleaded.

I slung a silencing glare in his direction. When I turned to face forward, Ilene was standing too. "Just ignore her. She's just doing this to tick you off."

"Oh no." Adelle leaned closer to the table, her manicured claws on the shiny surface. "If I wanted to piss her off, I'd tell her I was driving back to Hulett tonight, and breaking up with Tom now that Slade is free."

The taunt shoved me beyond words and into action. Lunging forward, I grabbed handfuls of brittle blonde hair and yanked her face inches from mine. "You touch him and I will finish what I started at Butch's." Pulling harder, I butted heads with the arrogant woman. "I made you bleed once, don't think I won't again."

She hung close enough for me to lean back and slap her, but I didn't. I turned my back and grabbed my purse from its place by Scott's leg instead. My jacket arm was bunched in a knot. I forced my fist through in time to miss the back of Adelle's head. "Beat it, bitch…"

She swung curses in my direction even as she retreated toward the center of the bar, but I ignored her. Watching me, Ilene signaled she was ready to do what I needed. The men huddled down in the corners of the booth and hardly looked toward either of us. I stood clutching my purse, fuming and feeling useless. Ilene hit Steve's shoulder. "Give me the keys. I'm driving Kally home. You can come or maybe get a ride with Switzerland over there."

Scott raised his hands in a helpless gesture, and Steve nodded. "S'okay, Ilene. I should explain the history between those two to Scott."

"I'll get him home later." Scott spoke to Ilene. He refused to look at me.

"Thank you, Scott."

"No problem."

I turned to look at him, even though he didn't acknowledge it. "For what it's worth, I am sorry."

"Thanks," he mumbled.

I expected to see Adelle in the parking lot or be blindsided by her. Nothing but moonlight and shadows moved among the parked cars. Everything was quiet and so was Ilene for the greater portion of the ride home. Finally, rounding the corner four houses from her driveway, she spoke. "I don't blame you, hun. I would have done the same thing in your position. Only I would have become an honorary member of Tribe Slap-a-Ho because I would have cuffed the bitch."

"I didn't want to mess up my manicure."

In the calm before the storm of laughter Ilene gave me the most comical expression. It was the girliest thing I'd ever said. The giggles didn't subside until we were in the house and the Pomeranians were in the backyard.

"I'm going to tease you about that manicure comment for years." Ilene shook out the blankets on the sofa.

"Wouldn't surprise me. It was...an inspired moment."

"Your cowboy would get a kick out of it too."

Those words drug up the ugliness from the bar and flung it into the bright lights of the living room. Without Adelle to pin my anger on, the emotion evaporated and left me filled with a sense of unease. My stomach soured and my head hurt. I sank to the sofa, examining the events of the past few days.

Such a tumultuous time, a rollercoaster of emotion, with hills built from Slade's calls, and valleys carved with news from Michigan and Adelle's taunts. The ride had started and stopped with Slade digging up information on Matt. A week ago, it framed every thought I entertained and choice I made. Distance and time to think had changed much, had taken out the sting. Now, it was the least of my concerns but still kept me from the arms of the man I loved when I most wanted to shelter in them.

Shadows obscured the hands of the clock on the wall, but by leaning against the sofa's arm and craning my neck, the digital clock on the stove was visible. *Nearly midnight. It's too late to call him.*

Ilene appeared from the kitchen with two snow-covered Pomeranians in tow. "I'm going to go to bed now. Only sleep is going to save Steve a serious tongue lashing when he comes home."

Yawning, I nodded and pulled the tie-dyed bull from my bag tucked under the end table. "I'm going to crash too."

Haloed by the light of the staircase, Ilene looked like a ragged angel. "You're going to call Slade tomorrow." I opened my mouth to argue. She shut me up with a raised finger. "Don't start with me. You will call him. Then we'll all feel better. G'night, Kally."

"Night, Ilene." I shuffled to the downstairs half-bath and changed into pajamas before dragging the blanket from the sofa to the armchair. Turning the chair to face the window, I pushed the curtain aside to look in the direction of the Fourth Moon. "I miss you, too, Slade. I wish I'd told you."

I closed my eyes and surrendered to the dream of the night he had held me.

Chapter Eighteen

The ranch was quiet. The shadows in the corners of his room whispered in Kally's voice when Slade awoke before dawn. Though he strained to understand them, the words fled quicker than his dreams.

Joints cracked when he stretched. His muscles were achy from lying on his side with his arm around an imagined Kally. He stood before the windows of his bedroom, curtain pulled aside while he looked in the direction of Gillette. He envisioned Kally, with her cracked porcelain appearance and a pained shadow over her eyes when she had put the last bag in the back of Ilene's Jeep. Sweet pain thumped through his chest. He drew a heart in the frost covering the windowpane, like Kally had the first morning. "I miss you, girl. Please come home."

The curtains whispered softly when they swished back in place. Slade turned from his moment of weakness, walked to the closet, pulled out work clothes and dressed for the day. The box harboring his mother's ring sat on the dresser, a silent sentinel to the hope Slade tenaciously fed for Kally to return to the ranch and him. He dusted the velvet top before closing the door.

Sunday mornings were always quiet on the Fourth Moon, and without the light and crackles of the fire, the Christmas tree and Santa Claus figures could well be Ghosts of Christmas Yet to Come. Adding more kindling to embers in the grate, Slade revived yesterday's fire and then added logs to the growing blaze. He donned his Stetson and headed to the foyer to pull on boots and a coat. Beams of vehicle headlights bounced and joggled through the pines lining the north drive, announcing the arrival of Slade's weekend helper, Red Baxter.

Reliable old Red. Baxter might shoot off at the mouth now and then, but if you needed help, Red was the man to call. Slade buttoned up his jacket, stepped out and then shut the door.

Slade's cheeks stung and crisp cold air tingled in his nose. He stomped his feet while he waited on the porch. The haphazard dance of high beams steadied to a smooth roll. The light blue vehicle rolled to a stop at the porch steps, the headlights shining past the carpentry shop when the wheels came to a halt. He looked at the shed and the packed trail beside it. He'd spent every afternoon out there while Kally was gone.

Red motioned for Slade to climb on. He stepped onto the running boards of the Rodeo, holding onto the luggage rack while his old partner and constant ranch hand drove down to the barn. Left running, the Rodeo's engine purred and the lights aimed at the barn. Red's door creaked when he opened it. It had since he had slammed it hard two years back. "G'morning, Slade."

"Morning." Slade stepped off the running board and skated across the packed snow to the barn door. "I appreciate ya helping me like this."

Red laughed, his cheeks round and nearly apple red in the morning chill. "You say it every morning, and I always say 'you're welcome' so...you're welcome. I'm happy to help. And Slade?"

He pulled open the barn doors and whistled to the horses inside. "Yeah?"

"I'm sorry I chased off your filly."

Oh, Kally. A sad heartbeat sent pain through him. "It's not your fault, Red. If anything, you just facilitated an earlier departure date for her. She's a smart girl, she would've found out anyway."

In the barn, yellow eyes followed every move he made while Kally's tomcat watched him from the rafters, swishing his tail if Slade got too close. When Red walked out of hearing range, he cooed to the cat the way Kally did. Red peeked around the edge of the door and Slade shrugged his shoulders and pretended to sneeze. Eyes traveling the edges of the barn, Red found the ginger kitty and then looked at Slade and snorted.

The oat mix his mother fed to the horses released dust into

the air when he portioned out meals for the animals. He wriggled into Jack's stall with a curry brush and a bucket, brushing the horse while he ate. While he repeated the process with Sunny, his helper tossed bales of hay into the bed of Slade's truck, which was parked nearby. Slade stroked the horses' noses before walking back out and pushing the door mostly closed.

He waved a glove at the truck bed. "Ready to go?"

Red nodded. "A-yup."

Out of early morning courtesy, Slade eased the Dodge down Rancher's Row without lights. In the dell where he had found Kally, he circled the back eighty pen to the right while Red's breath rose in white plumes and he chucked hay into huge tractor tires for the cattle. At the far end, Slade pulled to a stop and the two men checked the troughs and cleaned a pipe to get the water running freely. Sopping wet and smelling of soggy hay, they piled into the warmth of the Dodge.

Baxter dusted chaff from his pants and rubbed his hands in front of the vent. "You got plans tonight?"

"On a Sunday?" Slade cocked an eyebrow and tossed Red a curious glance. "I plan to sleep..."

"Why don't you come out with me? I'll buy ya dinner at Butch's. Call it Men's Night Out."

"Well..." Slade tipped his hat back and dabbed at sweat with a kerchief. He wasn't quite comfortable going out without Kally. The rumors flying around town bombarded the ranch house worse than any blizzard. He could just imagine the shit storm his appearance would blow up in a place like the roadhouse.

"Come on." Red pressed the issue. "Let me buy you a couple drinks and try to make up for screwing up your relationship with Kally."

"If it will assuage some of your guilt..."

Red's smile did not dissipate the rest of the morning, even through mucking the stalls. They talked about the good old days on the force, and by the time he returned to the ranch house, Slade had let go of missing Kally. He filled his day with ranch chores and discussed the coming Christmas sleigh ride with Rosie before dressing for a night out.

He paced in the foyer, debating on the wisdom of his decision. If he stayed home, he'd mope around and go to bed early. If he went to Butch's, everyone would see him without Kally. His musing was halted when Red dialed the house phone. Slade answered. "Hello?"

"I'm on my way...meet ya there."

"See you soon."

Butch's didn't look the same without the light of Kally's smile. The building hadn't changed, the same garish neon signs decorated the outside, and many of the cars in the parking lot were there the night he and Kally were there. The only real difference was his smile was gone. Slade put the truck in park and heaved a sigh when he pulled the keys from the ignition. *What the hell am I doing here? Oh yeah, easing Red's guilt...*

Suspicion was a wasted effort. He knew who would be in the roadhouse, and pretty damned near where they'd be sitting too. The snakes in the pit of his gut turned to slimy eels. Adelle was in there somewhere, and Slade without Kally was like a fish bleeding in the water. The bleached blonde shark would smell his weakness and be out for the kill.

Red Baxter's blue Rodeo pulled up alongside the Dodge. His too-big, too-clean bone colored hat perched atop his head looked like bobber floating on a pond. He waved and climbed from his rig, and then walked up to Slade's window and tapped on it.

"All right, all right." Slade stuffed his keys in his pocket and opened the door. "Let's get this over with."

"If you're uncomfortable, we don't need to go in there."

Slade's gaze fell to his boots. A shadow in the gravel looked conspicuously like his heart. His heel sunk into the darkness when he turned and shut the door. "I need to do something to get the girl off my mind."

In the entryway he caught sight of Cissy Rawlings, and any doubt he might have entertained about Adelle being inside evaporated. He pulled his Stetson forward and tucked his chin in the collar of his jean jacket. The chuckle beside him was only a precursor for the thump between his shoulder blades. Red's voice was in his ear. "Hiding ain't going to do you no good. Cissy already saw you, and everyone around Hulett knows Kally left for Gillette."

Yup, I'm bleeding in the water. Here comes a scout shark. Suzy Mitchell was on her way to the door. Her hair was piled exceptionally high, and her grip was exceedingly tight on Slade's wrist when she led them through the bar to a corner table near the dance floor.

"What can I get you, boys?" Her voice was close to a purr.

Slade ordered a bloomin' onion, the biggest chunk of steak on the menu, a basket of fries with a side of fry sauce, a shot of bourbon and a beer. Red's meal was meager in comparison, scaling the steak back to a sizzler and the fries down to a baked potato. Suzy's breasts nearly jumped from her blouse when she leaned closer. "A little hungry tonight, Slade?"

"Famished." He leaned back against the tooled leather cushion. "So be a good waitress and scoot your booty on into the kitchen and place our order, all right?"

"Mmm." Her eyelashes dropped in an attempt at a sexy come-hither look. "As you command." She turned fast enough to toss her tight-wrapped butt in Slade's face.

Suzy returned with their drinks and the bloomin' onion. Red lifted his glass and toasted. "Here's to a new tradition of Men's Night Out."

Here's to Kally. Slade clinked his shot glass against Red's tumbler and then tossed the shot back. He swallowed, felt it burn down his throat and wished to hell it would burn in his chest and warm the spot grown cold in Kally's absence.

Suzy walked past, on her way to another table. Red raised his hand, wolf whistled and shouted, "Yo, nurse!"

Her boobs reached the table before she did. "You boys ready for another round?"

"Yes, ma'am." Slade's empty shot glass pirouetted on her tray when she turned.

Slade averted his eyes, his gaze trailing to the corner of the dance floor where he'd held Kally tight to his chest. She had been soft, warm and her floral scent had wrapped him in wonder. A familiar pain bubbled in his chest. He wallowed in it and hated it. All he wanted was the happiness they'd shared before. He looked up in time for Suzy to slide another shot of bourbon in his direction.

His eyes slipped closed, he swallowed and the warmth of the firewater spread a little further in his chest. *A few more shots and the ache might just get numbed.*

Red watched his friend with a masculine sense of caring. "Think another shot might help?"

"Yup. It just might." Slade nodded his head and tipped his beer back. Suzy reappeared, laden with food and another shot glass of amber liquor. Red's eyebrows went up. "Where'd the shot come from? We didn't order another one."

Suzy's eyes darted to a corner table. "It's from—"

"Me." Adelle Crawford finished her sentence.

Great. Just what I need. The man-eating shark is here. Slade resisted the urge to check for open wounds and blood flow. Rolling his eyes, he took the shot glass from the tray while Suzy distributed the plates and Adelle forced her butt onto his bench. She smiled at him, her bright absinthe eye shadow sparkling above her venomous green irises. He gave her a lop-sided smirk and quaffed the amber liquor. "Thanks for the shot."

"My pleasure." Her smile reminded him of a cartoon shark's toothy grin. She leaned closer to Slade, the line of her buttons performing shiatsu massage on his arm. "You looked like you could use another drink."

Damn this alcohol. And damn you too, Adelle. "You always knew when I was hurting. Too bad you learned the lesson by firsthand experience of causing the pain."

"Oohh." She batted her eyelashes. "Point taken. I wasn't always good to you, and I'm awful sorry."

Nope, not listening to this crap again. Kally's right about "sorry". It loses its meaning after a while. Slade redirected the conversation. "So, where's Tom?"

She didn't even blink. "We broke up a few days ago."

Convenient coincidence right after Kally left. Too bad the shots were kicking his ass and he couldn't keep his tongue. "Right after Kally left for Gillette."

Her bottom lip sank, perfectly mocking of a sympathetic expression. The denim of his jacket buffered her patting his arm. "So I heard. When is she coming back? Will she be around for Christmas?"

Adelle's questions drove like a dagger into Slade's heart. *Christmas...the ring...* His cheeks were flushed with a bourbon blush, but he still felt the warmth of his tear. Holding his face like she used to, Adelle wiped his tear away with her thumb.

"Y'know, I ran into Kally in Gillette. She was sitting with some fancy pants accountant. Looked pretty comfortable too."

She should've just ripped his heart out and thrown it on the floor. It would have been less painful.

The raucous set of music died, and a tear-in-my-beer love song poured from the speakers and into his chest. Her hand slid along his jaw line, across his shoulder and down to his elbow, which she tugged toward her. "How about a dance, cowboy? Maybe we can take your mind off'n your hurt."

Against his better judgment, he nodded and excused himself from the table. Shock sat on every line of Red's face when he spoke. "I'll be here."

Adelle wove into his arms, pressing her curves against every sensitive point he had. She wasn't Kally, but the bourbon lied and told him it was okay to hold her. Slade's arm rode the small of her back. His other hand curled over her shoulder when his face tipped down close to hers. Adelle's curves were fuller, familiar in his embrace and smelled oddly floral. The heartache and alcohol nudged him down a reminiscent path and he lost himself in her voice humming in his ear, her hand stroking his body, grazing his belt line.

The moment the music died, he snapped back to his senses. He pulled away, enough for the greedy woman to paste her lips on his and grab the back of his head.

Surprise morphed into anger. Slade cupped her face in his hands and wrenched her lips from his. He seethed and the hot emotion rose through him and out of his mouth. "How dare you?" Her smile faded. "You're taking advantage of my weak moment. What did you think would happen? I'd pony up and be your pocket boy? Did you think you'd wiggle your way back into my heart as easily as you did my arms?" He pushed her away, fished a five-dollar bill out of his pocket and threw it at her feet. "Pay for the shot and keep the change. It's all you're worth to me."

Adelle's face sagged, tears welled up in her eyes. She balled her fists and stomped her foot. "To hell with you, Slade Carlson!"

"I'm already in hell. You just keep turning up the heat."

He turned on his boot heel and tromped to the table where Red sat with their meals in boxes, ready to go. "I'm sorry, Red. I just can't do this. Can't take being in the same building with...her."

"Not a problem." Baxter worked his way free from the bench, tossed money on the table and handed Slade his meal. "I had high hopes she would leave well enough alone, but the sniper had her sights set on you."

Slade straightened his coat and hat but wobbled on his feet. "If she ever picks up a gun, we're all in trouble!"

"Agreed. What an interesting call for the P.D. to run." He stepped even with Slade. "Why don't you let me drive you home? You slammed a couple shots more than me..."

The officer in Slade spoke up, agreeing with Red's suggestion. He didn't want to be another drunk driver on the roads. Even if he felt fine, he knew the effects a few shots of alcohol had on a person. Letting go of the reins, letting someone else take control was hard. Smart, but difficult.

He nodded and led the way through the bar. Adelle, Suzy and Cissy gathered in a tight knot at the waitress station, locked in conversation. He heard his name, a bit too loudly, Adelle was smiling and Cissy held a phone while she watched him walk up. A muscle along his jaw ticked, his shoulders tightened, and when he walked past Cissy Rawlings—an active agent of the Gossip Chain on her cell phone—Slade took the phone from her hand and snapped it shut. "You are not going to spread vicious rumors while I'm within earshot."

Yaps and growls similar to a pack of ankle-biting dogs rose from the women, and he suddenly understood Kally and Ilene's long running joke about sled dogs. He tossed the phone back to Cissy. "On second thought, gossip away. Tell everybody you know Slade Carlson is gonna get his girl."

The two men walked out, and Red slammed the door behind them. The cold air woke Slade up enough to realize he wasn't in any shape to drive. Skittering across the slippery lot, Slade locked up his truck and then piled into the front seat of Red's Rodeo. Red's door complained against the cold air and forced movement. Once he clambered in he slammed it again. "Easy on the door, Red."

"Sometimes you have to be a little...insistent. Even though it complains, I make it understand." He gave Slade a curious expression, one eyebrow raised, and Slade got the impression Red had meant much more than he said.

Slade stewed over the implications of Red's pointedly vague comment until the Rodeo pulled to a stop at the front door of the Fourth Moon. Looking at the carpentry shed, the place where Kally had poured out her heart to him, he finally understood. Kally might've complained about his actions and left because of them, but it was high time he made her understand why he tracked down Stransberg's police record. In his heart, he was sorry for hurting her, for not telling her. They needed to get past it and come back together, or the future would be miserable for them both.

Red caught his nod of understanding. His long time friend steadied his shoulder when he opened the vehicle door. "Go on. Make her understand."

"I'm damn sure gonna try."

"Don't try, man, do it." Red waved after Slade eased the door closed.

Monday morning came, heralded by a knock on his bedroom door. He yawned, and the motion set his brain to pounding. Rolling over with his hands on his head, he could empathize with the bourbon-induced misery Kally had suffered after their night out. The sour mash had kicked his ass last night, and that aftermath knocked his butt up around his ears this morning. The knock came again, through the door and into his skull. "Gimme a minute, please..."

Slade tumbled to the floor and staggered to the closet where he rustled up some thick flannel pants. He pulled them on over his naked behind and scuffed his feet into sweat socks while he walked to the doorway. The brass knob was cold when he opened the door, but Rosie's smile was broad and warm on the other side of the door. Her voice had a sonorous tone. "Phone for you."

"All right." He hitched his pants, adjusted the tie. "I'll be right down."

She leaned closer, her eyes sparkling. "It's Kally. Don't keep her waiting..."

Hell with getting a shirt! Slade hurried out, leaving the door open wide while he hurried down the stairs and passed the normal Monday morning workers and timeshares. He mumbled a good morning or two before slipping into the office and shutting the door behind. An accent lamp sat atop a cabinet in the corner, giving the room a deep shadowed appearance. His heart was in his throat when he picked up the phone and he had to swallow twice to get his voice back. "Hello? Kally?"

"Hi, Slade." Her voice was softer than the light of dawn coming through the window, and somehow sad. "How are things at the Fourth Moon? God knows I miss the ranch."

"Things are always busy here, with the feeding, the preparations for the cattle drive, and..." *Stop blathering.* "Things are lonely here without you."

"How can you be lonely with all the timeshares? I bet Rosie hasn't let a day go by without mothering you."

"You're right. Everyday, there's Rosie, trying to nag me into being happy. Okay, enough about the ranch and me. How are you?" *I miss you. I want you home, here with me.*

She was quiet a moment longer than was comfortable for him, but the entire conversation was stiff and awkward to this point. "I've been better. Sleep doesn't come very easy on Ilene's sofa, and her dog Tinker has taken a special liking to sticking her tail in my face to wipe away any rapid eye movement she senses." She paused, heaved a heavy sigh and then sipped something Slade was certain was strong coffee. "I've tried to fit in here, tried the whole girly thing. Ilene's friend even offered me a job in her salon." He heard the shaky breath she drew in. "I'm just not meant for this. I miss you. I miss the ranch."

"Then come home, girl. Whatever problems I've caused, we can deal with here."

"I'm thinking about it, Slade. I really am. The reason I left bothers me less than being away from you."

He wanted to reach out and hold her, bathe her in kisses, make her understand why he had done what he did. It was impossible with her so far away. "Kally, girl, come on, let's work this out together."

"Please just don't rush me. I'm not sure if I'm ready yet. I need this to be by my choice. I left and want to come home because it's what I need to do. If that makes any sense..." She sipped her coffee again. "God, I'm tired, I feel like I'm rambling and I'm scared."

"Scared? What's scaring you? Do you need me to come there?"

"No, no. Stay there. Steve is calling an attorney today anyway. What's done is done and it happened far away."

"Kally, what's going on? You're talking in puzzles."

"Ilene's mother still lives in Michigan, and she called here Saturday morning. She said she was harassed by a private investigator about Ilene's friendship with me. He put a copy of our high school yearbook on the table, so there was no denying we were in school together, but she didn't say anything more. And he made allusions about his client being impatient and forceful. There's only one person who would dig into my past and fits the description."

"Stransberg."

"Yes, he's on my trail and will soon figure out I'm with Ilene."

Slade didn't know what to say. If Kally was at the ranch, he'd do anything to protect her. She was vulnerable with the Rogers. He drew in a deep breath. "Kally, I don't want to push. I really think you should consider coming back to the ranch. No one in Michigan but your sister knows you're out here. I don't want anything to happen to you after all you've been through."

"Me either." She sighed. "Look, Slade. I'm going to get off the phone now. I need some time to think."

"All right." He hated hanging up the phone, but she left him with few alternatives. "Call me if anything happens, okay?"

"You will be the first. Goodbye, Slade."

"Bye, Kally."

He hung up the phone and lost his appetite for breakfast. The woman he loved was in danger and wouldn't allow him to help, to protect her. The office door shut loudly behind him on his way to examine the guns his father had hidden in strategic locations on the first floor. He checked the barrels, triggers, magazines. It was better to have the firearms and not need them than to need them and not have them.

Rosie caught up with him at the front door. Her eyes were wide with concern. "Is everything okay?"

"Not really, Rosie. Kally's trouble is sniffing out her trail, and she won't come home."

"Well, boy, if you need us, you just ring your mother's bell. Every rancher around will be here to protect you and her."

"She isn't here."

"Not yet. And when she arrives you love her with everything you have."

"Yes, ma'am, I promise."

Rosie patted him on the shoulder and headed off to the mailbox on the main road while Slade bundled up and headed out to care for the animals of the Fourth Moon.

Kally's call had thrown his normal Monday routine a

serious curve, and though he completed his daily tasks, Slade's mind was on Kally the entire time. He fed and curried the horses with Kally's bloody, muddy broken doll face in his mind. He knew some of those injuries hadn't been from her car accident. He thought of her vulnerable side, the one she had shown only to him and Ilene, while George assisted him with feeding and watering the cattle. He contemplated what possible move they could make to stop an investigation of public records while he drove back from the cattle pen. And when he collapsed in front of the Christmas tree and stared into the dance of the flames in the fireplace, he dreamt of bringing her home and never letting her go again.

Chapter Nineteen

The attorney Steve contacted offered us little, considering the Michigan P.I. had had the entire weekend to do his dirty work. He ended his consultation by recommending Steve contact local law enforcement, explain the matter and ask for stepped up patrols in their area. It was cold comfort in comparison to a hot fire in the Fourth Moon's hearth and Slade's arms around me.

After speaking with Slade, I knew he was waiting for me to come back home, wanting to work things out. I'd melted when he said, "Come home, girl. Whatever problems I've caused we can deal with here."

Were those his true feelings, or was he saying what he thought I had wanted to hear? I had dealt with the same behavior already in my life. There was bound to be anger in him somewhere. I'd learned from experience anger led elsewhere. In Matt, anger had led to violence against me, and I'd dealt with too much pain born of anger for one lifetime. Heart and mind conflicted, I twined my fingers in the fringe of a blanket, my foot on the windowsill to hold the curtains back and give me an unobstructed view of the skyline. Tinker's high-pitched bark jarred me from my musing. "What's up, fuzzball?"

Of course the Pom didn't answer. She put her front feet on my knee and bounced up and down like a toddler wanting to be picked up. I scooped her into my arms and deposited her on my lap. After a few circular paths, she settled down. The Pomeranian was small, nearly cat-like in size, but the fur, muzzle and big round eyes were far from feline. Still I stroked her back, thankful for a bit of quiet companionship.

Ilene emerged from the kitchen where I'd heard her

repeatedly cussing the roast. The yellow checked apron was a comical effect. She looked domesticated, such a mini-Sue, but her quizzical expression made me giggle. "Oh, hun, are you okay? You're petting the dog for God's sake."

"Desperate times call for desperate measures." I forced a smile. "Speaking of desperate, how are things going in there?"

She waved an oven mitt at a plume of gray smoke. "Umm...how do you feel about pizza?"

"Again?"

The fire alarm screeched. We both laughed, and then Ilene dialed Steve at work and asked him to pick up a pizza on his way home. She took the charred remains of the beef roast from the oven and set it out in the garage where the smoking carcass wouldn't set off the fire alarms again. Taking off her apron, she left the scene of the crime and settled on the sofa. "Okay, Kally, I think it's time to shit or get off the pot. Either you love the guy and you go back to him and make it work, or you can't get past the problem and make a go of it without him."

"Well, so much for broaching the subject gently." I knew it was time to make a decision. I just didn't want it to be the wrong one.

"It's time for straight talk." Ilene crossed her arms, an "I'm dead serious" expression on her face. "You can't hang in limbo forever. It's not good for you or him."

I sighed, my gaze falling to the small peachy dog on my lap. "I know."

"You know what?"

I didn't answer. I petted the dog instead while the storm I'd been avoiding raged within. Go back, or stay and lose the man I loved more than any other.

"Kally, look at me." I dragged my gaze back to hers. Inside, I stood on the edge of a great precipice—stay alone, or surrender to love? "Kally Jensen! What do you know?"

She cornered me, and with no place to hide in a house not my home, the truth came pouring out. "I know I love him. I know I can't stand being away from him. What I don't know is if he still loves me."

She shook her head. "Honey, a man like Slade isn't going to give his heart away and then ask for it back when things get rocky."

I didn't reply. Tears burned my eyes, and the only things

holding my bottom lip in place were my top teeth. Turning the armchair, I looked at Ilene and fought sobs. "Come on, honey, I'll help you pack." She stood and held out her hand. "After you've had a good cry, you can go and call him."

Together, we dragged my bags from the living room closet and packed everything, leaving out what I would need over the next day or two. No matter how my heart pounded or my body yearned to be in Slade's arms, I wasn't going to ask Ilene to drive me back to Hulett in the middle of the night. A few changes of clothes and a toiletry bag sat atop of the rest of the luggage, which we shoved into the corner underneath the computer desk.

Steve had arrived with two pizzas stacked precariously in one hand when we returned to the kitchen. Over dinner we discussed my talk with Slade, the decision Ilene helped me to make and then we talked over how to get me home to Hulett. Steve had the best solution. "Take the spare Jeep. It's under the tarp in the garage. It runs fine, Ilene just wanted a newer model."

"I don't have a Wyoming license."

"No." He winked. "But you do have a Michigan one. Do you think all the tourists and migrant workers have Wyoming licenses? No. And they drive all over this state."

"But what about insurance and the rest?"

"We're loaning it to you. You'll be covered under our insurance."

"You're not going to take 'but what' for an answer, are you?"

"Nope." Steve drained his glass. "Sounds way too negative. If this day is about decisiveness a 'what if' answer just screws it all up."

"Okay, okay. You win."

"Great," Ilene chimed in. "You can call Slade after dinner."

"I guess I have to, don't I?"

The remainder of the meal was spent in chitchat and Steve telling me the in's and out's of the Jeep I'd be driving home. By the last slice of pizza I knew everything there was to know about the Jeep, save how many times someone had farted in it. Even though he hadn't said it, I couldn't get the image out of my head of sitting in the driver's seat and having a weird funk floating in the air. A shudder ran down my spine, and I grabbed a blanket when I took the phone over to my favorite chair by the window.

Dialing the phone with Tinker on my lap and rooting in the blanket was a feat in itself. I held the phone with one hand, petted the dog with the other while I waited through the first two rings. Slade answered on the third ring. "Kally? Is everything okay?"

"It will be soon, if you still want me to come home. I've been doing a lot of thinking, Slade, and I think you're right. We can work through anything...together."

"Don't be silly." His voice sounded brighter than it had since running into Red Baxter in the Trading Post. "Of course I want you to come home. What time do you want me to pick you up?"

"I don't. I'm going to—"

"You don't want me to come? Is Ilene driving you then?"

"Calm down, cowboy. I am driving. I left you, and I am going to come back. This is something I have to do, Slade, a form of commitment, I guess."

His sigh was audible. "Commitments are good to make."

"Yes they are." Ilene peeked around the kitchen doorjamb, and I gave her the thumbs up sign. She whooped and threw her hands in the air. "So...I'll see you tomorrow then. I'm damn tired and want to get some sleep before driving on snowy roads again. I'll call you when I'm getting close, okay?"

"Sounds good, darlin'. G'night."

My heart pattered in a sweet, familiar rhythm. "Good night, Slade."

"Sweet dreams."

"They will be."

I disconnected the phone and nestled it in the blankets beside the Pom. Tinker and I sat looking out the window at the Christmas lights across the street for a long time. A sudden calm had settled in me the moment I had decided to go home. I enjoyed the sense of stillness and the snow falling softly outside the window. Steve and Ilene wished me a good night on their way up the stairs, and then I ducked into the half-bath to change into my pajamas before turning in for one last night on the scratchy sage green sofa.

Excitement and apprehension mixed in my stomach and chased away my appetite the next morning. I sipped a cup of Earl Grey tea and picked at a day-old apple fritter while we stowed my things in the back of the silver Jeep. Steve had left the garage door up when he left for work, a large and obvious indicator I should soon follow.

Ilene stood on the steps to the back door, a travel mug of fresh tea in one hand and the remains of my fritter wrapped in a napkin. "I kinda hate to see you go," she pouted. "I've really enjoyed having you here."

"I know." I stuffed the road food into the console of the Jeep. "I won't be far away. And I have to do this, Ilene. I love you, but I love Slade too."

"Then give me a hug and get your butt on the road."

"Yes, ma'am."

We both cried. Tinker barked, demanding to go outside. Ilene sighed and then giggled. "Duty calls."

"Yeah, take care of my dog."

She rolled her eyes and ushered me into the Jeep. "Get out of here, Kally. Go and love him."

"I will." I closed the door and waved farewell through the window.

The Jeep purred, rolling down the miles between Gillette and Moorcroft, where Steve's map instructed me to turn north. The buildings were decorated for Christmas, and I found myself looking forward to the holiday for the first time in weeks. Christmas at the ranch, hopefully in Slade's arms like it was before I left. I could picture the fireplace, the flames dancing, the soft cushions of the sofa. I could almost smell the clean scent of pine coming from the large Christmas tree.

A nervous sense of anticipation and fear danced on my nerves when I turned further north from Route 14 onto Route 24. *How will he react when I drive in?* "Time to find out," I said.

I pulled my cell phone out and pushed the speed dial number for the Fourth Moon. The first ring didn't even finish before Slade answered. "Kally?"

"Yup, it's me." I peered through the snowfall. "I'll be turning into the back drive any minute."

"Great! I'm hanging up then."

I couldn't respond. He had disconnected the call.

The Fourth Moon was more beautiful than when I had left. Christmas cookie pine trees drooped under the weight of thick layers of snow and weak sunlight lit the open spaces a shimmering white. The Jeep rounded the corner and coasted down the hill toward the ranchers' drive, where the warm earthy scent of wood smoke crept into the interior of the Jeep. I inhaled deep greedy breaths. *I'm home.*

Every occupied timeshare house was decorated with pine boughs, red bows and tiny white lights. Even the dream catcher in George and Rosie's window had a string of mini lights wound around it. I looked up the drive, and the main house captured my attention. The roofline sparkled with lights, pine garland festooned the wrap around porch. The breaks of the Jeep squeaked when I pulled to a stop before the ranch house.

I sat behind the steering wheel of the Jeep while it idled in the driveway. My legs were rubbery and my heart slammed. I yearned to run into Slade's arms, soak up all the cowboy goodness I could before he held me away from him and read me the riot act for not understanding, for leaving him. *Just go in and apologize. Say you were wrong. Beg him to take you back.*

Easier thought than done.

Pulling the keys from the ignition, I steeled myself for the coming emotional storm. Ruby firelight flickered through the living room windows and a familiar form paced in the foyer. Slade paused at the doorway and I pictured him there, holding the brass doorknob, debating on whether or not to welcome me. God, I wanted him to wrap me in his arms, ached to be held and cared for by him.

Cold, clean air, scented with fresh cut pine and wood smoke whipped into the Jeep after I opened the door. My nerves tangled inside, twisted in a sick sense of nausea, but the moment I put my feet on the ground, I knew I was home. I needed to convince Slade.

Any doubt about my reception disappeared when Slade threw open the door and rushed to my side, his boots skating the last couple of inches. Tears welled up, blinding me. I raised a hand to wipe them away. Slade caught my hand and pulled me to his chest. The warm scent of Stetson enveloped me. I drowned in it, drowned in his embrace. If the world stopped on its axis, I would be content to freeze in his arms. The flannel of his shirt wicked away my tears. "Slade, I am so—"

His arms circled tighter. "Hush now." He stroked my hair. "I know."

Enormous pressure burned in my chest. I had to speak, to apologize. "But I was wrong to get so upset, you—"

"*I*," he stressed the word, "am just damned happy you're home. You are in my arms, and nothing else matters. Leave the past where it belongs."

Slade scooped my legs into his arms and shut the Jeep's door with a bump of his butt. He cradled me to his chest, sheltering me from the wind, from the emptiness I had felt without him. On the front porch, he set me down only long enough to open the door, usher me in and then lock it behind us. He never locked the door, unless he was leaving the ranch. "What're you doing?"

The blue of his irises was an ethereal shade when the morning light caressed his face. His expression said everything. Inside I melted, only my skeleton kept me upright, and the bones pulsed with my speeding heart. Never had one man's gaze so completely silenced me and excited me at the same time.

My boots fell haphazard on the boot tray when he peeled them and my jacket from me. I opened my mouth to speak, but he buried his lips against mine in a desperate passionate kiss. Slade's arms were around me, his hands searching, touching as he reacquainted himself with my curves. The needs I had suppressed in the name of hesitancy dissolved in his embrace. I wanted him to hold me, to never release me again.

Entwined, we collided with the sofa. Pillows and cushions spilled onto the floor. Slade swept them aside and off the rug before the fireplace.

He pulled away, leaving an aching distance and sudden craving for his warmth. He stroked my cheek with his thumb, his gaze piercing my heart, my soul. "Let me make love to you, Kally."

Never had any words sounded so tender, so seductive and vulnerable. I nodded. "I've never wanted anything more."

Slade pulled off his shirt, exposing his ranch-built muscles and luscious tanned skin to my fingers before he guided my body down to the carpet. Drowning in my desires for him, I clung to his chest like a life preserver. His heartbeat was mine, my breath was his breath, given to me through a deep lip-tingling kiss.

Bracing his weight on his knees, he straddled my hips and unbuttoned my blouse. The fabric fell away, leaving my body and breasts exposed to the firelight and his touch. Shivers of delight climbed my spine and tightened my scalp. Then, he arched over me, pressing those rippled abs to me and cloaking my nipple in the hot wet velvet of his tongue.

Eager for more of the pleasure he gave, I curled my fingers in his wavy dark hair and guided his lips to the tip of my other breast. His tongue danced on the tingling nipple. Warm delight rushed from his mouth to flood me. I groaned, released my grip on his hair. Arching my back, I reached for his wide belt buckle, which I unlatched and pulled from his jeans. The leather strap whispered in the half-light, snaking through the path of belt loops and onto the floor. I wrapped my fingers around the edges of his fly and worked loose the first button before he held my hands and pressed me to the floor.

He pulled my jeans from me, the murmur of the zipper mingled with the crackling tones of the fire. Moans rose from me and above the ambient noise when he followed the waistband of my jeans with his tongue. Slade's leg slid along mine, a delicious sensation of denim on bare skin. I lay beneath him, reduced to twitching, desire crashing through me, until he hooked his foot between my ankles and eased my legs apart. Then, excitement fueled my desires.

He settled his chiseled chest between my knees and a shudder of anticipation rose through me. Light kisses blanketed my stomach, stopping at the edge of my panties. His fingers traced the lines of the fabric barrier, sending shivers up my spine and tightening my nipples.

His hot breath penetrated the cotton of my panties, and then he pressed his tongue against the material and slipped a finger beneath them. My heart pumped love and lust through me. I loved him, loved his touch and I lusted for more, more fingers, more tongue—less fabric between us. I wriggled my arms down, hooking my fingers in the waistband of the cotton chastity belt, but Slade smacked my hands. He gave me a warning glance, insisted on teasing me, prolonging and heightening my desires.

I twined my fingers in the rug's braided fringe. Slade touched the folds of my sexual core, and I lost my grip. My eyelids closed, my fingers clutched open air. Breath came in shallow and fast but exhaled in a groan. His fingers rhythmically slid in deeper and then out, while his tongue rubbed my clitoris through the thin cotton barrier.

Only one word passed my lips. "In...in..."

His fingers, his tongue, the hard rod I felt pressing and pulsing against my leg. I wanted it all.

Slade answered my desire, hooking his fingers over the edge of my panties and finally pulling them away. There was no embarrassment, no inclination to hide, I was exposed beneath Slade and loving it. I relaxed and he pushed my knees farther apart. Settling on his stomach, he kissed the edges of my crease before easing his tongue inside. Hot bliss throbbed through me, pushed in by his tongue. I whimpered for more while he stretched with one arm and grabbed his jeans.

His gorgeous blue eyes coursed over me. Slade reared up to his knees, deftly switching tongue for fingers to tease my tingling flesh. With his free hand he produced a condom from a pocket of his wallet. He pinched the corner of the wrapper between his teeth and ripped it open before bringing his hot mouth back to my slick opening.

I'd hardly caught my breath before his tongue returned, dancing on—in—around my sensitive points while he put the condom on. He pinned me with a searing gaze, my heart slammed against my ribs and then he curled over me taking a nipple in his mouth. Shivers of delight covered me. On his knees, lips pulling pleasurably on my nipple, he rubbed his rounded tip against my crease. Slipping past the sensitive edges he asked, "Did you say, 'in'?"

I wanted nothing more. Gazes locked, I nodded. "Yes. In..."

Slade obliged, driving pleasure deep into me and my mind into a carnal haze.

"Ohh." My chest heaved with panting breaths. "Again..."

Another plunge, deeper, and this time, Slade groaned too. He adopted an up-and-in slide, kissing me each time before he rode back out. Joined in body, bound in spirit, our hands wound tight together at our sides. He'd stolen my heart and now he took my breath away with his passion. The rhythm increased. He stiffened within then pulled nearly out.

Lifting my hips from the floor and twisting while I rose, I pressed against his pelvis and took him in. His pulse thumped against my walls. Slade exhaled a heavy breath, gaze on mine. He panted, "Do it again."

Repeating the motion, I watched his eyes pinch close and his face twitch. A fifth time seemed all he could handle. Slade pushed me back to the floor. Surrendering to the urges driving us both, he rocked until his rhythm had me whimpering and writhing beneath and against him.

Sweat bloomed on his skin, intensifying his cologne. Air raced through my nose in deep, greedy huffs. I abandoned our tangled handhold, grabbing his shoulders and rising to meet him, before I pushed him over onto his back. Slick and ready, I eased down his shaft. Slade sighed, his fingers convulsed on my hips. His obvious pleasure fueled my desire to satisfy his craving for release. I rode him until he came and I cried out in orgasm too.

He pulled me to his chest and wrapped me in a tight embrace. I closed my eyes, drank in the intimate moment, a libation for my heart and soul. The words, "I love you" begged to fall from my lips, but I wanted to hear them from Slade first. He kissed my cheek and then lifted my face and looked into my eyes. "Kally, please don't leave me again."

"I won't. I promise."

I eased off of Slade. In one fluid motion he rose and scooped me into his arms and then, naked, he carried me up the stairs and to the bath. I sat perched on the edge of the cold porcelain, chills creeping up my spine while a deeper, primal emotion filled me. The air was too much, and too thin. My heart raced and slowed to a lifetime between beats. The water thundered in my ears and the herbs swathed my sinuses. All I could see was Slade, my cowboy—my love.

Laughter and tears mixed. I pulled Slade to me, kissing him with every bit of love and passion I felt for him. We melded together, a perfect fit. He twined his fingers in my hair, pulling my head back to kiss my throat. Resting his forehead on my cheek, I felt a tear wet my skin and I wasn't sure if it was my own. I drowned within his sky blue gaze. "I know just how you feel."

With one last kiss, he eased me into the fragrant water by my shoulders. "You soak and warm up, and I'll get your things from the Jeep."

I raised an eyebrow. "Not naked you won't."

"Of course not. I'd be the poor sap to get caught locked out in the nude." He smiled his sweet, heart-melting grin and we both laughed. He dashed out the door, giving me a perfect opportunity to admire the exquisite sculpted nature of his butt.

He was so good for me. With Slade I knew I was loved, even if he hadn't said those words. He gave me confidence, comfort and a true sense of emotional intimacy. Things I never knew I needed until he shared them with me. I sighed, sank beneath the herbal-scented waters and listened when his bedroom door opened and then his feet thumped down the hall. Surfacing, I rested my head against the tub before using my favorite lavender sage body wash.

I had no more wished for Slade to wash my hair like he did the first night than he knocked on the door. The brass knob turned, and the panel swung in, followed by Slade in loose button-fly jeans, a pair of pajamas in hand and a sheepish blush on his face. "I hope you don't mind me getting these from your bag..."

How could I mind? We just made love. Why would it possibly bother me if he got in my bag? "Of course I don't mind, silly." I batted my eyelashes, a coquettish tilt to my gaze. I looked from him to the bottle, to the strands of damp blonde hair on my shoulders. "Would you mind?"

"Only if you told me not to." He winked and my heart fluttered and pulse sped. Placing my pajamas by a heater vent, Slade emptied the pitcher of its contents and knelt on a folded towel. His hands traced my arms into the water. He soaked a washcloth in the herbal waters and then folded the washcloth and placed it over my eyes. "Relax, darlin', and let me take care of you."

Leaning back against the porcelain, I surrendered to his touch, reveling in the intimacy we shared. The herbal scent soothed me. His hands gave comfort and took sadness. A warm sense of bliss bubbled up in me, flooding out into and weighting down my limbs. His face was beside mine, the Stetson cologne mingling with the steamy lavender and sage. The warmth turned to sleepiness while his hands worked down my shoulders, my arms, and moving back up, slipping in the lather to my neck and scalp in a physical lullaby. "*Mmm*," I purred. "I could fall asleep right here..."

"Please don't. It's only lunchtime, and I want you to sleep in my arms tonight."

"Then you best get me out of this tub."

"As you wish." His hands left me, and then he submerged the pitcher, filling it to rinse the lather from my hair and body. After the last pitcherfull ran from my skin, he gave me a loving, emotional kiss.

Replacing the pitcher, Slade pulled the drain stopper and handed me a towel. I stood and wrapped it around me, while he dried my arms and legs with another. Then, he wrapped me in the towel, grabbed my pajamas and brought me to my room. Tossing the towels in a wicker hamper, I pulled on the nightclothes Slade had set out for me. He returned from his room moments later wearing flannel pants and T-shirt. I ran a finger along the lines of blue and white on the quilt, happy to be home, wishing I could climb back into my bed. "We can't get under the blankets if you keep fondling them."

"But I thought you said it was lunchtime..."

His grin was enormous. "I didn't say we couldn't spend the day in bed." Slade disappeared into the hallway and then produced a tray of sandwiches and fruit. "I had these ready when you drove in. Thought we could eat them while we sat in bed and got caught up on the past couple weeks."

We nibbled and talked. Slade relayed the story of Rosie and the feather boa, and I laughed aloud. I told him about the war between me and the Poms, and he snorted. My blind date, his dance with Adelle was discussed, and any other awkward feelings were put to rest. After the sun had settled and the moonlight poured through the window, I snuggled down against Slade and yawned.

"Need to sleep, don't you?"

"Yup. Can you fix that for me?"

His smile was tender, and his eyes were tired. I yawned again. The distance I forced between us had strained us both. "I sure can." He lifted the blankets and scooted under, holding them up for me to slide beneath his arm and snuggle to his chest. Warm bliss enveloped me when his arm settled down and pulled me closer. I felt his every inhale and exhale against my back. His heartbeat drummed against my skin, slowing with his breathing until sleep took him and then me into the sweetness of dreams.

Chapter Twenty

Nothing was better than waking next to Slade. I lay there a long time in the dark before dawn and listened to his slow, steady breathing. Twitches in his limbs increased. The pace of his breathing quickened before he yawned and stretched beside me. "G'morning, darlin'."

"Good morning." I rolled and greeted him with a kiss.

He groaned and hugged me, pulling my head down to his shoulder. "I missed you. So bad."

"I missed you, too, Slade." I wanted to wallow in his closeness, bury my face and smell his warm skin and faded cologne. "Can we just stay here all day?"

"No, ma'am. We did that yesterday. Work calls. We got critters to feed, plans to make..." He arched up and straddled my hips, pinning me beneath him.

"Oh, dang it." I smacked a hand to my forehead. "I still have to mail Sue's package too."

"Okay, then, sounds like our day is planned." Slade climbed from the bed, grabbed a hand and pulled me up. "Let's get a move on."

In no time we were dressed, and Slade was putting boots on in the foyer. The cat food bag I had missed in our impassioned reconciliation was obvious now, especially when he shoved the bowl down into the kibble to fill it. "Y'know, your cat might appreciate seeing you..."

"I'd like to see him too." I shoved my feet in my boots, grabbed my jacket and we stepped out into the frigid December dawn. Sunrise softened the shadows in the east and washed the outbuildings in weak light. Even in pale light, I noticed the hard packed path around the carpentry shed. Slade however ushered me out to the barn without giving me a chance to ask about it.

He pulled the doors open and whistled to the horses. Jack whinnied, and Sunny swished her tail while Slade lit a battery-powered lamp for us to see. He pointed toward the rafters. "He's usually up there."

Taking the bowl of food, I shook it and chanted, "Here, kitty, kitty."

The yellow eyes peeked over a rafter, and then the rest of my ginger kitty appeared. He looked at me a moment, sniffed the air suspiciously before leaping from the rafter to the divider over the stall, to the bales of hay and then landed on the floor. I stooped down, bowl held out. His steps were cautious, deliberate until he reached the bowl. Placing the bowl on the floor, I scooted closer while Slade readied the horses' food, and when he entered Jack's stall, I petted the tomcat's head. "You're my boy, aren't you?"

Slade snickered. "He's been your cat since you came to the ranch."

After the kitty finished his breakfast, Slade walked me back to the house, where Rosie stood waiting beside the Jeep. My heart soared, and I let go of Slade's hand to run and hug my dear friend. She squeezed me, before she pushed me back and gave me a stern look. "No call? No note?"

My gaze fell to my feet, and I shoved my toe against the tire. "Sorry, Rosie."

Her bright smile returned. "Just don't ever let it happen again."

"No, ma'am, I won't."

Slade stomped his boots to get our attention. "Are you ladies going to be all right?"

Rosie lifted the tailgate of the Jeep and we each grabbed a box. "We'll be just fine."

"Then I'll leave you to it and get the chores finished."

"We'll have coffee and breakfast ready."

Rosie bumped me with the box. "Just one of the reasons he missed you."

I watched him walking toward his truck, where George stood waiting for him. Slade was gorgeous, and he was mine. "Just one of the reasons I missed him too."

Together Rosie and I emptied the Jeep and stowed the

luggage and boxes where they belonged, except the Christmas package for Susan's family. She nudged the box and regarded me. "I'm going into town later. They all know us at the P.O., and are very helpful with filling out labels and such. I can drop it there for you."

"I would really appreciate it, Rosie. Thank you so much."

In the kitchen we made a batch of breakfast mess and a pot of coffee while Rosie explained the Christmas traditions of the ranch. The timeshare ranchers gathered on Christmas Eve, and one of the male Carlsons would drive the sleigh around the Fourth Moon while the passengers sang Christmas carols and drank hot cocoa spiked with Pine's homemade Irish whiskey. Then, everyone gathered before the fire, sharing Christmas tales and good company. And, on Christmas morning, they would return to exchange gifts.

"Oh, Rosie, it sounds wonderful." I could have teared up just thinking about the loving closeness they shared. "I can't wait."

She covered my hand. "Me either."

Slade returned in time to eat breakfast with us, and before Rosie left, I hurried into the office, stuffed the remainder of Sue's money into an envelope along with a short letter of thanks and fond Christmas wishes. In my highest hopes, I wished Sue and Jerry would use the money to come to the Fourth Moon for the holidays. I scribbled their mailing address on it and handed it to Rosie, who shouted a farewell to Slade, kissed me on the cheek and disappeared out the front door.

In the office, I picked up the phone and dropped into Slade's mother's chair. My lover, my cowboy hero, peeked in the door and mouthed "Calling Sue?" My nod was enough to shush him and send him off to poke around in the fireplace. The metal of the rod clanked against the grate and soon the scent and crackle of pine drifted through the house. Dialing Sue's number, I inhaled the scent deeply.

Sue answered before the second ring. "Hello? Kally?"

"Yeah, Sue. I'm home now."

"And you were supposed to call me when you got there." Her tone carried her frustration from Michigan to Hulett with no lessening of intensity.

I sighed. "When I got back, well... We ended up..."

Her irritated tone disappeared, chased away by knowing

laughter. "Ah ha. So, your, ahem, reconciliation was pretty passionate?"

Whew! I was in my twenties. Why was I so apprehensive to talk to my sister about sex? "Um...yeah. But I didn't call to talk to a sexual therapist. There's a package on the way, a bunch of Christmas presents for the boys, and I also stuffed the rest of your money into a security envelope."

"Oh, Kally! You know you're not supposed to mail real money...you should have just kept it."

"Well, Sue, I don't have a checking account yet, and I haven't been home long enough to talk to Slade about it. It was a bit impulsive."

"I'd say."

"Okay, listen, if this is going to be a nag fest, I am going to hang up. I have lots to do to get ready for Christmas around here."

"Sorry, but you have to admit it wasn't the smartest move."

"No, it wasn't." I'd had enough of her nattering. "You want to know why I sent it? I was harboring a secret hope there'd be enough money for you and the family to come out here for a visit."

"Oh, honey..." She sniffed and I could picture her wiping her nose. "I'm sorry. We'd like to visit, we just can't with Jerry's work right now..."

This discussion had not gone as intended and I didn't want to deal with more heartache. "Well, look for the package and the envelope, call me when you get it, okay? I'm going to go now."

"I will, Kally. Try to have a good day."

"Bye, Sue."

The next week's morning meals were my domain, cooking while Slade and the timeshares cared for the morning chores. Our afternoons were spent shopping for gifts and generally letting all of upper east Wyoming know Slade and I were back together and any lies Adelle had spread were nothing more. And in the evenings, I wandered down the timeshares' drive to Rosie's or Grace's and learned handcrafts from them while I made a couple of Christmas presents.

Though we did not make love again, our love for each other grew with every glance, every touch, every embrace. My heart swelled until I felt my ribs could not contain it.

Slade and the timeshare gentlemen readied the sleigh, cared for the animals and prepared the home field cattle pen for the upcoming cattle drive. A few days before Christmas Eve, Red Baxter arrived to help drive the cattle from the back eighty to the more sheltered main pen. After the drive, the ladies had a massive meal ready of venison chili, beef stew, a pot of chicken soup Sue had taught me to make and loaves of homemade bread. At the table, Red apologized for his part in our temporary split.

It had potential for being a very awkward moment for us all. Slade swallowed a too-big spoon of chili, his eyes wide. I patted Slade's hand. "It's okay, Red. I would have found out and been upset either way. You didn't do anything wrong with following up on a friend's request. I know now he only asked out of love and concern for me."

Slade sighed in relief, pulled me to him by the collar of my shirt. He kissed me deeply enough for me to get a sense of the amount of Tabasco he'd used. "I didn't mean harm...I just—"

"You just need to eat your supper." I willed my understanding to reach him, to sink into his heart so he would know I had come to understand why he'd followed up on Matt's background. "Next time, just make sure you tell me what you're plotting on."

"Yes, ma'am."

After dishes were cleared, recipe books came out accompanied by bottles of beer and wine coolers. We'd decided to do something a little different for Christmas Eve at the ranch. Each family was going to find one dessert item and one party style finger food. It was going to be a fun night, not some fussed up affair and I looked forward to it.

Slade woke early Christmas Eve morning with Kally snuggled to his chest and softly snoring. He fought the desire to crush her to him in the gratefulness he felt knowing she loved him. Instead, he lay a moment longer, listening to her breathe before the urge to move became too strong to be denied. She mumbled something when he scrambled over her, then curled into the warm hollow he'd left behind.

Tucking the blankets around her, he caressed the silken strands of her blonde hair before scooting off to the bathroom.

The cold tile chased away any remaining tired tendencies, and after using the facilities he checked in on Kally. Her back was to the room, her breathing was rhythmic and regular. *Good, she's still sleeping.*

He tiptoed through the room and down the hall to his own room, where he quietly opened the door and snuck in. With a last check of the hallway, he closed the door behind him. In the corner beside his dresser stood rolls of plain brown wrapping paper—a family tradition—and assorted tapes, ribbons and twine.

Gathering up the wrapping necessities and a bag from his closet, Slade sat on his bed and wrapped the box his mother sent to him at Thanksgiving time. He pulled a decorative ornament he'd chosen for Kally while she was in Gillette and affixed it to the package, adding a tag with Kally's name.

He stowed the wrapping paper back in the corner and tucked the package under his shirt. After a second quick scan of the hall, he hurried past Kally's door and down the chilly staircase to the living room. He stepped on the light switch power cord and turned the tree lights on. It was a beautiful tree, the prettiest in years, but in Slade's mind, it was missing something. Slade had chosen the perfect spot to hide the ring box the day they decorated the tree, and he nestled the package in the pine boughs. The tree was complete, and Slade turned from it to stoke the fire.

Hurrying through the house, he lit all the lights and candles, even turned on a potpourri warmer of Christmas pine and berries. He wanted the next two days to be magical for Kally, days neither of them would forget, and he'd seen a magazine article or two about setting the scene to create a mood. He wasn't sure what it entailed until now—now he wanted everything to be perfect.

Ready to head up the stairs, he saw Kally standing at her favorite window on the stairwell, looking out into the snowfall. "G'morning, Kally. Did you sleep well?"

"I've never slept better in my life." She turned to him, and he wished he could get a snapshot of her wild hair, rumpled pajamas and tie-dyed bull in her arms. "These last few days with your arms around me have been pure heaven."

"For me too, darlin'." He nodded toward the stuffed animal. "What's up with the bull?"

She smiled sheepishly. "Well, I thought he might be nice to snuggle with on the sofa while you're out doing chores." A shadow of cracked porcelain passed over her face. Not the wounded kind, more a veil of sadness only he could see.

"Is everything okay? I don't want you to be sad today, Kally."

"Oh, I'm not sad...just missing the boys a little today. Before I met Matt, I spent Christmas Eve and Day with Sue and her family."

"Well then you go scoot your booty into the office and call them. Never mind getting breakfast, we can do it together when I get in."

"Are you sure?"

He knew she genuinely enjoyed cooking for him, but family was more important than his belly getting full. "Of course I am." He pointed to the office. "Now scoot!"

The melancholy shadow disappeared, replaced with a grin. "Yes, sir."

Kally reached up to kiss him, and he felt the sweetest sensation of becoming one with her, of losing himself in her arms, her lips, her heart. Heaven truly could be found in a kiss. She pulled away, her slim fingers following the lines of his jaw. He echoed her motion, savoring every curve, every nuance of flesh and flannel. Then he smacked her rear. "Get over there and call your nephews."

She saluted him, her hand swinging wide to return the playful spank. "Getting right on it."

She disappeared into the office, and it didn't take long for him to hear laughter and, "I'm glad you like it!" He smiled and then hurried to get dressed knowing George was probably waiting on him at the barn. At least with the cattle penned on the main ranch instead of a satellite pen the work would go much faster.

As expected, George was waiting, arms crossed, foot tapping and truck bed full of grain and hay. "Getting wrapped up in your girl are ya?"

Slade's gaze plummeted to the snow beneath his boots. Being chided by George was similar to a tongue-lashing from Pine and Slade braced for a reprimand. "Yes, sir."

George laughed then. "Good thing, damn good thing!" He walked to the barn with Slade to care for the horses. "My apologies, boy. I promised Pine I'd keep you in line."

"You and Rosie are doing a fine job of parenting, George." He stowed the curry brush and replaced the buckets. "I really appreciate it."

"Heck! We're honored to try to fill your folks' shoes." They climbed into the truck. "How are they doing on their business trip anyway?"

"Last time I spoke with them, it looked like financing was going to be secured for the expansion Beau's been pushing. And according to Mother, my brother has been causing quite the stir with the East coast ladies."

George snorted. "Certainly doesn't surprise me. He could charm a snake outta its oil."

"So I've heard." Slade had had to clean up a mess or two caused by Beau's dalliances and didn't appreciate his brother's mythic Ladies Man reputation.

George took a turn at driving the Dodge while Slade took up the post of pitching hay and pouring grain. He kept his eye on the livestock, ever mindful of Zeus, who'd been more than his fair share of cantankerous lately. He thumped his hand on the roof of the truck and George pulled to a stop and opened the door. "I think we should corral Zeus into the bull pen."

"I agree."

It took more than muddy boots and gentle persuasion to separate the bull from the herd, but he managed with George's help. The two men slammed the gate shut, then Slade tipped his hat to Zeus. "You are still the stud."

Two showers and a few hours later, the timeshares gathered before the Fourth Moon's main house. Grace clutched a huge thermos to her chest and Emma held a bottle of homemade Irish whiskey Slade knew his father had entrusted into her care. Rosie held two bags, one filled with cookies, and another appeared to be coordinating travel mugs.

Pride and love of his family's heritage swelled his chest when he hitched the horses to the sleigh and drove them to the front porch where his loved ones had gathered for one of his favorite holiday traditions. The sleigh bells chimed a high, joyful tune when his passengers clambered aboard. He wanted Kally by his side and extended a hand to pull her up onto the bench. Mugs inscribed with everyone's names were passed around, and then Rosie made certain to fill each with a healthy mix of cocoa and whiskey.

The snow squeaked beneath the runners, the horses' breath rose in plumes and his spirits soared. The yellow light of the lanterns mixed with the white moonlight, illuminating the pine branches and occasionally a pair of eyes or the paths they traveled. Kally settled a hand on his thigh and clutched her cocoa with the other mitten-covered hand. Simple carols were sung. Emma and Grace even did a tear-jerking round robin of "Oh Holy Night."

Ever mindful of the horses and the load they pulled, he kept the excursion brief, returning the carolers to the front door far before midnight. George remained in the rig to help him with currying the horses once the sleigh had been parked back in its place of honor. By the time they'd returned to the house, it danced with white lights and candle flames and happy laughter reached the foyer.

Slade took off his Stetson, hanging it on his antler peg, before settling into his favorite spot on the hearth. Kally left her spot beside Emma on the sofa and came to sit in front of him, with her shoulders nestled between his knees. Her sweet smell of jasmine and lavender mingled with the fire and the holiday goodies. He leaned closer, burying his face in her hair by her neck and took in a deep whiff before brushing aside the blonde strands to kiss her cheek.

Rosie stood in the middle of a loose circle of his family's dearest friends and a tingle of excitement climbed his spine. He nudged Kally and then whispered in her ear. "This is one of my favorite Christmas traditions."

Her hand slid down his calf to wrap his ankle in her fingers. "What is?"

"Shhh. Just watch and listen."

Kally snuggled deeper between his knees and he rested his arms on her shoulders, fingers playing with her hair. Rosie raised her hands, and in her Native American tongue blessed the gathering. Then, she reached into a pouch hidden beneath her sweater and cast dried powders on the flames behind him. A heady, pungent aroma soon filled the living room. "This is a gift Slade requested, an age old story to tell, one of many versions. This is the one passed on by my people."

"Many summers ago there were two brothers who lived in a village with their mother and father. They were good boys, but they sometimes wandered from the village. Their mother worried about this and warned them, 'Do not roam far from our village, for great Manitou will stalk and eat you, and I will die of a broken heart'.

"The boys were afraid of Great Manitou, for his fearsome claws and terrible teeth, so they listened to their mother and stayed close by.

"One day, while trying to catch a rabbit to eat, the boys wandered farther than they ever had from their home. They realized they did not know the country they were in and looked back towards their village. They could not see it. What they did see was Great Manitou stalking them. His fur was thick and shining like the sun. His teeth were long, like the roots of tree branches by the river. His claws were sharp like the arrows their father lashed to their bows. The boys were terrified and they began to run, but Great Manitou was fast. With his wide leaping runs he was almost upon them in no time. The youngest boy could see foam dripping from his mouth, for Great Manitou thought of the delicious treats the boys would make in his tummy.

"The oldest boy began to pant and falter. His brother tried to pull him along, but Great Manitou was coming closer and closer. The youngest boy turned his face to the sky and said, "Oh great Sky Father, protect us from mighty Manitou, so our mother's heart will not be broken."

"Sky Father heard the boys' cries and the ground beneath them began to grow and grow. It rose into the clouds. Higher it grew, until they were looking down at the earth below when Great Manitou reached the slippery slopes of the hill Sky Father created.

"Great Manitou jumped and leapt at the boys. He was not able to reach his lunch. He growled in frustration and anger, and began to claw at the sides of the hill. Each time he slipped back to the bottom, leaving deep marks in the wake of his claws.

"The boys watched in terror while Great Manitou clawed and pawed at the hill for two sunsets. Then, Great Manitou became exhausted from his efforts. He curled into a ball and fell asleep.

"Quietly, the boys climbed down the hill. On tiptoe, they passed the large sleeping bear. When they were safely past, they ran back to the village as fast as they could, right into the arms of their worried mother and they never wandered too far from the village again until they were braves.

"Great Manitou woke many sunrises later, angry his lunch was gone. He stalked off to find more foolish boys. Behind him, he left the great grooved hill. A reminder to all of his great strength."

The gathering was silent a moment out of respect, then erupted into applause. Kally trembled against Slade's legs, then reached back to pull him closer. "What an amazing story. I can see why you asked for it. I could almost see Great Manitou and feel the power Sky Father used to protect the boys."

He kissed her again. *She definitely belongs here with us.*

The rest of the evening was spent with people sharing their favorite holiday memories. Emma shared a story of the birth of a grandchild on Christmas Eve and the blessing the new life brought to their family. Grace recounted a tale of a Christmas program in their old church. Their husbands had more humorous tales about childhood memories, then Slade told the story of Grandpa Carlson's last sleigh ride. When it came to Kally, she smiled, wiped a tear away and said, "Right now. No holiday has ever been this special."

The clock chimed midnight and the gathering rose, giving hugs and good night wishes to everyone, before slipping in ones and twos out the front door to head home. Kally stood by Slade's side, her arm around the small of his back, waving to the ranchers, and when the last person left, she shut the door and yawned. "Wow. What a full, wonderful, magical day."

"Yes it was, and tomorrow will be special too."

"Promise?"

"Absolutely." He took her by the shoulders and guided her toward the stairs. "Now you get upstairs and get in bed. I'll be up in a minute."

"No, sir." She wriggled from his grasp and walked toward the back door. "I want to see if I can get Tom to come to the door."

"His name is Tom?"

"Of course. What other name could possibly fit?"

She stepped out onto the porch, chanting her normal "Here kitty, kitty" call. The cat appeared from underneath the porch steps and trotted right up to Kally. She patted his head and fed him a few scraps. Then when he rubbed against her knees, she scooped the cat into her arms. Slade half expected the cat to pitch a hissy fit. He didn't. When Kally carried him to the door, Slade braced for a mewling scratch fest, but the cat lay in Kally's arms like he was meant to be there. Slade eased open the screen door not to spook the cat, and then shut the door behind Kally. "Look at you, mighty lion tamer."

Slade could have sworn the cat cussed him, even though no noise came from the orange lump of fur except purring. Kally set the cat down on the sofa and then wrapped her fingers in his. "Come on, Slade, let's go to bed."

"Exactly what I'd encouraged a few minutes ago," he teased.

"Well...I wanted to get my kitty in the house. I've always dreamed of a Christmas morning with a cat on my lap."

"Well, I'm all for making your dreams come true."

She winked at him and it made his heart pound. "Maybe tomorrow..." She pulled him to the stairs. "Tonight I just want you to hold me."

"Happy to oblige, darlin'."

Kally disappeared into the bath, and Slade hurried down the hall and into his pajama pants. Then, creeping down the stairs while the bath water ran, he pulled a present from the supply closet and hid it behind the tree before he turned off the holiday lights and blew out the candles. He surveyed the room and his two hidden presents. *Yup, tomorrow is going to be a great day.*

Chapter Twenty-One

Sleep was elusive. I drifted off long enough to dream of Sue's family showing up on the Fourth Moon's front step with a huge truck behind them, but then Slade rolled over and shook me from the vision. I struggled to recapture it. Eventually, I gave up the fight, and around two in the morning I crept from the bed.

Slade dragged my pillow into his arms and nestled back into sleep. I pulled the door nearly closed and crept down the stairs. Soft shadows nestled in the corners of the great room and sat like pillows atop the cushions on the furniture. Darkness swathed the vaulted ceiling and the windows framed still life pictures of a snowy, moonlit Wyoming night.

Stopping beside the window at the bottom of the stairs, I drew a heart in the frost like I'd done the first morning on the ranch. The hewn log wall supported me while I watched the snowflakes dance in a lazy spiraling ballet. Branches from the pines lining the side yard sagged under the weight of the snow and blue-white light washed the world in ethereal tones. Winter had never been so beautiful.

I wrapped the quilt tighter around my shoulders and tiptoed to the Christmas tree beside the fireplace. I tapped my foot on the Christmas tree light switch and smiled when the lights flared to life.

A peppermint candy cane beckoned, and I plucked it from the branches. The metal tool was cold in my hand when I stirred the coals in the fireplace and added a few logs. Flames soon leapt and crackled, casting light and shadows across the furniture and tree. I soaked up the heat from the flames and then pulled the blanket close and sat on the fireside sofa. The silent grace of a Yule night, the beauty of twinkling lights and a dancing fire—if ever there was a magick Christmas moment for me, this was it. I pulled my feet up under the quilt and then cuddled into the pillows in the corner.

Tom joined me on the sofa nestling in behind my feet. Time ticked away on the clock, the brass pendulum swinging to the tune of Christmas carols in my mind. I sat there for over an hour, bathed in fire glow and Christmas glory. Then, incandescent glow poured down the stairwell, and I knew I was no longer the only one awake. Slade's slippers, pajama pants and then naked torso appeared in slow succession when he walked down the stairs. The heart on the window must have caught his eye, because he drew another heart interlocked with mine. He resembled a boy, with his tussled hair and huge yawn, but concern shadowed his blue eyes. He stopped at the bottom of the stairs and looked at me. "Kally, are you okay?"

The kitty leapt from his place of comfort and ducked under the sofa. I couldn't suppress the smile growing on my face. Even though my family was back in Michigan and I doubted that any of the presents beneath the tree were for me, it was the best Christmas Eve I'd had in many years. "More than okay, Slade."

A silly, too feminine tear trickled down my cheek and betrayed my emotions. I wiped it away and reached a hand out in invitation. "Will you sit with me?"

"Of course. You don't even need to ask."

I shifted closer to the corner and lifted the quilt for Slade to snuggle in the warm flannel folds with me. His arm settled around my shoulders and felt like nature had carved it only to cradle me. My gaze trailed from the fire to the Christmas tree. I wrapped my fingers in his free hand, pulled it across my chest to my face and wiped a fresh tear away with his warm fingers. I wanted to share the gratefulness in my heart. To make him understand how the comfort, safety and love he had so freely given had changed me. The words would not come. I kissed his knuckles and he held me closer to him, my head on his shoulder, my heart resting in his hands.

Neither of us spoke. We didn't need to. I felt him with every fiber of my being, and I knew he'd grown to love me. I only hoped he sensed the same emotions in me. When he rubbed his cheek against my hair and then kissed the top of my head, I knew. Wyoming had bewitched me. Slade had won my heart.

The rising sun warmed the window view, changing the world from midnight blues, to azure and gold. The irascible ginger barn cat I'd coaxed into becoming my house cat joined us on the sofa. Thomas curled into a ball on my lap and purred. Slade snorted.

"Now I know you are meant to be here. No one's ever been able to get that monster cat to cuddle, let alone come into the house."

I stroked Tom's ears, and down the back of his head to his neck. "He's a lover kitty, not a monster."

"For the past three years, I thought his job was to remind me he was too good for me."

"Well, I am nice to him, and he loves me." I stroked a finger along the cat's back and then up Slade's arm to stroke the stubble on his cheek.

"Makes two of us then."

The words were simple and no less right and proper than the fire in the grate. Slade shooed the cat from my lap and took my chin in his hand. I turned to face him. His eyes were shadow blue in the morning light, the stubble dark on his chin and his smile so soft it almost hurt. I would never forget his expression, or the words to come next. "I do, Kally. I knew the minute I saw you wrapped in my mother's quilt and my thermal underwear shirt, that I would love you forever."

Tears welled up unbidden, but they did not dampen my smile. I never truly lived until the moment he said he loved me, and I would live forever in his arms. "I cherish you, Slade. I love you more than I thought I would ever be able to. You rescued me from pain and misery and gave me this perfect life."

My words were minute in comparison to the passionate kiss Slade pressed to my lips. I wrapped my arms around him and melted into his embrace. He stood, holding me tight to his chest and smothering me with kisses. With my arms around Slade's shoulder, my toes barely brushed the floor when he walked backward toward the Christmas tree. Inches from the evergreen branches, Slade loosened his grip and helped me to stand, even though I was flying inside. He reached into the tree, pulled a small package from one of the branches and placed it in my hands. "Merry Christmas, Kally."

The package was small, the wrapping plain brown and tied with twine, like the rest of the gifts under the tree, only a ginger tabby cat ornament hung from the bow. I had to smile when I untied the ornament and hung it on the tree. "My own little tomcat."

The twining fell away, and the paper came off in one piece. Slade took the simple wrappings and crumpled them, tossing the ball into the fire. His eyes twinkled in the early morning light. "No going back now."

"Never."

The velvet-covered box was not new. The nap had been worn away on the corners. When I opened the lid the little metal hinges creaked. A silver ring sat nestled into the crease in the cushion. I lifted it from the bedding and held it up to the Christmas tree lights. The band was simple, but the mount was ornate, a wreath of ivy around an opaque stone. It was mottled, pinks and browns, and identical to any pebble the snowplows had pushed up, only highly polished. I ran a fingertip over the glassy surface before Slade took the ring from me and slipped it onto the ring finger on my left hand.

"This was my mother's." He stroked the skin of my hand. "The day my father signed the papers on the Fourth Moon, he picked up the first pebble he found. He brought the stone to a jeweler and had it mounted in the setting my mother liked. This was his promise to her. His promise of love and warmth on cold nights, of a good, simple life together on this ranch.

"I want to love you and give you a peaceful life." He dropped to one knee before me. "Marry me, Kally."

Tears fell in a mad rush, and though I cried, I laughed. "Nothing would make me happier, Slade. Nothing."

"So...you're saying yes, then?"

"Yes! A million times, yes." Thomas jumped from the couch then and trotted toward the back door. "Well I'd better take care of my kitty."

"Yep you should. I'm just a little terrified the bugger messed something while we were sleeping."

I snorted. "Ye of little faith."

After the life altering moment, we fell into our roles, he off to the chores, me to usher the cat outdoors and then get coffee and a pan of sweet rolls going. The house was abnormally quiet, but it only added to the solemn magic characterizing the season, and how Slade's love had changed me. I was in silent awe of how I had changed, toughened up and yet softened, how

I had let go of fear and embraced love.

Nose seeming to have sweet roll radar, Slade walked in as the timer rang. "Rolls done?"

"Just coming out of the stove." I donned oven mitts and pulled out the tray of sticky rolls. Slade peeked around the door, a jagged rip in his coat sleeve very noticeable. My heart leapt into my throat. "What happened? Are you okay?"

"Yeah." He pulled the rip in his sleeve open to demonstrate the lack of damage beneath. "Zeus got me. George and I were joking around, hooting and hollering and Zeus got agitated. He doesn't like loud noises. He was tossing his head and I got too close."

"Zeus?"

A silly smile lit his face. "Zeus is my favorite bull. Big, black, damn good stud. Okay, enough about the rip in my jacket. Let's get a shower."

"Yes, sir."

He closed the door, his heart pounding and blood raging. The word "yes" had released the floodgates in him, all the passion and desire he'd dammed up inside. Slade wanted Kally, wanted to hold her, taste her, make love to her until she cried his name. "Come here, girl. I want make you dirty before we get clean."

She batted her eyelashes. The mix of her pouting lips and sexy bedroom eyes fed the flames of desire in him. Slade loved it when she played coy. Stepping closer, he could smell yesterday's jasmine and lavender, and beneath, her warm skin. Her hands slid down his arms, and detoured to his belt buckle. He looked down. She locked gazes with him, a naughty, intent gaze to set his blood pumping and erection higher.

His jeans hit the floor once the belt was pulled free and a couple buttons were popped. Kally reached for her own shirt hem, and while he appreciated her fervor, he stopped her. Slade pulled her close, kissed her deeply tasting her tongue, her breath, and then held her shirt snug against her and tasted her nipple through the fabric. The feel of her body beneath the material turned him on. His hand roamed her body, caressing, teasing, slipping beneath hemlines and waistbands. She twitched, she moaned and his body responded, heating up, getting harder.

She whimpered, tugging at her shirt hem. "Please...make love to me."

"Strip for me first."

She locked gazes with him, pulling her shirt off while her body undulated from the chest down, accentuated at her pelvis. "*Mmm*," he said. "I like that."

"Then watch this..." She turned around, repeating the motion so her bottom rose in a delectable curve when her pants came off.

"Stay right there." Slade stood close behind her, bending her over the bathtub's edge to enjoy the curve of her butt while he unwrapped and put on a condom. Spreading her ankles with a foot, he bent her knees forward and out with his hands. Then, with her gorgeous behind propped up, he tasted her sweet honey when he licked her.

Her thighs trembled and Kally nearly vaulted the tub. "Light touches tickle."

"Let me fix that." He only wanted to make her happy, give her pleasure. Guiding her to bend further over, he pressed his erection up and into her. She moaned, taking him in, and he hardened to a pained persistence. The constriction, the friction when he ground into her set fires in his loins and built a pressure he needed to release.

Kally heightened his pleasure and his agony when she adopted his rhythm, rocking back against him, and then she shocked him by guiding his fingers between the folds of her flesh. She wiggled at the push and pull of each slide along his length, and the motion made him throb until he was panting and pumping into her. She cried out in orgasm first, and then he succumbed to the release he desired, clutching her hips and groaning her name.

Kally collapsed on the edge of the tub, panting. He stroked her butt and then guided her over the edge and into the tub. "Turn on the hot water, darlin'. I'll be in in a second."

She started up the shower while he disposed of his protection. Then wrapped in steam and his mother's herbal products, he washed Kally's hair and body, indulging in the simple pleasure of lather on her skin. When he'd rinsed Kally, she took the washcloth and washed him too. If touching her and allowing his hands to slide in the bubbles was a pleasure, Kally washing him, rubbing his chore-sore muscles was pure bliss. "I've never had anyone wash me...ever."

"No one had ever washed my hair before you did either. I wanted to return the favor."

"I'll take the trade." Her laughter was light and sweet, an honest gift on Christmas morning. And, with the thought of Christmas morning and presents, he knew there was very little time left before the ranchers arrived for the Christmas gathering. "We need to hurry up and get dressed. The ranchers will be here any minute."

She slipped to the back of the shower and pushed him into the spray to rinse. Twisting her hair tight, she wrung water from it before exiting the curtain and leaving him to turn the faucet off. Then he joined her on the rug, scrubbing the towel's nap on his skin to dry off. Wrapped in towels, they scurried to their respective rooms to dress with promises to meet in the kitchen later.

Flushed and hair still damp, Slade hurried down the stairs and directly into Rosie. Her knowing glance only intensified the heat of his blush. "Getting a late shower?"

"Yes, ma'am."

"Kally, too?"

He poked his toe at the Santa standing closest. Rosie had cornered and embarrassed him with motherly ease. "Yes, ma'am."

Her stern expression cracked and then fell away beneath the light of a smile. Rosie's dark eyes brightened in a knowing expression and deepened his mortification. Popping half of a cookie into her mouth, she sauntered off and Slade was certain within moments every woman in the house would know he and Kally had had sex. *Suck it up, Slade. Everyone knows you love her.*

Gaze averted, he shuffled into the kitchen and poured a mug of coffee. He rested his ass against the edge of the sink. The counter was covered with dishes of all kinds: cheesecakes, pumpkin pies, spiced apple turnovers, bacon wrapped shrimps and scallops, little sausages simmered in cherry preserves, finger sandwiches, even a seven-layer salad he was certain Emma had brought.

"Mother would be proud."

"She'd be proud about what?" Kally asked when she appeared around the corner.

"You and me, and the fine feast we amassed with our friends' help." He held out a hand and she cuddled up to his chest. It felt so good to hold her. The world could melt away and Slade would be happy if he could hold onto Kally. The world wasn't going away, it was Christmastime and the Fourth Moon was filled with guests. Anticipation bubbled up in him like a kid waiting at the top of the stairs for Mom and Dad to say it was okay to come down. He looked forward to the look on Kally's face when he gave her his present. Her expression would be his best gift this year.

"Hey, you two. Get out here and join us in the living room."

Slade sighed, reluctant to release her, but he knew in his heart, he'd never lose her. Kally wriggled free of his grasp, lacing her fingers in his when she led the way to the living room, to his favorite corner of the fireplace hearth. In her most adorable manner she stepped aside and motioned for him to sit in order for her to lean against his legs.

Normally his mother would pass out the gifts. With his parents in Connecticut, Rosie took over her role with consummate ease. She stood and addressed the gathering. "This year, our normal hosts Pine and Bonnie are away on business, and with Slade tucked behind Kally, I'd like to pass out the presents. And the first one is for..." She fished into the pile of presents. "Emma! And it's from Slade and Kally."

Slade felt the muscles of Kally's back tighten. He placed a hand on her shoulder, but there was no need to comfort her. The wrapping came away from the hardcover edition of the next book in her favorite series. Her eyes widened and she squealed. "Thank you, Kally! Thank you, Slade!"

"You're welcome." Kally relaxed beneath Slade's hand on her shoulder. He liked it there.

Rosie continued to pass gifts out one by one, and Slade could have gone the entire day without one, but a large, flat package was eventually placed in his hands to Rosie's announcement, "And this is for Slade, from Kally."

He hadn't expected a present. Her love was enough of a gift. "Kally, you didn't have to..."

Her blue eyes sparkled brighter than her smile. "I know. Rosie helped me."

With his curiosity piqued, Slade pulled away the brown wrappings and exposed a hand-wrapped, hand-knotted dream catcher. Strips of fabric dangled from the edge of the web and jogged his memory. He ran his fingers down the frayed lengths. With eyes half closed, replaying the memory of the day they had picked out the Christmas tree, he asked, "These were torn from your shirt the night you came here, weren't they? They were on the Christmas tree..."

"This way, a part of me will always be watching over you at night, catching the bad dreams and giving you good ones."

Healing had helped Kally so much, and now she even wore her heart on her sleeve and his mother's ring on her finger. Bending down to kiss her, Slade knew all was right in the world. When he pulled away, he stood and danced foot to foot through the wasteland of wrapping paper scraps and opened boxes. "And now, I have one last gift to give. Close your eyes, Kally."

He grasped the edges of Kally's gift and pulled it out from behind the tree where he'd hidden it earlier. The gasps started before he'd slid it to the front of the room, and people moved out of Slade's path. With the seat pointed toward her, he said, "Open your eyes, darlin."

The expression on her face was more than he could've hoped. Her jaw dropped, her eyes widened and then teared, and she struggled through the sea of paper and packaging to get to the rocking chair she'd first seen in pieces in the carpentry shed. She ran her fingers over the varnish, touched each slat and spindle. She even wiped away the tears splattered on the seat. "Oh, Slade." She twined the fingers of one hand in his and ran the fingers of her other on the arm of the chair. "It's beautiful. Thank you, so much."

"You're welcome, Kally. I hope you enjoy it for years to come."

With the last of the presents exchanged, the guests went into clean-up mode until all the packaging was broken down and Emma's husband Stewart offered to take it out to the burn barrel behind the shed. The men drifted away into evening ranch chores and returned when evening shadows had fallen and the ladies were ensconced on the sofas with cups of tea. Slade stomped the snow from his boots, hung his jacket on the hall tree and then wrapped Kally in a bear hug, sneaking his frozen fingers up her shirt.

The squeal and wiggle was worth it, and he enjoyed the

spanking she gave him once the guests were gone. He loved her playful side. It fascinated him in a completely different way from her soft feminine side or her feisty side. Together they blew out the candles and turned out the lights, but she wouldn't come to bed until her kitty came into the house for the night. Then, with the tomcat curled before the fire, she followed him up the stairs. After sharing the sink to brush their teeth, he left her room to hang the dream catcher above his bed and then returned to Kally's room. She was already in her pajamas and waiting for him under the covers.

"Hurry up and get in bed." She pouted. "I'm cold."

"So all I'm good for is a foot warmer?"

"Of course not. You saved my life, healed my heart and taught me to love again. You've given me a wonderful home and...I love you."

What more was there to say? "I love you too, Kally." Slade climbed into bed, snuggled up behind the woman he loved and soon lost himself to sunlit dreams of future days with Kally on the ranch.

Chapter Twenty-Two

A phone ring ruined the early morning silence. Slade woke with a start and climbed over me like an animal scrambling for cover. I rolled to the wall thinking it was a rancher calling about the morning rounds.

I was wrong.

Slade's voice bellowed up the stairs, a note of panic making it sound alien in the big house. "Susan's husband Jerry is on the phone, Kally."

Jerry is calling? My guts seized and the strength sluiced from me. *If Jerry is calling, the news can't be good.* I wrapped the quilt around my shoulders and forced myself to walk to the office, pushing through tension making it difficult to breathe. "Hello?"

"Kally, this is Jerry." His voice broke into sobs, and then he forced them under control. "Susan's in the hospital."

My heart stopped but picked up a rhythm echoing in my ears. "Jerry, what happened?"

His voice dripped acid. "Matt happened. I left to pick up the boys from an overnight party with my parents, and when I came home..." The sobs returned, but this time he spoke through them. "The front door was hanging by the hinges when I drove onto the driveway.

"I left the boys in their booster seats and ran in. Sue was lying in the foyer, unconscious. Her face was bloody... She..." Jerry couldn't continue with the sentence. "I called 9-1-1. The paramedics said she had a closed head trauma and she'd been choked. They had to put a tube down her throat."

"Oh dear God..." Tears fell unchecked. Slade took the phone from me and guided my head to his shoulder. Sobs shook through me. Air refused to enter my lungs. Slade stroked my back and rocked side to side.

"Jerry, this is Slade Carlson, Kally needs a moment. Is there anything we can do for Sue?"

Jerry's voice hummed through the phone. Slade stroked my hair while he replied. "Are you sure? We have plenty of rooms here at the Fourth Moon. Y'all are welcome to come here while she recuperates." The buzz of Jerry's voice took on a more stable tone before Slade spoke again. "No, no, you wouldn't be putting us out." He paused and I wiped tears and snot while Jerry responded. "Oh, one of our ranchers is a retired teacher. She could homeschool the boys... Well, please think about it okay?"

More under control, I nodded my head and motioned for the phone. "Jerry, can Sue talk?"

"Sorry, Kally. She's sedated. I'll have her call when she's awake and can talk."

My heart wasn't any better, even if my tears were under control. "Thanks, Jerry."

"Don't thank me, Kally. I think Matt's headed your way. We received the box Christmas—the return label was torn off—when I came home this morning, Sue was laying in the living room with brown paper bits littering her face. It was the return address, Kally. Printed out on a shipping label."

Shipping label? The helpful people at the post office had doomed me and my family.

I dropped the phone, unable to hold it any longer. Clinging to Slade, I shook while the old fear rampaged through me. Picking up the phone, Slade apologized to Jerry and then hung up the phone. "What is it, Kally?"

"He's coming."

"Your ex?"

The terror on my face answered his question.

"We'll be ready. He won't hurt you or anyone else again." Slade led me to the fireside armchair and wrapped me in the quilt I'd dragged down only moments ago. "You sit here while I make a couple of phone calls."

A numb sense of detachment flooded me while I stared at the lights on our Christmas tree. The warmth of the fire did not reach me. The whole season seemed hollow now. My utopia was gone, destroyed by Matt. Slade was here, and he was mine. I loved him more than I thought possible, but the monster from my past had come back to haunt me. He had hurt my sister and now he was coming for me. I curled my feet beneath me and shriveled inside, retreating behind the walls I'd erected within to keep my sanity.

Shutting the office door, Slade walked out into the great room and stood in front of me. Tears beaded up and blurred my vision when I looked up at him. I didn't want to cry, to lose myself to the fear in the shadows of my past. My lip trembled. He took off his Stetson, placing it on the antler rack beside the fireplace. Kneeling down, he took my hands and forced me to face him. His blue eyes were intent. The lines of his face were set. "Kally, come back to me."

The fear screamed inside. I bit my lip and my gaze drifted from his face back to the flames. Slade would not let me crawl any farther into myself. "Come on, girl." He tugged my hands, pulling me from the chair and onto his lap. "I'm here now. Nothing is going to happen to you, Kally." He lifted my face until our gazes met. "I love you."

I flung my arms around him, burying my face in his neck. "I love you too. I'm just so scared. If he hurt Sue so badly..." I shuddered. Only Slade holding me in the moment kept me out of my shell. "He would have done worse to me. She could have died. I could've died."

He grabbed my chin, forced me to focus on his eyes—those cool, pale blue eyes I'd fallen for, fallen into, with complete abandon. "Kally, I swear I will do everything in my power to protect you. I would lay down my life for you. And if he's stupid enough to come here, he's coming onto a ranch full of people armed to the teeth. He'll be biting off more than he can chew."

I nodded my head and collapsed against him, depending on Slade to hold me up while I fell apart. He rocked me side to side, stroking my hair and back until the storm subsided within and I crashed onto the bedrock of new love in my soul. He was my strength, the ranch was my shelter and the timeshares were my new family. I would not leave, nor be taken from it. I knew, however, there was no "if" where Matt was concerned. I was here, he knew it and he would not stop until I was in his sights, underneath his fists. "We need to prepare..."

"I've put calls in to the P.D., got Red coming this afternoon and the timeshares will be here in an hour to discuss the situation. I suggest we get showered and eat something. You're going to need your strength."

You have no idea. No sooner had I entertained the thought than I knew I was wrong. Slade did have some idea of what a domestic abuser can do. He had been a police officer. He'd run calls with victims like Susan and like me. I nodded and took his hand to lead him to the shower, but he shook his head.

"Nope, darlin'. I have a few more calls to make, then I'll get breakfast going. Rosie will be here to sit with you in a few minutes, then I'll get a quick shower."

I needed him with me, but I also understood this was Slade's way of seeing to my safety. If Matt had attacked Susan this morning, there was no telling where he was. He could be here in the middle of the night... An image of his bulking frame darkening the Fourth Moon's doorway burned in my mind and I shuddered. Wrapping my arms to my chest, I walked to the foyer and peered out the windows into the falling snow. How long would it take for him to get here?

"Kally." Slade's voice was soft, measured when he called my name.

"Yes...I know." My shoulders fell and I turned from the windows. Slade wrapped an arm around my shoulder, ushering me up the stairs and starting my bath for me before he shut the door and left me with my thoughts.

I stripped, sank into the water and greedily inhaled the herbal-scented steam. Lavender is supposed to soothe and calm, and I needed all the serenity I could muster. Sucking in a deep breath, I slid to the bottom of the tub, absorbed the heat, the quiet and willed my heart rate to slow. There, beneath the water, stubborn will rose within me, similar to the upstart emotion I had felt on the dance floor when Adelle had started yapping. I was no longer willing to be the victim. It was my time to stand up, fight back and own what I loved and knew was mine—my life and my love with Slade.

Dried, dressed and determined to win the war of attrition, I returned to the dining room, where all of the timeshares were gathered, even the Billings brothers. Slade, mug of coffee in hand, sat at the head of the table with a map of the ranch spread out in the middle. "Mike, I'd appreciate it if you and Mark could keep an eye on the north forty. Red is going to make sure patrols are stepped up along the highway. I'll be watching the northeast trails. Rosie?"

"Yes, Slade. The ladies are in agreement. We'll stay in the main house tonight." She noticed me standing in the doorway. "And Kally will stay at a different house each day until this criminal is caught."

Leave the main house? I tucked my hair behind my ears. I balked at the uncomfortable concept. The Fourth Moon's main house had become my home. I hated to leave its shelter, even in lieu of one of the other houses and families. If I was going to make a stand, I damn well intended it to be here, in this house. Shaking my head, I walked into the room and stood beside Slade. "I appreciate the effort and the offer to shelter me in your homes, but I ran away from this man once before, and I don't intend to do so again."

Emma spoke up. "It's only for your protection, dear, until he's caught."

"I understand, Emma. But you don't know him like I do. He's vicious and cunning. He'll come at you sideways instead of face to face. He won't hesitate just because the house has a different address."

Mike Billings spoke next. "So what do you propose, Kally?"

In the following silence, the fighter in me spoke. "Let the men guard the fences. Give me a gun."

"Kally!" Rosie's voice scaled to a high pitch. "You can't just shoot him."

"I realize that, Rosie, but reason doesn't work very well with him either."

The reasonable discussion flared into a shouting match, which died quickly, with solid decisions made. The men divided the ranch's borders into sections. Red would make certain patrols of the major roadways were stepped up, and the women agreed to rotate spending nights in the big house with me. With schedules set and watches synchronized, the ranchers departed for home. Rosie stopped in the foyer, grabbed my hands and hugged me. "You are going to be fine, dear. Slade and your new family will see to it."

I patted her shoulders. "Thank you, Rosie."

"And if anything happens and one of us isn't here, you ring the bell and we'll be here for you."

"I will."

The rest of the day was quiet. My appetite was non-existent. Slade pulled out the leftovers from Christmas, regardless, and covered the counter. "I know you said you're not hungry, but I don't want you to waste away with worry."

A sigh escaped me. "I'm sorry, Slade. The worrying comes from my Dutch mother. And loads of experience dealing with Matt."

He didn't talk, but took my hands and led me to the rarely used sitting room off from the great room. Slade called it the Trouble Room. It's where he and his siblings always ended up in deep discussion with their parents when they were caught doing something "less than right". Hard shadows crouched on the sofa, stubborn and unmoving in the light of the accent lamp he lit. The furniture was older, stuffy, almost Victorian looking and an unusual scent of museum air hunkered in the room.

"I don't like this room," Slade muttered when he unlocked a cabinet in the closet. "But there are useful things in here." He produced a handgun from the top drawer, a boxy looking semi-automatic, and then rummaged farther down in the cabinet for a loaded magazine and the keys to the trigger lock. He held them out for me. "These are my mother's. I called her and she said to give them to you."

I held the cold metal pieces in my hands and locked gazes with Slade.

"Do you know how to use them?"

"I took classes in firearms safety before I met Matt." I removed the trigger lock and then clicked in the magazine. He nodded, reminded me to keep the safety on until I needed it and we retired to the great room until Rosie arrived and Slade set out for night patrol. When I climbed into bed, Rosie was on the sofa sleeping with a shotgun next to her. My kitty was in my bedroom and my lover was out in the cold, hunting my ex-fiancé.

Needless to say, my dreams were haunted.

Chapter Twenty-Three

Slade dragged himself into the house after morning chores. I'd never seen him so tired, his head even nodded dangerously close to the pile of flapjacks on his plate. The coffee couldn't quell his fatigue, nor did the Tabasco liberally applied to his sausages. And nothing more than heartburn accompanied him to rest.

I tucked the sheets and blankets around him and sneaked out. In the office I called Jerry and got an update on Sue. Her condition had been upgraded, her injuries were not life threatening and she would completely recover. He also said they were considering Slade's offer of Sue recuperating on the Fourth Moon. That was followed by him asking if Matt had been sighted in Wyoming. "Not yet, Jerry. But I can't shake this sense of foreboding."

"Keep your wits about you, Kally. And call me when it's over."

"I will. Kiss the boys for me, okay?"

We ended the conversation with promises. He promised to pass my love to Sue and the boys, and I promised to keep them informed of events here. After breakfast dishes were cleared, I paced the confines of the house, nervous and unable to shake the sense of doom overshadowing me.

Late in the day, cagey as hell, I left a note for Slade, bundled up and walked to Emma and Stewart's to peruse her book collection. If I was going to be trapped in the house, I at least wanted something to read. Emma met me at the door and ushered me inside. Stewart bustled in the kitchen, making a stew and Emma scurried to bring me a cup of tea. I sipped Earl Grey and pored over books, looking for something to spark my interest. Years ago, I had read every fantasy novel I could get my hands on. I'd nearly surrendered hope of finding one among Emma's women's fiction and romance titles. Eventually, I found a copy of Tolkein's *The Silmarillion* on the bottom shelf.

Slade called the Edwards's to let me know he would be in the workshop until I came home. Looking out the window, I realized the lateness of the hour and, Tolkien tome in hand, I excused myself from the Edwards's to walk back up the drive while the meager sunlight held.

Emma stood on her porch watching me until I made it to the barn. The workshop was only yards away and the door was open. I could hear tools banging around in there, so I waved to Emma. She waved back and ducked inside the house.

The cattle milled in the huge pen beside the barn, and Zeus snorted. I detoured to the barn to grab my cat for the night. I knew it was foolish, but I could picture Matt finding the cat and hurting it because somehow, in his sick, twisted mind, he knew it was my pet. Pulling the door open, I noticed the horses were gone. *Must be out on patrol.*

I begged and pleaded, offered treats I didn't have and eventually coaxed the kitty from the shadows. With one hand I stuffed the book in my jacket, and with the other I scooped up the cat.

The light had died outside the barn. Jack was back, tethered to the front porch, and what little light remained spilled over his equine silhouette and lay, gray and weak, on the driveway. A sick sense of worry crept up through me. My legs turned to jelly and my guts knotted uncomfortably. In the driveway, Tom hissed in my arms and then leapt from my embrace and melted into the shadows under the porch. Light poured from the shattered frame of the front door. A light flickered at the east end of the house, and then darkness engulfed the dwelling. The soles of my riding boots slid in the snow. My heart skipped into a stilted rhythm and the bottom dropped out of my gut.

Matt was here, somewhere. I could smell his rancid patchouli cologne. It reeked like bug spray in the fresh winter air.

Checking my pockets for Bonnie's gun, I tiptoed across the porch. The gun was gone. I'd left it atop Emma's bookcase. I peeked through the door. Shards of colored glass peppered the floor and were embedded in the walls. The antler chandelier lay shattered on the great room floor. The Carlsons' beautiful home—my sanctuary—lay in ruin. Broken, overturned furniture sat at odd angles to the windows, casting surreal shadows across trophy mounts ripped from the walls. The kind of sick trepidation I thought I'd left behind flooded me. My muscles clenched and my stomach churned.

My boots crunched on the broken glass when I stepped in. I would not face Matt unarmed. I kept my eyes trained on the shadows in the center of the room, bent down and wrapped a broken antler in my fingers and lifted it from the debris on the floor. Having a weapon gave me a small measure of comfort, but when a crash rattled through the room, my heart leapt into my throat. I turned to run back to the workshop, back to safety—to Slade.

The shadows solidified behind me and around my neck in a vise grip. Matt was my demon in the dark. The beast haunting me for years had arrived. Panic flooded me. My only thought was to escape. He kicked my feet out from underneath me and dragged me into the living room. "Imagine me finding you here, Kally, on a fucking ranch in Wyoming, instead of taking care of our home like you should be."

Time froze. For one tight breath, the old me wanted to fade, to hide in my mind until the beating was over. The old me didn't exist any longer.

"This is my home now." I spent the rest of my air. "And you are not welcome here." Shifting my hip to the side, I drove the jagged antler back and down with all the force I had. The sharp end met flesh, and his howl rent the winter night. Matt released his grip on my throat and shoved me away from him in favor of pulling the antler out of his wounded leg.

"You crazy bitch! How dare you?" He pitched the antler backward into the great room. "Now I'm going to punish you."

"You can't punish what you don't own."

Matt's eyes narrowed, moonlight glared from his teeth when he bared them, and then he wiped the blood across his chest and lunged. I sidestepped the attack, raised my foot and buried the toe of my boot in his gut. He dropped forward and wrapped an arm around my leg, forcing his weight against me and driving me to the floor beneath him. My head bounced off the floor, glass bit into my scalp, spots swarmed in my vision but they could not blur the maniacal expression on Matt's face.

He was a man possessed, eyes wild, mouth agape and drool streaking his chin. Matt drove a knee into my stomach, pressing air from my lungs and bile up into my throat. Fists fell in a blizzard of pain. Cuss words hit me in a storm of belittlement and ended with the words, "You are mine!"

Anger blazed within me, higher and hotter with each strike he landed. The heat blazed through my limbs, pushed me to act, to fight back. His wrist was thick in my grip when I tightened my fingers around it and then elevated my hips like Slade taught me. Matt pitched off balance and tumbled to the floor. His limbs flailed, hands turned to claws raking me while I scrambled to my feet. He caught an ankle and dragged me forward. I refused to be his victim again. I was strong, I was a free spirit and I fought back. Using my heel for a pivot point, I twisted the ankle in his grip until my boot was over his wrist, and then I stood between his arms and kicked him until something cracked in his chest.

"I'm over me being under you, Matt."

He howled a sound worse than any coyote or wolf. Blood trickled from his mouth and his eyes were wild. I backed away and my boots skidded in the shattered glass. I came down in a pile of limbs and pain. Dazed, I forced myself to sit, keeping my eyes on the beast struggling to rise. My ears rang with the slamming of my heart. Breath came in short gasps and burned along my ribs. With sick clarity, I saw the butt of his old gun clenched in his hand. Boot heels slipped on the tile and shards of glass tore my palms raw when I skittered backward. I couldn't get enough air when I tried to scream. Words would not come out of my throat.

"Slade..." It was little more than a breath. Matt's grunts were louder than my cry when he struggled with the sight of the gun and the seam of his pocket.

The doorjamb felt like salvation beneath my fingers, but Matt's evil expression rivaled any demon in a Christian's hell. The strap of my boot snagged on an upturned rug and I dug my fingernails into the wood of the doorjamb until the expression on Matt's face froze the blood in my veins. He focused his hate black eyes on me, wrenched the muzzle free and leveled it on my chest. This time terror ripped a path in my throat. "Slade!"

Shocked, frozen—a deer in the headlights of an oncoming

car—I saw everything in the foyer and could not move.

Moonlight shone through the stained glass, painting the gun in his hand red. He pulled the slide back, and muscles around his eyes tensed. The muzzle blast cracked like lightning and the force of the bullet slammed me back through the door and onto the porch.

Fire exploded in my left arm. Red motes danced before my eyes and hot blood trickled between my fingers. The sound of the ricocheting bullet casing cut like brass blades into my ears. Motion returned and I rolled to my stomach, leaving a path of blood in the snow when I crawled across the porch. In a jumble of stars and stairs I tumbled down the steps. Matt swore, cursing his jammed weapon. The metallic clatter told me he had ejected the magazine and slammed in another.

I stood and then ran for the white horse tethered to the porch support. The reins came free and I swung up onto his back under the power of adrenaline and fear. Groaning, I collapsed against the horse's neck. "Find Slade, Jack! Find Slade."

Jack whirled and Matt charged through the front door. He brought the pistol up. I saw the muzzle flash. The bullet ripped past us, striking Slade's truck with a clanging *thunk*. The workshop door slammed open and I saw Slade standing in the doorway of the workshop, his rifle pointed at Matt, his eye pressed to the scope. "Kally, get down!" The horse stopped between the workshop and barn and I tumbled to the snow bank. Slade's chest expanded, he held the breath and fired. Matt's pistol hand whipped out to the side, the handgun tipping end over end through the air.

Matt's face contorted in a mask of rage, and then he charged, a snarling fiend on two legs.

I cowered on the ground, wanting to hide in Slade's arms, but too terrified to move. One gunshot wound was enough. The barrel of the rifle came down, cinched in his left arm when Slade pulled me up and then he thrust the gun into my hands. He stopped long enough to look at my ripped and bleeding arm. "This is gonna be man to man."

If only Matt had as much honor. I nodded and Slade stepped into the drive, bracing to meet Matt's charge head on.

Yards from where I stood bleeding, my cowboy and my monster collided in an audible crush of muscle and bone. Matt growled and shouted an insane language of rage. I leaned the barrel of Slade's rifle against a shoulder gone numb and rang the bell fixed to the workshop corner. The frigid night sank its teeth into my left arm, its numbing chill settling into the limb while I pulled the bell chord over and over.

Slade shoved Matt back and the crazed brute swung at him with an overhand right, mocking Slade, calling him a fake, woman-stealing cowboy. Slade only grunted when he sidestepped and countered with a jab and over hand combination. The short punch missed, but the second strike rocked Matt's head back. His knees buckled, and true to his football training, he lunged in for the tackle. His bulk knocked Slade off balance and he staggered backward, slamming into the barn wall.

The commotion stirred up the cattle, and they had nowhere to run. Penned, they started to pace and moo.

Bunching his fists in Matt's jacket, Slade spun the bigger man and rammed his head into the barn wall. Matt's head bounced from the red wall twice more, then, with blood running down his face, Matt drove an uppercut into Slade's jaw. The Stetson flew off, and Slade's hair swung out with the force of Matt's strike.

The fight was out of hand, well past honor and too far toward death. Slade crumpled against the barn wall and I screamed in horror. Then Matt took advantage of my cowboy's daze and buried his fist into Slade's gut. The men slid down the wall, Matt throwing everything he had at Slade, yet somehow, Slade ended up in a top mount position, raining down fists. The bell rang until other bells answered in the distance—the Fourth Moon's emergency notification system in action—and vehicles roared to life. The ranchers were coming and Matt would not get away with it this time. I left the bell and limped toward the barn.

The hulking beast rolled onto his side enough to unsettle Slade. Matt stood, despite the blows Slade landed, and then Matt launched a kick at Slade's crotch. Slade collapsed to the snow and Matt swung his leg out and connected with Slade's gut before taking the last few steps to the cattle pen. Dropping the gun and ignoring the pain in my shoulder, I ran to Slade's side, cradling his head in my lap. Matt laughed, a dark mirthless sound the Edwards's engine could not drown out. He pointed a finger at me and then dragged his finger across his throat when he lifted the latch to the gate of the cattle pen.

The crazed cows churned against the fence, lurching, kicking and bellowing. I refused to allow Matt to set the frenzied herd loose. A stampede could kill Slade who knelt only feet from the fence. I stood when Matt pulled on the gate and then I charged. He turned toward me, and I slammed my bloodied shoulder into his gut, knocking him into the cattle pen and onto his ass.

The cows milled around when he stood. "Get out of there!" Slade shouted.

I hated Matt, but at one time I did love him, and I didn't want to see him trampled to death. I begged him to come to the gate. "Matt, please."

He raised his middle finger and kicked at a heifer. "Fuck you, Kally."

"Don't be a fool, Matt!"

"Don't you dare call me a fool!" His voice escalated and he pumped his arms at his side.

It was more commotion than Zeus, Slade's prize bull, cared to deal with. He broke through the side of the bull pen and charged. I shouted for Matt to run. He only smacked his chest in a gesture of defiance. Slade clambered to his feet and ran for the gate, but Matt turned to face the rampaging bull.

Zeus's horn plunged into Matt's gut and then he flung him like a matador's cape. The cows scattered to the far side of the enclosure, and Slade ran into the pen, dragging Matt's semiconscious body out to the drive. Blood, thick and black soaked through his jacket. Emma jumped out of her vehicle and I screamed at her to dial 9-1-1 while I locked the gate to the pen.

Slade reached for me and I pushed his hands away when I dropped to my knees beside Matt. It wasn't supposed to end like this. He had been a decent man once. People back home loved him despite his faults. Seeing him lying on the ground, clutching his guts together, tore at my heart.

"Kally..." He coughed, blood trickling from his lips and running from the fingers he stretched piteously toward me.

His hand, the hand to cause me so much pain, hung in the air a silent petition for comfort. I averted my gaze, looked to Slade. "Is he...can he be helped?"

Slade's eyes were pale blue ghosts, hollow and horrified. He squatted down beside me, pulled open the tear in Matt's clothes. The gash in his stomach was huge, pieces of innards bubbled up past the edges. "The horn ripped his liver, chunks are torn lose...probably severed the artery...the blood is black..." He pushed a hand through the blood on his own lip, his voice was hollow when he spoke. "Kally, I've seen enough accidents to know, there ain't no coming back."

"H-how long?"

Slade didn't answer.

Matt moaned, begged for me again. "Kally...please."

I took his hand. In the name of everything good we once had, I would not let him suffer alone. His eyes rolled, blood seeped through the snow and faint, in the distance, sirens wailed. Matt's hand convulsed in pain around mine, then he opened his eyes. "Can you forgive me? Or...too much to ask?"

Slade's love had healed my heart, and life on the Fourth Moon had matured me. Forgiveness was a gift I was finally capable of giving. Tears fell and I choked back sobs while the patrol car careened down the drive. "Yes, yes I can. We had good times, and I will always remember them. Maybe someday..." He coughed, blood poured from his mouth. Black terror shadowed Matt's eyes. He nodded for me to continue. "Maybe someday, I'll forget all the pain you caused."

Slade's hand settled on my good shoulder and Matt's eyes drifted to my cowboy. "Do you...love him?"

There was no hesitation. "Yes, with all my heart."

Tears formed in Matt's eyes, washing away some of the blood and ichor, revealing the likeness of the man I once cared for. Headlights burned the image of his face in my mind. His hand tightened around mine, air, heavy with the scent of iron, wheezed from his lungs and Matt's ribcage raised no more.

My tormentor was gone.

"Oh my God," someone whispered. The world crashed back in on me then, and shaking I collapsed against Slade's legs, only vaguely aware I still held onto Matt's hand.

Slade stroked my head and I found myself mumbling, "He wasn't all bad. He wasn't all bad..."

Matt's limp hand slipped from my grip, and Slade pulled me to my feet. He pushed away the bloody hair clinging to my face. "No one is all bad, darlin'."

I crumbled against him, sobbing, until a paramedic asked if

I was injured. "I'm not sure. It's all a blur."

"You're bleeding, hun." She took my hand and led me to the ambulance where she tenderly checked my injuries. "The bullet tore right through. You'll need stitches for your bicep..."

I shook my head. I didn't want stitches. I just wanted Slade. Frantic, I craned my head out the back of the truck. "Slade?"

"Yeah, darlin'?" He excused himself from the officer he was speaking to and hurried to the ambulance. The paramedic explained my injuries, the risk of infection and permanent muscle damage, and the treatment needed. Slade nodded and then motioned to Rosie, who walked over. "Kally needs to get stitched up and the medic is worried about possible complications. Can you hold the fort until we call? I am going with her."

"Of course I can." She patted my leg, her bright eyes rimmed in sadness when she looked at me. "We'll be here, honey."

Slade sat on the bench beside the cart in the back of the ambulance while the medics strapped me in and locked the bed down. Looking at Slade's face, I fell apart. "I never thought I'd cry when he died. All I wished was his death—for months."

"You're a loving person with a big heart, Kally." He smoothed stray bangs from my eyes and then kissed my forehead. "The loss of life is never good, no matter how awful the person might have been. There's good in all of us, even if it is buried deep."

"What do I do now?" I sniffled and wiped at the snot and blood with an arm already stuck with an IV shunt. "Matt's been a shadow in my life for so long."

"Walk in the sun, Kally." Slade's palm covered my fingers where they rested on the blanket. "And I'll hold your hand."

"I want you to always hold my hand, Slade. You are my sun. You burned away the hurt and the pain, you warmed my heart."

"And I will always be here for you, darlin'."

"Well, you can't be right now, sir." The paramedic intruded, a bit of a smile on her face. "You'll have to ride up front. We only have patients and medics in the back."

Slade returned her smile, kissed me deeply and promised to be by my side in the ER for my repeat appearance. The medic closed the doors and I closed my eyes on the horror scene left behind. It would take ages to wash away the images of Matt, but I knew Slade would be with me every step of the way. And once we were back home, I planned to talk to my cowboy about arranging our wedding.

Epilogue

Spring breezes blew through the open expanse of the main ranch, pollen danced in the yellow sunlight, and Bonnie and I were deep into plotting the colors and flowers and food for my upcoming May wedding. The dining room table was scattered with papers, magazine articles and fabric swatches. Bonnie was rubbing her thumb over a sample of white silk damask. "This is nice, Kally."

"I don't know, Mom, it looks a little heavy for an early summer affair..."

The lavender iced tea was a sweet treat when I sipped it, and I twined my hair up into a bun and fixed it with a ponytail scrunchie. Pointing at an off-the-shoulder gown in a bridal magazine, I asked, "What do you think about this one? It's less formal, would cover my scar, and would look great with a bunch of your lavender for a bouquet and then I could have a sage colored sash..." I drifted off into my vision of a perfect wedding—sunlight, a simple white dress and my cowboy in inky dark blue jeans, nice white shirt and his Stetson.

The only thing to make it better would be for my sister and my best friend to walk with me. I knew Ilene was coming for the weekend, but Sue's husband Jerry just couldn't get the time off work.

Slade crashing through the back door roused me from my daydreams. Bonnie's normal nagging about removing his hat was conspicuously absent when he skated through the dining room. Before he disappeared from sight, someone knocked on the front door. "Kally!" Slade shouted from the front door. "You're gonna want to see this."

I looked at Bonnie, and she couldn't hide her smile. She

pretended not to know what was going on. I knew better. I stood, brushed off the frayed fabric snippets from my clothes, smoothed my hair and then hurried to the foyer. Rounding the corner, I saw Slade's back at the open door and the yellow front end of a big truck in the driveway. Falsely, I assumed a package had arrived for the wedding.

Slade stepped aside, and my sister Susan stepped in. My heart pounded, tears welled up and I loosed a squeal. "Oh my God, Sue! What're you doing here?"

"You're going to need a Matron of Honor. Beside, I couldn't let you stay out here in your Wyoming paradise alone."

I blinked, trying to make sense of it all when my nephew Samuel burst through the door and tackled me. "Aunt Kally!" He talked fast enough to make up for the months of lost time. "Did you hear? We drove all the way here! We're gonna have a house out here, too! The Carlsons are giving Daddy a job!"

Bonnie appeared behind me and shook Sue's hand. I lifted Sammy from my chest and stood with Slade's help. His smile was huge. "Is it true?"

"Yes it is, darlin'." He crushed me in a hug and then pulled Susan in too. "I will do whatever it takes to make my girl happy."

I kissed him and then gave Sue a peck on the cheek. "I am the happiest girl in the world!"

About the Author

To learn more about A. E. Rought, please visit www.aerought.com. Send an email to A. E. at aerought@gmail.com or join her Yahoo! group to join in the fun with other readers as well as A. E. at http://groups.yahoo.com/group/DarkInk.

Will Kate still want Chris when she finds out his secret?

Crazy for Kate
© *2008 Kelly McDonough*

Chris is the man of every woman's dreams. Not only is he a hot-looking construction worker who looks good in ripped jeans and a white T-shirt, he's also got a big heart he'd like to share with a wife and kids. But because of a childhood illness, he can never have the family he hoped for.

Fate has its way with Chris and he winds up working at a church picnic with Kate McKaye, an old classmate. She's more beautiful than he remembered, and is divorced with two young daughters. For the first time in years, Chris asks a woman on a date.

Chris falls deeply in love with sexy, sweet Kate. His only fear is how she'll react when she finds out she can't have all the babies she's told him she wants. Will she be like his ex-fiancé, whose maternal instincts lead her straight into the arms of another man? Or, can she be happy with him and her two daughters?

Available now in ebook and print from Samhain Publishing.

GREAT
cheap
fun

Discover eBooks!

THE FASTEST WAY TO GET THE HOTTEST NAMES

Get your favorite authors on your favorite reader, long before they're
out in print! Ebooks from Samhain go wherever you go, and work with
whatever you carry—Palm, PDF, Mobi, and more.

samhain
publishing ltd

WWW.SAMHAINPUBLISHING.COM

LaVergne, TN USA
07 October 2009
160171LV00001B/43/P